BENJAMIN

ARON BEAUREGARD

&

SHANE McKENZIE

BAD DREAM BOOKS

ISBN: 978-1-961758-48-3

Digital Animations by Jorge Jaramillo

Cover by Frank Walls

Interior Illustrations by Jim Agpalza

Edited by Lisa Lee Tone & Lucas Mangum

Printed in the USA

WARNING:
This book contains scenes and subject matter that are disgusting & disturbing; easily offended people are not the intended audience.

JOIN OUR MAILING LISTS AT:

aronbeauregard.substack.com

shanemckenziehorror.substack.com

For Jorge Jaramillo.

Without your hard work, creativity, and passion, the experience that is 'Benjamin' would never have reached its full potential.

IMPORTANT

Please read the following pages, scan the QR code, and watch a short video to ensure you get the best possible reading experience.

If you have any issues scanning the QR codes, please email: Follow.Benjamin100@gmail.com

NOT JUST A BOOK

BY ARON BEAUREGARD

The following story is *more* than just a book. Shane McKenzie and I have worked closely with several artists to ensure that *Benjamin* has a different feel than any other form of dark literature that you've previously consumed.

From the incredible, hand-painted cover by Frank Walls to the variety of interior illustrations by Jim Agpalza, you will be shown stunning imagery. But *Benjamin* spreads its wings even further than most artistic endeavors, also presenting you with a series of animations by the uber-talented Jorge Jaramillo.

Each animation you will view in the five parts of this novel is abstract, except for the final sixth video at the conclusion, which is an exclusive short film. None of the animations will spoil the story or merely be a boring regurgitation of what's already on the page. These animations are here to challenge you to look at the deeper meaning of this epic story. In addition to these videos, there are short poems that come along with each surrealistic nightmare. Will you be able to pick out the elements within the text to find deeper meaning?

The only way to find out is to follow Benjamin.

It should be noted that outside of the additional immersive content this experience offers, *Benjamin* also stands on its own. What makes this project special is that you can read or listen to the book by itself and still get every bit of the story that Shane and I desired to deliver to readers. It should also be noted that if you have photo sensitivity, brief parts of these videos may contain flashing. Viewer discretion is advised.

You are about to embark on an immersive entertainment experience like no other. We present you with our labor of love—a project that we've worked on for many months and poured hundreds of manhours and many sleepless nights into. I'd like to drone on more about everything that's gone into this venture, but getting you into the experience is much more important.

The story of *Benjamin* will be one-of-a-kind dark fiction, and we have just one more short hurdle before you begin. Please scan the below QR code with your phone and watch a brief introductory video before moving forward for the most optimal reading experience.

FEDERAL RESERVE NOTE
THE UNITED STATES OF AMERICA
THIS NOTE IS LEGAL TENDER FOR ALL DEBTS, PUBLIC AND PRIVATE
C00630261★
WASHINGTON, D.C.
C
3
C00630261★
100
ONE HUNDRED DOLLARS

PART 1:

THE CITY OF FEAR

FAST CASH

Violence has a heartbeat.

Inside the city, its pulse was healthy. It thudded with a resounding consistency. The soundtrack to delinquency was always just around the corner.

Police sirens.

Squealing tires.

Shattering glass.

Metal slicing flesh.

Automatic gunfire.

Screams of outrage.

Pleas of desperation.

The melody of malevolence touched everyone, forcing all inhabitants to either dance or decay.

Crane looked away from the street, trying to shield himself from the cold wind, and slipped inside the alley. Reaching into his pocket, he extracted a single hundred-dollar bill. Benjamin was in pristine condition, but the pair of ass cheeks it was about to be stuffed between weren't—the skin and rectal lining hadn't seen soap in some time. The remnants of prior anal expulsions had forced the white hairs that littered his exit to evolve. They were now either bronze, mustardy, or both.

Can't have you looking too crisp, Crane thought. *That'd be out of character around here. Always got to stay in character.*

As the vagrant squatted with his pants around his ankles, he forced Benjamin into his crusty cavity. Crane's wrinkled butt quaked as he expelled a moan that didn't quite sound like pleasure nor pain.

"There we go," Crane whispered, looking around the dark alley to ensure he was still alone. "Almost there—"

"Hey!" a voice yelled. "What the fuck is wrong with you?"

A cardboard box several yards away shifted.

Crane yanked the tainted bill out of his ass, pulled up his pants, and slipped Benjamin into his pocket. He wiped his browned, oily fingers against his ragged coat.

Another homeless man with a weathered mullet and scraggily beard peered out from his house of garbage. "Don't shit where you sleep, you ever heard that before?"

"I—I'm sorry," Crane said. "I'm new here and—"

"Damn right you are, and you better not come around disrespecting. You go into the wrong alley in this city doin' somethin' like that and you might not walk out of it. I been around here long enough to understand that the guys who don't learn the rules don't last."

Crane hung his head in shame. "It won't happen again. I'm just—I'm all screwed up."

"What's your name?" the man in the cardboard shack asked.

"I'm Crane."

"Hector." He allowed his glare to subside. "Listen, I know what it's like to be the new guy. And in this goddamn place, it's somethin' else altogether." Shivers made his body convulse as he rubbed his hands together. "If you gotta drop one, you don't gotta do it like a fuckin' dog. There's a bucket at the end of the alley, near the green dumpster. That'll give you a little more privacy too."

"Thanks," Crane replied.

"Now if you'll excuse me, I'm gonna try and warm up again."

As Crane watched him slide back into the cardboard, he took a step forward. "Is that the thickest jacket you got?"

Hector paused. "I'm sleepin' in a fuckin' box, what do you think?"

"I'd like to get you something warmer—my way of making amends."

Hector shook his head and laughed. "What's the catch?"

"No catch."

"I been around long enough to know nothing's free. One way or another, you're always on the hook. If there ain't no catch, then I don't want it."

"You never heard of a good deed?"

"Not around here."

Crane looked around the creepy alley in thought. He moved his coat closer to his face, trying to keep warm, before returning his gaze to Hector. "If I just made up a catch, would it make you feel any better?"

"Much better."

"Okay," Crane said, furrowing his brow. "I'll get you a nice warm jacket if you show me around the city this weekend. Nothing crazy, just—"

"Nothin' crazy?" Hector laughed. "Man, do you even know where you're at?"

He ignored the question. "Do we have a deal?"

Hector nodded. "Fine."

"Let's go, then."

Crane helped Hector to his feet, and they both made their way around the corner of the alley. Hanging above their heads was a glowing sign that read FA$T CA$H.

When they entered, bells jingled. A short Indian man in a turban, who also wore a tag with the name SINGH on it, sat behind three inches of bulletproof glass beside a door fortified with burglar bars.

While Crane hadn't been in the city long, the blatant lack

of trust was obvious. He'd never seen a pawn shop where *everything* was behind the counter. There was only a few feet of standing space and a small bench.

Singh looked them over like he wasn't about to let his time be wasted. "This isn't a goddamn shelter. How many times do I have to tell you people? I can smell you from—"

"I've got cash," Crane interrupted, holding up Benjamin. "You got any jackets—something nice maybe?"

The Indian man turned his back. "Just a moment," he said, disappearing into the backroom.

Hector sat on the bench and rubbed his arms, trying to get the blood circulating again.

Coughing, Crane turned to the large tube television flickering on the counter, illuminating a shotgun that didn't seem like it was for sale. It didn't offer a price tag—it was most likely there to offer a toe tag.

The news anchor's voice bled through the half-dozen holes in the glass. "And Mayor McKinney has still yet to comment on the police shortage. After the Broad Street bombing that severely damaged the precinct and saw thirty-seven officers slain, applications remain at a standstill."

Shaky footage of smoke billowing out of the flaming precinct was accompanied by a horde of horrifying screams. A small black woman with beady eyes in a blue suit appeared on the television, knifing her way through a crowd with security. As reporters prodded her, she pushed their microphones out of her face.

Footage from another, separate occasion of the press pestering the mayor was spliced in. An especially eager reporter with a microphone chased the mayor down a darkened street. She paid him no mind, briskly walking toward her limousine.

"Ms. Mayor, what do you say to the people who believe that you've fooled the public?" the reporter asked. "That your allegiance to the drug industry and your brother's criminal history indicate that the changes you promised, how you guaranteed things would be different from your father's political reign, are completely bogus?"

Mayor McKinney whipped around and pointed her finger at the reporter's face. "That man is not my father!" After avoiding the question, Mayor McKinney turned her back and continued down the street.

"What do you have to say about the thirty-first precinct going up in flames?" the reporter continued.

Mayor McKinney didn't bother to turn back this time. "The only heat I'm concerned about right now is blazing the campaign trail."

The picture on the screen transitioned to the news anchor with an image beside his head. The shadowy outline wasn't so much representing a particular person as it was the absence of one.

"Not only does the city's body count continue to climb, but another disturbing trend is suddenly on the rise—disappearances. Officials remain unsure if they're connected to the series of mass murders perpetrated by an individual known only as The Artist."

Crane watched as the police chief stared at the camera with raised eyebrows while the reporter barked a question at him. "Chief Tucker, why is no headway being made on the case? How many more people have to die or go missing?"

"Listen," Chief Tucker said, "if you..." He paused, emotion getting the best of him. "If you'd have seen one of these crime scenes—"

"Exhibits!" one of the reporters corrected.

The chief pointed his finger angrily. "That's exactly the goddamn problem! You people are afraid of offending this scumbag instead of being focused on nailing his ass! We can't let fear run this city!"

"What do you expect the people to do?" another reporter asked. "Catching The Artist is up to the police, whether there's one of you or a hundred, isn't it?"

"You try stepping into this gig, working with a goddamn skeleton crew in a war-torn headquarters. If it's not obvious enough, I'll just say it! We need all the help we can get!"

"What about the idea of rules for thee, not for me?"

"Excuse me?" Chief Tucker asked.

"It's not just The Artist who's getting away with murder in this city, it's many people. Some in higher positions What do you aim to do about it?"

The chief's boxy face somehow grew sterner. "When I took this position, I vowed to do everything I could to turn the tide. But it appears that my candidness may have enticed the very people who've run this city into the toilet. It wasn't my intent to stoke the flames of extremism, but one way or another, there will be justice—for those lives lost in the bombing and the people of this city. I just need the citizens to bear with me."

"It's as bad as I heard," Crane whispered to himself.

"I told you that already," Hector said. "But you're lucky you found me. I know who's who in this city. And more importantly, who not to fuck around with." He stared at the shitty hundred in Crane's hand like he was stuck in a dream. "You take care of me now, and I'll keep you alive."

"Understood," Crane said. "Mayor seems like a real piece of work."

Hector scoffed. "She played it smooth. Outed her own father in a political chess move. McKinney really looked like the hero for a while."

"Until what?"

"Until everybody realized that she was even worse."

The television displayed a picture of a wrinkled old man. Disgraced former mayor Horace Doyle's image transitioned into an advertisement for the very drug that the news indicated to be his downfall.

"Having trouble sleeping?" A soothing female voice found Crane's ears. He continued glaring at the tube, intrigued with all he was learning as the ad played.

A woman with an anxious look lay in a dark bedroom. Her eyes were wide and bloodshot as she tossed and turned in her dirty sheets. "Can't focus?"

The woman now sat at a desk with bags under her eyes, drinking coffee. "No appetite?"

The woman sat at the table with her husband and child while they all engaged in an intense argument. "Does your trauma and stress have a stranglehold on you?"

The woman was now in a dark alley while a grinning man with hosiery on his head held an arm around her neck and a knife to her throat.

"Just—just take my money!" she begged.

"I wanna take somethin' else," the evil man whispered, licking her ear.

The female ad voice returned as the woman awoke from the frightening dream, sweating in her bedroom. "Then you *need* Lobotozine."

The woman sat up in bed and lifted a bottle filled with black pills from her nightstand—she opened it and swallowed one. As she stood, the room brightened up. The sun shone through the window, and her demeanor shifted. Suddenly, she was cheerful and in control of herself.

Clips played of her busy at work, having a calm dinner, and sleeping peacefully. While she functioned properly, an aloof look stained her—like she'd just walked out of an electroshock therapy session. "Take control. Take your life back with Lobo—"

As the bells on the door jingled, Singh reemerged from the back with several coats.

An Asian woman entered the store carrying a small clutch purse. The cold made her shiver, but she looked like she had something on her mind more profound than the weather.

"Welcome back," Singh said over his shoulder to the woman. "Just a moment." He turned back toward Crane. "Okay, which do you like?"

Crane turned to Singh, who held up a couple of jackets.

Hector stood up from the bench and squinted at the coats. "Lemme have a look at that black one."

"Money first," Singh said, gesturing toward the drop drawer.

"How much?" Crane asked.

Singh grinned toward Benjamin. "This is a Bellacove peacoat, so it seems you have *just* enough."

Benjamin fell into the steel drawer.

Singh pulled it in and shuddered. "What is—ugh—why is it so warm and sticky?!" He retched, getting a whiff of the scent. "You people are fucking disgusting."

"Just a little dirt is all," Crane explained with a grin.

Singh glared at him but still placed the coat in the drawer.

"Step aside," Singh snarled, using a tissue to wipe his hand off.

Crane moved to the side of the bench, where he watched Hector try on the coat, but his eyes soon drifted back to the woman. She held up a ring with a modest diamond. But it was as if she didn't want to show it—like it hurt her when she did.

"This thing's pretty damn nice," Hector said, fiddling with the pockets and interior lining of the coat. "Warm as pussy." He licked his lips.

"Take your time," Crane said, his eyes still glued to the woman.

As she dropped the ring into the drawer for Singh, Crane listened closely to their conversation.

"A thousand?" she groaned, seeming stupefied by the offer. "But my—my husband paid like five grand for it!"

"This is a pawn shop," Singh said, "you're lucky to get twenty percent." Reports of local murders flashed on the tube. He pointed at the headline about a mass killing at a strip club. "Not exactly a lot of people falling in love around here these days."

Crane watched how the lady froze when she saw the reports. It was like she was no longer haggling, no longer in a conversation. Like her mind raced off to a memory and left her body behind.

"She got pretty eyes," Hector said. "All slanted like that."

Crane ignored him, captivated by her reaction.

"Take it or leave it," Singh said.

Tears welled in the woman's eyes. "How—how long do I have to get it back?"

"Exactly five days. After that, all bets are off."

She nodded. "I'll take the money."

Crane grinned as he watched Singh use several bills from his register to carefully handle Benjamin. Forming a small wad, Singh unloaded the stinky bill, dropping the stack and the receipt into the steel drawer.

The lady grabbed the cash, her expression heavy with shame and regret.

"Are you sure I can't interest you in a gun?" Singh asked as he inspected the ring. "Or at least a knife? From what they say on the TV, it's not safe out there. Especially for someone... like you."

She shook her head. "I figure you've seen me in here enough to know by now."

Singh raised his eyebrow. "Know what?"

She turned, a cold frown twisting her expression. "Mister, if someone decides to take me out, they'd be doing me a fucking favor."

Singh chuckled. "I wouldn't walk around announcing such things."

Crane's eyes widened. As the woman passed him and exited the shop, he stuck his arm out and held the door. He shifted his gaze to Singh. "We'll take the jacket."

"We will?" Hector asked.

"You like it, don't you? Warm as pussy, right?"

Hector rubbed the jacket again, checking its warmth.

"Well?" Crane urged.

"Yeah, I guess you're right."

"Then, follow me."

The derelicts stepped outside as the woman continued down the road, meshing with the night.

"What the fuck you in such a rush for?" Hector asked.

"When I offered you the jacket, you said you wanted a catch, right?"

"Yeah."

Crane kept his vision zeroed in on the woman and started to follow. “Well, the catch is you’re on the clock. Starting right now.”

THE FLOP FACTORY

Lola stashed the cash from the pawn shop inside her purse and kept walking. To reach her destination, it wasn't going to be easy. She knew the area well, but it was hard to tell if the backstreets were any better than the main roads. It wasn't as if there was any kind of pattern to the killings occurring across the city.

That might've been the most frightening aspect—*everyone* was fair game.

Her clutch purse hadn't had a wad like that in some time, and it made her think about what kind of gift she might buy Tanya in order to distract her—if there was enough money left over, that is.

She's gonna notice, Lola thought. *That girl never misses a chance to remind me that I'm an awful mother. And she's not wrong.*

Rubbing her empty ring finger, worry invaded her. Even in the darkness, she could see the tan line from the ring's absence. She always wore it—her hand felt strange without it. But stronger than her worry or the strangeness was another feeling—guilt.

Lola couldn't shake the feeling of betrayal weighing her

down. It was like a ghost looming over her, aching with dread and disappointment, eager to confront her from the afterlife.

The situation rattled her. Lola needed to forget again. Little by little, she was forgetting more each day, sinking deeper into oblivion.

I'll figure it out once I get the lobo. I'll figure everything out…

Distracted by her anxiety, she didn't think twice about her route until the structure became visible in the distance, breaking over the horizon bit by bit. She hesitated and started to tremble. Searching for an alternate path, she realized there was no way around it—she'd have to pass right by it.

The crime scene tape flapped in the icy breeze, draped all over the building. Her former place of employment looked about as sleezy as any spot in the city. With a name like Cheaters, it was hard not to.

Fuck.

Lola tried not to look at it but couldn't help herself. Flashes of the deconstructed faces and skinned bodies forced their way back into her head. Corpses displaying the most hellish expressions of the raging agony they felt when their lifeforces and aspirations dissipated.

Minus all of their skins, they were left only with their sins.

Whatever their lives had meant before no longer mattered. The Artist had stolen their purposes and repositioned their flesh to transmit his own abhorrent message.

Lola heard their screams from beyond the grave. They lived on in her mind, sharing their tortures with her.

The darkness surrounding the building seemed to manipulate itself. Now it wasn't just the wails in her mind—she saw clusters of haunting expressions.

No… Don't look at it. It's not real.

No matter how many times she'd told herself that, it didn't change how real it felt. Shaking her head, Lola focused on the sidewalk.

The sound of a tin can being kicked echoed behind her.

The hand holding the bloody fillet knife flashed in her head—the hand of The Artist.

She didn't dare look back. Her pulse accelerated with her pace. The clacking of her wide heels smacking against the pavement resounded as she left the rundown strip club behind and her true destination came into sight.

The dilapidated factory was massive. The silhouettes of deviants were projected against the windows by the continuous transitioning of neon lights.

The withdrawals were making her feel weaker, but she pushed. She didn't want to see the faces in the darkness again or find out the origin of the noise behind her.

Once she saw the gate to The Flop Factory, Lola made a run for it.

THE DRIP MAN

The thump of the bass made the building feel like it was going to come crashing down. The rap bars were about what one might expect in such a place—an endless limerick of money, murder, and muff with a splash of 'medication.'

When the cargo elevator brought Lola to the third floor, she rushed to the window. But as she looked outside, all she saw was the eerie night.

It was all in my head, she thought.

As she moved to the open factory floor, the decadence was on full display. Orgies involving every gender and race, under the influence of enough drugs and drink to fuel a mission to the moon. But with the chaos came the calm.

The zombies were there too.

Those—like Lola—who desired everything the ads on the television promised. A silencing of one's inner screams. A reprieve from the sickness that haunted most every nook in the city of fear.

Lola started to feel lightheaded. The weakness she'd felt from the Lobotozine withdrawal was starting to gnaw at her. Forcing herself to stagger forward, she used the railing to keep steady.

I need that fucking lobo right now, Lola thought. In that moment, it was more important than honoring her husband or parenting her daughter. In that moment, it was the only thing that mattered.

The mob of people dancing a short distance away transitioned from Lola's peripheral vision to her focus. She didn't want to look at them, but she had to. Each of their skinless faces, wet with blood and glistening with exposed muscle, held an unintentional grin, the ghastly teeth permanently exposed while their mangled bodies flailed about.

A man's sunk-in face flashed between the bodies. He stood out as the only one in the lot with his skin intact. His familiar bony knees trembled as he shook. His shriveled manhood oozed, moistening his overgrown pubic hair as he relieved himself on the dance floor. Wailing a spectral moan, he begged for death. All he wanted was for it to be over.

Oh, Gabriel. I'm sorry.

Lola wiped the gloss from her eyes. The Flop Factory wasn't the kind of place to show weakness. She needed to stay strong a bit longer. The torturous visions would soon be quelled if she could find the right person.

Where are they?

She continued to scan the frightening crowd, her gaze traveling to the back of the factory and falling upon a man who most certainly had the goods but sent shivers down her spine.

Lola knew him well—everyone knew The Drip Man.

In a city of darkness, The Drip Man still shined. In a place where lives ended on a daily basis over greed and envy, he openly flaunted all he'd taken. He was the type of cat who *wanted* people to try him. The golden stunner shades, platinum grill, long, gaudy chains, and glimmering rings told anyone with eyes that much.

Lola had seen him lose his cool in the club—she saw why everyone called him The Drip Man. She'd watched him pull his bejeweled burner and body several men at once in front of a whole room full of witnesses. Still, no one was dumb enough to talk. If they did, those would be the last words they ever spoke.

While 'dripping' anyone who opposed him might've been what solidified his street credibility, slinging lobo was what had made him rich. But even outside of the money and business, or even the killing, there was a certain darkness about him—one Lola couldn't put her finger on, though she could relate to the way it held dominion over him.

As The Drip Man adjusted his fedora from his platinum throne, the pelts that littered his shoulders became more visible. He lifted the drink to his lips and slurped. They weren't ordinary furs. They were what best represented him—wolf hides.

Lola knew she'd be much better off interacting with one of his minions than him directly. Even though his reach infected every boulevard and street, the more degrees of separation between her and The Drip Man, the better.

Despite Lola's depleted state and the demons whispering her name, her gaze drifted past him.

"You look like you lookin' for suttin'," a voice with deep bass said.

When Lola turned around, she was met with three hundred and twenty pounds of goon. His flab was abundant, and while he was a young man, the weight made him look like a veteran of the game. Big Vern was *exactly* the guy Lola was looking for.

"You look all kinda strung out." Big Vern reached into his pocket and extracted a bottle, shaking the pills like a box of Tic Tacs. "The usual?"

Lola nodded, pulling six crisp hundreds from her purse. But Benjamin remained safe inside. "Times three."

He looked at the money and hesitated. "You stockin' up or suttin'?"

"Please just… Give it to me!"

Big Vern took the money, letting his fingertips drag across her palm. "I only ask cuz, you know, I'd let that little ass of yours work it off, if you wanted to save some dough." He winked at her. "I don't just go around sayin' that to anyone."

Lola snagged the three bottles and shoved two of them into her clutch. Slumping down into the chair behind her with the other one in hand, she popped open the cap. When she tried swallowing a pill, her mouth was too dry. She looked to one of the abandoned cocktails on the table beside her and washed it down.

Big Vern plopped onto the couch beside her seat. "Why don't you let me get you a fresh drin—"

Another black man, with a sideways fitted hat and a smoke-colored Starter jacket, slapped Big Vern on the arm. Lola recognized him, having bought drugs off him countless times before—Nate Compton.

Like his counterpart Big Vern, Nate was a pusher, scouted and poached by The Drip Man. While anyone with their ear to the criminal underbelly knew the duo were stick-up kids, they weren't anywhere near as scary as their boss—their affiliation with The Drip Man bought them respect, whether they deserved it or not.

"Yo, Vern!" Nate said. "I just got a buzz."

"So what, nigga, everybody in here drinkin'," Big Vern said, trying to brush him off. "Can't you see I'm tryin' to talk to the lady?"

"No." Nate pointed to the pager on his hip. "I mean Ray Ray hit me up. Said they seen his whip over there when he passed by."

The drug was already starting to settle in—it was as trusted as Tylenol, as instantaneous as Advil.

"Oh shit." Big Vern looked at Lola. "I gotta bounce, but… think about what I said."

As Lola watched the two of them disappear into the crowd of mayhem, the dose crept deeper into her brain. She wouldn't be thinking about that or any other bullshit for a while. She was on the highway to Heaven, where demons aren't allowed.

Lola wanted nothing more than to just melt away into her chair like the rest of the zombies inside The Flop Factory, but if she made such a decision, she'd be ensuring an awful evening of uncertainty for her daughter.

I can't do that to Tanya.

Lola forced herself back to her feet and slipped the last bottle of lobo inside her clutch. She made sure to take just enough not to get too zonked out before she got home. If she could just get back to her house safely, she could finally get some rest.

HOMEBOUND

A subtle snarl of repulsion twisted Lola's lips as she looked at the spoiler on the back of the Mazda parked at the curb in front of her house.

It wasn't so much that she disliked Tanya's boyfriend, it was more that she disliked what he represented. Chino Anthony was small-time. Not the kind of guy she imagined would carve out a decent future for her daughter. And not the man who would protect her if something went sour—not that Lola was doing much better.

She felt at her bare finger again.

But maybe he's the distraction I need tonight, she thought. *Maybe he's a blessing in disguise. At least until I can figure out how to get it back or explain myself.*

She pushed the key into the lock and quietly crept inside. The lights were off, and she could hear music playing louder than she'd have preferred.

Lola knew what *that* meant.

That two-bit punk was inside her daughter again. As much as she didn't like thinking about it, Lola wasn't out to argue. Her only goal was to avoid conflict and get some rest.

Once she had her shit together, once she had some kind of gameplan, then she and Tanya could sit down and have a real talk—mother to daughter. Something Lola knew she should have done a long time ago. Like the talks she'd had with her own mother.

Lola slipped inside her room and closed the door.

Looking down at where her wedding band should've been, Lola's lean frame trembled—her terror was the puppet master of her flesh. The sparkle of the gem was no more. Her eyes darted from her bare finger toward the picture frame on her nightstand.

The photo inside was many years old. Before the look of worry and wrinkles of stress had reshaped her expression. Before she'd gone chasing the American dream.

In the snapshot, Lola stood near a well in her village, engulfed in the long arms of a handsome young man. The joy on their faces was unmatched. Their hopes and aspirations were inflated as much as Lola's belly was at the time. They were blissful and radiated their happiness to everyone around them. But now, falling in love back in the Philippines felt like another life.

Gabriel had fueled Lola. He was everything: her hope, strength, and purpose.

He never looked sick, she thought.

None of it made sense and none of it was fair. Gabriel was a healthy middle-aged man. The pillar who kept their family stable. When the cancer was discovered inside him, Lola had expected it to be just a small bump in the road. He was young—surely he'd beat it.

But he didn't.

Watching him lose all his fight and energy was hard. Gabriel was always the one with a solution. He'd fixed everything for both Lola and Tanya.

But he couldn't fix himself.

Lola had watched, heartbroken, as the nurses cleaned him and changed his diapers. As the humanity was siphoned out of him, in many ways it was siphoned from Lola as well.

The feeling that she carried after his passing was weight that would never leave her, a log of horrors that were ready to reactivate on command.

As bad as it had been for Lola, it was even worse for Tanya. A young girl who hardly knew what death was, so intimately introduced. Seeing her baby witness just a few of the horrifying bits that haunted Lola was another layer of agony etched into her weathered soul.

Flashes of his pale face, emaciated frame, and confused gawk erupted in her mind. The screams of agony ripped inside her head, accompanied by more imagery—Gabriel, bed-ridden beside a pair of smug doctors. The strong man who'd swept her off her feet now resembled his own daughter—a confused child.

The American doctors never seemed overly concerned. It was more transactional than emotional—like so many things in this city. Like Gabriel was some sort of science experiment they were monitoring. From the onset, they gave Lola and Gabriel little hope, refusing to remove the growth and urging 'treatment' as their only option.

Others had told her that the size of the malignant growth inside Gabriel was operable. A nurse had even pulled her aside and suggested they get a second opinion. But such things weren't financially possible.

She'd never gotten that second opinion. Instead, the doctors treated Gabriel.

They'd treated him to death.

Lola felt sick to her stomach. After they treated him, they were quick to offer treatment to Lola. They assured her that all the horrible memories of watching Gabriel deteriorate inside their filthy hospital would be subdued by the little black pills they prescribed her. And in a way, they were right. But, conveniently, the side effects of 'treatment' were never discussed.

Even worse, as of late, it wasn't just the horrors Lola had witnessed with Gabriel that she was dealing with. It was the repercussions of losing him. The devilish domino effect that the absence of love had on her existence. The wholesome, caring, and responsive woman she'd been was a ghost in the rearview. One that she further pulled away from with each waking moment.

As her watery eyes remained on Gabriel's youthful face, a vivid flash erupted in her head. The same vantage point from inside Cheaters the night of the massacre.

Lola didn't enjoy wearing her ring when she danced—it felt like bringing her dead husband along to watch her sin. But the selfish part of her needed that strength.

While circling the stripper pole that night, the ring had slipped from her finger—the weight loss from her stress came as a result of not wanting to eat. It hadn't taken much momentum to send the ring flying off her finger and through a crack in the rickety stage. She'd played it cool until after her set, when she'd frantically rushed to the back. Behind the curtain, she'd opened the hatch door, crawling under the stage to secure the ring, worried it might collapse down on top of her.

It wasn't until she'd gotten toward the front when she smelled a strange odor. As she retrieved the ring, she lost the ability to move her body. She'd lain frozen, looking through the cracks between the boards at the front of the stage—forced to watch.

The bodies of her peers piled slowly over time. The misshapen skins in the heap were frayed at the edges, a glistening wetness oozing from the carnal casings.

The memory of the mangled meat haunted her—the crack in the stage serving as a portal to mystery and mutilation. Lola had watched helplessly as the pair of blood-soaked boots moved about. The feet had taken several steps through the massive puddles of gore that had accumulated. A mini wave of warm blood had seeped through the base of the stage, inching toward her until it eventually caressed the side of her face. She'd lain immobile on the sticky floor, molested by the violence.

No! Not again!

She knew the dosage she'd taken back at The Flop Factory was enough to stop her hallucinations but not her thoughts. She needed more if she was going to stunt the horrifying visions. The shiny, raw muscle was even clearer in her head now, gleaming through the opening. The gore-caked blade of the steel filleting the rubbery skin of an unrecognizable female face. The flesh flopping around like a latex mask.

She wished that was the case.

Lungs inflating, Lola panted like she was there again. In many ways, she was. And there was only one way out. She removed the lobo from her clutch and set it on the nightstand.

Forgive me, Gabriel.

When she faced his picture, she felt her guilt start to bubble up again. Turning the frame, she angled it to hide his sweet gaze and then scooped the cash out of her clutch. Benjamin left a brownish residue on the other contents inside the purse.

"Ugh," she uttered, trying to shake off the smell.

It wasn't just the idea that she'd pawned her dead husband's ring, it was the symbolism behind it. Lola wouldn't have survived the strip club slaughter if the ring hadn't slipped off her finger. It was like Gabriel had looked over her—the guardian angel steering her away from harm. Without that ring, she would've been one of the ghosts she'd walked past.

And what had she done to show her gratitude?

You're fucking pathetic.

Lola hated what she'd become but didn't have the strength to be anything else. More tears ran down her face as she opened the bottle of lobo.

All she wanted to do was forget.

She quickly gobbled up several pills before falling onto the bed.

NO SHOULDER TO CRY ON

The door to Lola's bedroom opened gradually and without a sound. It was as if the person on the other side had employed the same stealthy tactics many times before.

Chino Anthony crept in like an assassin. His cornrows were tight, his lineup perfect—a gold tooth sparkled in his mouth. Wearing only his boxer-briefs and socks, his footsteps didn't make a sound.

He looked at Lola passed out in her thong and shook his head while he mouthed the word "damn."

Bitch got a better thumper than her fuckin' daughter, he thought.

He scurried over to the dresser, eyeing the cash. Moonlight leaked in through the window, causing the golden cap on his incisor to twinkle in the darkness.

Damn, where she get that much?

He always wanted to take everything in front of him, but

he restrained his urge. For his entire life, he'd stuck to the same method. When a crime is petty, people don't tend to notice.

Tanya's mom might've been a zombified, lobed-out bitch, but running out with that much dough was enough to wake the dead. However, if he just took a hundred, she was more likely to blame herself for getting so wasted that she lost track of her paper. His tried-and-true method would allow him to continue milking his cash cow, one sip at a time, until she dried up—or until the calf in the other room caught on.

Gotta be smart. Play longball with these bitches.

He snatched Benjamin off the dresser, knocking one of the pill bottles onto its side. The minute the paper touched his fingertips, he felt an *extra* grittiness, followed by a foul stench that nearly yanked a gag from his throat.

The fuck?

He didn't have much time to think about it as Lola's snore pattern suddenly changed and she rolled from her side to her back. Chino stayed still a moment, frozen in place as he watched her, waiting to make sure she remained asleep.

Once he knew he was in the clear, he slipped Benjamin into his underwear and tucked it under his nuts. Backing out of the room, he cautiously retreated down the hallway and slipped into the bathroom.

He knew Tanya would be listening, so he made sure to cover his tracks before exiting: he flushed the toilet, turned on the faucet, washed his hands. As Chino approached the door at the end of the hallway and adjusted his junk, he could feel the grime-coated bill wrapped around his scrotum like gift paper.

When he entered Tanya's room, she was still naked and trying to keep warm under the covers. But that was an impossible task. The heat had been shut off several weeks ago—Tanya's mom wasn't exactly on top of things. Choosing to feed her addiction rather than feed her daughter. The thought of it almost made Chino feel bad for stealing from them—almost.

The household had gotten so out of order that Chino wondered how much longer before they got evicted, which would fuck up his whole operation. Where else would he find such accessible pussy and petty cash?

Especially lately—all of a sudden, it was like Tanya couldn't get enough of his dick. He attributed the uptick to Tanya trying to keep her core temperature high on those cold nights rather than an insatiable craving for his cock.

When Chino looked at her face, she wasn't there. She gazed out the window blankly.

"You ain't cum?" he asked.

"No, I did," she said.

"What then?"

"Just wondering about my mom."

Chino nearly gasped but kept his cool. "Whatchu mean? You told me she was in her room."

"She's here, but she's not *here*. She never is anymore. I can't just keep watching her wither away. It's like…"

Chino furrowed his brow. Knowing he'd once again gotten away with it, he couldn't make himself care. But he'd gotten pretty decent at pretending.

"Like what?"

"It's like watching my dad all over again. It's actually worse. With her, it doesn't have to be this way."

Man, this bitch. She never shut the fuck up about her moms. My moms is fuckin' dead—shanked by a fiend when I was still shittin' in diapers. You don't hear me speakin' on it every fuckin' day, though. She lucky that pussy's bomb.

Chino picked up an outdated, dog-eared magazine with a group of iced-out rappers on the cover from the nightstand. He collapsed to the bed and flipped through the pages—not reading a word, only using it to avoid eye contact.

"C'mon, you know your moms been through all that shit at the club. It prolly fucked with her head."

"She was like this before the club," Tanya snapped back with a hint of annoyance in her tone. "Since my dad. And she just keeps getting worse and worse… When will she finally start getting better?"

Chino shrugged but kept himself hidden behind the magazine. "Ha, have you looked around? Ain't nothin' gettin' better for no one till they get the fuck up out this bitch."

She bit her lip. "Maybe I was right, then."

"Right about what?"

"Maybe it's time for me to stop fighting."

He laughed and finally tossed the magazine. "The fuck you talkin' about stop fightin'? You tryin' to run off?"

"In a sense, yeah—"

"Only thing worse than the local news is the national. You think this city's got it bad? The damn world's one big nightmare tryin' to kill you in your sleep. You gotta know the right spots to go—and I mean *exactly*. The grass ain't always greener on the other side because sometimes there's bodies buried underneath it, you hear what I'm sayin'?"

He watched Tanya chew this over, hoping his plan to keep her close was working.

"And speakin' of green, what money you got to be leavin' with anyhow? You broke as fuck in the cheapest city on Earth."

The look on her face had gone beyond blank—Tanya looked like a corpse. "Where I'd be going, I wouldn't need money."

Chino sucked his teeth. "You really ain't payin' attention. Regardless, you gonna need skrilla wherever you—"

Vibrations rumbled from the pager on Chino's side of the nightstand. He turned the face of the device toward him, angling it so Tanya couldn't read it.

"Oh shit…" He lifted the telephone and promptly punched in the number from the pager screen. He listened intently until someone picked up on the other end of the line.

"I need a driver to move a shipment," a smooth male voice said.

"Same spot as last time?" Chino asked.

"Yeah."

"Aight, I'm comin' through now."

After he hung up the phone, Chino scrambled for his pants. Money was calling, and he'd already spent enough time sitting around trying to cheer up pussy he'd already smashed. But when he saw the look of disappointment on Tanya's face, he quickly turned his pretending skills back on.

"I gotta do a play," Chino said.

Tanya still seemed delirious and despondent. "What's that even mean?"

"It means I'm makin' fuckin' moves for us." He finished tying his Timberlands, wrapped the bubble jacket around his upper body, and slipped on his skully. "Who knows, if I make enough of 'em, maybe someday the both of us'll raise up outta here together. Go plant our own grass somewhere, know what I'm sayin'?"

She said nothing in response.

"I'll hit you up," he said, slipping out of the bedroom.

Chino crept out of the house and jogged over to his Mazda under the glow of the moonlight. After unlocking the door, he sat down and stuck his key into the ignition.

High beams lit up his whip as the squealing tires skidded across the pavement. His hand instinctively reached for his hip, but there was nothing there. He patted his jacket pockets frantically as the fully-tinted SUV rocked to a halt right in front of him—both empty.

"Where the fuck's my—?!"

The windows exploded. A cascade of broken glass showered Chino as the slugs entered his body. He flailed like he'd been electrocuted as the barrage of bullets blew open portals of violence in his flesh. Red mist peppered the interior as he vomited the blood all over himself.

A second gun appeared out the driver's window and immediately started firing, blasting a barrage of bullets that destroyed Chino's face and neck. One blew his jawbone off, leaving it dangling from the side of his skull. Another sprayed his brains all over the headrest.

The last several landed in his throat, collapsing his Adam's apple and ripping a hole open that pushed a mini reservoir of crimson out over his chest.

By the time Chino Anthony's hole-punched body slumped over, he was already dead.

GETTING THE DROP

"There that nigga is," Nate said, watching Chino get into his vehicle. He cocked back the hammer on his Desert Eagle and nodded at Big Vern. "It's go time."

Big Vern put the car in drive. "Keep squeezin' till it's empty." He hit the high beams and screeched to a halt in front of the Mazda.

Nate stuck his arm out the window and started dumping rounds into the driver's side. "You like to shine, huh, mutha fucka?"

His words were swallowed up by the sound of the gunshots. When Nate's gun started to click, Big Vern scoffed.

"Man, fuck a body shot." He pulled his strap and disengaged the safety. "I told you before, aim for the fuckin' head."

Leaning out his window, Big Vern unloaded the gun. Several rounds blew Chino's head apart and opened his throat.

Nate sucked his teeth like the shots he'd let off would've been sufficient—frustrated that Big Vern stole his thunder.

Putting a fresh magazine in the gun, Big Vern pulled at his door handle. "You run his pockets. I'ma scope out the whip."

Nate nodded, reloading just in case. "Aight."

After opening the passenger door, Big Vern looked at the glove box. Bits of Chino's cranium clung to the handle. "Damn," he grumbled. "This nigga's melon's everywhere."

"Shit," Nate said as he tried to decide how to best get into the pockets of the bullet-riddled body. "I think we over did it. He a mess."

The glove box had nothing aside from a half-empty box of Dutch Masters cigars. "He don't even buy the greens." Big Vern huffed but snatched them up anyhow.

"Yo, Vern, how am I supposed to run his fuckin' pockets when he all like this?"

Big Vern looked at his partner with a raised eyebrow. "Man, you act like this your first time or suttin'. Grab him by the ankles and drag his skinny ass out the whip. But pop the trunk first."

Big Vern worked his way around the back of the Mazda and studied the contents of the now-open trunk: donut tire, lug wrench, toolbox, and a three-pack of wifebeaters—one of which was missing.

Big Vern shook his head in annoyance. "I thought you said he was paid. This nigga don't look like no baller."

Nate struggled with the body as he pulled it out of the vehicle. "That's what Ray Ray said."

Big Vern retrieved one of the shirts from the pack. "Man! You got us out here jackin' this fool on account a what that little dick itcher Ray Ray said? Is you stupid, or is you dumb?"

Big Vern approached Nate and tossed the shirt at his chest. "This mutha fucka look like he work at Home Hardware or some shit."

"What's this for?" Nate asked.

"So you don't get his fuckin' head all over your hands when you check his pockets."

Nate holstered his pistol and wrapped the shirt around his hand. He turned one of Chino's pockets inside out, revealing a pager.

Big Vern shook his head and glared at Nate. "Yo, I'ma lose my shit if this nigga broke."

"Chill, man," Nate said reaching for the other pocket. "He gotta have somethin'."

When the contents were revealed, Big Vern stayed true to his word. "What the fuck is wrong witchu?!" He kicked one of the tires, shaking the Mazda. "I should've known better." He clenched his gun as tightly as his teeth. "I should fuckin' smoke your ass."

Nate stood up and held out his hands, the bloody shirt still wrapped around one of them. "Bro, be cool."

"Be cool?! We just blasted this nigga for a half box a Dutches, and you want me to be cool?!"

Nate shrugged. "I'm sayin', we ain't searched *everywhere* yet. You feel me?"

"Huh?"

"I mean, when the five-o was out harder, alotta people stashed their shit."

"I'm past losin' my patience witchu. Just say what the fuck you mean."

"I mean, maybe he tucked his shit. Like under his nuts. He gotta have some crack, or cash, or somethin', right?"

"Well, what the fuck is you waitin' for?"

"What you mean?"

"Search his nuts, then!"

Nate raised his eyebrow. "Man, I ain't doin' no gay shit. You do it."

Big Vern cocked his gun. "I swear, I love you like a brother, but you trippin'. You dragged me into some dumb shit, now it's up to you to make it right." He aimed the gun below Nate's waist. "You can either lift his nuts, or I can clip yours."

THE EYES IN THE ALLEY

Crane's eyes bulged. It was as if the mayhem was a drug to him. He'd expected to see violence at the drop of a hat, but the utter disregard for human life was absurd.

Hector stood beside Crane as they watched the shooters bicker, camouflaged by the darkness of the alley. A smile remained on Hector's face as he enjoyed the warmth of his new coat. "This is every day out here. Everyone is so…"

Crane finished his thought. "Disposable."

"Yeah, unless you're the mayor or somethin'."

"What do you know about her?"

Hector scoffed. "She's a politician, what else is there to know? Horace Doyle was her daddy—corruption's in her blood." He pointed at the car riddled with bullet holes. "You think that cunt has any intention of stoppin' the crime here? From what I seen, keepin' the criminals happy and the citizens fearful is the foundation of her campaign. Whoever blew up the precinct should've put the bomb in her goddamn office instead. That would've made a lot more sense if you ask me—"

"Yo! This some gross shit!" The smaller shooter's voice echoed in the distance.

"Don't expect me to feel bad for you," the larger one said.

"Aw, man! Why his… why his dick smell like shit?"

"Maybe he had it in someone's ass."

Crane grinned, pleased with their exchange. Hector noticed and gave him a sideways look.

Glancing away from the murder scene, Crane focused on Hector. "What do you say after these two take off, we go for a little joyride?"

"Ride?" Hector asked. "You got a car?"

"No," Crane said, looking back toward the Mazda painted with brain matter. "But I can't imagine he's going to need that one anymore."

PICKIN' AT THE SCRAPS

"Oh shit, he got somethin'," Nate said as he yanked his arm from Chino's pants.

"What is it?" Big Vern asked.

"A Benjamin."

"Just one?"

"Yeah, but it's—aw, what the—it got shit all over it! You dirty ass—"

"Man, we can't be hangin' 'round here all night," Big Vern interrupted. "Try to clean it off with the shirt."

"I fished it outta his fuckin' nuts. How 'bout you do somethin' for once?"

"Cuz I got an idea."

Big Vern made his way around the car and removed a hammer and screwdriver from the toolbox in the trunk. Returning to Chino's corpse, he squatted down.

"Bro, what you doin'?" Nate asked.

"A hundred dollars and some Dutches ain't no come up," Big Vern said. "But that ice…" He gestured to the bedazzled tooth before aligning the edge of the flathead with the gumline above Chino's incisor. "That's prolly worth somethin'."

He slammed the hammer onto the handle of the screwdriver, sending the tooth exploding out of Chino's mouth.

"Fuck—no!" Big Vern yelled.

Nate had managed to wipe almost all the fecal matter off the bill. "What?"

"The fuckin' ice went down his throat."

"Couldn't have gone that far down, maybe you can still reach it."

"Nah," Big Vern said. "I can't." Nate's forehead wrinkled as Big Vern glared at him. "But *you* can."

"Fuck that shit!" Nate said. "I moved the nigga's nuts, cleaned his shit off the money. *You* do that shit."

"Man, look at the size of my arm!" Big Vern held up his ham hock. "You think that shit gonna fit down his little-ass throat?"

"The bottom of his jaw got blown off his face." Nate pointed at the detached mandible caked in gore. "It's fat nigga friendly."

Big Vern snatched Benjamin from Nate and slipped the bill inside his pocket. "You doin' it. It'll take two seconds, like fuckin' a bitch with a sketchy snatch. Just stick it in real quick and wipe it off."

"With what?!" Nate squawked. "The fuckin' shit shirt?!"

Big Vern shrugged and smiled. "And hurry up! Just because the cops ain't clockin' don't mean we should be hangin' around here all night. The fuckin' Artist out there still."

Nate shook his head in disgust, hunching in front of Chino's corpse while rolling up his sleeve and readjusting the shirt around his hand. "Man, fuck The Artist and fuck you!"

Big Vern grew serious. "I'm gettin' tired of your dumb shit. If it was me who suggested we pop this broke ass nigga, then I'd be goin' down his throat. But that wasn't me. That was you. Don't make me do some irreversible shit to you, bro." Big Vern's grip tightened on the hammer. "I don't wanna, but I will if I have to."

Nate seemed to comprehend the seriousness in his cadence. "Aight, aight, chill." Taking a deep breath, Nate looked at the ripped flesh where the missing jaw was and started to work his arm into Chino's throat. "Ughhhhhh, damn—I-I don't feel nothin'."

"Go a lil bit deeper then."

Nate pushed down farther until Chino's corpse was deepthroating up to his forearm. "Man, this some sick shit—"

Without warning, Chino's body interrupted, starting to spasm and convulse.

"What the fuck!" Nate screeched.

When he ripped his forearm and hand out of Chino's gullet, the carcass' insides started to rumble. Regurgitation commenced, launching a clumpy liquid with fierce rapidity.

The expulsion was the color and texture of past-due milk. Peppered within the porridge were pieces of Chino's face and blood. The mixture of half-digested food and gore sprayed all over Nate's arm and head.

Big Vern stood in shock. But as his eyes dropped down, his slack jaw tightened into a grin. Within the puddle on the ground, the golden tooth glinted.

MOUNTING FAILURE

Singh used his jeweler's loupe to examine the tooth. The gold had been scrubbed clean of the blood and vomit it was previously dipped in.

"So, what can we do with it?" Big Vern asked.

Nate stood by the side of his partner, eagerly awaiting the response.

"You can take this phony shit out of my store." Singh dropped the tooth back into the drawer and slammed it shut.

"Bullshit!" Big Vern pounded his fist into the glass.

Singh unlocked a rectangular flap and grabbed the shotgun off the counter. He stuck the barrel through the opening. "Get the fuck out of my store! Now!"

Big Vern threw his hands up. "Aight, aight, man."

"Yo, chill the fuck out, towelhead," Nate said. "He's just blowin' off some steam."

Singh pumped the shotgun, loading a shell into the chamber. "Call me towelhead again, and you'll need more than a towel for your head, my friend."

The doorbells jingled as they both exited the pawn shop.

Once the door was closed, Big Vern grabbed Nate by his Starter jacket and slammed him against the wall.

"The fuck you mad at me for?" Nate asked.

"Cuz you dumb!" Big Vern yelled. "You clearly didn't case this Chino nigga in the slightest. If you had, you'd have known he was broke!"

"What you mean? We got a Benji, didn't we?"

Big Vern squinted. "You think a man's life is worth a hundred dollars?"

Nate struggled with the query. "I guess it woulda been nice to get a G."

Big Vern's eyes widened. Clearly, they were thinking on two different stratospheres. It was like Nate's words had crippled him. Big Vern's grip on his collar weakened, and he shook his head. "I'm takin' you home. Let's go."

When he got into the SUV, Big Vern felt like a parent reprimanding their child—a parent who wished they'd had an abortion.

Nate climbed into the passenger seat. "But bro, we live together..."

Gritting his teeth, Big Vern huffed. "I fuckin' know that, but I ain't goin' home, not yet." He turned the key.

"Where you goin' then?"

"I'm goin' to try and forget about tonight and see if I can find the strength to forgive your stupid ass tomorrow."

"Stop playin', where you really goin', man?"

Big Vern caressed Benjamin in his pocket. "I'm goin' to get some pussy."

FEDERAL RESERVE NOTE
WASHINGTON, D.C.
C00630261
100
ONE HUNDRED DOLLARS

PART 2:

BARE & EXPOSED

A BOOTY FOR A BENJI

Sierra had been in front of her vanity, staring at her reflection, for what could have been hours when the knock rang out from her front door.

She couldn't be sure how long she'd been sitting there, wearing nothing but her crucifix necklace, studying her face and body. Remembering how her flesh used to be tighter and more supple. The once smooth skin of her face was now covered in wrinkles, drooping from her skull like a water-damaged Halloween mask. The skin of her neck bunched up and piled down around her clavicle like melting candle wax.

She ignored the knocking as she stood up and turned to the side, sucking in her stomach and arching her back. She knew she was lying to herself. She knew she'd never have her old body back, knew things were only going to droop more and more as the years kept ticking by.

You used to be so hot, she thought. *They used to call you Sierra Sacs. Now look at you… more like Sierra Sags.*

Sierra ran her fingertips across the rough texture of her chest. Sun damaged, loose, and speckled with spots and skin tags that poked out like dried oatmeal bits.

She nearly shed a tear as she studied her breasts. The way they sagged and hung down to her belly, striped with stretch marks, the nipples dark and chewed up.

When she started her line of work, back before Cheaters even opened its doors, her tits were the stuff of legend: perfectly round, smooth, and full. The way they bounced but stayed upright on her chest and her cinnamon-colored nipples perfectly placed at the center would drive any man crazy.

It was *those* tits that had caught Leon's attention—Sierra was his first hire, and they made a lot of money together over the years. But after more than a decade of abuse, from both men and gravity, those legendary tits of hers grew long and flat and looked like they probably tasted of cigarettes and day-old coffee.

That don't mean you're undesirable. You still got plenty to offer.

Sierra scoffed at her own thought—women with more to offer didn't get demoted to the day crew, especially after what felt like a lifetime of loyalty and devotion to a man who was fluent in broken promises. She recalled her past conversations with that man religiously. Leon—the owner and manager of Cheaters night club—was always on her mind.

It's not what you think, Leon had told her. *There's good money to be made from the lunch crowd, and I need someone I can trust to run that shit. Understand? None of these bitches mean shit to me, not like you do. You know that, right?*

Sierra had agreed, almost certain she was being manipulated again. It was near impossible to refuse Leon anything. Even something as demoralizing as shaking her aging body at construction workers on their lunch breaks as they stuffed all-you-can-eat chicken fingers down their gullets and ran their greasy, grubby, callused fingers across her flesh.

But she did it for Leon because she had still held on to the hope that—even after all the heartache and devastation he'd caused her—he would keep his promise.

One day, we'll leave this place, Leon had told her. *Just you and me.*

As she studied her figure, her hands roamed her belly and a wave of grief swept over her, remembering for a moment the small bump that once grew there, a dream she'd had to let go of, as hard as it was. While it seemed her breasts and hips were built for motherhood, God apparently had different plans for her.

When she would allow herself to compare the life she had always imagined versus the life she now found herself stuck inside of, it was enough to just throw in the towel and give up.

The knock came again, this time a hard pounding full of frustration and impatience. It ripped her out of her thoughts, which she was grateful for—the last thing she wanted to think about was Leon or Cheaters or all the things that could have been.

After what had happened, Sierra knew she should have been nothing but grateful. If she would have stayed on the night crew, she'd probably be dead like the rest of them. Or missing—she nearly picked up the red lips-shaped phone on her nightstand again but stopped herself.

Where are you, Cassie? Please just let me know you're okay.

Nobody was answering their phones, and everything she'd heard on the news was vague. Dwelling on it would only drive her crazy—she needed a distraction.

She threw on some clothes and started toward the front door but glanced over her shoulder toward her reflection one last time so she could admire her plump backside.

When she would complain about her body to Leon, he would always compliment her seemingly ageless booty.

Least God sees it fit to keep you thick where you shit, he would say before giving it a good hard smack to watch it jiggle and sway.

Leon's grinning face appeared in her mind again, but even as she managed to shoo it away, it was instantly replaced by Cassie's—that shy innocence that was always present on her expression flickered through Sierra's thoughts and made her eyes well up.

Sierra glanced up at the velvet Jesus painting hung just above her vanity, strategically placed as a reminder of her faith for the times she might have felt especially prideful or envious. But over the years, shame and regret had conditioned her eyes not to stray above the top border of her mirror, to avoid the judgmental stare of her Lord—she'd been a terrible Christian for far too long.

But since meeting Cassie—a Catholic girl who reminded Sierra so much of herself before life got a hold of her—she found herself thinking more and more about her faith and her relationship with God.

She questioned if she'd even be welcome after everything she'd done, all the sins she'd committed. She'd thought about going to confession many times in the past to beg God for forgiveness, but never quite made it to the church. Even if she'd gone and recited a thousand Hail Marys and Our Fathers and licked holy water off the priest's feet, she knew she'd be full of sin again by nightfall.

What good is God's forgiveness for someone who sins on a daily basis? she'd ask herself. *Sooner or later, He would stop listening. He would give up on me.*

Sierra wondered if *she* should give up on *herself*. She wondered if it was too late for her.

Sierra forced all thoughts of Leon, Cheaters, and God out of her mind as she marched across her small home toward the front door, where the knocking continued to grow in duration and intensity.

"Quit pounding on my door!" Sierra felt her scowl deepen, undoubtedly highlighting every wrinkle across her face as she yanked on the handle.

When she saw Big Vern standing on her doorstep, his belly pushing his XXXL T-shirt to its limit, she nearly slammed the door in his face. She knew why he was there. And from the way he stuck in his Air-Jordaned foot to block the door, it was obvious he knew that Sierra didn't want him there.

She pressed the door up against his foot anyway, just to make his toes ache. "Vern," she groaned as she rolled her eyes and shook her head. "Not tonight, all right?"

"Don't be like that," Big Vern said as he pulled Benjamin from his pocket and dangled it. "Look what I got for you."

The bill was wrinkled with a slight brown stain like a used napkin from a steak house, but still enough to make Sierra pause. Her stomach rumbled at the sight of it, just thinking about a meal that didn't come in a cup or a tin can. By the way Big Vern grinned, she knew he'd heard the growling of her hungry belly.

"With this, a girl could afford to treat herself. I know it ain't been easy, 'specially lately with what went down at the club. But shit." He leaned in as far as his gut would allow. "That don't mean you can't make money. Not when you got Big Vern, you know what I'm sayin'?"

Sierra scoffed as he waved Benjamin at her, waggling his eyebrows and licking his lips like a waterlogged LL Cool J. She hated herself as she stepped aside and let him in, already dreading what she knew would come next.

She tried to snatch Benjamin from Big Vern's hand, but he yanked it away and shoved the bill back into his pocket.

"You know how this work, girl," he said in his revolting version of a sexy voice before sucking on the front of his teeth like they were lemon Starburst. "You get your money when I get my honey."

Sierra shuddered with disgust. When Big Vern reached for her, she pulled away and felt another strong urge to shove this blob out of her house. But the rumbling in her stomach made that hundred in Big Vern's pocket seem like a winning lottery ticket.

And if she was being honest with herself, it felt good to still be desired—even by someone as disgusting as Big Vern. And so she took him by the hand—which felt like gripping a spiral ham—and led him toward her bedroom.

Big Vern didn't waste any time getting undressed. He kicked his Jordans off, slid his jeans and briefs down his rhinoceros legs, and then stood by the bed wearing only his T-shirt like some kind of ghetto version of Winnie the Pooh—

and this Pooh Bear wanted his honey.

Staring across the room toward Sierra, Big Vern stroked his stumpy dick with only his thumb and index finger. Little more than the head was visible from beneath his swollen belly. It looked more like he was trying to pop a zit than masturbate.

Sierra caught a glimpse of her reflection in her vanity as Big Vern struggled to pull his shirt off behind her. The last thing she wanted to see was her own nude body juxtaposed against Big Vern's, so she undressed and tossed her robe over the mirror before being reminded of who the saggiest one of all was.

Her eyes once again coasted up toward Jesus, who seemed to glare at her with disapproval. She thought about pulling the painting down, or at least turning it over, but then Big Vern stole her focus again.

"There goes Sierra Sacs," he said, "just the medicine a nigga need to fix the shit-ass day I been havin'. How 'bout you come on over here and get you a taste, huh?"

Sierra did nothing to hide her displeasure as she approached the tip of Big Vern's cock like it was a poisonous crab apple. Dropping to her knees, she took it into her mouth. As she sucked it, she tried to use only her lips to keep it aimed toward the roof of her mouth and away from her tongue to avoid tasting it, the dick too short to reach her uvula.

Big Vern moaned, a bit of phlegm rattling at the back of his throat. He gripped Sierra's head with both hands, mashing her ears and making the backs of her earrings poke her jaw. She tried to pull away, but he only held on tighter, pumping his hips like he was churning butter in her tonsils.

Her mouth filled with a smegma flavor like spoiled brie, despite Big Vern having no foreskin. The soft jowls of his gut smacked Sierra in the forehead, his gaping belly button peppering her head with moist kisses.

She finally managed to shove him off her, then spat a wad of foamy saliva onto the floor as her stomach lurched from the taste.

"You couldn't wash up first?" Sierra wiped the slimy moisture from around her mouth. "Should charge you triple for having no manners. Now pay up and get out of my house."

Big Vern smirked at her, stroking the underside of his cock with one hand while squeezing his balls in the other.

"You don't get paid till I bust this nut," he said, then reached down and lifted Sierra back to her feet by her shoulders. He gave her swinging tits a hard squeeze before shoving her onto the bed.

Glaring at her like a hungry hungry hippo, his eyes coasted to her fat ass. His tongue slithered past his teeth and wet his lips. "And you already know how I like it. Now spread 'em wide and lemme inside!"

"Come on, Vern," Sierra pleaded, covering her nakedness as his shark-like eyes glided over her body. "I've been eating nothing but ramen noodles and canned ravioli for over a month. I'm way too constipated for—"

"Ain't the customer always supposed to be right? 'Specially if you want that hundo."

Big Vern grabbed a hold of Sierra's hips and flipped her over before spreading her cheeks so wide she thought she felt something tear. He spat a tablespoon's worth of saliva into his palm and lubricated his cock, making it glisten like a skinned catfish.

"Take it easy," Sierra growled over her shoulder as he pulled her to the edge of the mattress and pressed his cock against her puckering anus. "I'm telling you, enter at your own risk—"

Big Vern rammed his rod into her asshole and pushed with all his weight. Even though his cock was short on length, the head was as wide as a cue ball, and his spit had done nothing but gum it up.

The pain was a shock, and Sierra wasn't lying about her constipation. And while she didn't think Big Vern's stumpy cock would be an issue, the sudden violent thrust caused her bowels to loosen their grip.

A torrent of liquid shit erupted and sprayed Big Vern's belly and groin and filled the air with an odor thick enough to chew.

"Ah, what the fuck?!" Big Vern gagged and turned his head away, but his hips kept thrusting, pumping harder and faster like they had a mind of their own.

As more shit flooded out, his dick made it spray in multiple directions like a thumb over a water hose.

"Thought you said you was constipated?!" he squealed. "I came here to fuck the shit out you, but goddamn!"

More than the humiliating and degrading circumstances, Sierra was disheartened by the way her flesh seemed to pour off her frame. Even when she defecated all over Big Vern as he humped her from behind, all she could feel was the way her tits slid across the mattress like two dead salmon hanging from her chest, her crucifix necklace swinging between them as if to remind her that, in God's eyes, she deserved this.

The fat folds of her belly flab and loose skin made wet slapping sounds as they collided with one another again and again. The rhythmic swinging of her own body was starting to give her motion sickness, but when her eyes coasted back up toward the Jesus painting, the nausea seemed to dissolve.

She saw Cassie's smiling, naïve face again and silently prayed that she was safe somewhere.

If she's with Leon, if she's still in this city, then she's not safe. One way or another, this place will drain all faith or hope or optimism. Cassie deserves better than that—I *deserve better than that!*

Sierra shut her eyes and tried to imagine a better life away from this godforsaken city and all the scumbags who called it home. Where she could start over, where nobody knew who she was or what she'd done. Where she could be a new, anonymous person.

Where she could reconnect with God and get back into his good graces, despite the lingering residuals of the betrayal she felt for being denied the joyous glow of maternity.

The thought made her smile, proud of herself, knowing she really meant it this time. Even when Big Vern pulled out and sprayed warm splashes of cum across her back and into her hair, Sierra held that rare thread of hope.

Dreaming about a future a million miles away from her past. And she knew just how to get it.

THE DAY CREW

"While obtaining any reliable information from our usual trustworthy sources has proved less than fruitful, people have been talking and speculations are rampant," the stuffy news anchor said from Sierra's staticky tube television. "Many were quick to credit The Artist, while others theorized anything from religious extremists, to domestic terrorists, to a robbery gone wrong."

Sierra—wearing a loose hoodie, tight leggings, and a towel wrapped around her head—sat on her ratty couch, the morning sunlight pouring in through the windows. Her hair was still wet from the refreshing shower she had taken—she took a long, scalding one seconds after Big Vern had left the night before, then another the moment she woke up and remembered the feel of his sweaty body against hers. When she'd turned on the TV, hoping for a distraction from the rancid memories of last night, it was already set to the news channel.

She knew it was a bad idea—both for her mental health and just the overall futility of it—but she still couldn't help herself from watching it and obsessing over any mention of the incident at Cheaters.

When the microwave dinged and Sierra rose from the couch to retrieve her shrimp-flavored Cup-O-Noodles, she kept her eyes glued to the television, anxious about potentially missing some minute detail that would somehow provide answers to her growing list of questions.

But it was the same as it had been since the night everything went down: the depleted police department was under a lot of pressure and was in no rush to conduct any kind of investigation, the mayor was more concerned with her re-election campaign than a bunch of dead whores and hooligans, and the media had no problem spreading misinformation and rumors as long as they had something titillating to broadcast.

As she blew on her ramen en route to the couch, she eyed the phone hanging from her kitchen wall. Out of all the girls she'd called, day crew *and* night crew, only one call had been answered: Lola Sulu, the ageless Asian wonder.

While Lola was only a few years younger than Sierra—and a decade older than the current roster of dancers working the night shift—she'd managed to keep her spot on the starting lineup.

Sierra couldn't blame Leon for keeping her on—Lola had always been a cash cow. She had a way of turning men into human ATMs. And despite all her troubles, she was always kind and respectful toward the other girls. When Leon had sent Sierra to the day crew, it was Lola who'd checked on her, saying how she admired Sierra's strength and resilience.

On Sierra's third attempt to call Lola, someone had answered the line but didn't say a word before hanging up a few seconds later. She figured it must have been Lola's daughter—*What was her name again?*—but all subsequent calls were unanswered.

Though it hadn't done much good over the past week, she told herself she still had to try calling everyone in her rolodex just in case—even the *one* number she'd been avoiding.

So far, besides Lola's phone, all she'd gotten were answering machines—none had called back despite the countless messages she'd left every day since she'd first heard the nauseating news.

"The only thing anyone can seem to agree on is that the Cheaters Gentlemen's Club was the setting of a gruesome mass murder involving over a dozen employees and customers alike. And our once great city continues to sink into a state of calamity." The news anchor's expression darkened as he seemed to glare through the screen toward Sierra before she finally snatched the remote control and changed the channel to some *Sally Jessy Raphael* rerun.

Benjamin was stuffed safely between her ample bosoms, and as she stared at her television, her hand absently reached for the bill just to feel its papery texture. That stained C-note now symbolized a new beginning for Sierra, the end of one era and the birth of the next.

This is my lucky Benji. The last cash I'll ever earn with my body. It's time to put my mind to use.

The details of her fledgling plan raced through her mind and filled her with anxiety. If the plan was going to work, she knew she couldn't sit around and wait any longer. It was time-sensitive. And while the police were dragging their feet, she needed to get in and out before someone else beat her to the punch.

It was no secret that Leon was loaded, not to mention a collector of rare, valuable objects—it was only a matter of time before the looters swarmed the club.

But along with the potential for a huge score, something else nagged at Sierra's brain—she had no idea who was alive or dead. She had become somewhat of a surrogate mother to many of the girls over the years, and imagining their mangled bodies scattered across the floor inside Cheaters filled her with panic and misery.

She knew the only way to find out for sure was to get over there and see it for herself.

I hope you're okay, Cassie. Please be okay.

Despite being discarded to decompose on the day crew, Sierra had maintained good relationships with most of the dancers at Cheaters, regardless of which shift they worked.

All but one, that is.

She figured the midday dancers were avoiding her call, probably holed up in their homes behind barricaded doors after they'd heard about the grisly incident. Sierra couldn't blame them. There were so many rumors and baseless theories circulating throughout the city over the past week—especially all the buzz and chatter revolving around The Artist.

One thing's for sure... I'm not going alone. If this really was the work of The Artist, who's to say he won't show back up to the scene? Or maybe he never left. Maybe... he's still inside!

Her mind became a flipbook of insidious images when she pondered why none of the night and weekend workers were picking up their phones or returning her calls. Were they doomed to haunt Cheaters for eternity? Their ghosts trapped inside, much like their bodies had been?

With her appetite ruined, she tossed her noodles into the sink and grabbed her rolodex on her way to the phone across the kitchen. The cord was long and tangled, and Sierra couldn't go further than a few feet before it would yank her back.

The dial tone hummed into her ear as she shuffled through the phone numbers, the receiver clamped between her cheek and shoulder.

She flipped past the names of all the girls she'd already tried—hash marks were etched into the paper to show how many times she'd called each one of them. When she reached the *only* name without a single hash mark beside it, she hesitated and wondered if she was making a mistake.

While The Artist was the media's favorite suspect to speculate over, Sierra could fill a notebook with other possibilities—Leon had a knack for inciting vengeful aspirations in the people he interacted with.

There was one name she knew for certain belonged on

that list—maybe even the first name below The Artist: Ivory Valentine. Cheaters' self-proclaimed star.

God must be cackling in the clouds right now, Sierra thought. *This is cruel, even for Him.*

Though Sierra never got along with Ivory—none of the girls did—she brought certain things to the table that made her an obvious asset to the plan, other than the lack of alternatives: one, other than Lola, she'd spent more time alone with Leon in recent years than any other girl, specifically in his office where he kept his safe, and two, she despised him even more than Sierra did after being demoted to the day crew.

Used to being one of Leon's top earners, Ivory took it extremely personally when he sent her away—still convinced she was just as hot as she ever was—and Sierra knew Ivory would jump at the chance to get back at him for humiliating and insulting her.

If she hasn't already.

Sierra started to dial Ivory's number but only got three digits in before hanging up. After taking a moment to center herself, she picked the phone back up, took a deep breath, and forced herself to punch in the whole number.

She paced back and forth within the boundary the phone cord's length allowed. As it rang and rang, she started to accept that nobody was going to help her, that if she wanted to claim a future for herself and find out which of the girls had met their fate, she'd have to do it alone—not even God would accompany her with so much sin blackening her soul.

God, I know you haven't heard from me in a while… I know I don't deserve any favors. But please watch over Cassie. Please keep her safe. If anyone is worthy of your mercy, it's her.

"Who's this?" Ivory's gruff and gravelly voice startled Sierra and made her drop the receiver. It clattered to the tile floor, cracking the plastic along the side. She could hear Ivory's tinny voice growing more impatient with every passing second. "Hello? Hello?!"

Sierra snatched the phone from the floor and shoved it

against her ear—she never imagined she'd ever be so happy to hear Ivory Valentine's voice.

"I hear you breathing, motherfucker—"

"Ivory!" The word came out as a frantic shout, and Sierra took a few deep breaths to calm herself. "I… it's Sierra. I can't tell you how much of a relief it is to—"

"Sierra motherfucking Sacs, my fellow reject," Ivory said with a mocking tone and a chuckle. "I bet those stanky hoes ain't laughing now, huh? Not after The Artist made 'em famous."

Sierra stayed quiet. Disagreeing with her mean-spirited remarks wouldn't be the best way to start off their interaction.

"Talking all that shit, thinking they're better than us. But we're still breathing! We're still alive, the ones they said had nothing left to offer. The ones downgraded to day crew status. Ain't that some shit?!" Ivory cackled and made Sierra wince. "Were you as glad as I was when you heard what happened? Wish I could've seen the looks on their faces, especially that crusty cunt Violet. Thinking she's hot shit just because of that stupid purple hair. Goddamn, I'd have paid good money to watch *that* bitch beg for her life."

This was a mistake, Sierra thought, instantly regretting her decision to call. *But there's no turning back now…*

"I've been trying to get a hold of someone for the past week, but you're the only one who's answered."

"You heard from Leon? I drove by his house a couple times, but ain't nobody home. Even broke in to make sure he wasn't trying to avoid my ass, but the place was empty," Ivory said with hot resentment in her voice. "Found a pair of that new girl's panties, though. Always white lace with that one. You know, the Jesus freak? Even her pussy smelled like holy water. But if I know Leon, that asshole will have God Girl's snatch smelling like sulfur in no time."

"That's enough!" Sierra roared as she took a step too far and got yanked back toward the wall by the phone cord. The very mention of Cassie got her blood boiling and her adrenaline pumping, especially coming out of Ivory's blasphemous mouth. "I didn't call you to catch up or to gossip… So if you could just *listen* for a minute, I'd appreciate it."

A pregnant silence hung on the line as Sierra considered hanging up while she still had the chance.

"All right, then," Ivory said with a mouthful of vitriol. "What the fuck did you call me for?"

"Because I need your help. I've got a plan I think both of us could—"

"Help? Why in the fuck would I help you, bitch?" Another burst of laughter. "You ain't never done a goddamn thing for me. Just another jealous heifer like all the rest. You think I don't know what you used to say about me behind my back? Think I didn't see you whispering in Leon's ear?"

"You'll help me because I know how bad it hurt when Leon betrayed you. Same way he betrayed me when he decided I'd outlived my usefulness. Same way he'll eventually betray Violet and Cassie and any other pretty young thing desperate enough to walk into Cheaters looking for an opportunity."

"Please," Ivory snickered. "You actually think I gave a damn about Leon or what he thought of me? You think I cared enough to let that son-of-a-bitch hurt *me?* You're funny… hilarious."

"Fair enough," Sierra said as she struggled to hold back her true feelings, wanting so badly to call Ivory out on all her lies, especially the lies she was telling herself. "I just figured you'd want a chance to get a little payback. Hit Leon where it'd hurt him the most—his wallet. Or more specifically, his safe."

Another long pause.

"All right, I'm listening," Ivory said.

Sierra smiled and wrapped the phone cord tightly around her fist like she was preparing to strangle someone with it. She realized that Ivory had a third valuable contribution to the plan: a car.

"Good to hear. Now how about you swing by my place so we can get moving?"

"Well, ain't you gonna tell me the fucking plan first?"

"I'll explain everything when you get here. And hurry. There's no time to waste."

Sierra hung the phone up.

Her eyes coasted to the ring of keys lying on her counter, focusing on the plastic keychain shaped like a voluptuous woman—the word CHEATERS was printed across the thigh.

THE ASSEMBLY

Sierra waited outside, pacing the cracked sidewalk in front of her ramshackle residence. Her neighborhood was like a life-sized playset for Meth-Head Barbie, and as various residents passed by, she avoided eye contact.

The countless wires of the telephone poles slithered through the skies, and even messier than the tops of the poles were their bodies. Staples upon staples pushed into the decaying wood, pinning various flyers.

The many sheets were a mix of information—to some extent—but the majority were missing persons. Sierra stared at the one closest to her, which bore the image of a Hispanic woman. While she didn't envy her situation, she did envy her state. The flyer read: MISSING ESTELA ALVAREZ

Sierra's eyes scrolled past all the specifics to the words that stood out to her under the Identifying Characteristics section. Several months pregnant at the time of her disappearance.

It felt like the fertility of others was constantly being thrown in her face. Sierra shook her head, trying not to think about it. Instead, she focused on how good it felt to be outside, to feel the cold wind biting at her skin as she took breaths of fresh winter air, especially after hibernating in her house for the past week.

Part of her was almost insulted that the neighborhood scum didn't catcall or whistle at her like they used to. They just shuffled on by with that same blank look in their eyes, seemingly oblivious of anyone else around them.

It was a look that was becoming more and more common throughout the city as the popularity of Lobotozine grew—the number of citizens crippled by fear and trauma seemed to increase on a daily basis.

The drug promised to make you forget, to give your mind a temporary reprieve, but the commercials and advertisements failed to mention one major side effect: when the drug wore off, the intensity of the nightmares would strengthen ten-fold, quickly turning desperate, damaged people into insatiable addicts—lobes, they called them—who would do anything to avoid the fangs and claws of their inner demons.

A man who looked like a skeleton wrapped in flesh-colored Saran wrap staggered by, ignoring Sierra as he passed. He wept as he mumbled incoherently to himself, repeatedly hammering his fists into the already-bruised flesh of his temples.

Sierra shook her head as she watched him go, thinking about all the girls at the club who had become slaves to lobo—including both Lola and Ivory.

She only hoped Ivory could hold it together long enough to get the job done. Her personality was enough to handle without her going through withdrawals on top of it—not to mention her motive for murder.

As Sierra watched the man scuffle away, a rusted two-door Plymouth Neon coupe squealed to a halt and jumped the curb, nearly hitting Sierra.

A TLC song rattled from the car's busted speakers as Ivory leaned across the passenger seat and rolled down the window. Sierra could tell right away by the dark circles around Ivory's eyes that the lobo had its talons sunk deeply into her psyche.

"Be careful, you almost hit me!" Sierra yelled as she glared through the window at Ivory, whose expression was all business.

"Get in," Ivory said in an aggressive tone that instantly made Sierra hesitate. "You said it yourself, right? No time to fuck around. So let's go."

After another tense moment of silence, Sierra reluctantly climbed into the passenger seat. The car's interior was spotted with stains and burn marks and smelled like ash and sun-damaged leather. She had to pull the door three times to get the latch to catch. She tried to buckle her seatbelt, but it was locked in place.

"Thanks for picking me—"

Sierra's words became a squeal as Ivory slammed her foot against the gas pedal and made the car rocket forward. Gripping the grab handle above her window, Sierra felt it tear a little as it bore her weight. "Take it easy, for the love of—"

"So I was thinking on my drive over…" Ivory's eyes stayed on the road as she spoke, her tongue clamped between her lips as she weaved around other cars. "Why in the hell would Sierra Sacs need my help? I know you don't like my ass. Always treated the other girls like they was family, like you was their big sister or some shit. Everybody but me."

"Where are you taking us?" Sierra winced and grabbed the handle with both hands this time as Ivory nearly rear-ended another car.

"But I ain't even mad at you for that," Ivory said as she finally made fleeting eye contact with Sierra and shot her a small smirk.

"Red light!" Sierra frantically slapped the dashboard. "Red light red light red light!"

Ivory's expression didn't change a bit as she stomped the brakes. The car skidded to a halt, half of the Neon sticking out into the intersection.

"Ivory, will you please chill?!"

"What's the matter, girl? You scared? Don't worry…" Ivory glanced at the golden crucifix between Sierra's breasts. "If anything happens, God'd save you, wouldn't He?"

Sierra held her tongue. As much as she wanted to lash out at Ivory, she knew it would do no good.

"Anyway, on the phone, you mentioned hitting Leon's safe." Ivory turned her body so she was facing Sierra, who stared back at her with nervousness worming through her. "He don't have one at his place. I know cuz I checked."

The light turned green, and Ivory mashed her foot against the gas, speeding through the intersection toward wherever it was she was taking them.

"I know," Sierra said, her body tense and rigid as she watched their surroundings zip by them. "And if you can just slow down a second, I can tell you—"

"But see, that's what's got me fucked up," Ivory said as she narrowed her eyes. "Cuz that would mean you were talking about the safe inside the club. And I *know* even you ain't crazy enough to try and break into Cheaters."

Sierra struggled to find the words, so she just shrugged and flashed Ivory a forced smile. Ivory shook her head and snickered as she cut the wheel into a sharp turn before finally pulling the car over beside a cluster of battered, crumbling buildings.

"You're fucking with me, right?" Ivory kept the car idling but threw it in park and turned toward Sierra with a smirk that looked more amused than shocked. "You know I heard they didn't even clean the place up yet? All those dead bodies laid up in there for, like, a week? Shit, the smell alone is bad enough."

"That can't be true," Sierra said with a dismissive wave. "Could the cops really just leave them there?"

"Bitch, what cops? And hell, even if we had double the police force, it ain't like they ever gave a fuck about people like you and me. You think a bunch of dead whores and criminals is a priority for them? If anything, The Artist did their asses a favor."

"We don't know it was The Artist, not for sure."

"Who else would take the time to skin everybody?" Ivory's icy gaze sent a shiver of dread down Sierra's back. "That's what I heard, anyway."

"From who?"

Ivory laughed. "No reason for me to tell you." She pointed through the windshield. "You can't fucking miss her."

GORGHI

Sierra peered through the windshield into the near distance, only then realizing where they were.

Scantily-clad women were already out on the corners hunting for customers. These weren't high-class hookers—they were in a class of their own. Girls who were as far away from traditional beauty standards as one could get, who most men would ignore or fling insults at.

Girls with disabilities, with physical deformities, with a set of cock and balls dangling between their shaved legs. The kind of girls who attracted a certain type of client with very particular tastes—a niche audience.

"There she is," Ivory said, tapping against the glass toward a station wagon parked in an alley between a couple of brick buildings. "I knew her ass would be down here. How'd she even fit in that fucking car?"

"Is that... is that Gorghi?" Sierra shook her head with confusion, suddenly filled with nerves and suspicion. "Why'd you bring me here? If you don't want to be part of this, just take me back home."

"I never said I didn't want to be part of this," Ivory said

as she honked her horn three times to get Gorghi's attention. "But if we're really breaking into Cheaters, then we need some muscle. Some fucking security just in case shit pops off."

"Not her. Not Gorghi," Sierra said firmly. "She's a nice enough girl and I feel sorry for her for all the things she's had to deal with, but she's too… unpredictable. She's not stable enough for something like this, especially if what you heard about the bodies is true."

Gorghi smiled and waved toward Ivory and Sierra before skipping across the street toward the Neon as her john sped off behind her. She wiped her mouth with her massive hand while adjusting her too-tight dress, the thick muscles of her arms and neck twitching.

Her wide, almost square face was caked in makeup, the dark maroon lipstick smudged across her chin along with a gelatinous pearl of cum she'd missed.

Built like a pro linebacker, most people assumed Gorghi was transexual, a behemoth of a man who'd realized deep down inside he was a woman behind the controls of a bulldozer body.

On the sporadic occasions Gorghi worked for Leon, she was sent to the 'secret' VIP rooms, where those especially-particular clients could request a private anything-goes session with her—and where she couldn't be seen by the rest of Leon's customers.

But Sierra had spent enough time with Gorghi in the dressing room and saw her naked body on more than one occasion, despite Gorghi always doing her best to keep herself covered. Not that it was all that possible in the tight confines of the Cheaters dressing room. Elbow to elbow, tit to tit, the women got eyefuls of one another's beneath-the-clothes secrets.

Gorghi's chest was swollen with plates of muscle that bulged at the edges with small wads of fat. Her nipples were tiny and almost the same color as her skin—just two small smudges of pink. Her bush was thick and curly like the ear of a poodle, with an almost purple clit just about the length of 'Big' Vern's cock.

Still, Gorghi was a moneymaker at one point—her regulars were loyal and willing to pay. But age caught up with her like it did the rest of them. Her gut growing and protruding past her pecs. Her pubis inflating, making the hair poof out like a raincloud about to storm.

"Oh, come on," Ivory said as Gorghi reached the car and rapped her thick knuckles against the driver's window. "Can you think of anyone better to have our backs? Just look at this bitch. She's big enough to climb these buildings and start swatting planes out the sky."

"Yeah, but what happens if things go south and all that size and muscle turns on us?" Sierra said as she flashed a forced smile toward Gorghi, who waved at her enthusiastically.

"Well," Ivory said with a shrug as she unlocked her door and leaned her seat forward, "too late now."

"Ivory, just hold on a—"

"Hey, you guys," Gorghi said with a voice full of bass as she climbed into the back seat. The Neon shook as she struggled to squeeze past Ivory, who was pressed tightly against the steering wheel. "What're you doing here? I thought you were both dead like everyone else."

"Glad you're still alive too, Gorghi," Sierra scoffed.

"Thanks!" Gorghi exclaimed as she crammed herself into the backseat, allowing Ivory to lean back and catch her breath after being nearly crushed. She leaned her head between the two front seats. "So where we going?"

"We're gonna break into Cheaters and rob Leon blind," Ivory said matter-of-factly, to Sierra's chagrin.

"Perfect," Gorghi said, the cum on her chin turning translucent as it dried. "This twenty I just got is all I have."

When Gorghi held up the wrinkled, moist bill, Sierra instinctively reached for Benjamin, which was still hidden safely between her breasts.

She slipped the bill out and studied it while the other two

women were distracted with greeting each other. She couldn't explain it, but there was something special about Benjamin, a feeling in her core that told her this was no ordinary hundred. As she stared at its matte green surface, Ben Franklin seemed to smirk seductively at her. And she smirked back before stuffing Benjamin into her front hoodie pocket.

That's just all that good fortune you're feeling, Sierra told herself, but she knew in her gut that wasn't quite it.

"What was that about?" Ivory asked with a raised eyebrow, studying Sierra with a suspicious glare as she threw her Neon into drive and took off. "Holding out on us already?"

Sierra narrowed her eyes at Ivory as she wiped her lips with the back of her hand. "It's my… it's my lucky bill, that's all. And I got a feeling we'll need all the luck we can get."

Ivory arched her mouth and shrugged—there was no denying that. Sierra even thought about saying a silent prayer for their collective success and well-being, but worried she may invoke His wrath rather than His grace, considering the task—and the company.

As Ivory started taking sharp turns and swerving through street traffic again, Sierra was forced to take hold of the grab handle to keep herself from getting jostled too violently.

Gorghi, on the other hand, sat as still and heavy as an anchor, her head still hovering between the two front seats.

"If it's luck you want," Gorghi said, "we should pick up Lola Sulu. She's gotta be the luckiest person in the whole city. Maybe even the world."

Sierra whipped her attention toward Gorghi, now clinging to the grab handle with both fists as Ivory's driving seemed to grow more reckless with every turn. "What makes you say that?"

"Tell her what you told me," Ivory chuckled, then elbowed Sierra in the arm. "Wait till you hear this shit."

"So you know me," Gorghi said as she sat up straighter, her tone like a teenage girl gossiping about high school drama. "Leon only lets me work during *special hours* or whatever, so I'm always the last to know if any shit goes down at the club. But I haven't heard from him in a while, right? So I head over there to see why he hasn't been calling me. Guess I beat the cops cuz the place was quiet and empty. Well, except for all the dead bodies, I mean."

Gorghi and Ivory shared a tasteless giggle, but when they saw Sierra's stoic expression, they both quieted despite the smirks that remained on their faces.

"So you actually saw them?" Sierra turned to face the backseat, switching her grip from the grab handle to Gorghi's granite pillar of a forearm.

Cassie's smiling face instantly filled her mind as a bubble of panic swelled in her belly.

"Could you tell who was… you know—?"

"Skinned?" Gorghi said with a shrug. "Not really. Without their skin, everyone kinda looked the same. I only got a quick peek. Didn't wanna go too far after what I saw."

"So it's true they were…?" Sierra started, but couldn't bring herself to say it as Cassie's smiling face morphed into a grinning, bloody skull in her mind.

Gorghi nodded with a fresh smirk.

"Like I said before," Ivory gloated. "The motherfucking Artist. No question."

"We still can't say that for sure," Sierra said, forcing the macabre images away. She narrowed her eyes at Ivory, taking note of her body language. "Leon made enemies of some of the most dangerous people this city has to offer. There's no telling which of them he might've pushed over the edge."

Ivory only scoffed and shook her head, looking more smug than guilty.

"I only saw them for a second, but I could tell it was a mix of girls and customers by how they were set up," Gorghi said, furrowing her brow as she seemed to relive the moment. She used her thick fingers as puppets to clumsily reenact the gory exhibit. "Like a bunch of Barbie and Ken dolls having a party. Except, you know, all peeled like bloody bananas or whatever."

"The Artist," Ivory said with another infuriating nudge to Sierra's arm. "Without a doubt."

"What about Lola?!" Sierra said this louder than she meant to, feeling Gorghi's arm flinch beneath her grip. "You said Lola was lucky. Was she *there?* Did you *actually* see her?"

Gorghi nodded. "Scared the shit outta me too. Came outta nowhere! I sprinted back down that hallway so fast and didn't stop till I felt the sun on my skin again. Thought she was one of the dead ones coming back to life or something. Blood all over her… It wasn't till she stepped outside into the light that I could see she still had her skin attached."

Gorghi frowned suddenly and deeply, her eyes going vacant. "And even though she was a gory mess and all freaked out, she still looked so… beautiful. You believe that? Perfectly petite and thin with firm tits and a tight ass that fit her frame just right…"

As Gorghi sunk deeper into her own mind, her mitts gripped the headrests of the two front seats and crushed them as easily as wadding paper.

Sierra and Ivory shared a quick glance, both sensing Gorghi's lunacy. It united them for just a moment before Ivory snorted with laughter and rolled her eyes—she was clearly still stewing about being demoted while Lola's popularity only seemed to grow.

"And then what?" Sierra asked. "Did you go back in? Did you see anyone else… alive?"

"Go back in? All by myself? No way!" Gorghi shook her head like a frightened child. "I only got, like, a glimpse, and it *still* gave me nightmares."

"Did she say anything?" Sierra asked with urgency.

"Who?"

"Lola! Did you talk to her? Did she tell you what happened? Did she mention anyone else?"

"Nope," Gorghi said with a shrug. "Didn't say nothing

to me. I don't even know if she saw me, now that I think about it. She just kinda walked away, dragging her feet like some kinda gorgeous zombie or whatever. But then I heard the cops coming, so I got my ass outta there before anyone saw me."

"So she's alive." Sierra said this more to herself than the others.

"Yep," Gorghi chortled. "Luckiest person in the world. Or probably the universe."

"If you call that lucky," Sierra said, still deep in thought.

"That's stupid," Ivory said. "There's no fucking people outside of Earth, so she can't be luckier than the world."

"There could be. I saw a UFO just a few months ago. I remember it clearly cuz I was shoving my purple strap-on down my client's throat right after I fucked the living shit outta his asshole with it." Gorghi paused when she saw the look of astonishment blossom across Sierra's face. "Oh, don't worry, pain and humiliation is his thing. He *loves* it. Anyway, I had to look away cuz watching him slurp his own shit off that rubber cock like it was a melting Fudgesicle was making my stomach turn, and that's when I saw it. I really did, I swear to—"

"Where are you taking us?" Sierra asked Ivory, only then becoming aware of the area of the city they were zooming through.

"Where the fuck you think?"

"No… not yet. Ivory, stop the car." When Ivory continued on her path, Sierra reached over and yanked the steering wheel hard. The car swerved and skidded across the pavement. "I said stop!"

When the Neon rocked to a stop, sitting diagonally in the intersection, Ivory threw the car into park and looked ready to throw down with Sierra.

"What the fuck is your problem, bitch?!"

"That was awesome," Gorghi said under her breath, smiling as other vehicles honked their horns in passing. "Felt like I was riding in a spaceship!"

"Sorry," Sierra said, taking her hand off the wheel and raising it in surrender. "We've got one last stop to make first."

It only took a second for Ivory to figure it out. "Oh, come on. The fuck we need that bitch for? She ain't nothing but another mouth to feed."

"A hot mouth too." Gorghi stared blankly at the ceiling as she seemed to speak her thoughts out loud. "No way her lips are natural, right? Been saving for a set of C cups, but maybe I should do my lips first. Tits are a dime a dozen, but if I can soften up this face, I'll be off the street and back in the club in no time. Don't you think?"

An awkward silence hung heavy in the car for a moment, Gorghi stretching her thin, shapeless lips into a grin as she waited for someone to respond.

Just as her smile started to fade, Sierra tried to speak up, give her a few words of encouragement, but Ivory beat her to it.

"Bitch, there ain't no club to get back into. And even if there was, you really think a fat mouth would earn you a spot on a Saturday night? All the silicone in the world couldn't soften your bulky ass. Lookin' like fucking Andre the Giant in drag."

"Ivory," Sierra gasped, her maternal instincts kicking in. "Take it easy."

"Oh, come on, it's what makes her so goddamn special. Well, that and that cum on her chin. Let me just get that."

As Ivory scraped at the gunky droplet of sperm from Gorghi's stiff jawline, Gorghi stayed still and stared ahead in a defeated stupor. She did nothing to hide her hurt feelings as she wrapped her muscled arms around herself, covering her bare midriff and humble cleavage.

"Lola is a dear friend, and now that I know she's alive, it only seems right to cut her in. Or at the very least, check in on her." Sierra made deep eye contact with Ivory as she flicked the cum flake out her cracked window. "That girl deserves this just as much as any of us. Might need it more than anyone here."

"Shit, the fuck she does," Ivory said with a snarl. "We're already splitting the score three ways, man. Ain't nobody else getting a cut of my money, especially not some stuck-up ass Chinese choad choker like her. Hell no!"

Your money?

Sierra sized Ivory up before watching Gorghi mumble incoherently to herself as she rocked back and forth in her seat.

Yeah, I can't go alone with these two. Even a strung-out, traumatized Lola would be a welcome comfort compared to these crazy cuckoos.

"She was the only one who was actually there," Sierra said in a softer, nonthreatening tone. "She might've seen something that can help us. With everything we *don't* know, wouldn't hurt to try and gather some information. As much as we can, anyway. Especially if your theory about The Artist turns out to be true."

Especially if she can tell us who's alive or dead.

Ivory ground her teeth for a moment, twisting her fists around the steering wheel. "Whatever."

Submitting to the idea, Ivory swung the car in the opposite direction before peeling out and rocketing toward Lola Sulu's house.

THE AGELESS WONDER

Ivory pulled her beat-up Neon to the curb and parked it a couple houses down from Lola's place. The fan belt squealed as the engine idled and filled the interior with the thick scent of burnt motor oil.

"Oh Lord." Sierra peered through the windshield toward a bullet-riddled Mazda with a ridiculous-looking spoiler mounted on the trunk. "What in the world happened here?"

"Those are bullet holes." Gorghi leaned forward and pointed with an almost child-like fascination—the sight of violence seemed to perk her up. "And blood too. Lots of it. Probably just another junkie drive-by."

"Guess maybe she wasn't so lucky after all," Ivory said as she cut the engine and quickly checked her makeup in the rearview. "But for real, though, this here is Lola's mess and ain't got shit to do with me *or* getting paid. And, Sierra, you know damn well the smart thing to do right now would be to put some distance between us and whatever the fuck this is. Don't act like you don't know I'm right."

Sierra had stopped listening to Ivory's rant about halfway through when she spotted the young girl sitting on the curb near the remains of the Mazda. Tears glistened from her cheeks and snot coated the rims of her nostrils.

"Just… stay in the car for a minute," Sierra said as she forced her door open and stepped out. "I'll be right back."

"Jesus," Ivory growled as she punched the steering wheel.

Sierra ignored Ivory as she tentatively made her way toward the girl, who was now looking right at her, wiping her face with her shirt sleeve. The girl furrowed her brow as if she recognized Sierra but couldn't quite put her finger on it.

Sierra knew who the girl was, of course, but was shocked to see how much she'd grown. From toddler to teenager in what felt like a blink of an eye.

"Hey there, uh… Tiffany?" Sierra said with a wince and a wave as she approached the girl.

"Tanya," the girl said with a hoarse voice, turning back toward the car dismissively.

"Right Tanya, of course."

As Sierra passed the Mazda, she caught a glimpse of the mess in the street beside it. A young man, or what was left of him, lay flat on his back, pants around his thighs with his cock out. His face and head were cracked open like a tree trunk struck by lightning. Bone shards stuck out from the gory nest of brains and cornrows.

"I'm Sierra. I don't know if you remember me." Sierra stopped short to give Tanya her space. She flashed a smile, but Tayna didn't bother looking at it. "Your mom's work friend, you know… over at—"

"What do you want?"

"What happened?" Sierra asked. "Are you hurt?"

"They—they killed him," Tanya cried through clenched teeth, a plume of fog wafting from her mouth. "They killed him, and it's all my fault!"

Sierra's instincts told her to console Tanya, to sit with her and comfort her as she told her all the details. But Ivory's voice filled her head, and despite all her feelings of regret for involving Ivory at all, Sierra had to admit she was right. They had to stick to the plan and stay focused, no matter what.

"Your mom around?" Sierra eased up closer, taking a seat beside Tanya on the rough pavement. Splashes of blood and vomit painted the street, along with chunky morsels of gray meat.

"Inside, probably asleep. Like always." Tanya kept her eyes averted, clearly wanting to be left alone.

"Mind if we go in?" She nodded toward Ivory's car. "Just to check in on her, you know, after what happened at the club and all that."

Tanya glanced over and spotted the other women. Shrugged and rolled her eyes. "Good luck waking her up. She's been strung out on lobo for hours. She's no different than a corpse when she gets like that."

Sierra started to reach out, pat Tanya on the back, but then stopped herself.

Stay focused, Sierra.

Sierra smiled. "Thanks. We won't be long."

Tanya stared into the bullet holes, not saying another word. Twin tear trails rolled from her eyes, and she wiped them with an angry swipe across her face.

Sierra nodded toward the Neon and motioned for Ivory and Gorghi to follow her toward the front door of Lola's home. She checked over her shoulder one last time toward Tanya, remembering what Lola had told her about her regrets as a mother.

My mother sacrificed so much to make a good life for me, and I know she'd be so ashamed to see how I turned out, Lola had said just a few months ago.

Sierra remembered how lost and desperate she'd seemed, not to mention the clear effects of the lobo she'd been taking.

My daughter barely speaks or even looks at me. I can't blame her either. I'm failing her, my baby girl... Since Gabriel left us, I just can't get right. And until I'm right, Tanya won't be. She always looks so depressed and unhappy. It's tearing me apart. I just wanna fix it, Sierra, but I don't know what to do to make it better!

Sierra hadn't known what to say without coming off as harsh or self-righteous. But what she'd wanted to say was something along the lines of, *You don't know what to do?! How about you kick the drug habit, save up enough money to move away from this city, and start somewhere fresh? No more drugs, no more clubs. It's your job to do whatever it takes to give Tanya the support she needs and the life she deserves. Do you have any idea how lucky you are to have a child? Do you know what I'd do to have what you take for granted?!*

"You good?" Ivory's voice yanked Sierra back into the moment.

Ivory and Gorghi were now standing beside her with troubled looks on their faces—Ivory's was directed toward Sierra, while Gorghi's was directed toward the house.

"You were looking a little lost in space just now," Ivory said before glancing toward Tanya. "So what's *her* deal?"

"Like you said before," Sierra said, "it's got nothing to do with us. Lola's inside, so let's just check on her."

"Lola's tips must be pretty damn big to afford a house like this," Gorghi said as she slid her palm across the uneven bricks of the house.

"This house is a pile of shit, Gorghi," Ivory said, shaking her head and pointing far down the road toward the downtown area. "This city never quite reached its true potential, which is why you have skyscrapers in some areas"—she turned her gaze back to Lola's house—"but then some bootleg residential brick housing in others."

Gorghi wasn't listening, that same dreamy look in her eye. "I'll have my own place one day. Once I fix my look just right and get back in the club—wherever that's gonna be, I really don't care. I'll make more money than Lola ever did, or *any* other girl." Gorghi finally seemed to snap out of it and smiled goofily toward Sierra and Ivory. "How much money do you think we'll get outta this, anyway?"

As Sierra studied Gorghi's face and body language, she was growing more and more uneasy about the delusional woman's mental health and what the ramifications would be if she eventually cracked.

"There's no telling. But I *do* know this," Sierra said as she started making her way toward the front door. "The one person alive who might be able to answer your question is on the other side of that door."

As Sierra approached the front porch, she heard the sound of the other women's footsteps following behind. The door was slightly ajar, and Sierra wasted no time as she shoved it in and stepped across the threshold.

The place was a mess, the air somehow colder inside than it was outside. Empty food boxes and filth-covered dishes littered the countertops. An overflowing garbage can was stuffed in the corner, surrounded by bulging bags that sat in a brownish-translucent puddle of juice leaking from their bottoms.

The living room had one couch covered in clothes, a musty smell drifting off them like wet towels. As Sierra stepped closer, it was obvious they belonged to Lola: thongs and garter belts and sheer tops—all unwashed, the stink of Cheaters still clung to them like putrid perfume.

"Let's check her bedroom," Sierra said before she crept through the hallway that led from the living room toward the back of the house.

She wrapped her hand around the doorknob before tapping her knuckles on the wooden door. No answer. Just a deep silence that filled Sierra with dread.

DOORWAY TO DEGENERACY

"Lola, you in there?" Sierra turned the knob but only opened the door a crack. "It's Sierra, just here to check on you, make sure you're doing all right."

Sierra flashed a concerned look toward Ivory and Gorghi, the silence putting her on edge. But they just stood there, waiting on Sierra to make a move. Despite the look of annoyance on her face, Ivory held tightly to Gorghi's arm, her fingertips dimpling her skin.

"I'm coming in, Lola, okay?" Sierra eased the door open and poked her head inside. The bedroom, much like the rest of the house, was in disarray. More clothes littered the filth-coated carpet, along with empty pill cannisters and liquor bottles.

Lola lay on her side atop a bare mattress, the sheets and comforter piled at her feet. Sweat poured off her body and soaked into the bed, strands of wet hair pasted across her face and neck.

Sierra quickly crossed the room toward the eerily still Lola, already thinking the worst.

"Is it just me, or does she look dead as shit?" Ivory said from the doorway, still gripping Gorghi's arm.

Sierra pressed her fingertips to Lola's neck, and when she didn't feel a pulse, she nestled her ear against Lola's chest. Breathing a sigh of relief, Sierra heard the faint beating of Lola's heart and the very subtle rising and falling of her diaphragm as she barely took in oxygen.

"She's alive," Sierra said, then spotted a few hundreds folded up on the nightstand, along with several pill bottles. A small pile of jet-black pills that shone like dolls' eyes sat near the edge.

Sierra picked one up to inspect it, noticing the capital L etched into its surface. "It's lobo. You take enough and it slows your heart and lungs to a whisper."

"What?" Ivory asked.

"I figured if anyone should know, it would've been you," Sierra replied.

"Well, how the fuck would I know?" Ivory spat. "I'm just taking the shit, not studying it."

"Yeah. It's not general knowledge, but they started to figure it out when a few folks presumed dead sat up at the morgue. From the looks of it, Lola must've taken her fair share."

Ivory dashed toward the nightstand, snatched a few pills, and popped them into her mouth, chewing them dry. When she saw Sierra glaring at her with disapproval, she shrugged. "What? Without it, I ain't good for nobody, trust me."

"And you think *this* is good for anyone?" Sierra nudged the nonresponsive Lola. "For the plan?"

"I only took a little. Just to, you know, take the edge off." Ivory grabbed a few more and stuck them into her pocket. "I know what I'm doing, all right?"

"Lola?" Sierra switched her focus to Lola, who was

nothing but deadweight. She poked her on the shoulder, then grabbed her arm and gave it a hard but firm shake. Still nothing.

"You *sure* she's not dead?" Gorghi said as she joined Sierra beside the bed.

Refusing to give up, Sierra sat down on the edge of the bed and wiped the hair out of Lola's face.

"Lola, wake up," she said as she tapped Lola's cheeks with a series of light slaps. When that didn't work, she put a bit more force behind her hand. "Come on, girl, I know you're in there!"

"Oh, for fuck's sake!" Ivory climbed across the bed until she hovered over Lola's motionless form. Then she cocked her hand back and slapped Lola with everything she had, the sound making Sierra's ears ring.

"Ivory!" Sierra yelled.

"She's deep in a lobo hole. Love taps and butterfly kisses ain't gonna cut it," Ivory said before slapping Lola again, even harder this time. "Wake up!"

Sierra wanted to stop her, but she observed Lola instead, watching for any signs of life. Lola's brow furrowed a bit, and her crusty lips twitched just slightly, but that was it.

"This is pointless," Ivory said as she crawled back off the bed, her eyes half-lidded as the lobo started to take effect. "She's no good to us. We ain't doing shit but wasting time here."

Sierra sighed, starting to lose hope. Starting to doubt herself and the plan and any kind of meaningful future.

"Lola... Lola!" Sierra shook Lola's shoulders. Light at first, then harder, slamming her back and head against the mattress several times. "C'mon, snap out of it!"

When she got no response, Sierra shoved Lola away and turned her back to the room, hiding from the others as tears of frustration pooled in her eyes. Then a large, warm hand pressed against her shoulder and eased her away from the bed.

"Let me try," Gorghi said in a calm voice. The giant reached down and picked Lola up as easily as a Raggedy

Anne doll, lifting her over her head and slamming her back down to the mattress. "Get up!"

Ivory snorted with laughter from the far corner of the room, enjoying the show as she popped another pill into her mouth.

When Gorghi backhanded Lola across the jaw, her knuckles like turtle shells, Sierra tried to intervene, but she bounced uselessly off Gorghi and plummeted to her backside.

"I said get up!" Gorghi grabbed Lola by the hair and crotch and tossed her like a bale of hay.

Lola's body slammed against the wall before dropping back to the bed and bouncing from the mattress to the floor with a hard thump.

"Gorghi, come on!" Sierra said as she climbed back to her feet and positioned herself between the two of them.

When Gorghi ignored her and reached for Lola again, Sierra planted her palms against her chest, but it was like trying to shove a parked bus.

"You want to talk to her or not?" Ivory said, grinning with amusement. "Toss that bitch again!"

Lola's tiny body nearly disappeared beneath the big girl's bulk as Gorghi straddled her. Grabbing hold of Lola's throat, she squeezed like she was testing her grip strength on a carnival game, digging her fingers in so deep her thumb and middle finger touched behind Lola's windpipe.

To Sierra's surprise, Lola's limbs started to buck, arms and legs thrashing and colliding with the carpet. A few seconds passed before her eyes finally popped open.

When her pupils landed on Gorghi's snarling face, a scream gurgled out past the constricting fist. Lola's wide, terror-stricken eyes glossed over, darkly bloodshot from the pressure.

"That's enough," Sierra said and shoved Gorghi with all her strength.

She managed to move her just enough to release her hold on Lola's neck, unleashing a shriek from the depths of Lola's gut that echoed through the room.

Gorghi's frenzied eyes coasted to Sierra, glaring at her hard. Sierra felt the heat like an open oven against her skin.

"She's awake," Sierra said. "Let her go. Give her some air." Sierra felt the tension but did her best not to back down.

"Well, well… the ageless wonder lives again!" Ivory cackled.

Gorghi finally seemed to snap out of her fit of rage, her expression turning almost apologetic as she crawled off Lola and rose to her feet. She backed away, giving Sierra some room.

The moment Gorghi's weight was off, Lola took in a huge lungful of oxygen. She sat up and scanned the room, kicking her feet to scoot away from them all.

"What… what's going on?" Lola asked.

"Relax," Sierra said, approaching her with her hands out, trying to look nonthreatening. "We just wanted to ask you some questions."

"What the fuck are *you* doing here?" Lola croaked as she spotted Ivory across the room. She wiped the blood from her mouth, staring at her red palm. "What did you do to me?"

Sierra knelt beside her, placing her hand on Lola's back and rubbing gently. Lola shuddered at her touch, but when she looked into Sierra's eyes, seeming to truly notice her for the first time, she instantly started to weep. Lola fell into Sierra's arms and sobbed into her shoulder.

"Please," Lola cried. "Just let me go back to sleep. It hurts too much to be awake."

Lola's eyes coasted to her nightstand, where the remaining pills sat, but when she tried to crawl toward it, Sierra held her back and wrapped her arms around her.

"I can't let you do that," Sierra said in a voice both gentle and stern. "Not until you answer some questions first. Just a few, okay?"

"Questions?" Lola asked. "Questions about what?"

"About Leon."

"Leon?" Lola's head shook violently from side to side. She clearly didn't want to see whatever was going on inside her head. "They're all dead …"

"Did you see *Leon,* though?" Sierra asked.

Lola shook her head.

"What about *him?*" Ivory took a seat on the bed, looking like she might pass out. She collapsed onto her back, staring across at Lola upside down. The drugs took her over more and more. "The Artist, I mean. What'd he look like? Was he hot? I bet he was hot."

"No, I… I crawled under the stage and hid. Then, everyone started passing out all over the club," Lola said with a faraway look in her eye. "Through the cracks of the boards, I-I saw past the showroom. I saw Leon pulling Cassie toward his office, but I-I couldn't move. He was hurt really bad… so much blood, and then—"

"Cassie?!" Sierra forced Lola to look at her. "Is she alive?! Tell me she's alive!"

"I don't know. I-I fell asleep. And when I woke up, everyone was dead, and their s-skin… it was…"

Sierra gingerly held Lola's face by the chin to keep her focused, like a child in the midst of weening off Ritalin.

"But when you last saw Cassie, she was still alive, right?" Sierra asked.

Lola nodded but still seemed unsure. But before Sierra could respond, Gorghi's shadow fell over them and her wide, makeup-covered face leaned down and glared toward Lola.

"How much money's inside Leon's safe?" Gorghi barked. "And what's the combination?"

Lola, startled by Gorghi's presence, shoved away from Sierra and crawled under the bed. She curled herself into a tight ball and hugged her knees tightly as she whimpered.

Sierra crept toward the bed and laid on her side, just close enough so she could talk to Lola. It saddened her to see her friend crashing and burning that way, losing her mind a pill at a time while her daughter kept a corpse company out in the yard, waiting for police who would never show.

Lola knew she had to do better—would consult with Sierra about it any chance she got—but the weight of the demons clinging to her back greatly outweighed her drive and desire to change.

Sierra remembered the way Lola would smile, all teeth and gums, when she would talk about her big plans and how she was finally going to do it this time. Get clean, connect with her daughter, go to school.

And most important of all, Lola had said some time ago, before the lobo had sunk its claws into her. *I'm moving as far away as fucking possible from this city. Or any city.*

Though Sierra had known every time that Lola would never follow through with any of it, she did her best to play along, to let her friend have even a day's worth of hope every now and then. *And where would you go?* Sierra had asked.

Some place open, where I'll have space to breathe. I want to dance with green grass under my feet. Lola had found a tiny patch of yellowed grass at the base of a telephone pole—littered with cigarette butts and broken glass and bullet casings—and she'd spun in place, arms stretched wide, her grinning face pointed toward the smog-choked heavens.

Sierra recalled the twinkle of hope in Lola's eyes when she'd spoken to her. *I want to find a place where me and my daughter can see the stars, where the sky's so clear my Gabriel can look down on us. And he would tell us that he loves us more than all the stars in the sky. Because Gabriel used to say that all the time. And he'd kiss us and tickle us and we'd scream and run. And Tanya would laugh… she'd laugh until her face was red.*

Sierra remembered the way Lola had broken down then, collapsing right there on that patch of dying grass and sobbing into Sierra's shoulder. She cried until the sun came up and shone its rays through the screen of pollution, sliming the carnivorous, nocturnal city with its mucus-colored luminescence.

Sierra scooted closer to the bed, both she and Lola lying on the floor. Lola's face was buried beneath the shadow of the mattress, but her wide, manic eyes shone like ectoplasmic orbs in a haunted house.

As she watched her friend squirm and scrape at her face and neck, Sierra knew she couldn't leave Lola in such a way. She knew that, if her scheme was successful, it could be the catalyst for the realization of Lola's dreams. It could be the first step toward dancing beneath the stars with grass under her feet and a laughing daughter in her arms.

Sierra couldn't help but think about how it would change things for each of them. *If we pull this off, there will be enough to make all of our dreams come true. Gorghi can get that surgical makeover. Ivory can get her new car and clothes, even though I know it's really attention and respect she craves. And me…?*

I want to start over as someone else—a completely new and different person. Someone who's worth loving. I want to feel the love of God, the love of a good man… the love of a child.

While the math of their ages didn't quite add up, Sierra considered Cassie to be somewhat of a daughter. The connection that had grown between them was the closest thing to a maternal relationship Sierra ever had.

And I'll be damned if I'm going to let that be taken away from me. Not again. Not the new *me.*

As those words echoed through her mind, they sparked a newfound determination. The sparks grew into a fire that burned in her belly and chest, and she knew that, one way or another, she was going to see this plan through to the end. No matter the outcome. She'd rather die trying than to live another day as Sierra Sacs.

"I have to get inside Cheaters. I have to see if Cassie might need my help," Sierra said before reaching out and touching Lola's back. "But you know how much money Leon keeps in his safe. That money could be ours, Lola. You can dance under the stars."

Lola's bloodshot eyes locked onto Sierra's. "I can't go back there. I-I can't."

"Lola, listen to me," Sierra said. "We can get out of here. This city, these people, they're—"

"They're all dead!" Lola interrupted.

"But we aren't! And we don't have to live this way! Your *daughter* doesn't have to live this way!"

Lola sniffled as she seemed to think this over. "The s-safe," she said in a harsh whisper. "It's underneath—"

Sierra saw the giant hand grip the edge of the mattress and fling it aside like it was nothing but a slice of white bread. Ivory jumped off just in time to see the mattress slam against the wall, leaving nothing but the metal bed frame.

Gorghi's blank stare had returned. The stare of a Great White closing in on its prey—pure instinct and bloodlust.

"Time to go," Gorghi said, then grabbed the bedframe with both hands and swung it against the opposite wall, denting the sheet rock. She grabbed a fistful of Lola's hair, lifting her off the ground with one hand, getting nose-to-nose with her—it was clear she was out of patience. "I'm done fucking around! Tell us how to get in that damn safe!"

Lola's lips trembled but offered no answer.

Gorghi flung Lola across the room toward Ivory, who had to sidestep to avoid being run over. Lola's slender body slammed against the doorframe of the closet, her back bending at an awkward angle before she dropped to the floor.

"Gorghi, stop!" Sierra said, rushing across the room and wrapping her arms around her Goliath waist.

"No more waiting," Gorghi said. She dragged Sierra along like a child riding their father's leg. "I want that money."

With one hard thrust, she threw Sierra off and stepped over Ivory, who just watched it all happen with a devilish grin on her face.

"I already know the combination," Ivory said over Lola's screams as Gorghi grabbed hold of her leg. "Didn't I tell y'all that?"

"Ivory," Sierra sighed. "Are you serious?"

Just as Gorghi's wild eyes locked onto Ivory's, she froze. The metallic click of a hammer stopped her cold.

Sierra turned, along with Ivory and Gorghi, and found the barrel of a chrome pistol shaking in Tanya's grip.

A newfound fear grew inside Sierra as she observed the manic look in the girl's eyes—it was the epitome of unpredictable.

Tanya steadied her aim. "Leave her alone!"

NO BRAINS IN THE BACKSEAT

After spending a night in the alley, Crane was grateful to be able to finally leave. Staying in one place was the last thing he wanted.

"Thought that fuckin' bitch would never leave," Hector said, staring at the house. "Almost ran out of garbage to burn." As he followed Crane, rounding the vehicle, his eyes turned to the corpse. "What'd she think holdin' his hand was gonna do for him anyhow? Bring him back to life?"

Looking down at the man's voided skull and hanging jaw, Crane grimaced. "Who knows."

The meager amount of brains that remained with the dead man had spilled out all over the curb like dog food from a can. Crane whipped his head back toward the house where all the women had disappeared into. Through the foggy window, he spied the ruckus—the women seemed to be clashing with one another.

"Fuckin' guy's all over the place," Hector said, using a fast-food cup from the street to scoop out the gore from inside the Mazda. He was extra careful not to get any bits of the dead man on his new coat. "So damn cold out here his brains feel like a slushy."

"We've got to move quick," Crane explained, taking hold of some newspapers he'd found on the floorboard. He stuck his head back into the car and checked for the keys—he was relieved when he spotted them dangling from the ignition. Looking down at the blood pool on the driver's seat, he frowned, realizing it had yet to dry.

The light coats of spatter that painted the interior of the car were starting to coagulate, quickened by the chilled air. The lethargic dribble looked as thick as caramel. Chunks of brain and skull fragments were scattered all over. Thankfully, Hector had gotten rid of most of the mess already.

Crane set some of the newspapers down and tried to sop up the blood. As he completed the task, he checked over his shoulder toward the house again. He could hear raised voices inside and saw the trio of middle-aged women through the window. He wondered if they were about to come back and stop him from claiming his prize.

"That's about as good as it's gonna get," Hector said, standing from his crouched position and stretching his back. "Let's get the fuck outta here before that hulk of a bitch comes outta there."

Crane studied the piles of sloppy meat strewn about the seat and floor. Hector certainly hadn't gotten everything, not enough to satisfy Crane.

Starting to reach in, Crane thought better of it. He turned around to face the dead man's body and began searching for something he could use as a glove. He looked at the corpse's feet and noticed one of the shoes had fallen off. The white wool sock was the cleanest part of him.

Crane reached down and yanked the other shoe off, then slid both socks off the young man's cold toes. He pulled the wool over both hands like he was about to put on a puppet show, then grabbed handfuls of the remaining beefy bits and tossed them to the street.

"The fuck you doin', man?" Hector yelled. "It's good enough. Let's get the fuck gone!" Hector glared from the driver's side through the broken window. "Maybe it's best we just leave the car. I'd rather freeze on foot than sit in there with all that mess. Besides, I got my jacket to keep me warm."

"Quit complaining," Crane snapped, pointing a red socked finger toward Hector that flung a ribbon of slime against his cheek. "If you did it right the first time, I wouldn't have to. The quicker it's done, the quicker we're out of here."

"You mother—" Hector gagged as he wiped the vile goo off his face with the shoulder of his coat. "Fuck!" He glared at the stain like it was a permanent bodily disfigurement. "Look what you made me do!"

Hector fought to keep the sickness inside his belly. The irony smell from inside the car only seemed to help vacuum the vomit from his gut.

Crane shook his head as he watched him, then gave up and ripped the socks off his hands. He tossed them on top of the corpse and then slipped into the driver's seat, plopping down on the newspapers covering the gummy mess.

"Come on, then," Crane said.

"Fuck that," Hector said just before another deep gag arched his back. "Told you already. No way in *hell* am I stainin' my new coat again." He looked at the splotch of blood with ire. "Best coat I ever had, I think. Even before I became homeless. Feel how soft it is."

"We had a deal," Crane said. "Remember who gave you that goddamn coat."

Hector grimaced, but the words seemed to resonate with him—he was a man of his word. Continuing to hold his vomit down, he opened the back door. "Didn't have to get all testy about it."

"There you are," Crane said. "It's clean as a whistle back there."

Crane started the car and turned up the heater before he peered toward the house again. The voices had quieted down, and he worried he'd see the women come flying out the door toward them at any moment.

Hector glared into the car and raised an eyebrow. "A whistle somebody swallowed and shit out, maybe…"

Carefully looking around in the backseat, Hector avoided the miniature morsels of brain and skull, sliding to a spot in the middle that was mostly devoid of detritus. He sighed a plume of fog and lifted his coat at different angles, frustrated at every spot of blood that made contact.

"Nicest coat I ever fuckin' had," he grumbled. "Goddamn shame…"

Crane stomped the gas, and they sped down the road, leaving the mutilated body in the dirt behind them. He held his icy fingers up to the vents as the warmth defrosted his digits.

GUN CONTROL

Tanya peered around the doorframe, doing her best to keep her shaking hand from accidentally pulling the trigger. She'd never even held a gun until mere hours ago. But as she stared at the three menacing women roughing up her mother, she was glad she'd had some practice.

Chino—the version with his brains still inside his head—had messed around with it in front of her a few times before. She'd seen him load it, clean it, and asked a few questions here and there.

But the questions weren't out of morbid curiosity—they'd served a hidden agenda. One Tanya had failed to follow through with when it mattered most.

Her lip quivered as she thought back to the moment. The lonely, empty feeling that ravaged her as she sat on her mattress was as cold as the night's air sweeping across her shivering bones.

Tanya had found a way to accept that she'd been robbed of a full life with her father. She was crushed when the cancer took him, but she fully expected the support of her mother to keep her steady through the storm of grief—not the other way around.

Before long, what was supposed to be a thunderstorm had evolved into a permanent hurricane, and Tanya soon realized nothing was ever going to change.

The semblance of life that she recalled was remediated to being a forgotten memory—overshadowed and outnumbered by much worse.

She'd swiped Chino's gun to put an end to her misery. But when she'd put the gun in her mouth and tasted the flavor of chrome, she realized that she was a coward. And while she might not have loved Chino, the weight of his death was a heavy burden to bear.

He might've had a chance if it wasn't for me, Tanya thought. She looked at the gun before shifting her glossy eyes to the altercation unfolding in her mother's bedroom. Rage manifested in her chest as she keyed in on the root of all her problems. *If it wasn't for her…*

Tanya watched as the huge woman—the one Sierra and Ivory had referred to as Gorghi—lifted Tanya's mother above her head.

As Sierra begged her to stop, Tanya was filled with equal parts regret and resentment like oil and water—refusing to mix. Her regret half shamed her for being too cowardly to help her mother, reminding her that in their Filipino culture, it was a child's duty to honor and obey their parents.

But her resentment half pointed out the pale ring of flesh on her mother's finger where her ring used to be. It reminded her that the sickness taking root in her core was a seed planted by her mother's neglect and watered by her mother's selfishness.

She sold the ring Dad gave her. She's not family—she's not my mother. I have no duty to anyone *anymore.*

Tanya was tearing at the seams with maternal disgust. Her sickness grew, blasting her innards with poisonous spores that transformed her resentment into hateful rage and vengeful vehemence toward her mother. It caused her to root for suffering over salvation.

Tanya's sickness grew thicker and stronger, taking control of her thoughts as it egged the monstrous woman on. It begged Gorghi to make her mother pay, to punish her for abandoning Tanya when she needed her most.

When she heard the sound of her mother's back cracking against the frame of the closet, the sensation was twofold: the sweet feeling of retribution echoed in her eardrums, followed by the sour realization that she didn't know who she was anymore.

Was she the girl with the gun in her mouth who was doomed to remain enslaved to a world without hope—a rabbit chasing a projection of a carrot while the hunters sharpened their knives? Or was she the daughter of a junkie whore who still cared—the only person who believed that the heap on the floor writhing in agony would one day rise from the abyss and piece together the strong woman she once was?

She wasn't actively thinking when she raised the gun and stepped into the doorway. But as the other women argued while the giant closed in on her mother, Tanya's instincts just kicked in. Instincts she never knew she had.

She pulled back the hammer. "Leave her alone!"

The women paused their frenzy, turning their attention and concerns to Tanya.

"Back up and get away from my mom." Tanya thrust the gun toward them with every word she spoke, clearly trying to show dominance. But when her hands started shaking again, they gave her fear away.

The one they called Ivory squealed and scurried to the other side of the room, pressing herself against the wall and hiding behind the dresser. The only things visible were her trembling knees. The presence of the pistol instantly evaporated the overly confident demeanor she'd just been displaying moments ago.

Sierra slowly closed in on Tanya, hands up, doing her best not to spook the teenager. She acted like this wasn't the first time someone had pointed a gun at her. "We didn't mean any harm. Things just got a little out of control."

"I said back up!" Tanya yelled.

Sierra obeyed her command, but Tanya had a much larger problem to worry about.

"Give me the gun," Gorghi said, still towering over Lola. That same emptiness in Tanya's eyes was amplified in the giant's—there was zero fear there.

While Sierra had stopped dead in her tracks, Gorghi started to move in.

"Stay there!" Tanya demanded.

Gorghi didn't listen, humming to herself as she closed in, the sweat beading on her face making her caked makeup run. Before Tanya could react, the tips of Gorghi's mammoth fingers hooked into claws and raked across Tanya's sideburns.

With a second swift swipe, Gorghi snatched the gun away. Tanya's finger had been tickling the trigger, and the violent motion caused her to inadvertently pull it. The bullet hit the dresser in a shower of splinters, blowing a fist-sized hole out the side of it.

Ivory shrieked from the opposite end before she stumbled out patting her body, checking herself for holes. A dark spot formed at the crotch of her pants where she pissed herself a little.

"Fucking little cunt almost shot me!" Ivory said, nearly in tears. "Knew we shoulda never came here! Am I still whole?"

She lifted her arms and spun in a circle beside Sierra, who only glanced at her, seeming far more concerned with what Gorghi was about to do.

"You're fine," Sierra said.

"Gorghi," Ivory said as she stormed her way across the room. "You almost got my ass killed. Give me that fucking thing before more bullets start flying around here!"

Tanya watched in shock as the insane women continued to interact. She remained fearful of what they might do to her and her mother.

Sierra looked surprised when Gorghi handed the pistol to Ivory with a shrug, as if her fists were far deadlier than any gun. Tanya felt like a five-year-old in that moment, staring up at Gorghi as if realizing monsters were real.

"It's okay," Sierra said as she crossed the room and positioned herself between Tanya and the others. "We're not here to hurt you or your mom or anybody."

"Maybe not before, but this little shit damn near put a hole in me." Ivory lifted the gun and pointed it at Tanya, narrowing her eyes. "Maybe I'll put a dot right between those slanted fucking eyes, yeah?"

Tanya gasped and dropped to the floor, hugging her mother, who seemed oblivious to their bloodline as she shook her head and slammed her fists against her temples. She figured her mother was lost in the trauma clouding her mind again.

Ivory's aim followed Tanya until Sierra shoved the gun away and pushed her in the chest. Stumbling backward a few steps, Ivory cocked her head and glared at Sierra as if deciding whether or not to point the pistol at her next. Instead, she just stuffed the pistol in her waistline.

"Lola," Sierra said, switching her focus back to the panicking woman. She leaned in and forced Lola to look her in the eye again—this time with desperation, like she didn't want things to spiral any further.

When Tanya looked at her mother's face, she wasn't sure if she was registering anything that was happening—her eyes looked lost.

"What were you saying about the safe?" Sierra asked, "Underneath… Underneath what? Was Leon hiding something? Tell me and we'll be out of here. Whatever it is you know, you tell me now and I'll make sure you get your cut."

Sierra grasped at the crucifix between her breasts. "You have my word. You'll have enough to make your dreams a reality, for you and your girl, just like you always talked about. The kind of life *your* mother sacrificed so much to give you."

The words made Tanya's eyes ooze. She couldn't tell whether her mother had actually said those words to Sierra in private at some point or if Sierra was just using them as the extra sizzle to sell the steak.

Lola just shook her head, seeming to slip deeper into the abyss of her traumatized, drug-dependent mind.

Sighing, Sierra rose to her feet and looked Gorghi in the eye as if trying to snap her out of her violent trance. "We should just go."

"That's what I *been* saying," Ivory chimed in. "This bitch don't bring shit to the table."

Gorghi seemed to come back to reality as she stepped toward Ivory. Sierra once again took the lead.

Tanya prayed that Sierra would stay true to her word. She wanted nothing more than the nightmare their lives had become to finally end—and for the dream to finally begin.

"Mom," Tanya whispered into Lola's ear as she turned her face until their eyes met. "Please…"

She wanted to say so much, but it was the only word that managed to slip past her lips. But she thought she saw something in her mother's eyes. Though weak, she thought she saw an acknowledgement there. An acknowledgement that she, too, wanted to make things right between them, that she, too, wanted to become the kind of parent that deserved to be honored and obeyed.

"Okay then…" Sierra nodded toward Ivory and Gorghi, motioning for them to follow as she stepped past Lola and Tanya into the hallway.

Gorghi moved past them in one large stride while Ivory scowled down at Tanya. The look in her eye was a warning, daring Tanya to make a move.

Tanya covered her head and squeezed her eyes shut. Wishing the monsters away.

"The safe," Lola croaked, making Sierra pause midway down the hall, turning to face her. "He changed it."

Tanya helped prop her mother up and gave her an assuring nod to continue. Hoping that what Sierra said was true, that this information may be their ticket to a new life. A life actually worth living.

"Leon, he..." Lola said, her voice trembling. "He got real paranoid... and so he changed it."

Sierra glanced toward the other end of the hallway, but Ivory and Gorghi were already gone and out the door. She raced back toward Lola and dropped to her knees.

"What do you mean changed it? The combination?"

Lola shook her head. "He *is* the combination."

Sierra locked eyes with Tanya for a moment, as if silently asking if she knew what Lola was talking about.

Tanya wiped the tears and snot from Lola's face. "Just say it, Mom. She wants to help." Tanya's eyes darted toward Sierra. "Right?"

"Yes," Sierra said before forcing a smile toward Lola, then toward Tanya. "Yes, of course. I've known you since you were in diapers. Your mom and I go way back." Sierra faced Lola again, taking her hand. "Now talk to me. Did he get a new safe? What's underneath it, a key?"

Lola squeezed her eyes shut and grimaced, grabbing handfuls of her hair and tugging as she plummeted back into the blackhole swirling inside of her.

Tanya kept a close eye on Sierra, bracing herself for a possible violent eruption of frustration—a feeling that was mutual between the two of them in that moment.

But her mother's former coworker said nothing, just nodded and backed her way out the door. And just as she stepped out of view, Tanya felt a breeze by her side.

She found her mother hunched over the nightstand, pushing pills of lobo into her mouth. And just as soon as Tanya's hope for a brighter future had arrived, it dissipated—her future promised to be darker than ever before.

IN-CONVENIENCE

"Pull into that store," Gorghi said from the backseat, thrusting her forearm between Sierra and Ivory as she pointed toward the corner store just up ahead. "I need to eat something."

"Seriously?" Ivory said as she swatted Gorghi's hand away. "Can't it wait?"

"Cheaters is just around the block," Sierra said as she studied Gorghi's expression, being careful not to awaken the beast she'd seen back at Lola's. "We really should get this going with all the delays we've had already. It'll be dark soon."

"It'll just take a second." Gorghi pulled her moist twenty spot back out. Sierra wondered where she'd been keeping it. "And trust me. You wouldn't like me when I'm hungry."

Sierra shared a look with Ivory, then shrugged. She'd much rather have a calm Gorghi on her team, especially considering what was waiting for them on the other side of the club's doors.

Ivory sighed as she jerked the wheel and screeched to a halt in the corner store parking lot.

A sick-looking dog was hunched over, barely able to keep its head up as its body trembled with thirst and hunger. Sierra could hear its pitiful whines as Ivory threw the Neon into park.

"Y'all want anything?" Gorghi asked and waggled her eyebrows. "It's on me."

Sierra shook her head and smiled politely as Ivory crossed her arms and remained silent, on the verge of throwing a tantrum.

As Gorghi exited the car, the balding, squat store clerk burst through the glass doors with a broom in his fists. His face was the color of raw steak as he stormed toward the dog and cocked the broom back.

"I told you already, you fucking fleabag!" He swung the broom and smacked the dog across the head, making it yelp and stumble onto its side. "Get your ass outta here! See you out here again and I'll grind you into sausage and sell you two for a dollar!"

The dog limped away but not fast enough. The clerk charged after the dog with the broom held over his head, but when he swung it, Gorghi's meaty fist caught it and clamped down on the wooden handle.

"Don't do that," Gorghi said through clenched teeth as she towered over the clerk. "He's just hungry is all."

Sierra sat up straighter, preparing for bloodshed, while Ivory chuckled and watched it unfold as if her windshield was a movie screen.

"This fucker's dead meat," Ivory said with a smile.

The dog trudged toward the corner of the building before collapsing to the dirt and lying on its side. The clerk glared toward the dog, but when his eyes met Gorghi's, his aggression deflated and he let go of the broom. He threw his hands up in surrender.

"Okay okay," he said before waddling his girthy body back through the store's glass doors. "I'll deal with it later. Come on in… how can I serve you?"

Gorghi glanced toward the Neon, and Sierra thought she

saw that blank darkness in her eyes again. She was about to step out and try to lure Gorghi back to the car, but then Gorghi flashed a wide, toothy grin, straightened her dress, and followed the clerk into the store.

A deafening silence filled the car, and Sierra turned to try and make small talk with Ivory, but her words caught in her throat when she saw the pistol.

Ivory turned the gun over in her hands, running her fingertips across its surface. The nail of her index finger traced the circular shape of the muzzle.

"How much cash you think we're looking at here?" Ivory asked, keeping her eyes on the gun as she spoke. "I mean, since you decided we're splitting that shit four ways now, I figured there must be enough to go around."

Sierra could feel the tension thickening between them. She wanted to snatch the gun away but decided to play it calm and convince Ivory that they were still on the same team.

"The way I remember it," Sierra said with a firm voice, "Leon would empty the safe Sunday evenings. Add up what he makes from cover charge, drinks, private rooms, plus his cut of the girls' money—"

"Don't forget his precious lunch buffet," Ivory said with a snicker as she finally switched her focus from the pistol to Sierra.

Sierra thought she sensed a moment of camaraderie between them, though the gun was still sitting on Ivory's lap, giving Sierra another vision of Ivory's name on the suspect list—just below The Artist.

"Plus whatever other shady shit he had going with his VIP customers, right?" Ivory snorted.

"No question," Sierra said before she and Ivory shared a small laugh. "So Cheaters gets, what, maybe a couple thousand customers in a good week?"

"Shit, on weekends alone. Some nights he had to turn folks away it got so busy. And Leon's clientele? You know they weren't stingy with their money."

Ivory gripped the lowcut collar of her shirt and pulled it down to reveal both of her perky, taut breasts. Though the rest of her body had aged and—thanks to her lobo addiction—sunken in, her breasts stayed preserved and in place.

"He even bought me these tits back when he still considered me valuable. Called them an investment. Don't tell Gorghi, though. I'm not trying to get body slammed."

Sierra felt a flash of jealousy crackle across her body as she studied Ivory's chest. There were crescent-shaped scars at the base of each breast, like twin C-sectioned bellies, and the nipples pointed in slightly different directions like a chameleon's eyes, but Sierra would have gladly traded her sagging, stretch-marked sacks of despair for a pair of imperfect implants.

I still had plenty of good years left, she thought as she squeezed her hands into fists and ground her teeth, Leon's slimy smile burning its way into her mind. *When I brought up the idea of a nip and tuck, you were so quick to dismiss it.*

That kinda thing's for these other bitches, he'd said as he forced Sierra to sit in his lap and ran his fingers through her hair. *You're way more valuable to me than a pair of tits, Sierra. You should know that by now.*

But Sierra knew, even if Leon had once actually had true feelings for her and meant the things he'd promised, things had changed after she lost the baby—his baby. After that, Sierra felt like more of a nuisance than the woman Leon had planned to build a future with.

Sierra had swallowed her pride and did what was asked of her. Watched from afar as Leon manipulated and burned through girl after girl, each one seemingly a symbol of Sierra's inadequacies. A small part of her still hoped that Leon would grow tired of that life and come crawling back.

But when Cassie showed up, it was the first time Sierra truly felt replaced and discarded.

Cassie, unlike the other girls, after finding her way to Cheaters by chance and circumstance, had bigger plans for herself.

Cassie, like Sierra, had so much more potential and deserved a chance to bloom. And Sierra knew she couldn't stand by and watch Leon wilt Cassie's spirit the way he'd done hers—she knew she had to do something while there was still time.

Even though Cassie had seemed like a younger, fitter version of Sierra, it felt more like a mentorship than an invasion. Leon had hired Cassie to make Sierra feel inadequate, his passive-aggressive attempt to tell her she was no longer worthy of his attention.

But Sierra flipped the switch on him when she took Cassie under her wing. She and Cassie had an instant connection, and it was Cassie who reignited Sierra's faith—her naïve optimism was contagious. But it was when Cassie, an orphan, first called her Mama Sacs that their bond was solidified. Each filling a hole in the other's heart.

Unfortunately, the incident at Cheaters happened before Sierra had a chance to rescue Cassie from Leon's menacing grasp. And while Sierra wanted the money in Leon's safe, she wanted to find Cassie alive inside the club even more. She prayed for it. Prayed she could take her away from the city, just like Leon had promised he'd do for Sierra.

"And he thinks that Violet cunt can ever hope to replace *me?* Just cuz her tits are fat and natural don't mean shit." Ivory pulled her shirt back up to cover herself. "See how those things hold up after a few year—"

"So where were we?" Sierra snapped. "We add all that up, and I'd say we're looking at two hundred grand. Maybe more. And that's just the cash."

"I was thinking the same thing," Ivory said as her hands found the gun again, caressing the metal. "Those motherfuckers might be peeled, but the clientele on a Saturday night? You know they came with fat stacks, not to mention their jewelry. We just gotta find their clothes or whatever."

"Not a bad idea," Sierra said, unable to keep her eyes from watching the gat being petted like a chrome yorkie. "But I had something else in mind. Something that could be worth more than a couple hundred grand."

Ivory glared at Sierra with impatience and annoyance, throwing her hands in the air to indicate she wasn't in the mood to guess what Sierra was referring to.

"Think about it. Other than money and status, what else was Leon obsessed with? What did he care about more than any one of us girls?"

As realization bloomed across Ivory's face, the women locked eyes and shared another brief beat of connection. They both smiled, and Ivory reached over and gripped Sierra's wrist.

"His collection," Ivory said as she shook Sierra's arm. "He was crazy secretive about that shit… but I managed to sneak a peek here and there. A lot of it looked like antique junk to me, but I saw some thangs that might be of value. It's worth a shot."

"He was buying pieces before he could afford them, and way before he even learned how to spot a valuable item," Sierra said with a hint of pride in her voice. "I maybe had a hand in teaching him how to recognize quality. You'd be surprised at how much some of that *antique junk* is worth."

"How the hell you know so much about that shit?"

"My dad was a collector," Sierra said. Just thinking about him made her emotional. It had been so long since she'd even thought of her father and was surprised by the reaction. "We'd spend full days hunting through shops or storage sheds or even junk yards. He taught me what to look for… guess it just kind of stuck with me."

"Oh yeah?" Ivory released Sierra's wrist and seemed to sink into herself. "So you were close, you and your dad?"

"We were. He died when I was twelve." Sierra almost told Ivory about her father's gradual descent into a crippling depression. A deep sadness that ate away at him until he eventually hung himself from a branch beneath the half-built treehouse—the one he'd always promised Sierra he'd finish someday. "How about you? Were you close with your dad?"

Ivory furrowed her brow, her eyes staring blankly toward the floorboard. "You could say that. We were close in the sense that he'd come into my room most nights and climb into bed with me. Even when I begged him not to." Ivory's grip tightened around the pistol as her hands began to tremble. "My dad's dead too…"

Another deep silence enveloped them. Sierra struggled to find the right words as she found herself wanting to comfort Ivory for the first time. She now understood how Ivory might've developed an attraction to a drug like Lobotozine.

"Ivory, I—"

The explosion of breaking glass ripped both women from their troubled thoughts. Ivory yelped and instinctively pointed the gun toward the sudden eruption of sound, her eyes wide and wild.

Sierra had expected the bite of glass shards to rain down over her but then realized it wasn't the windshield that had been smashed.

One of the store's plate glass windows was shattered and lying in pieces on the pavement. Along with the clerk's bloody, brutalized body.

His face was a swollen mess of pulverized flesh, the jagged glass fragments slicing into his exposed skin. The only signs of life were the weak writhing of his limbs and the tiny foggy wisps billowing from his shredded mouth.

"What did I tell you?" Sierra said as she spotted Gorghi stepping through the new opening she'd used the clerk to open up. Her arms were stuffed with as many hotdogs as she could carry, each weenie steaming against the chilly air. "She's too unpredictable for this."

Ivory laughed as she lowered her gun and watched Gorghi stomp across the broken glass on her way to the dog that hardly had the strength to lift its head as she approached.

"That asshole had it coming," Ivory chortled. "At least her heart's in the right place."

Gorghi piled the hotdogs beside the dog and whispered

into its flea-chewed ear as she ran her nails through its fur.

When the dog started to eat, Gorghi picked up a single hotdog and left the rest behind, crossing the parking lot toward the Neon. She used her teeth to open a mustard packet as she ducked into the car.

"Okay," she said with a mouthful of meat and bread. "I'm ready now."

CLUB HELL

Sierra, with Ivory and Gorghi on either side of her, stood in front of Cheaters. The yellow crime scene tape fluttered in the wind. Even from the parking lot, she could smell the funk of death oozing out of the building. She could hear the low hum of flies.

The familiar space that used to stink of hoes and Hennessy had been transformed into a potpourri of decay. Even from almost fifty yards away, the odor was so thick Sierra felt like she could feel it crawling across her skin.

"Y'all smell that?" Ivory grimaced as she scratched at her neck and chest. By the look on Ivory's face, Sierra could tell the lobo was starting to wear off.

"God help us," Sierra said as she gazed toward the yellow tape lazily stretched across the bright pink double doors. She turned to Gorghi, who still had a smear of yellow mustard at the corner of her mouth. "Did you actually see any cops?"

"Just heard them coming," Gorghi said with a shrug. Her demeanor was so calm and nonchalant it made Sierra even more nervous—somehow, seeing a hint of anxiety in

Gorghi would have been more comforting. "I didn't stick around long enough to see them. You know how they are. If they're not arresting you, they're molesting you."

Gorghi snorted with delight at her own joke, but neither Sierra nor Ivory joined her as their eyes stayed locked onto Cheaters. The place that once felt like a second home now seemed more like Dracula's castle, and Sierra wondered, for just a moment, if it was too late to turn around and call the whole thing off.

Maybe this was a bad idea. Maybe I should do like Gorghi and focus on fixing my look. Get back to the night shift somewhere and stick to what I know. Accept that I will always be unlovable—that I'll be Sierra Sacs till the day I die.

But before the idea could take root, Cassie's face surfaced in her thoughts. Smiling that wholesome smile of hers. A smile that reminded Sierra of the real reason her plan mattered and had to be executed no matter what was waiting for them on the other side of those pink doors.

Cassie deserved that much. Her and any other survivors who might be hiding inside, too scared to come out—especially for the crooked-as-a-broken-leg police force.

For that many days? Sierra thought, a question she'd been avoiding asking herself since the start of all this. A question that, according to her left brain, had only one logical answer.

The cops, The Artist, The Devil himself, it wouldn't have mattered who or what they were scared of. Nobody would stay hidden for that long anywhere, especially Cheaters! They're all dead inside.

Maybe Cassie's not hiding, Sierra's right brain clapped back. *Maybe she got stuck or locked in somewhere. Or hurt herself and has been incapacitated this entire time. If that's true, she'll need our help right away.*

Even if that's the case, her left brain argued, *a week is enough time to die without food and water. So the only way you're finding anyone alive in there would be a miracle.*

I believe in miracles!

But miracles aren't real…

"Sierra, you in there?" Ivory said with a furrowed brow

as she waved her hands an inch from Sierra's face. "Don't lose your cool now, not when we've come this far."

"Yeah. *Fuck* yeah!" Gorghi clapped her hands so hard and loud a flock of grackles burst from a nearby tree before disappearing back into the branches.

Sierra nodded, surprised to feel inspired by Ivory's words. The women all faced one another, each with an anticipatory smile on their faces, salted with fear.

"You're right!" Sierra said, putting on a stern, brave voice. "We've come this far, haven't we?"

She stepped away from the group and faced the building with her chest puffed out, reminding them who was in charge here—and reminding herself what was at stake.

"Maybe what happened here was an act of God. Against Leon… for creating his own Sodom and Gomorrah, a hub for sinners. And they were all punished with sulfur and fire. Maybe this was always inevitable."

"Inevitable?" Ivory said, her voice growing weaker and shakier.

"But if that's true," Gorghi said as she stepped up close to Sierra and stared down at her with an expression like a lost child looking for a hand to hold. "Then why aren't we dead like the rest of them?"

Sierra grabbed hold of Gorghi's giant hand and gave it a reassuring squeeze. "Exactly. If their deaths were meant to happen, then that means we were meant to live. We were spared for a reason. The question is…"

Sierra turned to face both women, feeling a new sense of power and confidence building in her chest. The feeling she used to get when she was a devout Christian—the feeling of God's grace. The feeling she'd felt weaken the day she found her father hanging from that tree—the feeling that was killed the day her baby fell out of her, purple and lifeless and spinning in gentle circles as it floated in the urine-tinted toilet water.

"What are we going to do with this gift of life?" Sierra asked with authority. "How are we going to prove that we are worthy of a second chance?"

While neither of them spoke, Sierra could tell by their expressions that her words hit home. A look of determination sparkled in their eyes, and they both straightened their postures, ready to execute the plan.

Sierra made eye contact with each of them, and though she still questioned whether or not either of them was trustworthy, she was convinced they were all on the same team—at least in that moment.

"Well okay then," Sierra said and turned back around to face Cheaters. She took a deep, soothing breath. "Let's go."

Sierra marched toward the building with Gorghi by her side, quickening her pace a bit. Ivory stayed a few steps behind, reluctantly following them toward the gentlemen's club that had fed on their youth and potential like a parasite for so long.

Reaching into the front pocket of her hoodie, Sierra squeezed the woman-shaped keychain, but it only seemed to amplify her anxiety.

The smell grew in intensity with every step. Like an invisible force trying to warn them, pushing them away like a repelling magnet. But the trio moved forward until Sierra pulled the ring of keys from her hoodie pocket and approached the door.

What did Lola mean about Leon being *the combination? Underneath… A tattoo maybe?*

Sierra hadn't mentioned Lola's cryptic message to the others, wanting to work it out for herself before complicating things by involving them. She didn't see either of them as skilled puzzle solvers—Sierra's dad used to tell her riddles, but she was never great at figuring them out.

Part of her wanted to figure it out on her own, maybe justifying a larger cut of the loot. Another part worried about what would happen if they got inside and couldn't open the safe, or even find it. More than anything, she worried about that pistol tucked into Ivory's waistband and Gorghi's muscle and unpredictable mental state.

The scent was so strong up close to the building that Ivory started gagging and coughing, her eyes watering. She pulled her shirt up to her nose and mouth, just high enough to show the bottoms of her breasts—a wave of resentment swept over Sierra at the sight of them, but she quickly looked away.

Gorghi stood still and waited patiently, watching Sierra as she fumbled with her keys. A small growl undulated at the back of Gorghi's throat with every exhale, like a mutt waiting for a treat.

Sierra tried to hold her breath but couldn't stop the funk from flowing into her orifices and assaulting her senses. She finally found the right key and managed to stick it into the door but then hesitated before turning it, realizing this was the last moment she could call it off.

Either she turned around and forgot about the whole thing or they pushed for the ultimate score.

Sierra used her free hand to clasp her crucifix.

Please, God. I'm sorry for neglecting You and for not making the most virtuous choices, but if You get me through this, I promise I'll—

"Well?" Gorghi asked. "What's the problem?"

Sierra took a deep breath. "There's no problem..."

As the door cracked, it squealed like the souls inside the haunted club had decided to cry all at once.

Once Sierra had it open a few inches and stuck the keys back into her hoodie pocket, Gorghi's sausage fingers swung in from behind her, gripped the edge of the door, and flung it wide. It slammed against the wall, sounding like a shotgun blast. Both Sierra and Ivory jumped, preparing themselves for whatever may be waiting to pounce on them.

But the only thing waiting on them was darkness, along with that smell pouring out of the building like rancid flood waters, a cyclone of rot that nearly blew Sierra off her feet, made more intimidating by the low hum of insects.

"Oh, Jesus, fuck!" Ivory turned her head and vomited onto the ground, the warm stomach acid splashing against Sierra's ankles.

Sierra gagged but kept her gut under control. She held her breath while taking tiny sips of air as she crossed the threshold and stepped inside. But before she could get two paces in, Gorghi shouldered by and nearly knocked Sierra over as she marched into the darkness.

"Time to get paid," Gorghi said with excitement in her voice as she continued on unafraid, pressing a single finger beneath her nostrils.

Passing the front podium of the windowless building, Gorghi moved by the walls decorated in glossy photos of women graphically posing for the camera, spreading themselves to show their glistening pink parts. They were only visible from the dying evening sunlight spilling in through the door, but just barely.

"Gorghi," Sierra called as she chased the giant down, desperate to cling to her as the shadows seemed to reach for them, as if trying to pull them deeper into the building's stomach.

"Don't leave me behind." The sudden surge of fear fueled Sierra as she ran up to Gorghi, staying close by her side and grabbing the fabric of her dress for comfort.

Gorghi glanced down at Sierra and flashed that big, dumb grin of hers, then held out her arm, which Sierra gladly accepted.

"Wait up!" Ivory shouted from the entrance. She glanced down at the locking mechanism installed on the inside of the door. "Don't y'all think we should lock it up? In case some motherfuckers got the same idea as us? Or, you know… The Artist comes back to admire his work or whatever?"

Sierra hesitated a moment, not sure she liked the idea of locking herself inside with these two, even though she alone possessed the key. But she had to admit to herself that Ivory had a point, and she'd come too far to take any chances. She rushed toward the door and locked it up tight, tugging on the handle to make sure it was secure.

The darkness deepened, the shadows wrapping themselves around the women. The weak, eerie glow from beneath and between the doors was suddenly the only light source.

Gorghi stood by and studied the nervous faces of Sierra and Ivory before they headed back into the building. Together, they moved further down the hallway, knowing that just around the corner lay the source of that stench. As they moved deeper into the building, the darkness became a void, seemingly blacker than black. Sierra tightened her grip on Gorghi's arm as they blindly moved forward, the symphony of bugs buzzing growing louder. Both Sierra and Ivory yelped and slapped at themselves as spindly legs landed and scuttled across their skin.

"Let's make this fast," Sierra said as she turned to face the women. "I don't know how long I can deal with this smell."

"Just breathe through your mouth," Gorghi said.

"With all these damn flies? Hell no," Ivory said with another gag that nearly doubled her over. "Why the fuck are the lights off?"

"Cops probably did it," Gorghi said, somehow calm as they inched their way deeper, running into tables and chairs along the way. "Bet they locked the door too. Cuz it was open last time I was here."

"So those assholes cut the power, lock up, but then leave all the damn bodies behind?" Ivory scoffed. "This fucking city, I swear to God."

"We don't know for sure they left the bodies," Sierra said, more to calm her own nerves than to debate with Ivory. "Maybe they—"

"Bitch, where the fuck you think that smell's coming from?"

"We need to find a light switch," Gorghi said as she ran her hand across the nearest wall, Sierra still clinging to it.

"No, it's not just the lights," Sierra said, trying to hold her vomit down as she waved more bugs off her face. "Power's out in the whole building. We need to find the breaker box."

They finally reached the end of the main hallway. Even in the dark, Sierra was so familiar with Cheaters' layout she could see it in her mind. Of course, her mind also conjured up nightmare images of a room full of dead, skinless bodies.

"Just… just stay here," Sierra said as she forced herself to let go of Gorghi's arm. She took a deep breath and turned in the direction of the main floor. "I know where it is."

And Sierra stepped away from the others and into the dark pit of the building's belly.

THE EXHIBIT

Sierra kept her eyes shut, the darkness behind her eyelids somehow less terrifying than the deep black of the club's interior.

She imagined the countless times she'd walked from the entrance hall to the main floor, seeing the floorplan in her mind clearly.

Yet, as she crept her way through, she kept bumping into things. Moist, slimy things that left gooey residue on her skin where they touched her.

Don't think about it. Just keep going.

The smell intensified, along with the never-ending buzz and scuttle of the flies. Whispering chaos into her ears, scurrying across her flesh as they sipped on her sweat.

She wanted so badly to swat them away but was afraid that swinging her arms might disorient her. And so she pushed on, breathing through her nose, her arms outstretched in front of her.

When her fingers touched the edge of the bar, she breathed a sigh of relief—even when her arm collided with something cold and damp… and fibrous.

Almost there. The DJ booth is fifteen, twenty feet from the bar. Keep going, Sierra.

She repeated this in her mind, counting her steps—ignoring the room's slippery inhabitants, the overwhelming odor, and the swarming insects.

...sixteen, seventeen, eighteen, ninet—

Her hands pressed against the far wall of the main floor. She knew the feel of the wallpaper, recalling when she'd run her fingers across its rough surface giving lap dances to customers who were as slimy as the figures sitting in the dark.

When she pushed up against the wall, she started scooting sideways, leading with her feet until they finally collided with the first step that led to the booth.

She climbed the steps carefully, sliding her palms across the wall, searching for the breaker box. Sierra knew it was there, knew she was close, but the flies closed in, crawling across her face, lips, and eyelashes. Their wings made her cringe, filling her ears with a hellish humming.

"Sierra?" she heard Ivory call out from across the room. "You almost there?! Hurry the hell up!"

When Sierra felt cold metal, she yelped with excitement and nearly tumbled off the short stairway. "I got it!"

With shaking hands, she managed to pry open the panel. Sierra slid her palms over a dozen switches but had no idea which was which. Desperate to get out of the dark, she flipped them all, one at a time.

The lights cut on simultaneously, the neon signs included. The speakers erupted with a steady bassy hip-hop beat that felt like atomic bombs exploding in her eardrums.

"Holy fucking—" Ivory started to gag again, covering her mouth and clutching at her stomach. Her frantic eyes darted in every direction, drinking in the display of depravity.

Sierra clutched at her crucifix, squeezing it in her palm. If there was ever a time when she needed God, this was it.

The bodies of all the clients and dancers were displayed like mannequins in a murder museum. Stripped of their skin, the muscle fibers glistened red and purple in the neon lights of the bar—the only light source, splashing pinks and blues and yellows across the dozens of bodies.

As if frozen in time, they seemed to have died the same way they lived. Stuck in their final moments like insects pinned to a foam board.

Sierra wondered if she knew any of these men, the countless regulars that either had more money than they could spend and loved flaunting their riches or the sad sacks who were convinced they were in love with whoever their favorite girl was, blowing their hard-earned paychecks for a little attention. But in their current state, it was impossible to tell who was who.

As Ivory recovered from her retching fit, Gorghi took it all in with more fascination than fear. Moving away from Ivory to weave between the tables, her eyes glided over the grisly tableaux.

Skinned men sat in chairs with fleshless women straddling their laps like slabs of fatty beef carved into human shapes. The women's breasts were globs of yellow fat tipped with nipples that clung like leeches. The men's testicles—scrotums removed—hung like fermented fishing lures from their groins.

Flies cut through the air, zipping in every direction, jumping from body to body as they feasted. The presence of flies was rare that time of year as winter settled over the city, but inside that dank, muggy building, they seemed to be thriving. Drinking in the putrid pudding, scuttling across the exposed, graying meat. Basting every inch of each body with their digestive juices. Laying their eggs so the next generation of flies could come into existence with a feast to grow fat on.

Sierra also couldn't keep herself from gagging, from feeling the sting of stomach acid at the back of her throat when she noticed the wriggling kernels. The pale maggots like grains of soft rice pulsating in the Swiss cheese holes of the bodies. Roiling and feeding, splashing in their own mucus as they ate away at the decay. Sierra wondered how long it would take before they stripped them down to bare skeletons like some kind of horny Halloween display.

"That fucking music," Ivory said through clenched teeth, trying to close her nose and cover her ears simultaneously.

Sierra realized she'd been focused on the room, ignoring the figure standing beside her. She turned to face the DJ booth slowly, as if she expected the skinned man to leap at her.

The peeled figure standing there resembled the rest of the corpses, but there was no question who he was. DJ BJ—his real name was Brian—was a decent enough guy, a young man with hopes and dreams like everyone else employed at Cheaters. And just like everyone else, he found himself stuck, slowly being corrupted the more time he spent with Leon and mingled with the clientele.

"Sierra, turn that motherfucker's music the fuck off already!" Ivory squealed as she tapped her fists against the sides of her head.

"I liked him," Gorghi said, her calm demeanor making Sierra more and more unsettled. "Always nice to me."

"He was an asshole like all the rest," Ivory said as she faced Brian's body. "And he had shit taste in music."

Sierra fumbled with the DJ equipment, the fleshless corpse looming over her like a zombie preparing to attack. She finally managed to cut it off, yanking a fistful of cables from the wall. "There, you happy now?!"

As the words spilled from her mouth, the body seemed to twitch—small spasms of movement in the head—as if Sierra shutting off his music resurrected him with vengeful energy. She just stood there, frozen with fear, her eyes widening with disbelief.

When the rat emerged from Brian's eye socket, its fur soaked in gelatinous body fluids, Sierra shrieked. She stumbled away, knocking over the equipment as she nearly tumbled down the small set of stairs. The plump rodent screeched as it scurried away, disappearing into the neon-laced darkness.

"Careful," Gorghi said as she caught Sierra in her arms,

keeping her from plummeting to the gore-soaked floor. "Don't wanna hurt yourself."

Sierra gave Gorghi a nod of thanks, then took a moment to center herself before facing the room and the task that lay ahead of them.

As Sierra walked between the chairs and tables, her feet stuck to the thin carpet, the coagulated blood gummy and clinging to the bottoms of her shoes. Every step made a ripping sound like walking across a movie theater coated with spilled soda and popcorn butter. And as her eyes adjusted to the neon lighting, she could see just how much blood had been painted across the floor. Like a red, spongey linoleum.

"Well son-of-a-bitch," Ivory said as she traipsed toward the center stage. The traumatized expression on her face pulled into a sneer. "Look who it is."

"Is that… Violet?" Sierra asked as her eyes followed Ivory and found the sickening display on stage.

A corpse, minus the skin, hung from the chrome pole, tethered to it by what appeared to be her own bra, like a lace bungee cord. The flesh still glistened with a soggy moisture despite the days it was left in the open, the air inside the building so dense and acrid it seemed to preserve the meat.

Sierra stepped toward the stage, staring up at the stripped stripper wearing her signature purple wig. The synthetic locks flowed from her fleshless scalp, her skeletal face lipless and grinning, triggering the hairs on the back of Sierra's neck to stand even taller. Her body hung limply from the bra—stretched to its limit and wrapped around her waist and the pole—her arms and hair dangling, knees buckled.

"She's never looked better," Ivory said with a snort, taking pleasure in what was clearly a horrific death. "What do y'all think?"

"She must've been new," Gorghi said with a tilted head. "Don't recognize her."

Lining the stage were half a dozen severed heads—all males, judging by the lengths of their hair. They were propped up by empty beer bottles, the glass necks lodged deeply into the sloppy throat stumps like diamond erections filling their windpipes with luxury. They all stared up at Violet with dead, lidless eyes. Her purple G-string clung tightly to her hips, stuffed with the peeled faces of the heads like moist leather dollar bills.

God, if you're listening…

But she stopped herself from finishing the thought—something in her gut told her that God was nowhere near this place. She might be on her own.

She finally had to look away, realizing that the side stages were also occupied by women she once knew. Similarly displayed, each of the dancers held their own grisly audience, blood-soaked dollar bills piled up around their feet, some stuffed between their exposed ribs. Gorghi shamelessly collected the bills, piling them into her arms.

"We should… uh… let's just get to Leon's office," Sierra said, wanting to escape the abattoir. "I can't stand to be in this room another second."

As she said this, her eyes scanned the bodies again, this time searching for any sign of Cassie, hoping she didn't find any identifying qualities in the human remains that surrounded her.

Now that I'm here, Sierra thought, *I think Ivory was right. This was no petty criminal. This is a psychopath's art exhibit—The Artist's work. Sending some kind of sick message about how beauty is only skin deep or whatever else his deranged mind had thought up.*

Relieved that none of the corpses appeared to be Cassie, Sierra took a moment to center herself before crossing the room toward the back. Both Ivory and Gorghi pulled themselves away from their respective stages and followed. Ivory still wore a satisfied smirk while Gorghi clung to the stack of bills, dropping several and causing them to flutter back to the blood-drenched carpet.

As they moved away from the main floor and toward the dressing room in the back, a feeling of dread struck Sierra as her mind began to wander.

What if he's still here? These kinds of whacked-out killers have been known to return to the scene. Clearly, he's a narcissist... What if he's biding his time, waiting for the right moment to spring an attack? What if I locked us all inside with him?

A shiver ran down her backside, making her ass cheeks shake and jiggle as if muscle memory had been taking control of her body from the moment she stepped inside Cheaters. But under those circumstances, it was a most unique gyration.

Where are all the skins? Is he sick enough to take them with him? Like a wardrobe's worth of fleshy trophies?

Sierra's mind flashed with the images of the skinned bodies, the reds and yellows and whites of the muscle fibers and fat and tendons. Their eyes still stuck in their sockets, staring blankly ahead—the terror of their final moments was captured in those abysmal stares.

Poor Lola. She deserves a bigger cut than any of us.

Just because she was the only survivor didn't make Lola the lucky one—there was nothing lucky about the mass mutilation before her.

Stay focused. Just get this done and you never have to think about any of this again, Sierra told herself, knowing deep down that this was not something one could unsee. This 'exhibit' was not the type of thing one forgot. The images were permanently tattooed to her frontal lobe, etched into the underside of her eyelids. And she would see them in the dark for the rest of her life.

But at least it will be a better life. A life away from this place and this city and all the sinners who call it home.

They followed a trail of blood that led from the main floor down the hall toward the back. A wide, crooked line, as if a giant with a paintbrush drew it with a shaky hand.

Ivory twitched and scratched, growing more agitated. It looked like her need for lobo had sunk its claws deeper into her mind. Mumbling under her breath, wincing either from pain or the traumatic memories that were surely starting to flood her brain.

"We're right at the finish line," Sierra said, praying there were no more surprises ahead. "Stay focused." She was saying this as much to herself as the others.

The dressing room was thankfully just as Sierra had remembered it, as messy and filthy as it always was but mercifully devoid of death.

Sierra only glanced at the chairs sitting in front of the mirrors that lined the room, each decorated with discarded clothing and strewn cosmetic kits. So many hours spent sitting at her station, staring at her reflection, covering up her imperfections, and sprinkling glitter over herself like she was salting a pork butt.

Further down the hall were the special VIP rooms where high-paying customers could enjoy their kinks and unusual cravings and urges away from the prying eyes of their judgmental constituents. Where girls like Gorghi could not only make a living but be worshipped as goddesses. Where pain was just as desirable as pleasure, and twice as lucrative.

While every other door in Cheaters was painted pink, these doors were black, like rectangular portals to other dimensions where the rules of the world didn't apply.

Sierra remembered hearing the screams of men and women echoing from those rooms and made it a point to steer clear of that hallway—she could only imagine the array of tools that were put to use behind those glossy jet-black doors.

Across from the dressing room stood the entrance to Leon's office. The door's rosy color glistened like a tray of raw ground beef, with a golden knob like a USDA certified sticker. It was behind this barrier, when Cheaters was just a fledgling club, that Leon had made his first promises to Sierra, filling her head with fantasies of a future where family would take precedence over finances and fornication. It was behind this door that Sierra showed him both the positive pregnancy test and, later, the slimy stillborn. She shuddered, remembering how she'd had to fish the fetus out from the shower room toilet and wrap it in a bloodstained bikini top.

It was behind this door that Sierra saw the change in the way Leon looked at her. From a potential wife and mother to just another soft body to profit from that was as disposable as his born-dead baby.

"Hey," Ivory said as she scurried through the dressing room toward the station at the back, opening drawers and rifling through items. A collection of purple wigs hung from hooks along the wall beside the mirror. "I knew this bitch stole my fucking lipstick. My favorite shade too. Didn't even fit her color scheme either."

She grabbed the lipstick off the station, opened it, and applied the red color with her trembling hands. Mushing her lips together, Ivory made them pop before turning to find both Sierra and Gorghi glaring at her. She looked at the girls, the circles around her manic eyes seeming to darken even deeper.

"After what we just saw," Sierra said, "you seriously just put on makeup?"

"What? It makes me feel good," Ivory said. "And right now, I'll take that any way I can get it." Ivory's eyes darted toward the mirrors as she passed them, as if unable to control her urge to see herself. Making sure she still looked presentable, still looked beautiful, even for clients who were long past dead.

When Ivory reached the others, Gorghi snatched the lipstick from her hands and applied it to her thin, shapeless lips, painting the skin above and below, expertly giving them the appearance of being twice as wide. When she smiled, she looked like a clown with gigantism who'd just escaped a mental institution.

When Gorghi tried to return the lipstick, Ivory wrinkled her nose like she was being offered a used tampon. "Nah… you keep it." She grumbled to herself, wincing more and more as the lobo in her system seemed to clear.

"Thanks, Ivory. How's it look? I mean, I know it looks

hotter on you, but… I still look hot, right?" Gorghi turned to Sierra and held out the lipstick. "Mind holding this for me? I don't have pockets."

Gorghi's big hand shoved the lipstick into Sierra's hoodie pocket.

Studying the girls, a strong feeling of pity washed over Sierra, and she hoped that when this was all done, these women would find lives where they would never have to worry about wearing lipstick or any kind of makeup again. Where what they wore could be chosen by comfort rather than considering the libido of strange men. Lives surrounded by a new class of people. People with real goals who didn't have a churning emptiness where their souls were supposed to be.

And the key to those lives is right behind this door.

"You look hot enough to set this building on fire, Gorghi," Sierra said and winked toward the larger woman.

Gorghi beamed and broke away to admire her reflection in one of the dressing room mirrors. Ivory watched her, shaking her head and scraping her nails across her scalp.

Sierra turned her attention back toward Leon's office, reminding herself not to get distracted, that it was up to her to accomplish this mission. The blood trail they'd been following led across the floor and disappeared beneath the door. And as Sierra reached toward the lock with the office key, the fear crept back to the surface.

Is that where The Artist would be? Waiting in Leon's office?

Her hand hesitated, pulling back a few inches. But her next thought overpowered her mind and shoved that fear to the sidelines.

What if Cassie somehow escaped The Artist's knife?

Sierra found her fist knocking against the door before she realized she was doing it.

The sound startled Ivory, and she immediately went for the gun. Whipping it from her waistline, she shakily pointed it at Sierra. The whites of Ivory's eyes glowed in the dim lighting, wide and panicked.

Before Sierra could tell her to put the gun down, Gorghi's hand appeared from above and behind Ivory and lowered the pistol to her side.

"You shouldn't point that at people," Gorghi said. "That's how accidents happen." She started to reach for the gun.

"Matter of fact," Sierra said, directing her motherly voice and stern tone at Ivory, "maybe it's best if someone else held on to the gun."

"I'm fine!" Ivory yanked the gat from Gorghi's touch. "We doing this or what?"

Sierra sighed, realizing that, sooner or later, she was going to have to get that gun away from her. She clocked the way Gorghi was staring down at Ivory and could tell she was thinking something similar.

The only thing worse than Ivory with a gun is Gorghi with it. I definitely *can't let that happen.*

"Hello?" Sierra leaned in close to the door and gave it another knock. "Anyone in there?"

"Guess you got short-term memory loss or some shit," Ivory said with a scoff. "Folks in here ain't much for conversation."

Sierra ignored her and cupped her hands over her mouth. "Cassie?! It's Sierra. Y-you in there?!"

Sierra pressed her ear against the door, doing her best to listen as Ivory made more disapproving sounds behind her. When she heard nothing, she took a deep breath, prepared herself for the worst, and stuck the key in. It unlocked without a hitch, but when she turned the handle and tried to shove the door, it held fast.

"What is it?" Gorghi asked, a hint of impatience in her voice. She was growing antsy to hold her prize in her hands.

"Locked from the inside," Sierra said, not sure whether this was good or bad news.

"Move," Gorghi said as she shoved Sierra aside with ease. She turned her neck, popping the joints, then cracked all her knuckles.

Approaching the door like she was facing a formidable foe, Gorghi refused to back down, preparing herself for battle.

LEON'S LAIR

When Gorghi rammed her shoulder into the door, it was hard and heavy, like a Mack truck slamming into a wall. The pink door rattled in its frame but stayed shut. Strong and sturdy, it refused to give.

Sierra felt the vibration of every impact in the soles of her feet as Gorghi continued smashing into the wood. The sleazy photos framed on the walls rattled, some falling and crashing to the floor. A spiderweb of cracks snaked across the doorframe and up into the wall.

"You got it, keep going!" Ivory cheered.

The molding trim along the frame snapped off, but the door wouldn't give. Still, somehow, it remained in place like a flamingo-colored bank vault door.

A familiar metal click rang out from behind Gorghi and Sierra. They turned to find Ivory pointing the pistol and baring a devilish grin on her now colorless lips. A streak of red lipstick was smeared across her cheek and caked on the front of her teeth.

For a moment, Sierra thought Ivory was pointing the gun at her. Maybe her need for lobo had finally made her snap and realize she wanted all the money for herself.

"Move out the way," Ivory said, motioning with the gun for them to step aside. "I got a key right here."

Not a moment after Sierra and Gorghi moved, Ivory fired a shot. It hit the door, cracking the wood but still not penetrating all the way through. The bullet lodged into it like a metal splinter.

She adjusted her aim and fired at the doorknob. The bullet hit the golden surface and ricocheted, Sierra ducking and covering her head with her arms.

"Watch it!" Sierra turned, noticing the red rivulets running down Gorghi's forearm.

Gorghi didn't seem to feel the pain. She just stared down at the wound with the same confusion and fascination as Sierra. Poking at it, she studied the blood on the tip of her finger, shooting a hard look toward Ivory that was deadlier than any bullet.

"You shot me." Her voice was flat and deep. No anger or agony, just a statement of truth. "You shot me in the arm."

Ivory averted her gaze, scratching at the side of her neck. Her sanity continued to dissolve as her addiction bubbled more and more to the surface, taking control—her fidgety demeanor made it obvious. The drugs seemed to be taking precedence over everything else, including her own safety.

"Well, I told y'all to step back," Ivory said, raising the gun again.

Sierra dropped to the floor and covered herself while Gorghi frowned and started to reach for the gun. But the pistol discharged before Gorghi could grab it. She smashed her palms against both ears as if the shot caused a painful ringing to erupt inside her head.

Just as Sierra looked back up, the door creaked open enough for her to get a glimpse inside. Enough to see the backs of the bare feet—both still wrapped in skin—lying lifelessly on the floor.

Wooden splinters and sheetrock dust were sprinkled and spread out everywhere. The smell of gun smoke swirled through the air, giving all three women a short reprieve from the stink of decay that filled the building.

Sierra glanced over her shoulder toward the others. Gorghi stared into the room, her wound already seemingly forgotten. Ivory still held the gun, shaking her head and rapping her free fist against her temple, mumbling something incoherent under her breath.

"Is that…?" Gorghi said as she stepped past Sierra and peered into the office.

"Leon…" Sierra didn't want to see him, but she forced herself to look. She knew Gorghi was right, not because she recognized his face but because she recognized the scar running across the back of his left calf. He'd been attacked as a child by his pet bulldog when it went rabid and lost its mind, ripping into him with its fangs.

Sierra's eyes slid up from Leon's legs, but then stopped at his thighs, just beneath his buttocks. Because this was where the skin ended and the glistening exposed fat and muscle began. His fleshless head lay sideways on the floor, his mouth wide and half-filled with what appeared to be masticated meat, as if he'd chewed his tongue to ribbons.

A bloody pocket knife lay near his hand, the small blade dull with bits of gore clinging to it. Sierra wondered if maybe he'd defended himself with it, if maybe that was The Artist's blood.

The way his arms and legs were positioned, Sierra figured he had probably managed to drag himself from the main floor to his office, somehow escaping The Artist after getting skinned from his crotch to his cranium. With his raw, exposed nerves sanded down by the rough floor, he'd painfully inched his way to safety.

Judging by the urine and excrement stains splashed across the office, Leon had stayed alive for at least a few days, suffering behind his pink door, somehow managing to hold on to life, as painful as it must have been.

Sierra found herself feeling sorry for the man, with maybe just a pinch of sadness. Leon had meant so much to her for so long, and even though he had betrayed her, she found no pleasure in seeing him that way: a mostly skinless mound of meat and sinew and tendon, ironically stripped bare so that all could see the true man who lay beneath the surface. It seemed that, before he met his demise, Leon finally learned the plight of his girls—what it was like to have to bare *everything*. And now, he was just a putrid pile of protein like everyone else.

It hit her so hard and suddenly that she audibly gasped. Sierra was so distracted by Leon that she hadn't even thought about it. Cassie's smiling face inflated inside her mind, shoving every other thought aside.

Lola said she saw Leon with Cassie… if he's here, then…

"Cassie?" Sierra stepped past Leon and scanned the small office for any sign of her. The walls were decorated with more framed pictures of girls from the past. The photo of Sierra in her prime hung just behind the large mahogany desk. "Cassie?!"

"Go inside already," Ivory said from the broken doorway. "You're wasting your time."

"Oh Lord…" The words puffed from the back of Sierra's throat like a soft burp. "Please no…"

Just visible from behind the desk, sticking out and completely still, were two feet clad in pearly-white open-toed heels. The toenails were painted white to match the shoes—Cassie's favorite nail color. The white nails and the pale skin were freckled with blood spatter. A thickened pool of blood was spread out across the floor beneath the legs, ending at about mid-calf.

"Oh shit," Ivory muttered.

Tears started to drip down Sierra's cheeks as more of Cassie came into view. The white garter belts strapped to her legs, attached to white laced panties that hugged her midsection. As she stepped closer, she saw Cassie's belly and bare, milky breasts. Her skin was so translucently white that Sierra could see the crisscrossing of blue veins beneath the surface.

Atop her shoulders, where Cassie's angelic face used to be, was now a mutilated mess of bloody flesh. The white bone of her skull shone starkly from the dark, gory chili that used to bear the sweetest smile. Her throat had been slit sloppily, the flesh ragged around the cut, as if a dull knife had been used.

"Cassie!" Sierra rushed toward her and dropped to her knees. Though it was obvious it was far too late—from both the state of Cassie's face to the strong smell of decay in the room—Sierra took hold of Cassie's shoulders and shook them. "No! Wake up!"

The office had been locked up so tight, the bodies inside had been spared the mega horde of flies, but now that the door hung open, the insects started finding their way in, scuttling across Cassie's face and suckling on her juices.

Sierra waved them away as she wept, burying her face into Cassie's cold, clammy arm.

Cassie's face looked like it had been carved on, the meat sliced right off her skull. And that's when she remembered the chewed-up wad inside Leon's mouth.

Just as this thought popped into Sierra's mind, a gurgling cough erupted from Leon's throat, spraying a fresh splash of blood across the floor.

Ivory screamed, nearly gagging again. "H-he's alive!"

LAST GASP

"Whoa," Gorghi croaked, staring with fascination at Leon's twitching body.

He shrieked in pain, his tongue stretched tight and rigid as he bellowed. More blood misted into the air like a crimson aerosol spray. His convulsions of shock caused him to flail as if having a seizure.

He's alive… He… was… eating her…

Sierra's stomach lurched, and she vomited into the corner of the room, spraying it across the framed photos of strippers.

Leon's body quivered violently, the hard ligaments and his exposed teeth rattling against the floor, making a sound like dice shaking in a cup. As Cassie's necrotic flesh fell from his mouth, his body continued to splash about in the coagulated blood. The red oozed from between the exposed muscle fibers, flinging droplets that freckled the floor.

Gorghi stood, silently watching and observing, seemingly unaffected by the grisly scene. Ivory paced just outside the office door, going back to murmuring to herself and pounding her knuckles against the side of her head.

Sierra wiped the puke from her mouth as a rage bubbled in her gut. With a roar, she ran and leapt on top of Leon, straddling his gory torso. She swung her fist into the side of his jaw, then hammered down blow after blow, each punch sending a mist of blood into her face.

"You killed her! You *killed* her!"

Leon's shriek shrank down to a groan that rattled at the back of his throat until it was nothing but a wet clicking sound. Whatever life he had left was beaten out of him by Sierra, and the moist gurgle faded into a heavy silence.

Nobody said a word—all eyes were on Sierra. The silence was somehow heavier now, despite Leon's gurgles replaying in Sierra's mind.

Sierra composed herself, catching her breath and climbing off Leon's body. She avoided eye contact with the other girls as she lifted one of Leon's coats from a rack nearby and covered Cassie's body with it.

I promise to honor you, she thought as she gave Cassie's icy hand a final squeeze, wiping the tears and snot from her face with her free hand.

Beside her, next to the coat rack, sat a wide cabinet. The area where Leon kept his safe. Before Sierra could move toward it, Ivory was already crossing the room.

"Move!" Ivory said to Gorghi as she stormed by her. "Let's get this shit over with." She opened the cabinet, staring blankly inside.

Sierra had expected to see the pale blue color of the same safe she'd seen countless times before. But instead, there was only darkness. The space was empty.

"No," Ivory grumbled before shaking her head violently. "No, no, no, no!"

"Where is it?" Gorghi growled as she grabbed Ivory's shoulder and shoved her aside with ease. "I *need* that money! Where the fuck is it?!"

"Gorghi, relax," Sierra pleaded. "We still have to—"

"Relax?!" Gorghi roared. "I've never had the luxury of relaxing! Not once, not for one fucking moment!" She accentuated her words with a hard punch to the cabinet, shattering the wood like it was made of glass.

"What, you think you got it worse than the rest of us?" Ivory used the barrel of the pistol to scratch at her scalp. "You think you need that money more than *me?!* Bitch, you don't know what I've been through!"

"You guys," Sierra said, trying to position herself between them. "Back at Lola's, she told me—"

"I know you were Leon's favorite," Gorghi said. "You knew what it felt like to be a star on that stage with men throwing money at you. But *me?!*" Gorghi towered over Sierra, barking toward Ivory with ease. Her spittle rained down on Sierra as she spoke. "I know about getting laughed at and called a freak! Being asked if I got a cock before they pull me into the back room! I know about this piece of shit"—she crossed the room and kicked Leon's body hard enough to break a few ribs—"pimping me out to the nastiest perverts and weirdos, creeps you couldn't even imagine! You think *you've* been through it? You have no fucking idea… I earned that money! And I ain't leaving here without it!"

Gorghi grabbed the cabinet with both fists and flung it onto its side, making Ivory yelp and jump out of the way. She leapt into the air and stomped down with both feet, smashing it to pieces. Needles of wooden shrapnel peppered Sierra's face, then her forearms as she tried to shield herself.

"Gorghi! Enough!" Sierra stomped toward her and took hold of her deltoid—as big as a head. "Enough from the both of you! Cassie's lying over there… dead! And you… you want to argue over who has it worse?!"

"Oh, fuck you, Sierra," Ivory groaned, dusting the wooden bits from her arms, that damn pistol still gripped in her quivering fist. "Trying to act all high and mighty like this whole fucking thing wasn't your idea in the first place?"

The tensest silence so far fell over the room as Sierra and Ivory glared hard at each other.

"You both need to stop fighting and listen," Sierra said. "Lola said something about the safe being underneath, but that's all that—"

"Hold on," Ivory said. "Lola what, gave you some kind of clue? And you kept that shit to yourself this whole time? For real?!"

Sierra watched as Ivory and Gorghi shared a quick suspicious glance.

"I wasn't trying to…" Sierra struggled to find the words, asking herself whether or not she was holding back for selfish reasons. "She just told me that the safe was underneath."

"Underneath?" Ivory scowled. "Underneath what?"

"Exactly the problem." Sierra shrugged. "I have no idea what it means."

"How the fuck am I gonna use the combination to a safe we can't find?" Ivory asked.

"That's the other thing." Sierra crouched down beside Leon and inspected his body—but only with her eyes, wanting to avoid touching him as long as possible. "When I mentioned the combination to Lola, she said that *Leon* was the combination. But I have no idea what she was talking about."

"What's this?" Gorghi dropped to one knee in the spot where the cabinet had been standing. Where a thick, red button stuck up from the floor.

Without waiting for a response from the others, Gorghi pressed the button with her girthy finger—a loud clicking sound filled the air.

"Oh fuck me!" Ivory pointed her gun at Leon's body, which had started to move again. "He's still fucking alive!"

Leon's corpse rolled over from its belly to its back, his fleshless face wiggling from the violent motion before resting on its side. Another mound of Cassie's chewed carcass spilled from his mouth.

"Wait a second!" Sierra shouted as Ivory cocked back the hammer. "He's not alive. It's something… under him."

A hidden compartment opened, and a gray safe rose from the floor with a mechanical whir. A red light blinked near what looked like a camera lens. Just beneath that was some kind of screen a few inches wide.

Ivory grinned. "That's what I'm talking about!"

EYE OF THE BEHOLDER

Ivory dashed across the office and squeezed past Gorghi, a confident smile on her face as she searched the safe's surface. "Where the fuck's the combination dial?!"

There is no combination, Sierra thought, remembering Lola's words. *He* is *the combination...*

"Gorghi," Sierra said as she reluctantly positioned herself at Leon's feet, preparing to take hold of his ankles. "Help me with him."

Before Sierra could wrap her fingers around Leon's ankles, Gorghi grabbed him beneath his armpits and lifted him effortlessly off the floor.

"Where do you want him?" Gorghi asked.

"Um... over here." Sierra stepped over the large bloodstain and approached the safe.

"You see this here?" Sierra pointed to the camera lens.

"Hold his face up to it. I think this is one of those eye scanner things."

Gorghi balanced Leon's face up against the safe, his eye hovering just above the lens.

Beep! The red light turned blue as a high-pitched tone filled the air.

"Like that?" Gorghi asked

Sierra furrowed her brow, wondering the same thing. Before she could answer, the light turned red again and the tone disappeared.

"I… I don't get it," Sierra mumbled. "What are we supposed to do?" Sierra rushed to the safe and studied every nook and cranny.

"The hell with this," Gorghi said through clenched teeth. "I'll get it open myself!"

Gorghi shouldered Sierra aside and wrapped her arms around the safe. She positioned her feet, took a few deep breaths, and then lifted. The veins that crisscrossed around her muscles were filled with fiery blood as she growled, attempting to rip the safe from its stand.

As powerful as Gorghi was, the mass of steel didn't budge as sweat poured down her face and moistened her dress. Strands of wet hair hung over her face like squid ink pasta noodles.

"Damn it!" Gorghi howled, refusing to give up.

Sierra gasped. Looking past Gorghi's quivering form, she spotted the small screen. It was just large enough to rest a finger on. But her hope was quickly replaced with frustration as she stared down at Leon's skinned hands.

"What is it?" Ivory asked, studying Sierra's facial expression.

The skins… where are all the skins?

Gorghi finally gave up and collapsed to the floor, panting heavily for air. Energy spent, she stayed down on all fours, sweat raining down.

"I'll be right back," Sierra said, grabbing Leon's pocketknife before rushing out of the office.

"Famous last words," Ivory said, looming in the doorway, watching suspiciously as Sierra turned the dressing room upside down.

Sierra looked everywhere but found nothing. Storming out of the dressing room, she headed back toward the front of house. Her eyes widened when they found the floor, and she paused for a moment, understanding the solution had been in front of her the entire time.

Of course!

The macabre streak of blood Leon had left behind might as well have been a road map.

ROADMAP OF RED

The blood trail looked like it was glowing when she zeroed in on it. Sierra followed the ruby path back to the source of the smell and the low hum of the flies.

She did her best to prepare herself to face the carnage once again, holding the knife out in front of her. As soon as her feet left the hallway and crossed into the main area of the club, the squish of the blood-soaked floor echoed in her head. From her vantage point, she could only see the tables and chairs. The skinned victims were displayed here and there, glistening in the neon.

When she entered the main room, the trail of crimson didn't disappear, but it became much less obvious. The massive space was littered with blood spatter and various pools, causing the trails to all intersect within a giant knot of necrosis. Sierra looked to the stage where The Artist's Violet exhibit lay.

I'll be able to get a better look of the entire room up there, she thought.

Climbing up onto the main stage, a shiver took hold of her as her mind once again contemplated the idea that The

Artist could still be inside the building somewhere. After all, he had spent so much time getting every element of his twisted vision just right—his exhibit was a spectacle to behold. Would someone who paid such painstaking attention to detail want to revisit their masterpiece? Or live inside of it to relish its genius? Sierra couldn't shake the feeling that she wasn't alone.

She tried to ignore the thoughts and moved a few feet behind Violet, but found herself squeezing the hilt of the knife tighter. The severed heads with their withering eyes seemed to stare at her, the festering audience mocking her for her failure, blaming her for being alive when so many were dead.

If I would have stayed on the night shift… if Leon never demoted me… She forced those thoughts out of her head too, refusing to let herself fall into survivor's guilt. *I'm still here for a reason. This is all God's design.*

As Sierra walked past Violet, she could feel the stage shifting beneath her, the old, rickety platform an issue that Leon knew he needed to fix but had never found the time or the desire to. No matter how many workers pleaded with him about safe working conditions or how the pole would wiggle in place, coming loose from the ceiling where the bolts rattled, nothing ever changed.

From up high, Sierra could see the entire club. The remains of DJ BJ were still propped up, headphones strapped to his fleshless head, flashy rings and gold bracelets clinging to his exposed muscle tissue, stuck in place by the gummy blood evolving into gelatinous ooze.

Her eyes scanned the place, glancing over all the clientele and the workers, the air alive with the movement of flies. Sierra kept waving the critters away as they orbited around her head. She spat in disgust when one of them landed on her lip and scuttled across, leaving a trail of putrescence that filled her mouth with rot seasoning.

The headless bodies of the annihilated audience lining the main stage sat at the bar. The seats had been removed from the stools so the long chrome poles could be shoved up their rectums, holding them upright at odd angles like cadaver lollipops. A dark-brown liquid clung to the poles like maple syrup. The pests frenzied over the putrid rectal slime, dotting the fluid streams like buzzing raisins.

There was no sign of the origin point of Leon's blood trail. The room was too much of a mess to pick out any kind of pattern.

Where could the skins be?

Sierra was filled with worry when she considered again the possibility that The Artist had taken the skins home with him. Killers did that kind of thing: take gruesome trophies. The casings could've been displayed on his walls at that very moment. Or maybe he'd hung them in his closet like freshly peeled leather jackets.

The closet!

As Sierra started to march off stage, she forgot to step lightly. The ground shook with each step, and just as she passed Violet, the bra holding her up snapped. Violet's rotten head bounced off the stage beside her. Dark blood splashed across Sierra's feet. The ghastly stripper's once beautiful face was now aimed toward Sierra, jaw propped open, the fetid tongue swollen and brown like a wad of raw liver.

A shriek of surprise erupted from Sierra's throat and she stumbled, losing her footing. She tried to catch herself, but the stage rocked again, sending her tumbling toward her dead peer. As the stage collapsed, Sierra dropped her knife, leaping as it turned to rubble.

Sierra's face slammed into Violet's buttocks, nose jamming between the yellow fat of the cheeks. The necrotic juices of the body basted Sierra's face with room temperature oils—the fat ripped off in chunks and jiggled beside her like fermented flan.

Crawling away in a panic, Sierra spat and coughed, desperate to get the rich lard taste out of her mouth. Gagging, she tried wiping it off her face with her hands and forearm, but her efforts did little to erase the funky flavor.

Violet's custardy eyeballs glared across the floor at Sierra, her pupils wide and black, the side of her face pressed against the floor. The impact from the fall crushed her right cheekbone, causing her eye to ooze out of the socket.

Sierra tried to regain control of herself, fighting off the panic and revulsion. She searched for the knife, her only defense, but it was lost in the debris. Back on her feet, she turned away from the stage and walked deeper into the room. Before long, she reached the opposite side where the closet sat.

They had passed it on their way in, but it had been too dark to see. Written in dark blood across the pink-painted wood of the door were the words: THE SKIN YOU LIVE IN.

As she stood there reading the words, another wave of decay slapped her across the face. The vile aroma was accompanied by the buzz of flies inside the closet. The flickers of their wings were frenzied and wild, sounding more like an angry nest of hornets. A translucent slime expelled from beneath the door—chubby maggots writhed and thrashed in the bodily porridge as they rode it onto the floor like limbless beachgoers caught in the tide.

Sierra took a quick moment to center herself, wrapping her fist around the doorknob and pulling it open. Hot air washed over her, spiced with decay. A cloud of angry flies burst into the air and swarmed over her, making Sierra scream and wave her arms frantically. It was like the pests had grown an insatiable fondness for human flesh. Swatting at them, Sierra rustled her hair when she felt them scuttling across her scalp.

And once the flies had dissipated, she gazed upon the monstrosities inside the closet. She saw all the human hides hanging from the thick metal hangers. They came in all shades and sizes. Scars and tattoos. Needles of body hair. The skins glistened like oiled leather, the edges pink and white like raw thick-sliced bacon. The emptied flesh of their head flaps hung from their necks and shoulders, draped over their backs like hellish sweatshirt hoods. The pink slime dripped steadily from the fleshy wardrobe, adding to the salmon-tinted puddle beneath them.

Her mind wandered to Cassie again, and she wondered whether or not she would have been better off letting The Artist have her. Would he have made it quick, flaying the skin away only after death had already taken her? Did she suffer more at the hands—and mouth—of Leon?

I'm so sorry, Cassie. I should have rescued you from this life, from Leon, the first day you stepped foot in this godforsaken place.

Sierra took a deep, calming breath and faced the skins.

Okay… here we go.

She stepped into the puddle of goo and reached into the closet, flipping through the moist pelts one at a time, searching for Leon's. Flying right past the female skins, Sierra shuddered. Their empty breasts sagged worse than hers. They were caved in like deflated beachballs.

She tossed aside any male skins that were extra-large or devoid of tattoos, remembering specifically a tattoo etched into Leon's stomach: an ouroboros symbol circling his belly button, the snake head swallowing the tail.

As Sierra shuffled through them, the sting of bile burned the back of her throat, but she held it down. Scanning every skin up and down, finally, she saw it.

There you are!

She recognized his skin tone, the patterns of hair across his chest and back. The size of his cock, which hung loosely beside the elongated scrotum skin. The snake tattoo was looped around his naval, more faded than Sierra remembered.

She reached in and pulled the hanger off the rack. Once it was free, she was surprised how heavy the skin was, even without the flesh of his legs.

She grabbed Leon's floppy wrist and dragged his hide across the floor on her way to the back. She walked past all the other dead bodies and the collapsed stage. The skin kept getting hung up on the sticky ground, and Sierra would have to give it a hard yank to unglue it from the gore.

When she reached the dressing room, Ivory was now sitting at one of the stations, fully doing her makeup. She had reapplied a different shade of lipstick, her eyelids shimmering with dark-blue eye shadow. She used a brush to apply pink blush to her cheeks, stretching her mouth to the side to widen her canvas. Her body rocked back and forth, sweat dribbling from the crown of her head, causing the new makeup to streak. Sierra knew her addiction was gnawing at her—trying to stay busy was probably the only way she was able to help distract herself from the horrors her withdrawals were forcing her to relive.

As Sierra trudged by, using both hands to drag the heavy hide, Ivory paused and raised an eyebrow.

"What are you doing?!"

"I found the key," Sierra said.

Gorghi was still inside of the office, back on her feet, her arms wrapped around the safe, trying to pry it free from the steel stand again.

Growling, sweat poured off Gorghi's face as she struggled and strained. A frustrated whimper sprayed from her mouth just before she gave up again. Leaning over, Gorghi rested her hands on her knees as she fought to catch her breath. Then her eyes coasted over and landed on Sierra—and Leon's pelt.

"What's that?"

"Lift him up," Sierra said, pointing toward Leon's lifeless body. "Aim his eye in the same place as before."

When Gorghi cocked her head in confusion, Sierra grimaced. She was still trying to work up the nerve to do what she knew was necessary in order to open the safe.

God forgive me.

Sierra reached down and slid her hand into the flesh of Leon's arm. As her skin wormed its way inside Leon's, it felt like her limb was on a serial killer's Slip 'N Slide ride. Pushing her way further into Leon's casing, Sierra donned his flesh, although it fit her like an oversized glove. She winced at the cold, squishy feeling inside but held her composure as she reached toward the fingerprint reader.

Gorghi seemed to catch on as she grabbed hold of Leon's body and lifted it up without issue. Even in her weakened state, it was nothing to her.

"Okay," Sierra said through a grimace. She held her finger, wrapped in the hollow flesh of Leon's digit, over the scanner. "One, two, three!"

Gorghi held Leon's eye against the camera lens, making it squish like an overripe grape.

Beeep!

The red light turned blue again, followed by that maddening tone. Without wasting another second, Sierra pressed Leon's fingertip across the scanner, rolling it back and forth to make sure it got an accurate reading.

Beep Beep Beeeep!

The blue light flashed three times before turning green, and the safe door popped open.

THE REAL MONSTERS

"You did it!" Ivory's eyes darted between the open safe, Leon's peeled body, and his crumpled-up skin lying a few feet away.

Sierra's imagination flashed images of tall, fat stacks of cash. She imagined the inside of the safe to be piled to the brim. But when she opened the door and stared into it with hopeful eyes, a wave of shock swept over her. Followed by an immediate feeling of danger.

Sierra positioned herself so the others couldn't see inside, peering into the narrow space as she slowly cracked the door open.

The safe was near empty. There were no countless wads of cash—just one item sat in the center of the steel box. An item she'd never seen but could tell right away by how the light sparkled off it that it was the real deal. Probably more valuable than any amount of cash a safe that size could have held.

"What is it?" Ivory begged.

Sierra looked over her shoulder at the girls who shared an impatient look. Quickly reaching inside, Sierra snatched the diamond. Concealing it in her fist, she squeezed it, the rock's sharp edges cutting into her palm.

Money is one thing… but how are we going to split a diamond?

They could take it to a jeweler or a pawn shop to get it appraised, but she could already feel the heat of impatience burning on their faces. Their hunger wouldn't be quelled by such suggestions. Ivory's withdrawal wouldn't wait another second—her pistol would be ready to spit fire so she could take that diamond for herself. And by the look on Gorghi's face and the way she rocked her weight back and forth, she appeared ready to crush anyone who came between her and the cash.

"How much?!" Gorghi grabbed hold of Sierra's shoulder and squeezed it hard enough to make Sierra wince.

Sierra tightened her fist around the diamond, hiding it behind her back as she was forced to face the other women. Both of them looked into the safe, and when they saw that it was completely empty, their eyes landed on Sierra.

"You're fucking with me, right?" Ivory asked. "I know we didn't do all this shit for nothing!"

"How was I supposed to know?" Sierra scanned the room, doing the math on how difficult it would be to run through them and make a break for it. "We talked about what could *potentially* be inside, but we couldn't have known for sure. It was just a theory."

"What's that?" Gorghi asked as she grabbed Sierra's elbow and twirled her around, holding her in place.

Sierra winced and hissed but didn't attempt to get away. She knew she was no match for Gorghi.

"What is it?" Ivory said, reaching behind her back as if going for the gun. "This bitch trying to double-cross us?"

"No, I was gonna… I was just thinking, that's all!" Sierra's hand was finally pried open by Gorghi's crowbar fingers. She felt despair suffocate her as the diamond got snatched out of her palm.

No! It's mine, I earned it!

"It's… it's a diamond!" Gorghi shoved Sierra away as if

swatting a fly. The diamond looked like a nose ring in her massive mitt. Her eyes sparkled as she looked at it, as if already thinking of all the possibilities. "A *big* diamond."

Ivory's eyes snapped toward Sierra, her hand swinging back around with the pistol in its grip. "You think you're real slick, huh?"

"I was gonna tell you guys."

"That was a rhetorical question. After all we been through, you think you can just cut us out?"

"I-I thought this thing would be stuffed with cash, maybe a collection of valuable items," Sierra said, her eyes bouncing between the pistol in Ivory's hand and the diamond sitting in Gorghi's grip. "Just like we talked about. Cash would've been easy to split, right? Chop it up evenly, everyone gets their piece, and we're done. But this?" Sierra reached for the diamond, and Ivory pointed the gun at her.

"Don't fucking touch it," Ivory threatened.

Sierra stopped her motion and let her hand rest by her side, her eyes still mesmerized by the stone.

Ivory furrowed her brow in anger. "And so your plan changed, right? Can't split a single stone, so you figured it belonged to you?" Ivory stepped up to Sierra and pressed the barrel of the gun to her forehead.

Sierra held her breath, staring past the gun and into Ivory's eyes—searching for some kind of humanity but finding only the blackness of greed and the madness of addiction.

God help me.

"No, I-I was just as shocked as you guys. I was trying to think of a way we could split it without drawing attention to ourselves. It's not like we can take it to the pawn shop."

"Why not?" Ivory thrust the gun harder into Sierra's forehead as she spoke, each word pissing her off more and more. "Seems like an easy enough solution to me. Trade that shit for some cash, split the cash, just like we talked about. Just added a small step, that's all. Out of all the crazy shit we've pulled already, it'd be a pretty easy step."

"It's so beautiful…" Gorghi held the diamond up to the light, staring at it with mesmerized eyes. In her own world—just her and the rock.

"Let me see that thing," Ivory said, snapping her fingers.

"No." The diamond glowed in Gorghi's eyes, casting a nefarious twinkle. "I'll keep it."

"You'll what?" Ivory swung the gat toward Gorghi, clicking back the hammer to show she wasn't messing around. "Sure about that?"

"Put that thing down." Sierra felt the tension in the room thicken. The energy between the women darkened, each one of them feeling entitled to the gem. The prize at the bottom of a cereal box full of raisins and skinned corpses. "We can figure this out together. We can't start turning on each other."

"You the one who tried jacking us!" Ivory yelled.

"You keep pointing that at me…" Gorghi said as she closed the distance between her and the pistol. She pressed her muscular body against the barrel so it was dimpling the skin of her chest. "And I'll rip it out your hand and butt fuck you with it."

"Oh, you think so?" Ivory locked eyes with Gorghi, refusing to back down. "How about you go fuck yourself instead. I'll give you some extra holes to make it easier."

"Try me," Gorghi growled.

Ivory unlocked her gritted teeth. "I already put one inside you before, you think I won't do it again, you big, ugly cunt?"

Sierra felt the heat in her gut rise to her head, boiling her brain and making it feel like steam was spitting from her ears. Her fists tightened and knuckles cracked like walnut shells just knowing that diamond was still nestled inside Gorghi's kraken of a hand.

And why shouldn't I keep it for myself?

Sierra glanced back at Cassie again before dashing across the office toward Gorghi.

God wants *me to have it! God will protect me!*

Her sudden explosion of motion made Ivory flinch.

The pistol shifted slightly as it spat fire, blowing a hole right through Gorghi. The bullet blasted through her shoulder above her clavicle, going in and out with a fireworks display of blood that splashed against the wall.

Ivory just stood there, hands shaking as she stared in shock at the gaping hole in Gorghi's shoulder. She kept the gun raised, sensing how badly she messed up—knowing she would pay a price for her itchy finger.

"Gorghi… I-I didn't mean to—"

"You shot me," Gorghi said, her voice sounding more amused than angry. "Again…" She looked from the smaller wound on her arm to the larger one near her shoulder. Reaching up, Gorghi ran her fingers over the damage, then stared at the blood staining her fingertips. Her hard eyes slid from her fingers to Ivory. And her mouth turned into a grimace of fury.

Sierra's ears rang from the blast, but her full attention was still on the diamond swallowed up by Gorghi's monstrous grip. Gorghi slowly crept toward Ivory.

Ivory turned the gun on Sierra, backing away toward the office door an inch at a time. The cheap rings on her fingers rattled against the metal of the pistol as she trembled, still trying to force her face to be intimidating. "You made me do that. We were just talking, that's all. And you—"

Gorghi's fist smashed into the side of Ivory's head. The same fist that held the diamond inside, as if channeling the power of the rock and injecting it into her foe's skull.

Ivory's legs went limp and she collapsed, plummeting to the floor. Her eyes rolled to the back of her head, and when she hit the floor, so did the gun.

Blam!

Another deafening explosion erupted, and the bullet whizzed right by Sierra's ear before ricocheting off the safe. She didn't have time to duck or react. She looked on in horror, watching the red circle form on Gorghi's belly—the stain on her dress growing in size as the shade of red darkened.

"Oh… no," Gorghi groaned.

BLOOD DIAMOND

The bullet didn't go through Gorghi this time but got lodged somewhere in her gut, turning on a crimson faucet. Blood trickled down her stomach and splashed onto the floor, painting her shoes.

Sierra felt a sting on her ear. Reaching up, she touched the edge and hissed at the pain where her finger made contact. The blood and uneven edge made it clear that the bullet had taken a piece of the cartilage.

It happened so fast that she was still in shock, her pain only then making itself known. Sierra quickly checked the rest of her body for holes, thankful to learn she hadn't been hit anywhere else. She was glad to be alive when she looked at Gorghi's hand.

It felt like time stopped when she watched the diamond fall from Gorghi's palm and bounce off the floor. The fluorescent lights sparkled against the gem's surface, throwing prism patterns across the walls like the sun reflecting off a lake. And before she knew what she was doing, Sierra found herself moving toward it. But as she closed in, she was stopped in her tracks by a strong grip.

One of Gorghi's mitts was clamped onto Sierra's shoulder, the other clutching at her own stomach as she bit her lip in pain. Blood dripped from between her fingers as she dropped to her knees, groaning. Her furious eyes met Sierra's before she lost consciousness, collapsing forward.

The motion and Gorghi's strength clamped down on Sierra's clothing. The giant's meaty fingers got hold of Sierra's hoodie and the bra underneath, pulling everything off. Sierra's massive tits poured free and swung heavily from her chest.

Gorghi's meaty face bounced off the carpet before settling, leaving a stunned Sierra standing half-nude over her. While monitoring the giant's actions closely, Sierra remained motionless. Gradually, the blast of the gun and the ringing in Sierra's ears finally started to fade.

With both women now disoriented, Sierra found herself the last one standing, her pendulous breasts hanging down to her waist. Her ear pulsated with agony, but she only cared about the diamond. It was calling her name, promising her things from the office floor. Gorghi's blood crept toward it as if trying to claim it for itself.

I never meant for this to happen, she thought, a barbed balloon of guilt inflating in her stomach. *I wanted this to be* our *way out… Not just me but everyone.*

She turned and looked at Cassie again, trying to force her mind to remember her smiling face rather than the meaty skull staring back at her.

"I swear I never meant for anyone to get hurt," Sierra said, not meaning to speak her thoughts out loud, but hearing the words felt good. "My intentions were good. I… I swear to God they were."

But even as she said it, she knew she was lying to herself. She knew the events of the day had altered her intentions.

This diamond, however much it was worth, no longer symbolized freedom. It wasn't just a way to start over somewhere. If Sierra was being honest, it had now become a chance to live the sort of life she never thought possible for someone like her. The sort of life she only saw on TV or in magazines. The sort of life that would transform who she was and how the rest of the world saw her forever. It represented the amount of money that would not only get respect but demand it.

Sierra slipped into total tunnel vision, like a horse with blinders on. It was like she wasn't even controlling her body—the motion was almost magnetic.

Just as her hand grabbed hold of the diamond, she heard the cocking of the pistol. Ivory pressed the still warm barrel against the side of Sierra's face.

"I knew you'd stab me in the back." The hatred in Ivory's stare faded. Her eyes looked dreamy, still half in concussion land, half in the grip of her lobo addiction.

Seeing her opportunity, Sierra made her move. Pivoting her body as she palmed the rock, she smashed it into Ivory's left eye. The devastating blow made her scream and stumble back, firing a wild shot that hit the ceiling and filled the air with dust. A second round fired in succession as Ivory looked like a punch-drunk boxer staggering sideways. The slug missed Sierra by mere inches, instead plunging into Gorghi's back. The fatty tissue of her flank blew apart, shredding the flesh and fabric en route.

Gorghi didn't move or react, even though Sierra could feel her breathing. Long, labored breaths that rattled with phlegm at the back of her throat.

"You fucking bitch!" Ivory pointed the gun around the office, clutching at her eye, pouring tears that blurred the room and made it impossible to aim. "You—you blinded me!"

Sierra saw her chance, bum-rushing Ivory and slamming her fist into the underside of Ivory's chin.

Ivory lost her footing, and as she flipped backward, the harsh crack of her skull hitting the floor echoed. It was like Sierra could hear Ivory's concussion multiplying.

Sierra thought about going for the gun, but Ivory still held on to it despite her fall.

Sierra raced out of the office, moving with ultimate conviction in the direction of the main floor. Part of her expected to hear the rapid gunfire ringing out behind her, bullets chasing her across the strip club like a pack of dogs after a cat. But she heard nothing.

Sierra made her way past the depressing dressing room. She took resolve in knowing that she wouldn't have to be humiliated and subjected to being a piece of meat ever again. She might have to run home naked tonight, but after that, it would be over.

As she passed the bar, peeled strippers, and mutilated johns, she felt a weight lifting off her shoulders. She was so close to freedom, so close to the next chapter of her life that as she ran down the dark hallway just steps away from the entrance, she could taste it. God had shown her mercy, guiding his child toward the light.

As she scrambled and reached for the door handle, emotion overwhelmed her.

You did it.

But when Sierra turned the handle, it didn't open.

NOWHERE TO RUN

"I'll fucking kill you!" Ivory's voice exploded from behind Sierra.

Sierra instinctively reached for her keys but found her bare belly instead. She could see in her mind's eye her hoodie, with the keys stuck inside the front pocket, lying on the office floor.

It was obvious Ivory was out of the office by the way her voice echoed, and so Sierra shoved away from the front doors and raced back toward the main floor.

When she spotted the bar, she sprinted toward it, the only place close enough to hide. She dove past the four headless corpses sitting upright on the poles shoved up their asses.

Sierra's body soared over the bar, even surprising herself. Managing to leap over the counter without knocking any glass over, she landed directly on top of the skinned bartender.

Sierra's face and body slammed into the slimy exterior of the corpse's exposed muscle, coating her bare torso in equal parts coagulated blood and translucent goo. She held still, trying not to make a sound.

"Sierra?!" Ivory screamed. "You washed up, saggy-titty slut. Where the fuck are you?"

Ivory's voice had lost all its shake. There were no more signs of fear in her tone. Each of her footsteps ripped loudly from the sticky, gore-strewn floor, growing closer and closer.

Sierra pressed her back against the other side of the bar. She clutched the diamond in her fist until it bit into her palm.

The footsteps grew closer as Sierra fought the urge to peek over the bar. Her eyes fixated on the collection of liquor bottles standing side by side along the wall, illuminated by the neon signs that splashed vibrant colors across their glass bodies.

Sierra focused, just barely able to make out Ivory's reflection in the glass. Contorted and disfigured, her image rode the bulbous shapes of the bottles, all at slightly different angles. Sierra's foe clenched her bloody eye socket with one hand, the gun with her other.

As Sierra watched, she did her best to hold her breath, waiting for the perfect moment. The tension tightened as the gun aligned with Ivory's good eye, pointing in the direction of its stare. She methodically took in the entire room, searching for hiding places.

Once Ivory turned her head toward the DJ booth, Sierra rose to her feet. Quickly and quietly, she snagged one of the half-empty bottles by the neck and ducked back down.

Ivory either sensed the movement or heard it, because not a second later, she aimed her pistol toward the bar. Narrowing her eyes, she crept toward it. She clicked her tongue in an unh-unh-unh rhythm, mocking Sierra as she closed in. Both of her hands were steady on the pistol, as if she'd grown tired of missing.

"I knew I couldn't trust your ass. And you wonder how Leon could move on from a flabby hag like you?" Ivory asked, taking a sticky step up to the bar. "Always talking about your loyalty, how reliable you are. Please, bitch. You just as slimy as all the rest! An old dog with tits sagging to the floor whose purpose in life dried up a long time ago!"

She fired a shot that hit one of the bottles displayed behind the bar. The glass shattered and sent a waterfall of shards and liquor crashing down on Sierra and the skinned bartender. The fragments speckled the exposed muscle tissue, bedazzling the cadaver.

"And it's time to put Old Yeller down!" she barked.

Sierra stashed the diamond beneath the cash register before slowly grabbing the corpse by the armpits and sliding it toward her. Hoisting it up to a sitting position, she then angled herself and wrapped her arms around its torso. As she planted her feet, she took a series of quick breaths like a bodybuilder preparing to powerlift.

"I was supposed to be his favorite!" Ivory continued. "Do you have any idea what I did for him?! What he made me do?! I deserve better! I deserve to live in fucking luxury!"

Sierra lifted the bartender, mustering every ounce of strength and adrenaline she could scrape from the depths of her body. He was heavier than she'd thought he'd be, and the liquor and slime coating his body made him as slippery as a wet bar of soap. But she managed to get him up, just high enough for his head, shoulders, and chest to peek up over the top of the bar.

Ivory roared like a lioness as she unloaded the pistol, pulling the trigger as fast as her finger could twitch. Blasting fist-sized holes through the flayed corpse. The chest, shoulders, and head all took catastrophic damage as bullets ripped through the bar's back wall. Room-temperature gore splashed and splattered down on Sierra. She turned her head just in time to avoid getting bloody goo in her eyes.

The headshot made the cranium rock back and created an exit wound large enough for Sierra to fit her foot into. Brain and bone erupted, painting the remains of the back wall. And then the shots stopped.

Click, click, click.

Sierra had been waiting for that sound. Relief washed over her, but some dread still lingered. Once she knew the gun was empty, Sierra tossed the corpse aside, jumping to her feet, and flung the liquor bottle like an axe. As she watched it spin through the air, the bottle tumbled end over end en route to her foe.

Ivory didn't see it soon enough to brace herself. The bottle crashed against her face, exploding on impact, splitting the skin from her forehead to her jawline before drenching her in bourbon. The unforgiving broken glass drew red lines across her skin and shattered her cheekbone as she collapsed backward.

The empty gun fell from her grasp, sticking to the layer of gore coating the floor like a fly caught in petroleum jelly.

Sierra leapt over the bar, snatching a shot glass from the counter. Her massive breasts flopped and swung as she hit the ground in a full sprint, racing toward her enemy.

I'm sorry, God, she thought as she closed in on Ivory. *It's either me or her.*

Diving on top of Ivory, Sierra smashed the shot glass into her already bleeding face. Crushing it over Ivory's one good eye, she ground the now broken, extra thick bar glass into the socket. The pit welled up with blood and enveloped the panicking eye, drowning it in a lagoon of ruby.

Ivory shrieked as Sierra twisted the jagged edge of the glass deeper into her orbital bones, turning the skin around her socket into shredded pork seeped in sweet and sour sauce.

"This is what you deserve!" Sierra shrieked.

As most of the shot glass disappeared inside her orbital cavity, Sierra felt the flat bottom sink deep enough to be flush with Ivory's exposed cheekbone. With the glass merging into her face, the disturbing bellows intensified, piercing into Sierra's brain like voodoo needles.

Ivory's body thrashed, looking like she was having demons exorcised from her soul. In some ways, she might've been. But Sierra needed to make it stop, to put an end to the madness. Without the glass, there was only one way to do so. She would use the only other weapons she possessed. The ones Ivory and many others had ridiculed her over. The ones Gorghi so desperately desired.

The ones God gave her.

Lowering her chest, Sierra draped her massive mammaries over Ivory's face. She used her hands to press them into her like she was smothering her with a pair of memory foam pillows. As she shoved her tits over Ivory's airway, hard jolts of pain ripped through her chest. Fragments of the glass sliced into her bosoms while Ivory's teeth bit down on her flesh in desperation, but still, she soldiered on.

Ivory bucked more violently. Her lungs ached for oxygen, and she made it known, continuing to gnaw and claw at Sierra's chest in extreme distress. But Sierra rode her like a rodeo horse, unfazed by the small amount of fading fight Ivory had left.

Sierra could feel warm blood splashing across the undersides of her breasts as it spat and gurgled from Ivory's mouth. Her groans of pain and screams of terror were drowned out by the piles of dense fat.

"And that's a hundred percent *all* natural!" Sierra roared.

Ivory let out one final muffled scream before going completely silent. Her arms and legs, falling to the floor, spread out like a dead starfish. Her rapidly undulating chest stopped pumping.

Sierra held her tits in place for another minute just in case, letting all the death rattles pass and watching Ivory's twitching fingers before finally pulling away. When she revealed Ivory's bloody frown of agony, she winced for her. One of her eyes was swollen and bruised, the other mutilated and bloody, trapped behind the base of the blood-soaked shot glass. Her smeared makeup resembled that of a clown who'd been beaten to death.

Blood continued to pour from Ivory's wounds, adding to the widening pool beneath her—the carpet was already too saturated with red to soak up any more.

Sierra's knees ached as she rose back to standing, panting as she struggled to catch her breath. The front of her torso was covered in blood.

She caught a glimpse of herself in one of the many mirrors surrounding the room. A few maggots wriggled inside her hair, trapped in the strands like moths in a spider's web. Panicking with revulsion, Sierra grabbed fistfuls of her hair and shook it out, watching as the maggots rained down and thrashed between her feet. The blood, brain, and slime that coated her was bad enough, but there was something about the chaotic roiling of the larvae that sent her over the edge. She stomped down on them, mashing them into paste beneath her feet.

Her eyes coasted back to Ivory's corpse, and a hot wave of guilt swept over her.

What have you done, Sierra?

The thought filled her mind, but in Cassie's voice. Sierra imagined Cassie sitting with God above, staring down and watching. Judging her every move.

I had no choice! You know that, don't you?

After a deep, calming breath, she forced herself away from Ivory and back to the bar, this time walking around it. Shuddering, Sierra remembered the hot, throbbing feeling of bloodlust that pumped through her veins during the murder.

The bite marks on her breasts ached, leaking a steady trickle of blood. Ivory's teeth went in deeper than she thought—the fatty flesh below her right nipple was chewed and shredded.

She plucked the diamond from beneath the bar where she'd stashed it and squeezed the rock in her palm, thinking about how much of a shame it would be to sell it. She wondered if any amount of money would be worth giving up the thing she'd worked so hard for. The thing she killed for.

Oh Lord… Gorghi.

Her heart reignited with fresh guilt. She had to go back and check on her. Just in case she was still alive. It was the right thing to do.

The key to the front door is in the office too. One way or another, I'm seeing her. If she makes it outta here, I'll keep my promise. I'll split everything with her. And Lola too.

As the thoughts rattled off in her head, she absently reached for her crucifix but found only bare skin. She felt naked in more than one way since Gorghi had ripped her hoodie off. With her crucifix no longer around her neck, she felt less connected to Him. She was aware she'd accidentally left Him behind, and while the thought was literal, as she looked down at Ivory's ghastly final expression, it was also metaphorical. Maybe that was why she was staring at the ceiling, having to imagine the heavens in front of her.

He wanted me to do this, to set her free. That's why He stayed behind. It was the only way…

Sierra held the diamond tight in her fist.

Without Him against her skin, without His protection, she felt suddenly susceptible to evil. Not just the darkness inside of her, but inside the building around her.

If The Artist is here, this may be the moment he's been waiting for. What if he's closing in on Gorghi? If she's still alive, that is…

The realization that everyone she'd walked inside Cheaters with just a short time ago might be dead hit her hard. Was it her fate to become one with the morbid décor too? Had he been waiting in the darkness, watching them all turn on one another and chuckling to himself?

Still, regardless of what might lie in the shadows, Sierra knew she had to go back. There was no way around it.

It's time.

NAKED NO MORE

Sierra weaved her way through the bodies on her way to the dressing room, then searched through the various stations until she found a top. The only one that fit was a shimmering shirt with no back on it that looked like a flattened disco ball. The inside of the garment was rough and sharp, grinding into her injured breasts and torso. But it felt good to be covered, to hide her shame even though she was the only one there.

Sierra listened closely as she made her way into Leon's office. But after taking just a few steps inside, she paused. Leon still lay where she'd left him, along with Cassie's partially eaten corpse. But Gorghi was gone. Just a massive bloodstain where she'd been lying.

Where did she go?

Heavy footsteps approached from behind. Each step, like a wrecking ball against the floor, coming fast and hard. Sierra barely had time to turn and face the noise before Gorghi was on her. Driving her shoulder into her gut, the giant lifted her in the air and slammed her body hard to the floor.

Sierra landed right beside Leon, the back of her head crashing into his arm. Thankfully, the decaying flesh was squishy enough to cushion her skull and avoid any serious damage. The wind hissed out of her lungs as she struggled to breathe, kicking her legs in a panic.

Gorghi stood over her like a bleeding, muscular skyscraper. Her dress was nearly soaked through with blood, and more continued to leak from her belly and arm wounds. Her psychotic, bloodshot eyes landed on the diamond that remained in Sierra's death-grip. It was going to take much more to pry it free.

They said she was a freak of nature, but this is something else.

Sierra's mouth opened to plead for mercy, to try and talk some sense into Gorghi. She wanted to let her know that they were on the same side here, that they didn't need to fight now that Ivory was out of the picture. But no words would come, only more gasps and squeaks as her lungs pinched shut, refusing to cooperate.

"Give it to me," Gorghi said, reaching her clawed hand toward the rock. "Now!"

Even as Sierra struggled to breathe, she clutched her fist and held firm as Gorghi grabbed her wrist and lifted her off the ground. Sierra dangled from Gorghi's grip, legs kicking as the behemoth dug at her fingers, trying to get her fist open.

No, Sierra thought, refusing to let go despite her finger bones threatening to snap. *Nothing and nobody is taking this from me!*

With every passing second, Gorghi's fury grew in intensity. Her almost vacant eyes rattled with otherworldly anger as she snarled.

"I said…" Gorghi growled as her free hand struck out like a rattlesnake and took hold of Sierra's throat. She dug her fingers in like she was kneading dough and pulled Sierra in close while she strangled her. "Give me my diamond!"

Frustrated by Sierra's refusal to submit and obey, Gorghi launched her across the room. Her body collided with the mahogany desk, the momentum sending Sierra over the top and crashing to the other side.

Sierra clutched her spine, still struggling to breathe through her aching lungs. The anguish in her throbbed as she turned and found herself staring into the dead eyes of Cassie. The lids had been eaten off with the rest of her face, leaving the eyes to float in slime-filled sockets. A mournful surge erupted in her chest, and when she was finally able to take a much-needed breath, a powerful sob exploded from her lips.

But she was forced to swallow her sadness for Cassie down once again as the thunderous sound of Gorghi's charging footsteps filled the office.

Keeping the desk between herself and Gorghi, Sierra reached out and hooked her fingers around Cassie's lace panties. Tugging at one of Cassie's high heels, she unbuckled the ankle strap. Sierra screamed as she swung the shoe like a spiked mace, the pointed heel slamming into Gorghi's front teeth. The blow stunned Gorghi, but she kept her balance as she grabbed a fistful of Sierra's hair. Growling and lifting Sierra off her feet, Gorghi made her scalp feel like it was about to rip free from her cranium.

"We don't have to fight." Gorghi spat a wad of blood from her mouth, along with one of her central incisors. "But things are different now. You know I need this more than you, more than Ivory or Lola or *anyone*. Just give it to me and I won't have to do something awful."

Sierra dug down deep and found a small reserve of adrenaline. She bellowed a war cry as she wrapped her fingers tightly around the shoe and thrust the pointy heel upward, stabbing it crookedly into Gorghi's nostril.

The pressure on her scalp instantly disappeared as Gorghi released her, sending Sierra plummeting back to the floor. She landed on her feet, standing over Cassie's body, as Gorghi tumbled backward off the desk.

Landing hard on her back, Gorghi gurgled and groaned in pain as she rocked like an overturned turtle, clawing at her face as blood gushed from her nose. The heel was lodged halfway up her enormous nostril, tearing it like a cracked peanut shell.

Somehow, Sierra managed to keep the diamond in her hand. She felt like God himself would have to reach down from the sky and take it from her.

Despite all the pain crackling across her body and blood steadily pitter-pattering against the floor, Sierra forced herself to move. She glanced down at Gorghi as she jetted by her, just as the behemoth yanked the heel free and flung it across the room.

Spotting the crumbled-up hoodie lying beside the safe, Sierra paused. She knew without her keys, there would be no place to run or hide from Gorghi's rage. But as the giant rose back to her feet and pounded her chest like a rampaging silverback, Sierra knew there wasn't time.

"Gorghi, stop!" Sierra screamed over her shoulder as she sprinted out the office door. With no place else to go, she turned left and raced down the dark hallway, passing the inky black doors of the VIP rooms, each filled with the ghosts of unspeakable depravity. "Ivory's dead! We can still split it."

Something collided with Sierra's spine like a battering ram, throwing her violently off her feet. She didn't notice the door to the shower room at the end of the hall until her face was smashing into it, her lips meeting the chipped metal in a car crash of a kiss.

Teeth breaking and shattering, cutting into her lips and gums, the impact threw the door open and sent Sierra flying across the tiled floor, sliding the full length before smacking the far wall. Rusty shower heads gleamed in the dim lighting above her, the one just over her face leaking a drop at a time. Water dripped against her forehead in a steady Chinese-torture-rhythm.

Gorghi appeared in the doorway, wincing and clutching at her stomach again. Her eyes blinked slowly, half-lidded. She wavered a bit on her feet, losing blood and hydration as her flesh expelled beads of sweat. Shaking her head, she knocked the cobwebs loose.

"You lie!" Gorghi roared as she charged toward Sierra.

Sierra gasped for air as she rose up to her hands and knees. She had nowhere to go. The only thing she could do was brace herself for the incoming collision.

The storming Gorghi lowered her shoulder and smashed into Sierra, crushing her against the water-stained wall, leaving a sizable dent in the tile.

Blinded by pain, Sierra scrambled to find something to defend herself with as Gorghi stomped toward her, but her hands only found smashed bits of tile.

"Wait," Sierra pleaded through gasping breaths.

Gorghi showed no mercy as she reared her foot back and kicked Sierra hard in the gut. The pure power lifted Sierra off the tile, sending her crashing face-down back to the shower floor.

More blood filled her mouth and marinated her tongue in gamey flavor. Her nose was busted, turning to the side, and when she touched it, a screech of agony erupted from her throat. A shrill whistle squeaked from her nostrils as she breathed. Sierra only had time to take a couple of blood-basted breaths before Gorghi was coming for her again.

But using every last ounce of willpower she had left, Sierra firmly gripped the diamond.

"Let me have it!" Gorghi screamed as she grabbed Sierra by the throat and shoved her hard against the wall. Pinning her there, she lowered her face until she was nose to nose with her. "Don't make me kill you."

Sierra had been waiting for the right moment, and when Gorghi threatened her life, Sierra lifted her fist, full of broken tile shards, and thrust them into Gorghi's face, grinding into it like she was trying to scrub the rust off a cast iron skillet.

Gorghi growled, more in frustration than pain, and lifted Sierra higher off the ground, her fist squeezing tighter around her throat.

Just high enough to reach the showerhead.

Sierra ignored her aching, oxygen-thirsty lungs as she focused on wrapping her fingers around the metal pipe that connected the showerhead to the wall, the remaining bits of tile precipitating down on her. With her other hand, she lifted the diamond like a butcher knife and drove the pointed end down into the top of Gorghi's knuckles—again and again and again, a quick series of stabs that shredded the top of her hand and the webbing between her fingers.

Gorghi finally let go, staggering back a few steps as she cradled her injured hand to her already bloody dress.

Once Gorghi's hold on Sierra disappeared, gravity took over—along with Sierra's weight—and she hung from the shower pipe. As the metal began to bend and break, water sprayed and leaked, soaking Sierra and splashing over the floor beneath her.

Sticking the diamond into her mouth, Sierra held it in place with tightened lips and used both hands on the pipe. Wiggling and thrashing her body, she tried to break the steel tube free as the gushing water made it slippery. The taste of Gorghi's blood washed over her tongue.

"You… you bitch!" Gorghi flexed her muscles, making the cords in her neck bulge like tree roots. "You're so fucking dead!"

As Gorghi charged at her, Sierra felt the bent metal finally give, snapping from the wall. She let gravity do the work as she dropped, swinging the pipe and showerhead like a mallet, the diamond still nestled in her mouth.

The showerhead crashed into the top of Gorghi's head, splitting her scalp and instantly staining her hair red at the roots. As she grimaced from the sudden burst of pain, her gigantic foot landed on the now slick tile floor. A loud squeak filled the air, like the dying squeal of a stuck pig, as Gorghi slipped. Both of her feet flew up, and she tumbled, the back of her skull hitting the floor before the weight of her legs bent her back awkwardly. The blood leaking from her head mixed with the widening pool of water, turning it a diluted crimson color.

Though Gorghi looked dazed, Sierra didn't hesitate to attack, taking advantage while she still had the upper hand.

God forgive me for what I must do.

When Gorghi tried to sit up, Sierra swung the shower-head like a golf club, smacking the giant hard under the chin and causing her head to crack against the tile floor.

She hammered the metal into Gorghi's nose and mouth, causing another eruption of blood to burst into the air.

But it only seemed to anger Gorghi more. She snarled through the blood and her swollen lips, and when Sierra swung again, Gorghi caught the metal pipe one-handed. She squeezed so hard it bent in her fist before she jerked it from Sierra's grip and tossed it away.

Sierra opened her mouth to plead with Gorghi, maybe even apologize in an attempt to avoid the violence that was surely about to ensue. But when Gorghi's bloodshot, narrowed eyes bored into Sierra, her instincts kicked in, and the next thing she knew, she was dashing out of the shower room and back into the hallway, pulling the diamond out of her mouth and squeezing it in her palm.

She knew she had to reach her hoodie, her keys back in Leon's office, but by the sound of Gorghi's pursuing foot-steps, there was no time. Instead, she tested the handle of each black VIP room door as she rushed through the hall. One after another, each one was locked tight.

"Where the fuck you going?" Gorghi stood at the end of the hall, looking more powerful than ever. As if she'd grown in size somehow, the hallway hardly wide enough to fit her frame.

Sierra quickened her pace, rushing to the next door as Gorghi methodically trudged toward her like a slasher in a horror movie.

She yelped with surprise when a handle finally turned. When she leapt across the threshold into the deeply dark-ened room, Gorghi sped up, galloping toward the door just as Sierra slammed it shut and turned the lock.

VIOLENT, INJURED PEOPLE

Gorghi's fists pounded against the door, making it rock in its frame. *Boom boom boom!*

"If you make me break this door down, I swear to God I'll rip your fucking limbs off!" *Slam slam slam!*

Sierra backed away, panic swelling in her chest. Something bumped up against her back, and a scream ripped free as she blindly swung behind her. She felt the cold touch of metal against her skin, followed by the twinkling sound of rattling chains.

Oh Lord… what was that? Sierra thought.

As her eyes started to adjust to the dark room, she spotted a light switch along the wall just to her left. She carefully made her way forward as Gorghi continued to assault the door, the wood already starting to splinter.

"I'll huff!" Gorghi roared.

Sierra hit the lights, hoping to illuminate the room with brightness, but instead, it was flooded with a deep red color that made the room look splashed with blood. The overhead lights buzzed as they glowed hotter, revealing the objects in the room with a crimson hue.

What Sierra had collided with moments before was some kind of leather harness hanging from the ceiling by metal chains. It still swayed from the punch she'd thrown at it.

"And I'll puff!"

Along the wall opposite from the door were a series of shelves, each lined with all manner of tools. Every tool had a very specific function, and while Sierra was aware that these were all designed for various degrees of sexual pleasure and kink satisfaction, all she saw were torture devices meant to inflict pain on flesh and orifices.

There were whips and zippered masks and ball gags and nipple clamps and countless other objects that Sierra didn't even recognize, many with sharp points and serrated edges.

One shelf was stacked with dildos and butt plugs of all shapes and sizes and colors. The lengths and girths and amount of anatomical detail varied greatly between the vast collection—not to mention the degree of cleanliness. It was obvious to Sierra that at least a quarter of the phalluses hadn't been cleaned since their last use.

The door exploded inward as if a bomb had gone off from the other side, and Gorghi stuck her head through the wide hole and grinned with demonic glee. "And I'll rip your fucking heart out!"

Gorghi's mitts reached in and pulled the rest of the door apart like she was breaking pieces off a chocolate bar. Her hulking body still barely fit through, her deltoids breaking more wood as they rubbed against the obliterated doorway.

Sierra had nowhere to go as Gorghi stormed across the room and wrapped her fist around her throat, slamming her into the shelves. Dildos and butt plugs and all manner of toys rained down as Gorghi choked her, growling into her face.

Sierra did her best to fight back, slamming her knuckles against Gorghi's face, but they seemed to have no effect. Gorghi reached behind Sierra, grabbed a long, thickly veined purple dildo, and held it under Sierra's neck, pressing hard with a hand on each end until it became a silicone staple clamping her into the wall.

Her lungs begging for air, Sierra still held the diamond, scraping it across Gorghi's face, leaving crooked red lines across her skin. But despite the fight she was putting up, the pressure of the giant phallus against her neck was draining her. She felt her senses starting to dull—her mind considered giving up while her body wanted to stop working. The deepest sense of desperation set in. Deeper than the consolidated desperation of her entire lifetime. She was fading fast.

"Give it to me!" Gorghi roared.

"You want it?" Sierra barely whispered, zeroing in on Gorghi. As she fought off the sleepy urge, she understood she only had one shot. "Take it."

Sierra tapped into a sudden reserve burst of energy. Her hand shot up in a flash and shoved the diamond into Gorghi's massive mouth, as deep as she could get it. Gorghi's teeth scraped Sierra's hand when she pulled it back out, anxious to see if the gem was deep enough to put an end to their battle.

Gorghi released her grip, and Sierra crashed to the floor, riding a wave of sex toys. She grabbed a filthy butt plug, and before Gorghi had a chance to spit the diamond out, Sierra bulled her into the wall and shoved it down Gorghi's gullet like she was driving a wooden stake through a vampire's heart.

Gagging and coughing, Gorghi sprayed blood from her ripped nose like water from a whale's blowhole. She desperately clawed at her throat as the diamond worked its way deeper, slicing her flesh open on its way down—shredding her neck meat like roasted pork.

Sierra reached above the dildo shelf and found a long leather whip. Giving it a twirl over her head, she lashed it toward Gorghi, who was stumbling backward as she choked. The whip wrapped around her thick forearm with a *whack!*

Even as she violently suffocated, blood gushing from her mutilated throat—the red light sparkling pink as the diamond cut its way to the surface—Gorghi grabbed hold of the whip and yanked Sierra toward her. Then in one hard motion, she tossed Sierra over her head like she was trying to make a trick shot in basketball.

Sierra soared over Gorghi, upside down, feet arching above her. As she went, she pulled the whip tight between her fists, and looped it over Gorghi's head and around her minced throat.

The momentum threw her all the way over, and she clung to the whip as it tightened over Gorghi's neck. Despite Sierra's speed and weight, Gorghi somehow managed to stay on her feet, stumbling a few feet back, spewing blood from her mouth and nostrils. As she raked her nails across her throat, she only worsened the damage, tearing off fleshy ribbons.

Sierra held tight to the whip like she was dangling from a tree vine, even as memories of her father hanging from beneath her tree house swirled through her mind, followed by the gory faces of Cassie, Leon, and Ivory.

She bounced her weight against the thick muscle of Gorghi's neck, making her take a few stumbling steps backward.

Sierra planted her feet but used most of her body weight to keep the whip taut around the monster's neck. Gorghi groaned and choked as a fresh mist of blood poofed into the air.

Sierra could feel the giant tree of a woman starting to tip backward, and the shift in leverage made her lose her footing.

Stumbling toward the wall, Sierra landed in a mesh comprised of several leather harnesses, her limbs getting caught in the chains like a metal spiderweb. She stayed that way, watching as Gorghi's body dropped to the floor, twitching and thrashing, her hands still clawing and digging at the diamond lodged in her throat.

Her legs spasmed and kicked, shoes rattling against the floor as the last jolts of life exited her flesh.

And then she went still. The only sounds were the beating of Sierra's heart and the wet splashes of Gorghi's blood gushing from her wrecked neck.

Still tangled up, Sierra breathed a sigh of relief and looked up toward the ceiling. Toward heaven. Imagining God's judgement shining down on her.

"I'm sorry," she said, suddenly very aware of all her injuries. The screaming wounds across her head and body raged. But Sierra could handle the pain.

I deserve the suffering. It's the least I can do…

After finally releasing herself from the harness' hold, she knelt beside the massive carcass and dug her fingers into Gorghi's ruined throat. It didn't take much to pry the diamond free and pull it out with a wet *schluck*.

After wiping the blood from her hands over Gorghi's dress, she traipsed down the hall and into Leon's office. She found her hoodie lying in a pile beside the still open safe and tore off the sparkling shirt she'd borrowed from the dressing room in exchange for it. She reached into the front pocket and felt a wave of relief sweep over her when she found the keys, along with the lipstick Gorghi had asked her to hold. There was something else there too.

She pulled out Benjamin and peered into Ben Franklin's eyes.

Lucky bill, huh? I'll show you.

Remembering Leon used to keep his cigars in his drawer, she circled the desk, but then paused when she found herself face-to-fleshless-face with Cassie.

"I'm sorry," Sierra said, her voice quavering a bit. "Don't worry. I won't leave you here like this. You deserve better than that. I won't let them think of you—or anyone in here—as just another body inside The Artist's sick exhibit."

Sierra opened the desk drawer, and along with a box of matches, she stared at stacks and stacks of cash. The drawer was deeper than most and filled to capacity with money. She couldn't help but laugh. A small chuckle at first that grew into a full cackle.

She started to pull the money out, looking for some kind of bag she could use to carry it out. But then her eye caught something glinting on the floor across the room from her: her crucifix, the tiny Jesus painted with blood.

She looked up at the ceiling as her laugh died down to a knowing smirk.

I always knew You had a sense of humor. Sierra shook her head, contemplating her next move. Looking down at the money, she nodded as her grin returned. *This cash is just a drop in the bucket compared to what Leon's stone is worth. And this cash belongs to the girls who sacrificed everything for it.*

The haunting image of Ivory's mutilated face flickered in Sierra's mind, along with the wet gurgles of Gorghi's choking. Ripples of guilt electrified Sierra as she lifted the wads of cash.

They deserve their share. Her cracked nails dug into the bills as she gazed upon the bloody crucifix. *And mine.*

After piling the stacks around Cassie's body like kindling, she struck a match and held the flame an inch away from one of Benjamin's corners. But she stopped herself. After everything she'd been through, Benjamin symbolized something more, something deeper. She dropped the match onto the piles of money and stuffed Benjamin back into her pocket. As Sierra walked out of Cheaters—diamond in hand—the smell of smoke followed her.

GODDAMNED

Sierra crept out of Cheaters—which was now billowing smoke—and was instantly greeted by the cut of the cold air. The various fluids coating her skin turned frosty at once as she shivered and hugged herself. The skin-tight leggings she wore and the loose hoodie did nothing to warm her.

Her brain told her to just go home. Back to the safety of her walls, where she could wash the gore off herself and sit down and start figuring out what in the hell to do with the diamond. In this city, she knew it wouldn't be too hard to find a decent buyer if she was willing to let them haggle. She'd probably only get a fraction of what the stone was worth, but no one would ask any questions and she'd be done with it.

Sierra looked down at the gore-caked stone—she was well aware of what a diamond that size might fetch.

Even if they paid me a tenth of what this thing's worth, I'd be set for life, she thought. *Or at least pretty close to it.*

But as her brain told her these things, her heart told her something else. Her heart told her that she didn't deserve that diamond, not after what she'd had to do to get it. That burning the money was only her first step toward making amends. Sierra realized her intentions were corrupted from the very start. She'd dragged the others into it, ultimately costing them their lives.

They'd been so concerned that the city's monster might return to the scene of his most recent massacre. Sierra shook her head. It was never The Artist she'd had to fear.

It was Ivory.

It was Gorghi.

It was herself.

They were the real monsters.

And as she stood in the cold, polluted air, the only one of them who'd ever be able to breathe it in again, Sierra realized something horrible.

She was the scariest monster of them all.

You call yourself a child of God, but that diamond in your hand won't do anything but pay your toll to Hell.

Despite the winter assaulting her from every angle, she suddenly felt a burning sensation. She could feel The Devil's flames licking her flesh, tasting the grease of her sins. The diamond felt like hot coal in her palm, a gift only fit for those on the naughty list.

Another heavy sigh blew a cloud of smokey fog from her mouth as she turned toward the darkness. Her entire life had been darkness. She yearned for the light.

In the distance, she saw it. Like a sharpened gargoyle crouched and ready to take flight into the black sky. The steeple looked like a massive sword. She took the outline as a warning: live by the sword, die by the sword.

Sierra saw the flashes:

Ivory's mutilated face, one eye swollen and the other buried under the blood-filled base of the shot glass.

Gorghi's bulging throat, the sharp point of the diamond cutting through her neck, eyes bloodshot and horrified.

Those final images were created by her hand. They would now be with her forever.

She turned and watched as Cheaters burned, and a fresh

splash of hope hit her and flowed over her body. *At least Cassie can be at peace now. Cassie and Ivory and Gorghi… and even Leon. They finally escaped that godforsaken place.*

Her eyes coasted from the burning building to the church and then back to the diamond.

A murder of black crows flew over her, cawing their raspy cries as they soared from one building to the other. A speckling of white bird droppings freckled the street around her, missing her by inches.

Sierra sighed as she felt the rock rolling around in her palm. She trudged toward the church as a few of the city's night folk started to creep out of their hidey holes. Feeling their eyes on her was like being surrounded by glowing cigarette cherries thirsting to burn into her.

She ignored them, keeping her focus on the church as she quickened her pace. After a few minutes of walking, the holy structure was in eyeshot. The moonlight sparkled against the stained glass windows, lulling her in, promising relief from her guilty conscience.

A catcall and whistle rang out, making Sierra hug herself, holding her pendulous breasts in place to avoid calling any more attention to her.

"Ay, mami," a voice called out to her. "Look like you need a friend. I'll be your buddy, baby!"

Sierra kept her eyes straight ahead, that voice growing closer behind her, footsteps clopping against the pavement like a horse's hooves.

Sierra sprinted the last twenty yards, speeding up the church steps and nearly slamming herself into the doors. She wrapped her fingers around the brass handles and yanked them open.

Once she was inside, an entirely new feeling washed over her. Sierra felt a warm, welcoming sensation that started on the surface of her skin and soaked in deep through her meat and into her bones.

The eerie moonlight spilling in through the stained glass windows splashed a kaleidoscope of color across the floor and pews.

Tears instantly welled in Sierra's eyes, and before she could even reach the pews, she fell to her knees. Pressing her forehead against the floor, she wept, the deep sobs boiling up from the pit of her gut. The profound sadness she'd been holding on to for years mixed with her grief and guilt from what transpired inside Cheaters.

It weighed her down.

She regained her composure, looking around to make sure she was alone. At such an hour, she wouldn't be surprised if she was. Sierra thought she could hear some voices in the distance, somewhere deeper within the church, but she was the only one in sight. And for that, she was grateful as she trudged her way from the entrance, past the rows of pews, and up to the altar.

A realistic Jesus grimaced in pain above her, nailed to the cross, blood running down his face through the puncture wounds on his head from the crown of thorns. As Sierra stared up at the statue, she lowered herself to her knees rather than collapsing. Squeezing her hands together, the stained diamond, still there, reminded her of the atrocities she had committed. The sharp rock felt like a nail slowly burrowing itself into her palms, a sign that she deserved to suffer for what she'd done.

"I'm… I'm so sorry," Sierra cried, banging her fist against the floor, the diamond cutting into her palm as she hammered it down. "Forgive me…"

The Jesus statue swam in the tears filling her eyes, making the image blur into a ghost comprised of browns and reds.

She spotted a series of confessional booths along the wall to the side of the altar. But there were no priests in sight. A couple of voices, like the moans of spirits, echoed from further down the hallway. Maybe someone else giving confession, but Sierra needed to get it out of her system. She turned to Jesus again and bowed her head.

"I know I don't deserve Your forgiveness for what I've done. For all the sins I've committed over a lifetime. I could feel Your presence. I knew You were there… but I chose to sin anyway. I chose greed and lust over charity and chastity. I chose pride over humility… envy over kindness." The tears rained off her face. "But I want to do better. I want to *be* better. And I promise… I will earn Your love back. I will earn Your forgiveness and my place by Your side."

She reached into the front pocket of her hoodie, pulled Benjamin out, then crumbled the hundred in her hand. Squeezing the bill in one fist and the rock in the other, she was ready to make her proclamation. "This I promise You… Amen."

As she stood up, she opened her fist and stared down at Benjamin, which opened like a blooming, bloodstained flower.

It's time to make my own luck.

Just as Sierra stepped away from the altar, she spied the donation box nearby. She continued forward, approaching the gothic chest. Pulling the red lipstick from her pocket, she applied a thick coat. She flattened Benjamin and kissed the back side of it, stamping the paper with the shape of her plump lips, before shoving it inside the metal slot.

The front doors suddenly flew open, and a figure stood in the doorway just beyond the threshold. A striking silhouette that sent a shudder across Sierra's body, the moon blasting a silver beam like a spotlight in the night sky.

Sierra knew who he was before he stepped into the church. She could tell right away just by the shape of him. She could *feel* his presence.

The Drip Man…

Sierra wanted nothing to do with him. It would be in her best interest to get out of the church immediately. Besides, she knew what she had to do now. And nobody—not The Drip Man, not even The Devil himself—was going to stop her.

The Drip Man glared down between the rows of pews, his dark eyes stapled to Sierra. She hugged herself again, feeling naked in front of him, suddenly fully aware of how bloody and exposed she was.

The Drip Man, draped in furs and sparkling jewelry, grinned. The platinum in his mouth twinkled.

Sierra lowered her gaze and made her way down the aisle, thinking of The Drip Man as Satan's last attempt to corrupt her. If anyone could move the boulder of ice in her hand, it was the demon standing before her. Her redemption was right outside of those doors.

All she had to do was walk past him.

This isn't the future I imagined, but it's the only future that matters.

She held the key to proving both her spiritual sincerity and corporeal loyalty, and it was like God himself set the path in front of her. Sierra held her breath and walked toward the doors, averting her gaze from The Drip Man and keeping the diamond hidden in her hand.

THE UNITED STATES OF AMERICA
IN GOD WE TRUST
ONE HUNDRED DOLLARS

PART 3:
HOME OF THE HEARTLESS

ON HALLOWED GROUNDS

As the dim beams of light filtered through the stained glass windows, they made Mason Moons look like a god—but not the benevolent, sympathetic type. The Old Testament hellfire and hatred was always at a mild boil beneath the wolf husks, jewelry, and charismatic swagger. While the gaudy treasures dripping off his frame were the reason he'd gotten his name, it wasn't the *only* reason.

Mason's gaze fell upon Sierra and her oversized rack. It looked like she had hammers hanging from her chest. He remembered when she was still young and fresh. When the fellas would pay top dollar to poke her. But it wasn't just the haggard state of her body that drew his eyes.

That bitch look beat, he thought.

Sierra's clothing had a few bloodstains—too many to be her own. Not to mention the piece of her ear that'd gone missing and claw marks around her throat. She staggered forward in her hoodie, hampered by various injuries, looking like she'd gotten taken for more than her lunch money.

Mason kept his hand ready under his furs. The diamond-speckled barrel of his gat was always ready to take a life. A bitch *that* busted up couldn't be trusted. He saw the fear in her eyes as she walked down the aisle toward him, past the steel donation box.

She look fuckin' unhinged.

Just because she kept her head low while approaching him didn't mean he was prepared to let his guard down. Mason didn't let his guard down for nobody. He'd bodied countless people over the years but refused to live a life of fear. Still, that didn't mean he was going to just let some random fiend take him out either. There were plenty of people in the city gunning for him, he accepted that. He lived like every day was his last.

He was *always* ready.

As she passed him, her head remained down. He turned, staying zeroed in on her. He couldn't help but admire her booty as the thick cheeks jiggled enticingly.

"Have a good night, baby," Mason whispered.

She still didn't dare make eye contact with him. "Th-thank you," she whispered.

Mason let his shades fall to the tip of his nose and looked over the top of them. Biting his lip, he shook his head.

Even with all that blood on her ass, that thickness is a treat.

Once she disappeared out the door, Mason turned to the donation bin and looked around the rest of the church. He removed a set of keys from his jacket, located the small silver one, and stuck it into the box. When the mechanism clicked, he swung the top of the contraption up.

He furrowed his brow.

Ratty ass niggas.

The inside of the bin was empty, save for a single donation. Benjamin was showing age: wrinkles, a brown smear, blood splatter, and a lone, voluptuous lipstick print.

He scoffed, snatching up the bill, immediately flaring his eyes. Such an amount was unacceptable. The church was supposed to be a source of hope for the depressed populous—a syphon for the smaller section of the city who didn't depend on lobo for support. No matter which way people lived their lives, Mason wanted his cut. And it was clear the church wasn't doing its job.

That had to change.

"Where's that mutha fucker?" he mumbled.

He looked around, angered as he zeroed in on the four confession stalls. Pulling his strap, Mason moved in on the first door. Gently, he pressed the barrel against the entrance. Empty. He did the same to the second and third. Empty. But when he arrived at the fourth, the door wouldn't budge. Cocking his leg back, he kicked it open in one shot.

Quiet audio of a woman moaning leaked out of the booth. A cassette player lay on the floor beside a penis pump—the end of which was hardened by dried semen. A bottle of dick pills was spilled on the tiny sill. Soundproofing foam lined most of the stall, including the sliding vent that connected to the other booth. A heading that read Best Sins was attached to the wall in an olden font. Underneath, the wall was littered with countless printed sheets of paper and Polaroid pictures. The photography was of an extreme and pornographic nature.

The areas of the thinner pages looked like they'd been soaked—stuck to the wall with a 'natural' adhesive. The photos represented different perversions, each labeled with a different sin at the bottom.

A morbidly obese woman with advanced rot lay dead in a recliner. The hollows of her body where the flesh had been devoured writhed with pools of plump maggots. The image was marked GLUTTONY.

Another snap of a woman with several broken teeth sucking on the barrel of a Desert Eagle pulled his gaze. Black tears ran from her terrified eyes. Blood leaked from her broken mouth. The bottom of the picture was marked LUST.

A square mirror was positioned in the center of the collection of sinister stills. As Mason stared at his reflection, he realized that he had a buffet of sins that could've taken the place of the swarm of pictures, but there was something about the underlying meanness and immorality of the ones surrounding him that caused him to cringe. When he dusted someone, it was a business decision, usually tied to a dollar figure. Killing was evil, but the enjoyment that seemed to be associated with the pictures was what sickened him.

"Father Fletcher?" Mason said, letting his voice boom throughout the decaying building.

He looked to the doors, past the cracked statues and unkept altar, at another door leading to the back of the church and started walking.

When he crept over the threshold, a series of black curtains shrouded the room. The area was filled with many religious trinkets, a cot soiled by sweat, several bookcases, a desk, and another confessional. But unlike the ones up front, this one seemed to be private. Mason heard a mumbling coming from behind the two doors. Turning his ear to the booths, he listened intently.

"I've intentionally been taking less," the man's voice said.

"Why is that, my son?" Father Fletcher asked.

The man paused. "Because I'm—I'm just trying to deal with it myself, not be so dependent."

"There's no better way to address it than confronting it. The devil is in the details, you're brave to face him again."

"We both know that's not why I'm here."

"Regardless, you're here to find God. Now tell me, what did you see?"

"It was after they'd broken into her room. I could see her body. Not the arms or the legs, it was after they'd been removed—when I'd only just discovered her."

"And how was she then?"

"She was in pain—complete agony. She was crying, a shrill kind of screech that was almost animalistic. The shock had worn off on her… it was like she'd found a new world." An unsettling despondency saturated his tone. "But she was still here."

"Mmm… but how did she *look?"*

"Her stumps looked like shredded rags—stringy veins and muscle twitching at the ends."

Father Fletcher sounded like he was breathing heavier. "Please, continue."

The confessor's voice started to crack.

"She was vomiting on herself, and at first, I didn't realize why—I was too distracted. Then I saw the bloody screwdriver next to the pillow and the gaping hole in the side of her abdomen. They must've ruptured her stomach or something."

"Oh, good heavens," Father Fletcher moaned.

"It has nothing to do with Heaven."

"And what happened next?"

"I…" He broke down into tears.

The priest's voice grew stern. "Quickly! And what happened next?"

"I couldn't just leave her there, in her crib like that."

"What did you do, my son?" he begged.

The pain in the confessor's voice had reached a pinnacle. "Those savages, they fucking tore her apart. Left her in a pile of piss and shit. I—I had to…"

"Had to do what?!"

"I put the pillow on her face. I stopped her screaming."

Mason listened to the priest wail. The oozing pleasure and exhaustion sickened him, but still, he listened on.

"All right, I told you the fucking story again, with extra details this time. Now give me my money, you sick fuck!"

It sounded like the priest was drinking. He paused his chug. "Of course, my son. But first, I want to pray—pray not only for you, but for your daughter. We know she's in a better place now. And—"

"Just give me my goddamn money!"

Mason kicked the door in, gripping his sparkling barrel.

"That ain't his money to give." He cocked the hammer.

The middle-aged white man inside the confessional shrieked. "Wait, what the hell is this?!"

Mason lifted his lips, his platinum grill sparkling. "But don't worry, I'ma give you something better than a little come up. I'ma give you peace."

Mason unloaded five shots into his chest, spraying blood all over the crucifix hanging on the wall inside the booth. Stepping to the side, he muscled his way into the next chamber, but the reveal was different than he'd imagined.

Father Fletcher didn't even acknowledge Mason or the gunshots. He stared forward with a crazed look in his eyes, holding a picture of the mutilated baby in his hand. The nude, dismembered child had police evidence markers positioned around it. The word GREED was written in red marker on the corner of the picture. His cum drenched the vile image, dribbling down onto the floor, but he wasn't focused on the snapshot any longer.

The chalice filled with wine sat on the sill as suds of purple saliva leaked from the corner of Father Fletcher's mouth. His eyes widened, zeroing in on the crimson holes and labored final breaths escaping the confessor's lungs. While his manhood looked shrunken and spotted, the pills had somehow still found a way to solidify it. The old man used the fresh cum, stroking it over his wrinkled shaft violently like an entranced pervert. He was wholly captivated by the murder—it was like being on the set of a porno rather than watching one.

Mason's lip curled ever so slightly, looking at his gat. "Shit's too good for you."

He put the safety back on and slipped the piece inside his holster. When his hand reappeared from underneath his furs, his fingers had slipped into a new piece of jewelry—one that wasn't just for show. The golden brass knuckles were speckled with various gems. Mason let his finger run over some of the stones until it rested on a tiny button at the base of the brass.

"That's too good for you too," Mason whispered.

Father Fletcher was still entranced by the confessor's final wheezes, stroking his cum-coated shaft with a flare of madness in his eyes.

Mason drew his hand back and sized up the priest's cheekbone. "Gotta make sure you feel it long and hard, like the bitch you is."

When the brass split open Father Fletcher's cheek and shattered the brittle bone beneath, the old bastard had no choice but to take his eyes off his latest obsession. The old man's dentures fractured and partially dislodged. Faux teeth ejected from his mouth, and the chalice of wine spilled all over his robe.

Before the priest could get his bearings, Mason sent his glimmering fist into Father Fletcher's torso several more times. The bones in his ribcage sounded like firecrackers, some breaking and splintering while others burst into shards.

The old man's gurgle morphed into a moan and was trailed by a luge of crimson ooze and saliva.

Mason put his hands around the pervert's neck. Ripping him out of the booth, he tossed Father Fletcher into the desk. When his hip connected with the wood, a popping noise echoed throughout the chamber. Mason lifted him off the ground and smashed his head against the glass candleholder on the table. His eyeball extinguished the candle's flame, and hot wax engulfed it. The glass shattered and burrowed into his face, tearing a flap of lined flesh from the bottom of his jaw up to his other cheekbone and shattering his nose.

Father Fletcher's body went limp, but Mason didn't let go. He reeled him back in and threw him into the bookcase. The holy manuscripts were now bathed in blood, and as he crashed down against the stone floor, several volumes accompanied him.

"I don't remember giving you permission to use my paper for your little jerkoff sessions," Mason said, slipping his fingers behind the heavy wooden case.

The broken dentures in the priest's mouth hung, coated in a cherry sludge. He tried to respond, but a series of bubbly gurgles was all that manifested.

As Mason tipped the heavy case forward, a shower of bloody scriptures rained down along with the weight of the furniture. When it connected with the priest's legs, a sickening crunch exploded. His brittle femurs fragmented, sounding like a wooden baseball bat exploding after a home run. The agony caused Father Fletcher to wiggle and spit what remained of his dentures out. He looked like a man on fire without the flames.

"You thought you could play me," Mason said, kicking the leg of the old desk repeatedly. Once it was loosened by the blows, he slipped his bejeweled knuckles into his pocket, leaned down, and pulled at the leg until it broke free. "But everybody gotta pay me."

He lifted the wooden leg off the floor—two thick screws sticking out the side of it. When the leg hit the side of Father Fletcher's ribcage, the unforgiving screws punched through his flesh and shattered more of the bones. Mason focused on the outer abdomen next—the same area of the baby that the 'holy man' had been so pleased with during the confession.

When the next blow landed, a sickening wheeze and surge of blood erupted from Father Fletcher's mouth. His gummy grimace and twisted nose looked nightmarish. Mason tried to retrieve the leg, but as he pulled, there was no give. The steel fangs were lodged deep in the perverted priest's stomach.

Father Fletcher let out a hiss of horror, and when he closed his eyes, Mason relinquished his grip on the furniture leg. As he looked up from the bloody mess, he noticed a much younger priest standing near the back exit, his body rigid with stress and terror.

Mason's glimmering grin manifested. He kicked Father Fletcher in the side of the head as hard as he could while maintaining eye contact with the younger man. "You better be ready to step up."

Adjusting his hat, Mason headed back to the door he'd entered from. But as he reached for the knob, he thought better of it and turned back. His cold gaze pierced through the religious costume of the petrified priest. "And if you're smart, you'll keep ya mutha fuckin' hand out the cookie jar."

SMALL WORLD

When Mason exited the church, the stretch limousine waited. The driver hurried out and opened the door for him. As he sat down in the limo, Mason had a pissed-off look on his face. But it wasn't directed toward his driver or even the disgusting incident that had just unfolded inside the church. The current issue on his mind was now seated before him. Mason glared at Big Vern and Nate Compton, who nervously awaited him.

"Where to, sir?" the driver asked.

Mason thought about it carefully before he spoke. "Bring us to Food Plus."

"Understood." The driver rolled up the window, allowing them their privacy.

"Y'all don't realize how lucky you are," Mason said. "I almost said the graveyard. Maybe I'll change my mind."

An uncomfortable silence bloomed inside the vehicle.

Mason shook his head, beside himself with the situation. It was difficult to find the words, but finally, they came. "You monkey ass niggas. What did I tell y'all?"

The pair looked confused—too afraid to talk.

"If I told you once, I told you a thousand fuckin' times," Mason continued. "You don't drip a nigga without my say so!" He punched the tray that held the champagne, making ice spill onto the floor.

"I—we"—Big Vern turned to Nate—"we would never do some shit like that."

Mason tried to calm himself and lit up a blunt he had pre-rolled in the ash tray. He took a deep puff in and then exhaled.

"Then riddle me this," Mason said. "Why'd Chino get clapped to the future last night? And then, mutha fuckas in the hood sayin' they seen your Humpty Dumpty ass and Tweedle Dumb runnin' the nigga's pockets?"

The pair kept quiet like children caught in a lie. Nate looked at the floor.

Mason's eyes grew wide, and his tone sounded more baffled as he expounded on his thoughts while selecting his words. "I don't even wanna know why they found the nigga with his dick out."

He shivered in disgust as he took another hit. "Did y'all know Chino was a runner for me?"

They shook their heads, and Nate started to fidget.

"That's right, you didn't," Mason said. "Because you don't run shit! I run shit! We missed a mutha fuckin' delivery because of y'all! And I know your lil baby brains can't comprehend it, but lobo's bigger than this city—we expanding! We ain't playin' with no Monopoly money! This is Risk, and we out to conquer! I'm over here rolling the dice, and you two out here fuckin' shit up." He tried to bring his tone back to cool but struggled. "You faggots ain't even have guns before I put you on. Y'all worked at the damn grocery store."

"We still work at the grocery store," Nate said.

Mason gritted his teeth. "Nigga, that ain't the point. I gave y'all power. I gave y'all a common goal—a purpose. I got capable players. We out here blowing up police stations, movin' weight that'd give Schwarzenegger a fuckin' hernia, and y'all killin' the help."

The notion was gnawing at him, forcing his hand into his fur. When Mason pulled his strap, Big Vern and Nate gasped.

"Y'all are more trouble than you're worth," Mason said.

"Wait—we—it wasn't supposed to happen like that!" Big Vern yelled. "Ray Ray said that—"

Mason put the burner to his eye.

"Oh, Ray Ray said? Nigga, do I look like I give a *fuck* what Ray Ray said?! You gettin' work tips from fiends now? Every time you open that fat mouth of yours, you disrespectin'. And the sad part is, you too fuckin' dumb to realize it. Since it don't seem to be workin' anyhow, maybe I should just shut your brain off for good." He cocked the hammer back.

"Please, man, we—we gotta be able to figure some shit out," Big Vern begged.

"For real, we'll do anything, just chill," Nate said.

As the limo came to a stop, Mason took a deep breath, put the safety on the gun, and put it away. Hitting the blunt hard, he pondered for a moment. Mason looked through the tinted window at the dark alley beside them, then through the other window at the glowing red letters of the Food Plus sign. "I like that attitude. Maybe I will give y'all one last chance after all."

"We'll come through—for real, for real," Big Vern said.

"Let me break it down again. This is the city of fear. The shit we slingin' is predicated on terror. When things happen—like that shit that went down at Cheaters—that fattens our pockets."

Big Vern and Nate looked unsettled by the mere mention of the strip club massacre. It was plainly visible that neither of them liked where the conversation was going.

"While that particular act of violence didn't have our fingerprints on it, we ain't necessarily mad at it. But that shit's old news, people have already settled down. That's bad for business. I think it's time to get folks scared again." Mason grinned, brandishing his bling. "That was a bunch of whores and gangstas. I want you to pick a public building for this. I need y'all to kill people who mean something to the common man—a lot of them. I want you to body fifty in one night."

Big Vern's eyes nearly popped out of his head.

"When the headlines drop," Mason continued, "I want niggas in therapy. I want *everyone* outside our circle to suffer. You got until tomorrow to decide. Once you figure it out, hit me on the hip." He tapped his pager. "I'll ensure our people stay clear of the target location so you don't go killin' my assets again."

"F-fifteen?" Big Vern asked.

"I know you got shit for brains, so you probably got shit in your ears too," Mason said, raising his voice. "Five-o, like the boys in blue. Fifty dead, tomorrow night. Make me back the money y'all lost me and we cool. But fail me again… and I'll make that shit The Artist done look like some Sesame Street shit compared to what I do to y'all."

Mason opened the door of the limo and looked at the grocery store. "Y'all don't gotta be at the bottom of the food chain. If you pull this off, there'll be opportunity in the future. But fuck up this time, and it's maggots and worms. Understood?"

They both nervously nodded.

Mason returned the gesture and knocked on the glass behind him.

The driver rolled down the tinted divider. "Yes, sir."

"Gimme their guns," Mason said.

The driver handed them through. Big Vern took his Beretta, and Nate grabbed the Desert Eagle.

Mason relit the blunt and took another big puff. "You've re-earned those, for the moment anyway. Now raise the fuck up outta here before I change my mind."

They both exited the limo, and Mason watched as they headed in toward the back parking lot of Food Plus. Looking away from the window, his eyes fell on the small square glass mirror resting on the mini table in front of him.

He shook his head.

Them niggas think they got it hard? Mason thought.

Even through the dark lenses of his shades, he could still see his jewels sparkle. The gold, platinum, and gemstones shining as the lighting bounced off them brought him back.

They don't know what hard is…

Digging his fingers under the many bangles of bling, The Drip Man felt the deep scarring around his wrist.

Rather be a slave to the paper than that man.

His mind saw flashes of his wrist when it was much tinier. The weight of the rusted steel pulling down on him. The smell of the buckets for pissing and shitting. The coldness of the stone basement floor. The sight of the old man's grinning face. Everything was burned into his memory.

Old white bastard.

His young sister's face was adorned with a mixture of agony and horror as his liver-spotted cock emerged from his slacks half erect. The girl's fingernails scraped down that moldy wall, cracking alongside her voice as she wailed for help in a place where only the helpless and that old bastard could hear her. The sound of her chains dragging over stone with each pump that jarred her tiny body played over and over inside his head.

He didn't even love her like I did. She was just his fuck thing.

Mason shook his head. He'd often tried to make sense of it, to look at it from a different angle that would have shown him in a more powerful light. But no matter how he spun it, he could never shake the feeling it left him with. So instead, he covered it up.

His hand toyed with the chains around his neck and the additional patches of scar tissue beneath them. One set of chains for another. And while the layers of jewelry and Mason's countless trinkets could cover the scars on his flesh, the ones in his mind would live on forever.

"Sir?" the driver asked.

"Just a minute," Mason said.

The driver rolled the divider back up.

He needed to shake off the thoughts of the past and

knew just the right medicine to do the trick. No way was he getting high on his own supply—that was for the lobes. Mason reached into his jacket and opened a small baggie of cocaine, dropping a few lines onto the little square mirror. Once it was divvied up to his liking, he pulled out Benjamin.

Rolling the bill into a tight tube, he aligned it with the blow and sniffed. Mason immediately retched. "The fuck?"

The scent that wafted up his nasal cavity was like having a sleepover in a sauna during a colon cleanse.

This fuckin' dope tainted? he wondered.

He hovered his nose above it and sniffed.

There was nothing abnormal about it.

He immediately recalled the horrific state of Benjamin as he reinspected the bill. The plethora of stains and its disgusting condition repulsed Mason. Promptly, he rolled the window down and tossed the bill to the sidewalk.

"Dirty ass mutha fuckas," Mason mumbled. He knocked on the divider again. "Yo, let's be out."

The glass slid down.

"Where to this time?" the driver asked.

Mason took another deep drag of the blunt. "Bring me to Mayor McKinney's."

LUCKY NIGHT

"I'm fuckin' starving," Hector said.

He stood beside Crane in the alley, under the cover of darkness, bored with watching the limo.

As the two thugs headed into the entrance of Food Plus, the window of the limo went down a quarter of the way and Benjamin flew out onto the concrete.

The fancy ride zipped away, and Crane grinned. He turned to Hector, whose gaze had already landed on the crumpled bill. "Ask and you shall receive."

Hector's eyes stuck to Crane an extra second before he snatched up the money. He smoothed it out and looked at the lipstick kiss and various filth impressed upon the bill. "I'll be damned."

"Most of us already are." Crane stared intensely at him, maintaining his unsettling smile.

Hector furrowed his brow. "You know, you got pretty nice teeth for a bum."

"There's enough decay in the world already without me adding to it."

"You're fuckin' weird, man."

Hector scratched the side of his face, thinking about how his teeth ached every time he needed to chew.

Lucky motherfucker, he thought.

Crane exited the alley and started walking back to the shot-up car that they'd stashed near the dumpster.

"Hey, where you goin'?" Hector asked.

"Didn't you say you wanted to get something to eat?" Crane replied.

"Yeah, but I'm hungry now." He pointed at the Food Plus sign. "There's a grocery store right here."

Crane nodded. "All right, as you wish."

As they crossed through the parking lot, they passed only a handful of cars. When they entered the store, it became evident why: they were just minutes away from closing time.

"Better hurry," Crane said.

"I just want a rotisserie chicken, somethin' to drink, maybe grab a paper," Hector replied. "Won't take long. You want anything?"

Crane shook his head. "Nah."

The chicken Hector selected was overcooked and an odd size—pumped to the max with hormones. He also made Crane carry two forties of Olde English for him.

When they approached the register, a clean-cut white man in his mid-fifties awaited them. His wrinkles weren't overly defined, but he was on his way. As they approached, he turned off his lane light and swung his eyewear retainer up, setting his black frame glasses on his nose. The early stages of a potbelly hung over his belt. His flattop haircut was a mixture of salt and pepper. JAMES was the name on the work tag pinned to his collared shirt.

"Good evening," James said.

"Depends who you ask," Hector replied.

James sighed. It seemed like there was more on his mind than wrapping up his shift. "Will that be all?"

"I'll take a paper." Hector pointed to the rack beside James. The headline inked across the front said: THE ARTIST REMAINS AT LARGE, WILL HE KILL AGAIN?

James glared at the headline, pausing momentarily. When he reached for the paper, his hand shook. The newspaper flapped as he set it on the counter.

Hector caressed Benjamin between his dirty fingers. "Why don't you give me a pack of those Swisher Sweets and a lighter too, and—and what's that come to?"

He tapped a few keys on the register.

Hector noticed James had a shaky hand. He'd watched the cashier delete and reenter the totals several times, appearing to grow frustrated with himself.

"Just cuz I look like this don't mean I'm gonna rob ya," Hector said. "No need to be nervous."

James' cheeks grew red. "I'm not nervous. It's a medical condition. I can't control it."

"Oh." Hector looked at Crane unsure what else to say.

James finally was able to hit the correct keys and looked up. "Ah, that'll be nine seventy-three."

Hector set Benjamin down on the counter. "Gimme nine of those ten-dollar scratch tickets."

"What kind?" James asked.

"A few of each."

As James started to tear the tickets away, Crane rolled his eyes. "You're gonna blow it all on that? Right away?"

"I'm feelin' lucky," Hector said raising his eyebrows. "Gotta ride the wave."

James bagged up the bottles and food, opened the register, and drew out the change. He handed him the scratch tickets and receipt. "Good luck, buddy."

"Thanks," Hector said.

As they exited the store and headed for the Mazda, Crane turned to Hector. "You really like putting all your eggs in one basket, huh?"

"What do you mean?" Hector asked, gazing down at the tickets. "This is, like, nine baskets."

"You don't get it," Crane mumbled.

As they got closer to the car, Hector sighed. "Weird."

Crane glanced at him. "What?"

He turned, looking back through the doors of the grocery store at James, who was still at his station watching them. "My receipt's blank, they musta run outta ink or somethin'."

Crane kept walking toward the car. "What the fuck do you care about a receipt, anyway?"

CLOSING TIME

James Wellwood discreetly slipped Benjamin into his pocket, being careful to keep the register drawer slightly open with his pinky. He grabbed from the pile of loose change under his counter, replacing the exact amount that he'd given the last customer, and let the drawer close.

"James," a booming male voice said. "My office, please."

James swung around like he'd been caught with his pants down. The store manager, Glenn Gaither, stood near the customer service desk waving him over.

Fuck, last thing you can afford to do is lose your goddamn job, he thought.

Leaving the register, James started to limp toward the office as he rounded the corner. He couldn't put too much weight on his leg—it had been extra sensitive as of late. When he saw Glenn, he was hunched over, restocking a massive pile of newspapers on a rack. The same headline stared back at him: THE ARTIST REMAINS AT LARGE, WILL HE KILL AGAIN?

James curled his lip and shook his head. It felt like his face was getting hot.

In smaller print, another mini headline read: BOMBING FALLOUT, POLICE REMAIN UNDERSTAFFED.

This place is pure chaos.

The final front page article was written in an even finer print and read: FEDS SAY TRAIL OF MISSING MILLIONAIRE KENNETH C. STARKS GONE COLD.

"You got a call in the office. It's Shelly," Glenn said.

"Oh." James exhaled in relief. "Thanks."

James continued gingerly down the hallway and entered the office. As he reached for the telephone, his hand trembled. When he lifted the receiver off the desk, he attempted to steady himself, but the phone made tiny circles around his ear as he listened.

"Hi, sweetie," James said.

"Hi, babe," Shelly replied. "I hate to bother you at work, but…"

James could hear that she was trying to hold back tears, and it broke his heart. "You don't have to apologize, call anytime, okay?"

"O-okay."

"Is something wrong? Is Eli all right?"

"His blood pressure was really, really low today. He lost his balance and fell—but he's fine, just some bruising is all."

"Jesus Christ."

"I know, it's my fault."

"No, that's not what I meant."

"He—he just doesn't like me helping him to the bathroom. I mean, he's almost twenty. At that age, I wouldn't have wanted my mother watching me… well, you know."

"It's not your fault. You've gotta stop blaming yourself for all this."

Her sobbing was getting louder. "I just—his heart isn't pumping like it should. And I'm scared… I'm scared that he doesn't have much time left."

"Baby, I told you already. I promise I'm working on it." His lips quivered, but he successfully fought back the tears. "I'll figure out a way."

"Those fucking doctors!" Anger burned in her voice. "What are they waiting for, him to—? Eli, just a moment, don't get out of bed yourself. I'll be right there, honey."

"Is he okay?"

"He—he's fine."

James was trying his best to keep calm. The subject that Shelly had broached was beyond sore.

"Could you bring some eggs back with you?" Shelly asked. "That's all he's been wanting to eat lately, and we're all out."

"Of course."

"Okay, I've gotta go."

"I love you," James whispered.

Shelly hesitated. "I love you too."

James hung up the phone, broke down, and quickly recomposed himself. Wiping the wetness from his eyes, he made his way out of the office. Glenn was still adjusting the newspapers when he approached him.

"Is there anything else you need from me tonight before I balance my drawer?" James asked.

"Nope, how's Shelly doing?" Glenn asked.

"Ah… she's pretty good. It's just tough with Eli and everything."

Glenn nodded solemnly. "Well, I'm pullin' for ya, Jimmy."

"Thanks."

"Have a good night."

"You too."

James started toward his register, then paused. "Oh, hey. Would you mind ringing me up for a dozen eggs really quick before I leave? We're fresh out at the house."

"Eh, just do it yourself." Glenn turned back and smiled. "I trust you."

James nodded. He held in tears as he staggered down the snack aisle to the rear of the store. When he approached the cooler, he couldn't help but wonder if his wife's hesitation to tell him that she loved him was more than being distracted by Eli.

Does she think I've failed her? Failed Eli?

Her words echoed in his head.

Those fucking doctors.

It was hard not to wear his heart on his sleeve when he was still waiting on one. Whether his only son lived or died depended on it. While he understood the wait list at Memorial Hospital was massive, time was running out. Facing a corrupt system that saw politically connected officials pulling favors for themselves, their friends, and their families wasn't something he could sit by idly and watch any longer.

It wasn't like he hadn't been working on it forever already. But James knew he needed to take action now—stealing a few hundred dollars a week from the cash drawer wasn't going to be fast enough to pull the type of bribe he'd need to bring to the table. Eli would be in a box before he hit drinking age if James didn't sort things out soon.

They're rotten—just like the rest of this godforsaken city.

He wiped away the first droplet that beaded from his eye and pulled open the refrigerator door. The first thing he heard was the loud hum of the cooling unit, but as he grabbed a dozen eggs, he heard something beyond it. An argument between two of the night shift shelf stockers.

"What if we just leave town?" Big Vern asked.

"And do what?" Nate asked. "Compared to the rest of the country, this city looks like fuckin' Disneyland."

"I don't know, but it sounds like he gonna drip both our asses if we stick around."

Nate sucked his teeth. "Man, even if we leave, what makes you think he won't find us still? You heard him in the limo—he extendin' *outside* city limits. He'd find us. Even if we lay low, the fuck we gonna do? You want us to end up like them two fuckin' bums in the alley outside?"

James had previously had a handful of interactions with Big Vern and Nate. Their communications were infrequent and courteous. The way they were talking wasn't like anything he'd heard before. While he didn't understand the full context of their conversation, it was clear that their lives hung in the balance of it.

"We couldn't pull off that kinda killin' by ourselves, though, could we?" Big Vern asked.

James' eyes widened.

"What don't you understand?" Nate asked. "We ain't got no choice. *Where* we gonna do it is the real question."

Big Vern paused. "Man, I don't like killin' no strangers. If I'm killin', there gotta be a reason. I ain't no fuckin' psychopath. This shit is crazy."

"The reason's that big ass of yours," Nate said. "If you wanna keep it intact, it's the only choice."

"I don't wanna be involved in this shit."

"Listen, I don't wanna do this shit neither, but you know it's them or us."

An awkward silence crept up.

"I know," Big Vern said.

"We don't got much time to think about it," Nate reminded. "We need a location, and we need it fast."

James' heart started to race as an idea formed in his head. He knew that he had at least one thing in common with Nate and Big Vern: they were all running out of time.

RECIPROCATION

James had to wait about another hour before Glenn pulled out of the parking lot. With his manager gone, he knew it was just Big Vern and Nate inside Food Plus restocking the shelves. That was exactly what he wanted. As his car rounded the back of the building, he took a deep breath.

He stopped a few feet short of the loading dock and looked at the carton of eggs on the seat. They made him think of Eli and how little time remained for him to find a solution. Drastic measures were in order. Dark things he hadn't thought about for what felt like ages.

I got no other choice, he thought.

When he rang the service bell, his heart fell into his stomach.

You've got to.

The door swung open, and a boatload of beef stood in front of him. Big Vern looked at him sideways. "James? What you doin' here?"

"I need to talk to you… and Nate too," James said. "Can I come inside?"

"What we got to talk about?"

James struggled to find the words. "I—I think I can help you."

"The fuck you mean?"

James brushed passed him. It felt like every minute he wasted was dragging him closer to Eli's demise. He didn't have time to wait for Big Vern to step aside. James limped his way into the loading dock.

Closing the steel door, Big Vern turned and raised an eyebrow. "Man, you better watch where you goin' if you know what's good for you."

Nate appeared beside a partially unwrapped pallet of eggs. "What's goin' on?"

James nodded and pointed back at Big Vern. "I was just trying to tell your friend here, I can help you guys."

"Help us with what?" Nate stepped closer to James.

James used the pallet to bridge himself up and take some of the weight off his leg. "I overheard the two of you discussing your… problem." He threw one of his hands up. "Look, I don't wanna know why you're doing it—the less I know, the better, really. But I can do the deed."

"Nigga, who said your old crusty ass was gettin' in on anything?" Big Vern said.

Nate laughed. "Fuckin' Lame James rollin' up in here, tryin' to call the shots. How you gonna help us when you can't even help yourself? You got a bum leg, man. You can't even walk straight."

James' demeanor hadn't changed since he'd entered the storage room. His gaze was ice cold and collected. "Keep running your mouths and I'll make you both believers." He pushed himself off the pallet, cracked his knuckles, and stepped up to Nate.

Nate laughed again—this time in James' face. "I ain't below stompin' out a cripple. Honestly, it's been a fucked-up day, I wouldn't mind gettin' out a little aggression. But I'm tryin' to do your dumb ass a favor." Nate pushed his chest hard, causing James to stumble a few steps backward. "If you know what's good for you, you'll raise the fuck up outta here, *now.*"

"I'm not leaving until you give me a chance to—"

"Man, fuck this nigga!" Big Vern punched James in the side of the head.

James stumbled back into the pallet and used it to bridge himself up. Nate pounced on him, but James was already spinning around with a backhand that landed on his jaw and stunned him.

Big Vern was on him before James could make another move, but as he fired a combination of straights and hooks, James kept his head on a swivel.

He bobbed and weaved, then fired off several punches into the big man's belly. Despite James' blows having some bite behind them, the amount of blubber that lined Big Vern's exterior protected him from any significant damage.

He put his big mitts around James' neck and tossed him across the dock into a broken box.

James let out a moan of agony and pressed his hands against the floor, lifting himself to a plank position. Before he could even get his head up, Nate's boot blasted into his brow. The shot cracked his glasses and split open his forehead.

When Nate saw him roll sideways, he lined the next kick up with his ribs. "Whatchu, crazy?" James felt a hard thud when the kick connected with his torso. "I should fuckin' kill your ass!"

James did another revolution, pain piercing his body as he landed in a pile of pulled boards. As he felt around, his fingertips suddenly touched steel. The blood oozed from his head as a grin manifested. When he saw the crowbar, he knew the odds had evened.

Nate swung the next kick at his ribs, but James leaned to his side, swinging the crowbar into the Achilles of the leg that remained grounded. When he hit the concrete, Nate cried out, and James pounced on him with the metal, following up with three rapid strikes to the gut.

As the air hissed out of Nate's lungs, James retook his footing. But Big Vern was now closing in on him. His huge hands banged against James' mouth and chin.

As James fell against the forklift, his lips started to swell, and he regained just enough awareness to see the follow-up strike.

Big Vern's punch flew, but James ducked it. As the fat man's fist collided with the side of the forklift, a loud cracking noise exploded from his knuckles.

"Mutha fucka!" Big Vern yelled, immediately clutching his hand.

Fury burned in his eyes as he charged, but James was ready. Putting his weight on his good leg, he rotated, spin-moving Big Vern and whipping the crowbar into his back, and then landed a follow-up hit on the side of his kneecap.

As Big Vern cried out, he dropped to one knee. His head hovered over the pallet of eggs as James brought the crowbar down on the back of it. When Big Vern's head hit the shells, they exploded. Yolk and translucent goo slimed Big Vern's entire face as he fell over sideways.

When James looked back, Nate was finally getting to his feet. As he saw Big Vern knocked out, the urgency of the situation seemed like it was starting to hit him.

"Ready to talk yet?" James asked.

Nate held his sternum in agony—as if it had been bruised almost as deeply as his pride. He couldn't swallow that, no matter how far things went. "You think you hard?" He lurched to the door and pushed through it. "I got somethin' for your ass."

James had no idea what he was talking about but didn't like the sound of it. He promptly followed him outside, grimacing as the pain grew deeper with each step. There were only two cars in the lot: James' and the SUV Nate was opening the door of.

Right when James saw the barrel of the gun, he swung the crowbar. Nate dodged the blow, which dented in the door of the SUV. When he tried to turn the gun on him, James knew he needed to lose his grip on the crowbar or lose his life.

"I'm here to fucking help you, goddammit!" James yelled, clasping his hands down on Nate's wrists and keeping the gun low.

"I'ma fuckin' help you, nigga," Nate replied. "Help you to the next life."

The gun went off twice, shooting James directly in his bad leg. Nate probably expected him to crumple to the ground, but instead, James drove his other knee directly into Nate's groin.

"Mutha fucka!" Nate wailed as James wrestled the gun away, then fell onto his ass.

Leveling the Desert Eagle at Nate's head, James watched him slowly slide down the side of the SUV. He cycled through a mix of potent emotions. His astonishment, disappointment, and anger were all palpable.

The shock Nate displayed when he realized the bullet holes in James' leg weren't bleeding was priceless.

James adjusted his prosthetic while keeping the gun fixed on Nate. The rawness he felt on his nub had bothered him the entire brawl—he could feel a tingling pain dancing around the piece of his thigh that remained.

James cocked the hammer back, making it clear to Nate that it wasn't his first time holding a gun. "I'm running the fucking show now. And you better make damn sure that computes, because right now, as I understand it, neither of us have a hell of a lot to live for. Don't fucking test me, got it?"

Nate shook his head. "Man…"

"I said you got it?!"

"Aight, aight." Nate nodded.

"Good. Now let's go back inside and see if we can wake up Vern."

EGG ON YOUR FACE

"Now what we had here was a failure to communicate," James said. "Let's do our best not to let that happen again. There's no need for us to keep knocking each other's dicks in the dirt. We should be working together."

Big Vern and Nate both sat on some boxes while James stood with the gun fixed on them.

"All I wanted to do was help you," he continued.

"The fuck you wanna help us for, man?" Nate asked.

James exhaled. "I'm not saying I ain't gonna get anything out of it."

"What's in it for you, then?" Nate asked.

The stress inside James' belly was bubbling. "I'm gonna be straight with you. Someone close to me needs a heart. They've been on the transplant list, but between the money these dirty fucking doctors want and the corrupt nature of the scheduling, there ain't no way it's happening. I need to make it happen myself. You need to kill someone—I need to save someone. In a way, it's the same shit. You tell me who you need killed, and I'll get it done. But when I make good on my end of the deal, I need the two of you to help me break inside the organ refrigeration unit at Memorial Hospital and get that heart."

Big Vern was still wiping egg off his face and rubbing the lump on the back of his skull. "That actually kinda sound good. I was tellin' you to fuck off before, but clearly, I was under the assumption that you was useless. And for a cripple, you capable. But there's just one problem."

"What's that?" James asked.

"It ain't just one person who gotta die. It's ten."

Nate raised his eyebrow. "Wait, but don't we gotta—?"

Big Vern smacked him in his bruised sternum. "Let me do the talkin'. The man was straight up with us, so let's be straight up with him."

"Ten…" James said. "Why ten?"

Nate huffed. "Cuz—"

Big Vern slapped Nate in the chest again and grilled James. "When you first walked in here, didn't you say the less you know, the better?"

James shook his head. "When I first walked in here, I thought it was one. Who are they?"

"That's actually the easy part," Big Vern grinned. "It don't matter who. It can be *anyone.*"

James' eyes widened—a light bulb activated. He thought about the callous doctors and rotten hierarchy he'd had to deal with for the last several years. They didn't seem to care if his boy lived or died, so why should James care if they did?

He lowered the gun. "Maybe we can kill two birds with one stone. I'm sure I can think of ten people who deserve to die in that building."

"Wait, what buildin' you talkin' 'bout?" Nate asked.

James grinned. "Memorial Hospital."

A CALL TO THE PAST

When James returned home, he stumbled out of the car, the bottom of his thigh scraping against the prosthetic. The irritated flesh was ragged and bleeding. The napkins from the console he'd stuffed inside absorbed most of the fluid but not all.

Once he'd entered the house, he dropped the eggs off in the fridge and headed for the bedroom. His adrenaline was still going too hard for him to sleep, and he wanted to check on his family.

As he peeked inside Eli's room, Shelly was laid out sideways on the recliner, a faint snore occurring with each breath.

I'm glad she finally got some rest, he thought.

She was constantly taking care of Eli, with little time for herself. Some days he'd return home and find her wide awake, just staring at him while he slept. James and Shelly were the same in the regard that neither of them was going to be able to live their lives until their child's problem was resolved—*if* it could be resolved. In that way, they were ideal parents and partners. But how cruel the universe could be.

James' gaze drifted to his sleeping son.

Just need a little more time.

The thought pushed him to not wallow in his misery like he did most evenings.

Tonight's different. Tonight, I've got a gameplan.

He quietly closed the door and moved into the living room. There was no doubt in his mind—he knew what came next. But getting himself up to the task terrified him. He stared at the telephone as if it had done him wrong. The discomfort inside him swelled.

I'll do it. I've just got to unwind a little.

He stepped into the kitchen and poured himself a sizable shot of whiskey and instantly fired it back. Then another. While the burn set in, he snagged a beer from the fridge. James waited until he returned to the living room and quietly opened it.

When he sat down in the recliner, it only made sense to switch on the television.

Get my fucking mind off it for a few.

The stunning woman in the green top had her makeup applied perfectly. The graphic beside her head contained a picture of city hall with a headline above it that read: MAYOR MCKINNEY SPEAKS.

"And we here at WPNS have obtained an exclusive audio quote from Mayor McKinney regarding the recent rash of immigrants who've gone missing. Let's have a listen."

The television displayed an image of a grinning black woman giving a thumbs-up. "I think that we need to be extremely careful about how we approach this issue. These hardworking people are the literal backbone of our city. If we didn't have them, who would clean our toilets, mow our lawns, wash our dishes—I mean, I could go on all day. But at the same time, we don't want to assume anything. Maybe they aren't missing at all, maybe they've simply gone home or somewhere else."

"But, Mayor," a male voice said on the recording, "isn't it their families who are reporting them missing?"

"In some cases," she replied, "and I can assure you, we're most certainly looking into those."

"What do you have to say about the allegations that you've carelessly allowed direct-to-customer marketing of experimental drugs, such as Lobotozine, because Garland Pharmaceuticals—the company that created the drug—was and is the main contributor to your campaign?"

"Dan, uh, Dan?" the news anchor who set up the clip said as the screen transitioned back to her. She made a throat cutting gesture. "And, ah, that's all that was available from the mayor's conference. But as you can see, Mayor McKinney is committed to finding a resolution on this issue and continues to go to bat for the less fortunate still trying to gain their footing in this terrible country. And now, a brief word from our sponsors."

James glared at the TV. It was obvious what they were doing, and it disgusted him. Sometimes, he just had to watch it a moment to even accept that it was real.

My ass. What a crock of shit—

The ad for Lobotozine cut in before he could finish his thought.

"We know life can be hard," a soothing female voice said as a man in his car yielded for traffic on a bridge. A criminal with brown hosiery distorting his face crouched beside the car window and pressed the barrel of a gun to the side of the man's face.

"Take whatever the heck you want!" the driver cried.

The criminal pulled the terrified driver out of his car by the neck and dragged him to the rail near the bridge.

"I wanna see you fly," the criminal said.

The criminal dumped him over the side of the bridge, and the man's body went plummeting down. Just before he connected with the water below, the shot switched to the man awakening in the middle of the night. He was sweating profusely and riddled with anxiety.

"Don't let fear control your life," the woman's voice continued.

The man now drove down the street, petrified.

"Let the past stay in the past," she said.

The ad flashed to his bedroom, where he stood looking at a noose he'd hung to kill himself with.

"With Lobotozine, you can stay strong."

The man swallowed a handful of black pills and changed his expression instantly. He turned to the camera and smiled, taking the noose down.

"You can forget about your worries."

After exiting his home, the man was using the same rope from the noose to build a tire swing on a tree in his backyard. Once he was finished, he sat on top with a big grin on his face and swung in the breeze.

"This world is fucked," James whispered, turning off the television.

His eyes returned to the telephone.

Just do it.

James lifted the phone and tilted the base, examining the underside. The small, green button was carefully hidden. After pressing it down, James held the phone to his ear. With his hand shaking, the concern multiplied with each extra second until the ringing suddenly stopped. The other end of the line remained silent but active.

"It's me..." It took James a few moments to put together what he was actually trying to say. "I never imagined I'd ask you for a favor again—especially after how things ended between us—but I've got no one else. These last few years have been hell. Eli doesn't have much time left. If he doesn't get a new heart soon..."

James paused. The thought of losing him wasn't something he'd battled with enough to block out the pain.

"He's dead." Sniffing, James wiped away a tear. "You two remind me of each other a great deal. I've thought about our relationship a lot over the years. And you were right—now I realize who I was, that I failed you. I know my son and my problems are as far away from a priority as they can get for you. But please, I'm begging you."

James dropped down and knelt—the prosthetic leg ripping deeper.

"As God is my witness, I'm on my fucking knees right now." He broke down completely. "I'll do anything to make it right. I know I left you behind, but I can't leave him. I can't let him down. And tomorrow night, one way or another, I'm coming out of Memorial Hospital with Eli's heart."

James waited and listened intently. The fear inside him was braising. The silence was killing him.

"Please, help me. I know you can still do what I taught you. Y-you can save him—"

The phone went dead.

James continued crying on his knees until he was able to corral his emotions. As he slowly hung up the phone, the uncertainty of the interaction gnawed at him.

I've done what I can. Just gotta hope for the best.

A CHANGE OF PLANS

It was past lunchtime, but James wasn't hungry. That wasn't abnormal, considering what he was getting ready to do. He'd felt such a loss of appetite in his past. He didn't like doing evil things, but it would take something wicked to make things right again.

As he pulled over by the payphone, a lurking feeling of dread loomed. The overcast sky felt like a bad omen, but in the city of fear, he couldn't be sure. Regardless, there were so many questions.

Was he about to ruin his life?

Did he still have what it took to execute his plan?

If shit went south, would the hugs he'd given Shelly and Eli that morning be his last?

Don't fall into that trap—don't think negative, James thought.

He took a deep, icy breath and hopped inside the booth. After he fished a quarter out of his pocket, he dropped it into the slot and punched in the number. The phone rang several times before the line got picked up.

"Sup?" Big Vern asked.

"Hey," James replied, "everything's a go on my end."

"Yeah, well, we got a little problem."

"Huh? What do you mean?"

"Me and Nate been doin' some thinkin', and we need more manpower. Three of us ain't enough."

James was already on edge but achieved a new tier of fury. "Why the fuck couldn't you tell me yesterday so I had some time to prepare?"

"We needed to make sure whoever else get brung into this wasn't sitting around plottin' with you all day. Wouldn't want you to think you can get the drop on us."

James shook his head. "But there's not enough time!"

"You still got a few hours." Big Vern laughed. "Somethin' tells me you'll figure out a way to make it work. We'll see you at the spot real soon. Peace."

"Wait—"

Tired of getting hung up on, James smashed the receiver of the payphone repeatedly.

"Fuck, fuck, fuck!"

He stepped out of the booth, clawing his hands through his hair.

What the hell am I gonna do now?

As James let his hands fall from his head, he stared blankly across the road. The desperate look on his face soon dissipated.

His solution was just a stone's throw away.

THE PICKUP

When James pulled into the Home Hardware parking lot, many spaces were occupied. Property was always being damaged or vandalized in the city, and to say the building supply store was important to the community was a gross understatement.

At the back of the lot, his miracle awaited. Several pickup trucks sat parked, surrounded by Guatemalan immigrants wearing parkas and hoodies. As James parked and left the car running, several men swarmed him while smaller groups of men remained in the background. One was at the passenger window knocking on the glass while two others fought for the driver's side window.

A middle-aged man with slicked back hair and a wispy mustache extended his hand to greet James as he commenced his carnival barking.

"Allo, sir. I'm Miguel Flores," he explained in broken English.

James shook his hand and nodded. "It's a pleasure, Miguel."

"Sir, I has tree strong, *very* strong men. They work all day for you—only two hundred dollar."

Another man with a full salt-and-pepper beard, who was the spokesperson for a different group of workers, tried to undercut him.

"I give you four men, only one-fifty dollar," he yelled.

James looked at the other man, considering the counter.

"Vete de aqui, Rolando!" Miguel growled before turning back to James with a follow-up offer. "Three men, all day, one hundred dollar."

"What about night?" James asked.

"Night?"

"Yeah." James' face grew tight, and his tone was dead serious.

"What you want for them to do?"

James leaned in closer to Miguel. "What if I paid you triple, and you don't ask me that question?"

A grin appeared on Miguel's face, revealing the plaque caked on his teeth. "Deal." He opened his hand to receive the money.

Reaching into his pocket, James' fingertips brushed up against Benjamin. He thought about giving Miguel a partial payment, but something stopped him. He was thinking about handing the bill to the man, telling his body to, but it didn't respond. Instead, James started to convince himself that it was the wrong choice.

What the fuck's he gonna do if I deny it? They're all working off prospect out here, James thought

"You get the money after the job," James said.

The smile melted off Miguel's face. He now spoke with a deadness to his tone. He gestured to the pickup truck where his men stood. "Fifty more dollar and they bring the truck. All the tools—everything."

James popped the handle and stepped out of the car. He opened the back door. "I already got tools." Looking over at the laborers, he pointed inside. "They can ride with me."

Miguel allowed his cold stare to linger a moment before calling his team over. The trio of men stood at a modest height. Two of them had short black hair that had been buzzed down. The third man, breathing into his hands to keep warm, had a longer mullet with curls

Miguel put his hand on the shoulder of the mullet man and pulled him close. "Filipe, haz lo que este hombre te pida, pero si regresas después del trabajo sin trescientos dólares, me aseguraré de que tu familia nunca vuelva a ver el sol. Diles lo mismo a Jorge y Diego. Esto es mucho dinero, no lo arruines."

James wasn't sure what he'd said but didn't much care. They needed to get moving.

"Are we ready?" James asked.

Miguel glanced back with a grin. "Anything for you, my friend."

THE MEET UP

Driving the three immigrants around in the back of the car felt strange. James had done little else during the drive besides asking them their names—hopefully, he'd be able to remember them.

When he glanced in the rearview mirror, he observed the men whispering amongst themselves. The nervous nature of their exchanges was warranted. James could only imagine being new to a strange country and forced to operate under the guidance of other people like the cold carnival barker in the parking lot of the hardware store. They were probably nervous about continuing to get work, doing a good job, or learning the language.

If they only fucking knew, James thought.

He felt bad about it. The immigrants looked like decent enough folks. The way they were being treated in the city was hard enough to deal with. They didn't need him thrusting his problems onto their plates. But James was short on time. He was kind of impressed that he'd been able to figure something out on the fly.

At least they'd all be going into the volatile situation

together. Hopefully, he could protect them. Hopefully, they didn't go apeshit when he explained to them what was on the agenda. Even so, deceiving people wasn't something James had done on such a scale in a long time. But lying's like dying—even if you don't want to do it, eventually, everyone must.

"What is yob for?" Filipe asked.

Several letters in the Memorial Hospital sign had shorted out, but James pointed at the ones that still glowed blue. "This is the building. I'll show you right after we meet our partners."

James imagined it might've been feasible to the men that this was the building they were set to work on. Especially considering how much of a shithole the place was. James had been forced to roam the halls many times when Eli had to stay overnight or go through procedures and tests for his failing heart. It wasn't as if he wanted to bring his sick son to such a place, but there wasn't exactly an alternative—not that he could afford.

The paint-peeling walls.

The insect and rodent infestation.

The burned out and broken light fixtures.

The unsanitary and hazardous equipment.

The unempathetic and aggravated hospital staff.

Memorial Hospital was one big metaphor for the larger problems of the healthcare system.

A rotten building filled with rotten people.

He saw Big Vern and Nate sitting in their SUV inside the visitor's parking lot, just as they'd agreed.

Those fuckers better be ready to kick in some cash if we make it out of this place.

As James parked the car beside his shady partners, the feelings of guilt he'd been battling with since he'd formulated his plan resurfaced.

Are ten of their lives worth one heart?

He knew the staff was corrupt and viewed money as their master, but was that enough to justify the killings?

James wasn't used to thinking about such things. He was already in too deep for a change of heart. Subconsciously, he knew the answer to any question he had: saving Eli trumped all else. He'd just have to deal with the feelings of culpability after the fact.

Rolling down the window, James looked at Nate in the passenger seat. He and Big Vern were both already masked up. "I've got three to back us up inside—good men. They shouldn't ask too many questions neither. They ain't the type who'd be eager to interact with the cops."

"My nigga." Nate grinned. "Got you some Mexicans?"

"Guatemalans," James corrected.

"Same shit. Gwizzies are a good choice, though. They green as fuck, so you know they gonna listen good. You tell 'em whassup yet?"

"I figured we'd do that together."

"Aight. Let's get it poppin', then. Hop in, there's plenty a room."

James nodded.

The Guatemalans filed out of the car along with James. They all took their seats in the two rows of the SUV—the shorter haired men in the back, while James and Filipe sat in the middle behind Big Vern and Nate.

"Time to gear up," Big Vern said.

Nate reached down to the floor and turned around. He handed four ski masks to James—three of them were black and one was hot pink.

James furrowed his brow. "Pink? Aren't we trying to be lowkey?"

"Man, that's what they had," Nate said. "Stop bitchin' and just give it to one of them gwizzies."

James took a black mask for himself and handed the rest to Filipe.

When the laborer took hold of the mask, he scratched the side of his head. "Why?"

"You definitely don't want them to see your face," James replied.

Filipe looked even more concerned, but not as concerned as James would've imagined. It was almost as if he'd expected he was coming into a royally fucked-up situation.

Big Vern looked at the pink mask through the rearview. "That pink shit kinda fire if you ask me. It's all about how you rock it. I have Jordans that would be murda with that."

"Speakin' of murda," Nate said, raising up a revolver, "why don't we stop worryin' about what kinda fuckin' fashion statement we makin' in this crack house of a hospital and find out if any of these dishwashers ever used a blicker before?"

"Revolvers?" James asked. "That all you got?"

"For the help, yeah." Nate checked the cylinder to ensure it was loaded and spun the shit out of it. "They shouldn't need much. We just need 'em to look intimidating and lead the way when shit's about to get hairy." He lowered his voice and leaned in so only James could hear him. "So if shit pop off, we ain't gettin' killed first."

Big Vern cosigned the idea. "Can't go wrong with a revolver—them shits can't jam."

As Filipe finished sliding a black mask over his face, he handed the final black and pink ones to Jorge in the back seat. He whispered directions in Spanish before Diego pounced, snatching the black one from his clutches.

"Aye! No—kay—no!" Jorge yelled.

He stuck his fingers into the eyeholes and mouth of the black ski mask, yanking violently. Diego held tight, but that didn't halt Jorge's attempt. The cheap yarn at the crux of the dollar store masks started to unravel. When Diego tore the hood back, a loud rip could be heard throughout the vehicle.

"Yo!" Nate yelled. "Both of you niggas chill!"

The men looked at the gun in his hand and promptly obeyed his orders like siblings reprimanded by their parents.

Filipe's eyes bulged when he saw the gun. But he kept quiet.

Miguel really has these fucking guys under his thumb.

"This is for them," Nate said, checking the other two revolvers.

James took all three of the guns and carefully passed them to Filipe.

"And *this* is for you." Nate pulled the sawed-off out of the duffel bag between the seats. "The bitch is loaded, but put a few of these in your pockets in case shit really pops off."

He handed the shotgun and box of shells to James. When James took hold of the piece, a strangeness overcame him. A tremor ran down his spine, and as he contemplated pulling the trigger, imagery exploded in his head.

The memory depicted the last time he'd been inside the hellish hospital. James recalled the maddening sound of cockroach legs scraping against the metal sink in the examination room. Eli had been laid out on a table, his heart being examined by Dr. Robert Finkelstein.

As Dr. Finkelstein listened intently to the irregular beat, the sweat made his toupee adhesive ooze down the sides of his head. It married to the black dye that remained in what was left of his actual hair, creating a dark slime around his ears and the bushy sideburns he overcompensated for his baldness with.

Dr. Finkelstein grinned. His sharp, yellow incisors appeared almost vampiric. Considering what he was doing to James and his family, such attributes seemed appropriate.

He probably doesn't have too much time left, Dr. Finkelstein had said.

Eli's face and body quivered. He rolled to his side and started to cry into the sweatshirt he'd taken off prior to the examination.

Rubbing Shelly's shoulder, James snapped.

James, Shelly cried.

Stay with Eli! James yelled.

He grabbed the doctor by the collar and white jacket and pulled him out of the room. After James flung the door shut, he slammed Dr. Finkelstein against the wall.

H-hey! Dr. Finkelstein barked. *Get your goddamn hands off me!*

He's not dead yet! James screamed. *You might be ready to give up on him, but say that again in front of my family and I'll break your fucking jaw!*

The doctor wormed his way out of James' grip. His rug was no longer properly set atop his head—it was twisted sideways, and the hair dye sweat storm had traced over the sides of his face several more times.

Put your hands on me again and I'll make sure that boy never gets a heart! He pointed at James menacingly, his hair piece flopping around as saliva exploded from his cracked lips. *I'll make sure everyone in your foul little family tree is put onto a wait list that'll see them rotten long before their appointment days arrive. No procedures! No antibiotics! You won't be able to get a fucking Advil in this city! You catch my drift?!*

James clenched his jaw, reluctantly nodding. He would've liked to rip the bastard's head off, but for Eli's sake, he needed to control himself.

Dr. Finkelstein fixed his toupee and swiped the sides of his face with his jacket sleeves. The black slime discolored the doctor's already dirty coat and left a thin layer of disgustingness on his cheek.

Now, Dr. Finkelstein said. *Since you've calmed yourself a bit, maybe we can talk business. What's say instead of getting so emotional you actually focus on getting the money required to… expedite Eli's heart transplant.*

James shook his head. *And how the fuck do you expect me to find that kind of money?! I'm just a regular guy now. You damn well know I don't make a salary like yours anym—*

Well, that's truly regrettable, Dr. Finkelstein said, *but in case you haven't noticed, regular people die every day! No one cares or remembers them! It's only the exceptional who survive. Not only do they survive but they thrive. You should've thought about such things before forming a family. The sad part is you could've been special. I understand it's frustrating, having your body betray you.*

It took everything for James not to snap—thoughts of swinging wildly on the doctor clouded his mind.

But I'm not here to throw a pity party for you, Dr. Finkelstein continued. *You know as well as I do where you've come up short. You've failed your son. You've failed your wife. And you've failed yourself. Don't return here unless you're ready to pony up. Now take your pathetic family and get the fuck out of my hospital.*

"Yo! Lame James," Big Vern said. "Wake the fuck up."

James gripped the shotgun tighter and gritted his teeth. His hands trembled and the gun rocked as the words echoed in his head again: *your body betrayed you.*

"What's up with your hands?" Big Vern asked. "You scared or suttin?"

James laid the gun over his lap. "I am. But not for myself. I'm scared for the people inside."

"Man, we don't need to know all that, just answer the question," Nate said. "You know how to use that thing or what?"

"Let's go inside and I'll show you," James said. There was a new iciness to his tone.

"Hey, bro, you ain't gotta impress me," Nate said, setting his Desert Eagle on the dash. "How 'bout you save the tough guy shit for inside?"

James said nothing. He just continued to stare through the windshield at the hospital. It was like he wasn't even looking at the building but past it.

Nate retrieved two TEC-9s from a separate bag and handed them to Big Vern.

"Aight," Big Vern said. "It's on you to make sure the gwizzies know how to use a cannon and, more importantly, what the fuck we 'bout to get into."

James slipped on his ski mask and turned. Filipe had his mask on—pieces of his curly mullet stuck out of the eyeholes. Jorge wore the pink ski mask, momentarily looking down the barrel of his own gun.

"Hey! Christ, man, keep it aimed at the floor!" James said, quickly grabbing Jorge's hand and lowering the gun.

Filipe rambled on, translating James' words just in case it wasn't clear.

The final immigrant, Diego, sat nervously with his gun on his lap. While he was wearing his ski mask, the massive rip where the eyes and mouth normally connected left his entire face exposed, defeating the whole purpose of wearing it.

James exhaled his agitation, looking at the glorified ear warmer. He couldn't just pretend his anxiety wasn't crippling or that they'd assembled a crew who were even remotely capable. But what the fuck else could he do?

Looking back at Nate, James pumped the sawed-off and loaded a shell. "We might just have to wing it."

BUILDING OF SICKNESS

When the immigrants passed through the doors of the hospital, from the waist up, it looked like they were in stadium seating. Big Vern, James, and even Nate—who wasn't the tallest—all stood behind, towering over them. But the heaters each of the three laborers held would make anybody who didn't respect their stature sweat.

They'd waited until no one was around the front of the building. James knew the layout well and directed them through a secondary entrance. They all successfully slipped inside the stairwell without getting noticed, just as James had hoped they would. The space smelled like rust and piss. Stairs that were once metallic now looked as brown as shit. In James' eyes, it was almost too fitting for such a place.

"This place look more like a porta potty than a fuckin' hospital," Nate said.

"For real," Big Vern added. "They curin' diseases in here or creatin' 'em?"

As a squealing rat ran into a hole smeared with filth and rodent fecal matter, the immigrants quietly bickered with one another. Still, Filipe seemed to have them under control. Even though they didn't know what they were doing, they must've assumed they didn't have a choice.

James looked over at Nate and Big Vern. "All the more reason to do what we came here to do and get the fuck out. Moving forward, I'll take point. Remember, be cool until we get upstairs. The ones who deserve this..."

He paused, biting his lip. The images of his sick son groaning in fear and agony flickered in his brain, further motivating him.

"Their offices and the main security office are all on the third floor—same as the ICU. As we discussed previously, it's best for us to handle security first before we take care of any business. Once we have them under control, I can trigger the lockdown."

"What you mean lockdown?" Nate asked. "You ain't mention that before."

"Some years ago, when the murder rate reached an all-time high, hospital administration implemented a lockdown system. If the city goes into a state of emergency, the guards—who are understaffed to begin with—can instantly secure the building."

Nate furrowed his brow. "How you know so much about this place?"

"That's not important," James said. "What *is* important is that we get inside that security office *quietly*—before anyone gets out of this building in a panic."

"Aight," Big Vern said. "But we gotta be ready on the way. We masked up, niggas might try to come at us."

"That's fair," James replied, "but let's do our best to get to the security office without incident. Otherwise, this'll be a lot harder than it needs to be."

James looked back at the group of immigrants. "Like I

said before"—he pointed to the gun—"no shoot yet, just scare, comprende?"

The men all nodded. They looked wholly terrified. Especially Diego with his entire face exposed. James still wasn't sure if the poor kid even realized it. His smooth, youthful skin held more expression to digest. The wrinkles in Diego's face made it seem like he didn't believe he was walking out of the building.

"Let's get this over with," James said.

They ascended the flights as quickly as they could—the less time they spent in the sewer-stench stairwell, the better. When they reached the floor, James cautiously opened the door and peeked outside.

The yellow lighting stretched down the hallway as a lone nurse walked under a flickering tube. When she reached the end of the corridor, she turned right, disappearing as she passed under a sign directing toward the nurse's station.

James' eyes darted to the side. The security office was just a short distance away. "It's clear. Let's move."

All of the men scurried up to the security office door. James pushed his way through into the small room. An overweight guard sat at his desk with a half-eaten cold cut shoved into his mouth. James kept the gun fixed on his head. "How many on?"

The security guard's eyes stretched as he dropped his sandwich and tried to quickly swallow his bite. "What—what is this—what do you mean?"

As the men finished filing in and locked the door, James stepped closer and put his sawed-off to the guard's head. "Do not fuck around with me. If you play it straight, no one gets hurt. How many other guards are in the building?"

"Two! That's it—I-I swear it!" he cried.

James could see he was already getting emotional. As Nate disarmed the big boy, James was grateful the security guard had been an easy nut to crack.

Looking back at the control panel and monitors behind him, James noticed the screens were all mostly vacant.

"Where?"

The guard kept his shaking hands up. "One downstairs at intake and another on the fourth near the coolers."

Inspecting his name tag, James got even closer to him. "Listen, Richie, I know you're new around here. You don't strike me as a hero. It would behoove you not to play one."

"I ain't gonna try nothing," Richie said.

"Good." James nodded. "Just let us take care of what we need to, and we'll be out of your hair. But while we're taking care of business, I'm gonna need you to show me how to put the building in lockdown."

"Why—why should I do that?" Richie asked.

"Nigga, is you stupid?" Nate asked, raising his Desert Eagle to Richie's eye socket. "Ask another question and I'll blow your fuckin' wig all over your hoagie, fat boy."

"Okay! I'll do it!" Richie cried.

"Damn right you will," Nate said.

ON THE LOW

Nate looked at Big Vern as he watched the security guard explain the control mechanisms.

James loomed over the guard. "I just want all entrances and exits locked. But skip the first responder flag. Don't alert *anyone,* understood?"

"Yeah," Richie said.

"You better, because if someone shows up, I've got no choice but to shoot you."

Nate's eyes shifted to the security monitors. He leaned into Big Vern, keeping his voice at a whisper. "I don't see a whole lotta people in the hospital."

"Could you blame 'em?" Big Vern asked. "This place nasty as hell."

"No, but, bro, that ain't the point. If you don't wanna get dripped, then we better figure out a way to pad the fuckin' numbers soon."

Big Vern narrowed his eyes. "Did you look at that monitor on the top left?"

"What? Ain't no one there."

"I know. But read the sign on the wall."

A chill ran down Nate's spine. "Oh. You really wanna do all that?"

"No." Big Vern shook his head. "But if we have to, we have to."

A key turned on the control panel, and the green light below the hole transitioned from green to red.

"All right, it's done!" Richie said.

"Now disable the cameras," James commanded.

The immigrants seemed to be getting more nervous as they watched the events unfold. They were mumbling to themselves and trembling.

Nate looked at them and furrowed his brow. "Fellas, just chill, you'll be aight."

Filipe nodded.

After hearing a few pecks of some keys, Nate returned his gaze to the monitors and watched them all go dead.

"I—I've done everything you asked," Richie said. "Please, just don't hurt me."

James removed the handcuffs from the guard's belt and set them on the table. "Close your eyes," James said. "Look at my face and you die."

Richie did as he was told. James looked at Nate and Big Vern as he took his mask off.

"Slap these on him for now," James said. "I've gotta find Finkelstein on the fourth floor."

"Finklestein?" Nate asked. "That sound like a fuckin' diddler's name."

"Just keep the door locked until I get back."

"Aight, but you better hurry," Big Vern said. "We got shit to take care of too."

"Understood," James said. "You have my word." He loosened his belt buckle and wedged the sawed-off in the back of his waistband. "No one leaves until everyone gets what they came for."

CREEPIN'

As James stepped out of the security office, he heard the door lock behind him. He saw a maid inside one of the vacant cleaning rooms changing the sheets on a bed. James swiftly approached the unattended cart outside one of the empty ICU rooms. The bag of various linens also contained several sets of scrubs and a white doctor's coat.

Once he slipped on the white coat, he filled one pocket with shells and was able to better conceal the sawed-off.

Time to find that cocksucker, James thought.

James retreated back to the stairwell while the stress swelled inside him. He figured that route gave him the best shot at reaching Dr. Finklestein without running into too many people. As he opened the door, the squeaking and scurrying of more vermin could be heard. When he saw the sneaky and cowardly reaction of the rats, he was immediately reminded of Dr. Finklestein.

You always liked bragging about being in the 'penthouse.' Let's see if you're still there.

What Richie had said to him was still fresh on his mind. When he reached the top of the stairs, he knew there was a good chance he was going to have to confront another security guard. He removed the sawed-off from his waistband and took a deep breath. A feeling of sickness budded in his belly as he realized what the grip of the cold steel in his trembling hands actually meant.

If it's between Eli or him, it's gonna be Eli…

As he limped his way to the final step, James leaned up against the door. He cautiously peeked through the sliver of rectangular window.

The hallway was clear.

Here we go.

The sound of the door opening at the bottom of the stairwell echoed. Panic washed over James as he considered his options. He didn't know who was coming, but for the moment, he had the jump on them. Above all else, he needed to ensure he didn't lose that advantage.

He pushed the door open and wormed his way inside. Careful to close it quietly, James leaned up against the wall in the exact spot the door would cover upon opening. As the tension heightened, sweat oozed down the side of his face. His eyes darted from the office door he remembered to be Dr. Finklestein's to the light at the end of the corridor. The organ repository was just around the corner.

I'm so fucking close.

The muffled conversation drew toward him. He tried to listen closely, but the steel door didn't allow him much detail. As it opened, James bit his lip.

There was more than one voice.

"I don't know what it is, but every time a patient goes stiff while we're working together, so do I," Dr. Finklestein said.

James saw the large ass of the nurse by his side—it was about three times the size of his own.

"I ain't mad at it," the nurse said. "The faster they go, the more time we have to ourselves."

He laughed. "Rene, you know I have an oath to uphold."

"I know, but I have something I need you to look at."

"Hmm, that sounds urgent."

James quietly crept up behind them as they approached the office.

Rene lowered her tone. "It is. From the first moment I saw you today, my pussy hasn't stopped leakin'."

The sound of the sawed-off cocking stopped them dead in their tracks.

James wrapped his hand around Rene's mouth and pointed the gun at her head. "If the two of you lovebirds don't shut the fuck up and get in that office, it's gonna be more than just your pussy leaking."

When Dr. Finklestein turned around, his jaw dropped. "James, what the—"

James switched the aim of the barrel to Dr. Finklestein's face. "Not another fucking word or it'll be your last. Open the goddamn door. Now."

The doctor obeyed his commands.

James gestured toward the door with the gun. "Get inside."

When the door closed, James pushed Rene into the desk before locking them in. He tried to steady the gun, but his hands quaked.

Rene started crying. "Please don't kill us."

Pointing the sawed-off at the nurse, James gritted his teeth. "Quiet!" His eyes darted back to the doctor.

"What the hell is this?" Dr. Finklestein asked.

"This is what desperation looks like," James said. "This is what *you* created."

"Now, James, I-I'm sure we can solve this without violence. Just tell me what you want."

"It's not about what I want and you damn well know that. This is about what Eli *needs.* And if you wanna survive the night, you damn well better make it happen."

THE SCORE

Rene lay on the office floor with both of her stockings removed—they'd been used to gag and hog-tie her. As Dr. Finklestein exited the office, James did his best to conceal the firearm under his doctor's coat. He watched the sweat drip down the sides of Dr. Finklestein's face, tinted by the cheap hair dye that had been overapplied in an attempt to match the greasy hairpiece atop his head.

"Hey, wait," James said. "You need to look natural. Wipe the sweat off your face before we go."

Dr. Finklestein did as he was told and used the inside of his jacket to clean himself off.

James nodded. "All right, let's go. No stupid shit or I'll leave that ratty rug splattered all over the wall—got it?"

"Understood."

As they approached the corner, James' heart pounded. This was the part he couldn't prepare for.

Is the security guard going to be a problem? How might the doctor react? Doctor? He doesn't even deserve the title.

The jugs were some of the biggest he'd ever seen. The guard's titty magazine was on full display. He seemed distracted by the full-color pages of luscious ladies. James watched him closely as his eyes elevated up for a moment. He still wasn't able to see the guard's face.

"Hey, Doc. How goes it?" the security guard asked.

"Not too shabby," Dr. Finklestein said. "Just gotta… ah, check the inventory."

The guard's eyes narrowed as he looked at the side of Dr. Finklestein's face. A black bead of sweat and hair dye slid down his cheek as he fumbled to remove the keycard from his pocket.

"Everything okay?" the security guard asked, eyes transitioning from the nervous doctor to James.

When he dropped the magazine, James saw the guard's expression, and they mirrored each other's shock. He keyed in on the bulge in James' jacket and then his face.

"James?" the guard asked, looking back to Dr. Finklestein. "What the hell's going on here?"

Dr. Finklestein swiped the badge over the room's door, unlocking it while yelling, "He's got a gun!"

"Winston, don't!" James yelled.

As the doctor slipped into the refrigerated room, the security guard reached for his handgun. James had no choice but to elevate his barrel. As he pulled the trigger, the shotgun erupted and the spray-fire ripped through Winston's right cheek and neck.

The guard fell sideways off his chair and started to choke as the blood gushed from the massive crater in his throat. As James watched him squirm in agony, he knew it would be cruel to allow Winston's life to continue. Aiming the gun at his face, James winced before forcing himself to pull the trigger again.

The close-range follow-up shot blew even more of the meat off his neck, exposing his spine—a kill shot that gave James confidence that poor Winston wouldn't be creating any more issues.

He scooped up the pistol and slipped it into the back of his waistband. Glaring back at the door, he popped a pair of fresh shells into the sawed-off.

"Son-of-a-bitch!" James grumbled.

The steel door before him wasn't one he was just going to kick open. He looked back to Winston and grinned.

James glanced at the badge affixed to Winston's belt, immediately bending over and snatching it. He then slid it over the card reader.

When the door slid open, a cloud of gray smoke hit James in the face. He staggered backward, planting his prosthetic leg in Winston's blood. As his heel slipped, he went tumbling to the floor, his white coat overrun with crimson. Out of the cold fog emerged the doctor, a fire extinguisher raised above his head.

The hard casing smashed into James' nose, causing a mass exodus of blood and snot. James winced, stunned by the unexpected violence. The shotgun went sliding down the hallway, its path greased by the slick of blood.

"You stupid fuck!" Dr. Finklestein yelled, raising the canister back up again.

James' eyes watered as the taste of blood filled his mouth.

"We've known each other for some time now," the doctor continued. "Long enough for me to know this was your fate. You were always weak! Of course your seed was going to be defective! After all, it came out of your—"

"Hey, Rob," James whispered.

The doctor shook his head and laughed.

"I think that extinguisher's defective." James whipped his hand out from behind his back and cocked the pistol.

It took everything in him to tighten his body enough that his hand didn't shake. When he took the shot, the bullet tore a hole in the top of the canister. As the device rocketed downward, it pushed Dr. Finklestein face-first into the floor. His jaw cracked as it slammed into the hard tile, and several of the doctor's teeth ejected.

As Dr. Finklestein's eyes fluttered, three more shots entered his nose and forehead. A mass of gore shat out the backside of his head, turning his expression into a sickening void of horror.

James couldn't stop the twisted grin from contorting his mouth. "And so's your face."

THE PRECURSOR TO CARNAGE

When the door to the security office opened, James stood covered in blood, nose smashed, the sawed-off in one hand, and a small cooler in the other.

The men inside were shocked when they laid their eyes on him. A new terror surged inside the eyes of the three immigrants. James wasn't sure if they understood how far they were taking things, but if they hadn't realized it before, they did now.

"Looks like you got shit poppin' early," Big Vern said.

"Nigga lookin' like Michael Myers," Nate said.

"That's two for the books," James said. "I've got what I need." He held up the cooler and squinted down the hall. "We can hit the doctors' lounge on the way out and clip the other eight there. Nurses are fair game too but no—"

Nate fired the Desert Eagle. The round ripped through

Richie's head. A crimson mess vomited all over the desktop as the overweight security guard keeled over.

"Whoa!" James shouted.

The sound of a nurse yelping in the hall could be heard. "W-was that a gunshot?!" she asked.

"It's time ta get it poppin'," Nate said.

"We waited on you," Big Vern said, "now we gotta get our shit in."

"How about we use a little strategy?" James asked. "Why let 'em know we're coming, for Christsake?"

"Man, how about you shut the fuck up and lead us to the room with all these doctors already?" Nate asked.

"Yeah." Big Vern looked to the immigrants. "And these gwizzies need to put in some work too, otherwise, the fuck we bring 'em for?"

Nate pointed his gun at Filipe. "Ándale, nigga! Tell 'em! 'Fore we add y'all mutha fuckas to the count!"

The immigrants appeared terrified. They looked to James for guidance, but he couldn't save them. He nodded his head, gazed down the hallway, and waved them in.

KILLING SPREE

It was locked. James carefully leveled the gun at the door-handle to the doctors' lounge. There was no way to be sure how many of them were inside—after Nate fired the shot in the security office, many might've tried seeking cover.

If it's locked, someone's gotta be in there, James thought.

Gritting his teeth, he turned to the trio of immigrants and nodded. "Uno, dos, tres!"

Blam!

When the shot ripped through the door, just as they'd planned, Filipe kicked it in and bulled forward. Jorge followed him with Diego in tow.

James heard the drill before he laid eyes on it. The half-moon of the bone saw spiraled hastily. As the revolving teeth met with Filipe's head, he tried to raise the gun. But when the unforgiving steel smashed into the motor cortex of his brain and scrambled it, his arm went haywire.

The barrel of his gun ended up under Jorge's chin, the bullet exploding through his soft tissue and sending a wave of gore cascading over Diego's face.

"Ay, Dios mío!" Diego shrieked.

Falling backward through the doorway, Diego screamed as he dropped his gun, frantically wiping the blood out of his eyeballs.

The screams of nurses inside the room could be heard. The doctor holding the bone saw dropped it. He stepped into the doorway and made a move for Filipe's gun.

"Man, these mutha fuckas," Big Vern said raising the pair of gats.

As the doctor lifted the revolver, two balls of fire appeared in the front of the gridded barrels of TEC-9s. The green scrubs the doctor had donned were instantly shredded. The rapid gunfire tore up his body, and he dropped to the floor like a sack of shit.

"One," Big Vern said.

The big man stepped over the bodies and into the lounge, where another doctor and three nurses tried hiding under the tables. One of the nurses bravely stood up, trying to reason with him.

"Please, I-I-I won't say—"

Before she could finish her pitch, a half dozen bullets penetrated her chest. Blood splattered all over the vending machine as she crashed into it. When her body fell back into the glass, the shards broke apart and showered the ground, leaving the nurse hung half into the machine, propped up by the metal spring-shaped racks.

"Two."

Big Vern didn't stop there. He unloaded the rest of the magazines into the other members of the medical staff taking cover. Screams and shell casings multiplied as the hole-riddled bodies were left immobilized, with some still twitching in agony. When Big Vern approached the dying healthcare workers, he inserted fresh magazines into each gun. He methodically walked past them, sending a final slug into each of their forehead's execution style.

"Three… Four… Five," Big Vern grumbled.

James watched the big man find his way back to the door. As a tearful Diego and curious Nate watched on, Big

Vern loomed over Filipe's convulsing body. After gazing into the gaping hole in his head, he decided to add to it.

The bullets from the TEC-9 flung knotty wads of Filipe's already scrambled brains all over the floor.

The heartless shot made James jump, while Diego cried out, still curled up on the ground and traumatized.

Big Vern looked up. "Six."

"What the fuck are you doing?!" James cried.

Big Vern raised the gun up and, this time, fired in James' direction. Losing his balance, James tumbled backward.

When the screams behind James erupted, he quickly realized that the shots weren't intended for him. A security guard—the third and final—crumpled to the blood-soaked ground behind him, the gun he held falling out of his reach. Deep wails of intense suffering echoed throughout the halls.

"Savin' your ass," Big Vern said. "Gotta have eyes in the back of your head, homie."

As the man continued to squeal like a crucified cat, Nate fired several more shots into his writhing frame, causing any movement to cease.

Big Vern approached the dead security guard and lifted his firearm from the floor and a pair of handcuffs from his belt. He nodded at Nate and tossed the handcuffs at him. After catching them, Nate slipped them into his pocket.

"S-so that's seven," James said. "Plus my two! One more and we're home free." He thought about Rene locked in Finklestein's office on the fourth floor. There was no way in hell he was heading back up there.

Should've just fucking lied and said I killed three! he thought. *We'd be on our way already.* He picked up the cooler off the floor. *Nah, a deal's a deal.*

"Oh, shit, Father Fletcher?" Nate said.

Nate stood looking into one of the ICU rooms. The men huddled around and peered inside.

The priest was laid up in a bad way. He looked like he'd been in a train wreck, but his heartbeat continued with the assistance of the machines.

"I'ma have a few new shits to confess to you once you're back on the level," Nate said.

"Man, why not smoke his ass?" Big Vern asked, raising the gun. "That's a easy come up."

"Yo yo yo, chill," Nate said. "That's a fuckin' holy man. You crazy?"

"Hey!" James yelled. "The fuck are we standing around here for? We need to get this last one in and get the hell out of here!"

"He's right," Big Vern said. He looked at Diego. His mask was still ripped open, and most of his face was stained with gore. He was a total mess. "Man, you better fuckin' hold it together."

"I'll handle him," James said. "Let's just get to the stairs and we can pick one more off on the way out."

"We takin' the elevator," Big Vern said.

"What?" James shook his head. "Why? That's fucking dumb, we don't even—"

"Because I fuckin' said so!" Big Vern yelled. He pointed to the cooler. "You got what you came for already. Now we callin' the shots." He elbowed Nate. "Let's go."

"Aight, Father, I'ma say a Hail Mary for you," Nate said.

Big Vern narrowed his eyes at James. "Now, show us the way."

THE ELEVATOR

When the elevator doors closed, Big Vern and Nate stood behind James and Diego. Big Vern slowly turned to Nate and nodded. "Now!"

Each of the men drove their gun handles into the back of the man in front of them. Diego hit the ground, out cold, but Nate followed up with a couple more strikes, causing a lump to swell on his noggin.

"Fuckin' gwizzies is useless!" Nate yelled, continuing to throttle him.

James wasn't out cold, but Big Vern had rocked him enough that he looked like putty. But that wasn't the only thing he felt. As he heard a metallic clicking noise, James realized that his hand had been cuffed.

"Relax," Big Vern said to Nate. "Don't kill the nigga, we might need 'em on the way out."

When Nate stopped pistol-whipping Diego, James noticed the other side of the restraint. It went behind the steel handrail inside the elevator and had been tightened around Diego's limp wrist. Blood poured from the crack in his head and saturated his frayed ski mask.

"What the fuck is this?" James asked. His speech was slurred and groggy.

"This is business," Big Vern said. "Don't worry, we still gonna hold up our end of the bargain."

Ding! The elevator started to descend. The only problem was neither Big Vern nor Nate had hit a button.

James reached out and was able to get his fingers around the handle of the cooler and pull it toward his body. He would protect the heart with his life.

"Be ready!" Big Vern said, pointing to the side door on the elevator. "You take that one, and I'll cover this one."

"If you're planning on keeping your word, then what the fuck is—"

Big Vern reached back and smacked James in the mouth with his burner. As a wide gash spread across James' lip, he could taste the blood on this tongue.

"Stay quiet!" Big Vern said.

As the elevator came to a stop on the second floor, James watched the doors with fear and anticipation. When the steel parted at the main entrance, the back of a black man's head with twisty braids bobbed. His clothing and body were dirty, and he scratched at his arms and crotch in unison like he wanted to peel his skin off them.

"Fuckin' shit better make it stop burnin' when I piss," the man yelled. "If I gotta come back here again, there's gonna be problems, man."

When he turned around holding the prescription paper, his tough guy act melted away.

"Ray Ray?" Big Vern uttered. He was calm, but James picked up on the mixture of anger and excitement in his tone. "Just the nigga we wanted to see."

"Aww shit," Ray Ray said.

"Yeah, thanks again for the hot tip," Nate said, leveling the gun. "Got a couple for you now."

When Ray Ray tried to turn away from the elevator and run, Big Vern and Nate simultaneously unloaded. A barrage of bullets froze Ray Ray momentarily as they tore deep tunnels of violence throughout his body.

The scream of a nurse could be heard down the hall, but Big Vern paid her no attention. He looked back at Nate. "Hit it."

"You… you sure, man?" Nate asked.

"It's the only way," Big Vern replied solemnly.

James' eyes drifted over to Nate's finger as it pushed the control near the smaller door in front of him. Beside the white circular button was the label: Maternity Ward.

"This city's full a death, but they can't stop folks from fuckin'," Big Vern continued. "That might just be what saves our asses."

"Wait, you—you just fucking killed him!" James said. "That's ten! The gig is up!"

"That'd be true if ten was what we came for," Big Vern said. "But I'm afraid we're just getting' started, partna."

"No!" James screamed as the elevator slowed. "They're just fuckin' kids! Babies!"

Big Vern looked back at him. "We gotta handle business. But don't worry, when we're finished, we'll cut you loose. A deal's a deal."

When the doors came open, James could see several nurses huddled together talking beside a pregnant woman in a hospital gown who was hugging an older man. It was a picture-perfect image… before it was torn apart by a hail of gunfire.

DEATH BEFORE LIFE

James listened to their screams of terror, the pitch cutting lower and lower. As the gunfire continued to erupt, James listened to the chorus get killed off.

The door had closed, but the elevator hadn't moved. He looked at Diego—he was still incapacitated from the stiff beating. The blood had stopped raining over his face, but he was motionless. He would be of much greater use if he was conscious.

Fuck... at least he's still alive, James thought.

A sickness was marinating inside James. He knew he was responsible for the deaths of the laborers. And if Diego died, he'd be responsible for his death too. It wasn't like he wasn't prepared to sacrifice his purity to achieve his goal—he'd done that before—but it was never something he felt good about.

Another blood-curdling scream ripped off, only to be instantly snuffed out by the gunfire. How far were they planning to go? He couldn't help but think of the babies. An image of Eli as a baby flashed in his mind.

Don't got time to think. I've gotta stop them!

Nate had stripped Diego of his revolver and stolen it, but the sawed-off was too awkward for Big Vern to take along with his TECs and remained in the corner of the elevator. James still had a pocketful of shells in his bloody coat, but they were of little use—the gun was too far for him to get his hands on.

Think! Think!

The idea struck him out of nowhere. In such a situation, his biggest disadvantage in life was suddenly an advantage. But as he unbuckled his belt and started to slide his pants off, the elevator door opened.

With one blood-drenched hand over her crimson stomach, the soon-to-be mother fell to her knees. She gagged on the gore oozing from her mouth, trying to apply pressure to the cluster of gunshot wounds on her belly before losing the ability. Her shocked body landed sideways in the path of the elevator door.

"Jesus fucking Christ!" James cried.

The door tried to close but, instead, just pressed firmly against her blown apart belly before retreating when it finally realized there was an obstruction. The elevator door continued to attempt closure over and over, repeatedly juicing the shot woman's womb.

As James finished taking off his pants, he couldn't help but look away from the dying woman. Once he got his prosthetic exposed, he unstrapped the faux limb from his nub. After removing the shoe, James flattened out his thumb against the steel wall and angled the heel of the fake foot at his joint. He bit down on his lip and jammed the hard plastic into his finger.

He tried to subdue his moans of agony, but as James repeatedly struck himself, they grew louder than the maddening sound of the door. Still, the screams of the horrified nurses and patients that Nate and Big Vern had forced around the corner of the hall overshadowed anything else.

Crack!

The sound of James' thumb bone breaking echoed in his ears. Whimpering in pain, he tugged his limb, maneuvering the destroyed finger to the side of his hand. He put the toes of his prosthetic leg into his mouth and bit down as he savagely yanked. After several more attempts, his hand was finally able to slip free from the cuff.

As the gunshots continued to rip off, James scrambled to get his leg back on. He knew there wasn't enough time for his pants and moved on to the sawed-off. Hands trembling, he loaded the barrels. He looked back at the heart in the small cooler, then to the dead woman in the doorway.

As long as she's there, this elevator isn't moving.

He still didn't feel comfortable leaving the cooler inside, but there was no way for him to keep it with him and fire a gun at the same time. Diego was still knocked out, so he was of little help. He picked up the cooler and set it just outside the elevator door. But once he broke the threshold, it felt like James' stomach filled with lava.

The lights cut out.

"Fuck, just what I need," James mumbled.

Along with the lights, it seemed like the screaming and gunfire had cut out too. The red emergency lighting basked the hallways, making the metaphor that James saw the hospital for come to life.

This is Hell.

The simultaneous silence and darkness triggered a grave feeling in his belly as doubt crept into his mind.

Damn it, am I too late? Either way, I have to know.

James started to stagger down the hall in his tighty-whities, the blood-soaked doctor's coat flapping at his sides. The bullet-riddled bodies of several dead patients and hospital workers lined the corridor. James looked into the room beside him, where a pregnant woman's body lay in front of an examination table, blown to bits and oozing rivers of crimson. Each subsequent room he passed had the doors shot up or kicked in and held a slightly differing arrangement of extreme violence.

As he approached the corner, there was a sign that read *Neonatal Intensive Care Unit.* Due to the city's overwhelming dependence on Lobotozine, more and more babies were being born with complex health issues. But as James drew closer to the dozens of bassinets, it was clear the problems were far more serious than when he'd first become aware of the issue.

"Why *I* gotta do it?!" Nate yelled. "I always gotta do all the fucked-up shit! Why can't we just get the fuckin' gwizzie to do it? Ain't none of them niggas done shit yet!"

Big Vern crinkled his face like it was hard to swallow his stupidity. "Oh, you mean the mutha fucka whose ass you beat senseless? After what you done to him, he might never wake up!"

"What's the count up to?" Nate asked.

"Nineteen," Big Vern said.

"Nigga, if you think I'ma shoot thirty-one babies myself, you crazy!"

Big Vern looked down sheepishly. "I-I can't shoot no baby."

"Man, how you know until you tried? Here, let's take it slow. I'll do one, then you do one." Nate raised his gun, angling it down into the bassinet.

Fire exploded from the tip of James' sawed-off. He'd tried his best to keep his arm steady and shot high. But his hands weren't what they once had been. While his intention wasn't to kill a kid, as Nate's blood sprayed into the bassinet, causing the baby to cry, he couldn't be sure if he had. Nate held himself up, trying to turn around and elevate his gun, while Big Vern hit the floor and took cover.

James let off the second shot, turning Nate's face into cherry pie filling.

"Fuck," James mumbled, using his busted hand to try and retrieve more shells from his pocket.

Big Vern popped up over the shrieking infants and let the TECs unload.

James fell backward and lost the grip on the shotgun.

He'd avoided the bullets—but not for long if he didn't move his ass. As he found his footing and staggered forward with his bum leg, he heard Big Vern inserting fresh magazines. Before James could make the corner, the shots rang out again.

He didn't get lucky like the last time he'd been shot—instead of his prosthetic being damaged, it was his flesh. Two bullets blew through his thigh and another into the small of his back. James cried out as his blood painted the floor. He used a hospital bed in the hallway to pull himself around the corner before bridging himself up against the wall. As he struggled onward, he finally made it back to the elevator. He collapsed, landing on the ground several yards away from the cooler.

When he hit the floor, he couldn't feel his leg. He was devastated. James was thinking outside of his own personal wellbeing—about the heart and tight time limit associated with it. A few strides now felt like a marathon to his bleeding body.

"Fuck!" he cried, pounding his fist into the ground.

He dragged himself forward. Why he wanted to be close to the heart, he didn't know. Maybe because it symbolized hope. He still wanted to protect it. Protecting the organ was like he was protecting Eli. When his body slowed, James realized that he no longer harbored enough energy to reach it. He winced in pain, rolling onto his side, and stared up at the ventilation duct defeatedly.

As if it mattered anyway.

"You mutha fucka!" Big Vern yelled. "We had a fuckin' deal!" He walked up to James and aimed the TEC at his forehead.

James looked like hell. His breathing was labored. "I didn't agree to an infant genocide. I'm not *that* selfish."

Big Vern shook his head in disgust. But before he could respond with words or action, the ventilation grid above flew open. A scrawny man in an overcoat and raggedy pants descended on him. The lengthy fillet knife glimmered in the emergency lighting of the hospital—the blade was almost as filthy as him.

He came…

"Ahhh!" Big Vern yelled. "The fuck—"

James thought back to the phone call he'd made at his house as he watched the gaping slash open up Big Vern's knuckles, cutting down to the bone and severing several of his digits. As the TEC-9 hit the ground and slid away, the big man reached for the other tucked inside his waistband. But before he could grab it, the long blade disappeared in his massive gut.

As James stared into the black eyes below his disheveled hair, he remembered the man once had a name. But that was no longer the case. He was now only a headline. A creator of morbid exhibits with an often vibrant and always violent approach. Now, he was known only by the name the media had branded him with: The Artist.

Jerking the knife up, the carnal slit released what looked like twice the entrails of a normal man. As Big Vern screamed, The Artist ripped the knife out of his midsection and, with the swiftness of a swordsman, drove the tip into his face several times over.

Big Vern fell back, belly open wide as a window. When the intestines oozed out, accompanied by a wave of crimson sludge, The Artist bent over and plucked the blade from his head. Returning his gaze to James, The Artist squinted, examining the blood-soaked attire.

"Playing doctor again, are we?" The Artist asked. "This reminds me of the good ole days."

James' eyes grew wide as he lay helpless. He watched The Artist walk to the cooler and pick it up.

"I suppose this is it?" The Artist asked. "What you've worked so hard for?" He moved the bloody blade, gesturing to the various corpses that littered the room. "How you've twisted your reasoning to justify the deaths of these people, not to mention the ones before them…"

James subtly shook his head, knowing The Artist had

done exactly the same in his work. But it was no time for a debate. Time was running out.

"Please," James whispered. "You're the only one who can save him. I beg of you."

The Artist set the cooler down, popped off the lid, and looked inside.

"What are you doing?!" James yelled, suddenly coming back to life.

The Artist lifted the slimy organ up in his palm, looking down upon it with deep adoration—and also disgust. "It's only fitting. After all, you did the same to mine."

"Noooooo!" James yelled.

The Artist stabbed the blade into the heart—it was like a voodoo doll absorbing a thousand pinpricks. Except the tip of the fillet knife opened far wider holes. So many that when The Artist held up the face of the organ in James' direction, it looked like an oozing cheese grater.

"Why?" James wailed.

The Artist squeezed the heart as if the question was the ideal fuel for his rage. The countless holes bled a mixture of ruby and translucent fluid like a rash of pimples puking in unison.

The Artist squinted his eyes, which somehow grew blacker. "This is called reciprocation. And it's *long* overdue."

James tried to think. The extreme agony from his broken thumb, smashed cranium, and the gunshot wounds clouded his brain. But when he closed his eyes and pictured Eli's face, the words finally came.

"By that logic, as of right now, we're even!" James yelled. "But why leave this place such a mess without a purpose." James' bottom lip quivered. "Please, give us a purpose—give *me* a purpose."

The Artist watched on as James winced in pain, peeling off his blood-soaked shirt and the doctor's coat. "I offer you mine. Your materials are here." He tapped his chest. "Just promise me you'll put it inside Eli. He has nothing to do with what happened between us."

The Artist stood, looking down at him, contemplating and digesting all James had laid out. "Even if I could, the equipment that would be required would be imposs—"

"It's all at my house," James interrupted. "I swear to you. Piece by piece, I built it over time—it was my life's work. Everything you need is waiting."

It seemed The Artist was seriously considering the idea.

James put his hands together. "Just think of it: the transfer of a sinful heart into an innocent body. It could be your most profound exhibit yet—"

The Artist raised the blade at James' face. "You don't tell me about *my* exhibits! They are to transmit *my* messages, not yours! Understood?"

James hung his head. "Of course. I-I apologize. That was foolish of me to say."

"As foolish as it was, you do have a point," The Artist said. "It would be a shame to waste such extraordinary materials, and not to mention… circumstances."

The Artist removed a mini cassette player, pressed the record button, and set it on the ground.

James laid back, tears streaming from his face and exhaustion setting in. As he prepared himself for the pain, he tried to see the positives. But when The Artist grinned and reached into his overcoat, the outline of the rib cutters filled his entire body with dread.

THE ARTIST

The Artist set the still beating heart inside the cooler and sealed it shut. Looking at the chasm of butchered humanity inside James' quaking torso was a relief. Such ecstasies couldn't be explained with mere words. He hadn't even planned on making an exhibit that evening, but when it came to collaboration, even he wasn't a total narcissist.

Best idea wins, The Artist thought.

The sound of a baby crying startled him. He looked over at the corpse of the pregnant woman laid inside the doorway of the elevator. As the door continued to open and close, each time, it rammed into her wounded stomach. Finally, the pressure had squeezed the baby out enough that it had partially made its way out of her cadaver. It looked like something that had been spawned in the inferno. The child's introduction to Earth was the bullet that shot its nose off. As the baby hissed and wailed, The Artist could tell that it was utterly horrified by the idea of life.

I know exactly *what you mean.*

But it wasn't just the infant's expression that drew his attention, it was the expression of the man beyond that mirrored the child's. The man held his bleeding head in a state of confusion. A ripped ski mask pointlessly surrounded his blood-smeared face, the torn center doing nothing to obscure his identity.

"Who are you?" The Artist asked.

"I-I just here to help," Diego stammered.

"Why are you involved in this?"

Diego started to cry. He looked at the baby half stuck in the dead woman. It was as if, to him, the symbology of the event meant even more than the horror. "The man…" Diego pointed at James. "You cut his heart. He come to hardware store, hire me and—and my boss make me come here. I no want to come here!" He slammed his fist against the side of the elevator.

The Artist squinted his eyes. "Settle down, just try to relax."

"These"—he gestured with his hand to the bodies of Big Vern and James—"they want to kill all people. I just trying to earn money for my family…" As he trailed off, his sobs became hysterical.

"Ah, I see," The Artist said. "Some cheap help. Probably thought you were fixing a toilet or something." He glared at James' glistening organs. "You wouldn't be the first he's used… Did he at least have the decency to pay you?"

Diego shook his head.

The Artist furrowed his brow. He looked at James and remembered his pants were missing. Then he eyed the pair on the floor of the elevator.

As The Artist approached, Diego held his hands up, continuing to gush tears. "Please, I-I help you instead now! Please don't kill me!"

The Artist squatted down and ran through the pockets of the pants. He found a wallet with a lone hundred-dollar bill inside. The Artist stared at Benjamin's disgusting exterior, hating everything it represented but, at the same time, understanding what it represented was a necessary evil.

"Looks like he was holding out on you," The Artist said,

extending Benjamin toward Diego. "Go on, it's the least you deserve."

Diego hesitantly reached out, snatched Benjamin, and pushed the bill into his pocket. "Gracias." The tears continued to trickle down his cheeks.

"You know, I'm reconsidering your suggestion," The Artist said. "For a procedure the magnitude of what our friend is asking,"—he tapped the cooler—"I could in fact use some assistance."

Diego's eyes widened with dread.

The Artist grinned. "Another pair of hands is exactly what I'll need."

THE UNITED STATES OF AMERICA
C 00630261 *
100

PART 4: UNDERGROUND CULTURE

NOTHING TO FEAR

Diego burst through the hospital doors, finally ripping the useless mask off and tossing it into some bushes lining the hospital's entrance. He cradled the bleeding, red bump on his head as it throbbed, grimacing from the searing pain that tunneled through his skull.

The Artist strode away, his movements almost cat-like, fluid and smooth. The cooler with the fresh heart inside was clasped in one hand—holding it firm so it wouldn't swing—his long filet knife, dripping fresh blood, in the other. Diego watched him go, knowing he was expected to follow.

While he didn't have the firmest grasp on the English language, Diego was able to put two and two together when James had his exchange with the man. He didn't want to attach himself to James—but he didn't want to end up like him either. Offering to assist this killer felt like he'd made a deal with The Devil.

Despite his fear of the bloody man in the overcoat, he wondered if he could dash back into the hospital, pull an alarm, and somehow avoid being murdered while he waited for the cops to arrive. He could plead his case, explain that this whole thing was a mistake and that he got suckered into it—that he was an innocent man. Surely, they would understand that he was just as much a victim as the rest of the people lying dead inside.

But he knew better. If he could somehow avoid being stabbed to death like the gun-wielding fat man, he knew the police would see him as a criminal on sight. He wouldn't even have the chance to defend himself.

Not that the cops would show up soon anyway. Even with a screaming alarm and a building full of dead bodies…

When this was all done, he wondered if this killer would just let him walk away. Diego would do what the man required of him, ask no questions, and then go back to his original plan: work hard, make enough money to pay Miguel, and hope his boss would stay true to his word.

Maybe he will finally tell me something. Anything for just a glimmer of hope.

Diego doubted it. This city, from what he'd seen, wasn't a hub for honesty and honor. He had already paid Miguel thousands over the past nine months, working job after job, keeping just enough to minimize his hunger pangs.

The Artist stared at him from across the street. Sweat and fresh blood were soaked into his overcoat, glistening on his chest—rising and falling as he breathed—that long knife still in his hand, its chrome surface no longer visible under the layers of blood.

Crimson fingerprints striped the cooler, reminding Diego of the grisly scene he'd witnessed. The sound the knife made as it cut into James' sternum and split him open.

But there was no animosity there, at least as far as Diego could tell. Though admittedly, this man was impossible to read. Seemingly devoid of all human emotion. Even when he killed, he seemed more fascinated than thrilled.

"Don't be afraid," The Artist said, his voice calm and nonchalant. He cocked his head to the side like a curious dog as he studied Diego, his eyes black and intense. "You have no reason to fear me—what is your name?"

"Uh… Diego… And you?"

"I have no name. The media labeled me The Artist, and while accurate, if you ask me, that's a gross oversimplification."

Diego had worked so hard when he'd entered the country. His accent remained, but out of all the guys who hung around the parking lot of Home Hardware looking for work, he was one of the more well-spoken. Initially, he'd thought that reading English would be a great asset, but he quickly learned it more so served as a mechanism for fear. Right when he started reading the headlines, that much became obvious.

He'd seen and heard that name all over the city: The Artist. The notorious killer who dominated the newspaper headlines and who he'd seen reports about on television—he couldn't fully understand it all, but he was able to get the gist of it. It was a name muttered from the mouths of the citizens, regardless of class or social status. In a city where fear was the currency, all were united by their fear of The Artist.

"Follow me, Diego." He smiled, but it looked more like the snarl of a predator than a genuine human grin. "I'm in an uncharacteristically generous mood. Consider that you're the first person—outside of me—to ever exit an exhibit alive. Consider yourself fortunate, but don't press your luck. We've got four hours tops before this heart is useless. So please… follow me."

Diego had one last thought of making a run for it, but the next thing he knew, he was crossing the street. The madman would've likely run him down and slit his throat. He hugged himself as he moved in, feeling like a bunny rabbit in a forest full of grizzlies.

Diego tried to look the man in the eyes, but the intensity staring back at him made him avert his gaze. It was like staring directly into a solar eclipse. The Artist only grinned and sheathed his knife.

Trying to keep loose, Diego followed the strange man into a dark alley between two abandoned buildings. Stray cats and rodents scattered as they strode into the shadows.

Diego's mind was full of questions, but he held them back as he watched The Artist kneel beside a rusty manhole cover. The man ran his fingers across the etchings on the thick metal surface as if petting it, letting it know that he was a friend. The cooler sat beside him. A rat snuck out of the shadows and darted straight for the ice box, sniffing it and licking the bloody prints before scurrying away, as if sensing The Artist's dominant presence.

The same presence that kept Diego rooted to his spot—he envied the rat for running away while it still had a chance.

And then The Artist's intense eyes darted up and landed on Diego. Once again studying him, sizing him up. He was reading him like an instruction booklet, sniffing the air like a hungry animal.

His fingernails made a scraping sound as they stroked the sewer lid. "You still worry I'm leading you to your death."

"I… I read about you," Diego said, shoving his hands into his pockets to hide how violently they shook. "I see what they say on the news. In the hospital… I see what you do… Sí, I'm scared of you. Everyone is."

The Artist rose to his feet and tilted his head again, those eyes holding Diego in place like pins in a butterfly. "Diego, my new friend. Please take no offense to this, but the reason you have nothing to fear is simple. Your death would be meaningless. You aren't comprised of the proper…"—he used his fingers and gently brushed them against Diego's brown skin—"materials to warrant a new exhibit. I choose my materials *very* carefully."

Diego thought about his words. The man before him wasn't a killer who murdered chaotically, choosing random victims. This was a methodical murder machine who killed to make statements.

I'm a dog in his eyes—not important enough to be a statement.

"However," The Artist said as his eyes somehow intensified, as if they had their own gravitational pull. A sharp, predatory smile crept back across his mouth, and he tilted his head to the other side. "It could be interesting, couldn't it? To highlight a person who is invisible to the citizens of this city. To emphasize such… insignificance. To show them the beauty and complexity of those they ignore. Just imagine what that could mean for others in your shoes. Your death would not only elevate you but all the others like you. Your death could spark a revolution."

Diego felt like butter in a microwave under The Artist's stare. Melting into the grimy alley, becoming one with the sludge that glazed the ground around him. His innards felt like they were churning in his stomach, like dirty clothes spinning in a washing machine. He tried to breathe, but his throat seemed to pinch shut, his own fear evaporating the oxygen around him.

"But like I said before," The Artist said as he straightened his head, his smile fading back into a straight line. He reached down and picked up the cooler, holding it against his chest as if trying to feel the heartbeat. "I'm in a particularly good mood. And I give you my word. You have no reason to fear me. Now, let's move."

Diego smiled and nodded, though he struggled to calm his nerves. Still had to take strained, shallow breaths, his fists tightening into petrified chunks of wood at his sides. His pulse blasted in his ears like hurricane thunder.

The Artist reached toward the belts strapped across his stomach, lined with knives, vials of liquid, and other tools of various size and purpose—what appeared to be a gas mask hung from his hip, the reflective surface of the eyes sparkling like that of a giant insect. He pulled out a small rod, like a miniature crowbar, and shoved it into the opening on the sewer lid. Propping it open, he slid the heavy cover aside.

"The work we are about to do…" The Artist said as he sheathed the rod. He held out the cooler with the fresh heart inside like grim treasure. "Is very meaningful to me. I trust you'll give me your best effort."

Struggling to understand exactly what the man was saying, Diego forced an enthusiastic nod. That seemed to satisfy The Artist, who nodded back, smirking ever so slightly.

Glaring across at Diego with his dark, burning eyes, he clamped the handle of the cooler in his teeth and started to climb down, expertly descending the slippery metal ladder, clearly familiar with every rung. After a moment, he was gone—swallowed up by the mouth of the manhole.

Diego listened and heard a faint splash as The Artist reached the bottom. He approached the sewer, finally able to breathe normal again, trying to stay centered and in control. He hesitated, but when he looked up into the backstreet and saw all the red and yellow eyes of the alleyway creatures starting to close in, he planted his feet on the ladder rungs and climbed down.

"Don't be rude," The Artist's voice echoed. "I wouldn't leave the door to your house open. Pull the cover over."

Diego did as he was told. He was fortunate that many jobs left his arms toned and strong. Muscling over the manhole cover, he sealed himself in with the darkness.

The air was humid and moist, thick with the odor of human waste and standing water, with a pinch of rot. Diego held his breath as he climbed past half a dozen scurrying cockroaches, each one big enough to strap a saddle to.

The brick walls were wet and beaded with moisture like sweating skin. The sound of dripping water surrounded him as he reached the bottom of the ladder, being careful where he stepped as he lowered himself down to the ledge beside the river of gray water.

Diego watched in disgust, pulling up the collar of his shirt to cover his nose and mouth, as a dead, puffy cat floated past him, surrounded by chunks of feces and a cornucopia of garbage. The scuttle of verminous legs seemed to come from every direction.

The Artist stood a few feet ahead, waiting patiently. The main corridor of the sewer seemed to stretch on forever in both directions, countless tunnels branching off every twenty yards or so, leading to various areas around the city.

"This way," The Artist said, his face mostly cloaked in shadow. Everything but those eyes seemed to shine. "And steady those hands. We're going to need them."

The Artist strolled down the corridor, ignoring all the filth and waste around him. This was clearly his domain.

Diego had no choice but to follow.

THE SEWERS

Diego stayed a few steps behind The Artist as they walked through the tunnel. While it felt aimless to Diego, he could tell The Artist moved with purpose. He seemed to know exactly where they were going.

Something splashed from the river of waste, somewhere behind them. It was a good distance back but still too close for comfort. Whatever it was sounded far larger than any rat. Diego spun in place, both of his fists up in front of him. Across the tunnel, about twenty yards away, he saw ripples fan across the filthy water. A pair of twin orbs glowed yellow before they dunked into the liquid and disappeared.

"Hijo de puta…" Diego backed away, his eyes scanning the murky water, the surface littered with waste floating between the islands of trash.

The Artist patted Diego on the back, showing the confidence of a man who didn't fear death, who knew he reigned supreme in these sewers and no creature, large or small, would dare cross him. The sudden contact made Diego yelp and jump, causing him to nearly fall into the water. But The Artist caught him just in time and pulled him to safety.

"We've really got to do something about that, don't we?" The Artist said.

"About… about what?" Diego asked.

"That pesky fear of yours." He smirked, continuing through the sewer.

Diego followed, but The Artist's words did nothing to quell his fright. And he knew it was useless to lie about it or try to hide it. The Artist, the mightiest monster of all, would be able to sniff it out.

"Can I ask?" Diego said tentatively as they turned down a tunnel branching off the main corridor. "They call you Artist because… how you do your killings?"

The Artist glanced over his shoulder at Diego, a look in his eye that made Diego's heart immediately start racing. He kept walking as he spoke, his voice calm and smooth.

"Art is far more than what you simply see, Diego. Art is experienced through all of our senses. The sounds and smells… the flavors and textures. Like a symphony, each sense is a different instrument, all working together to create a single message. To make the audience feel something they may not have known they had the capacity to feel. To think in a way they'd never even considered. Do you understand?"

Diego's defenses were alerted by the monotone, emotionless tenor of The Artist's voice. The sound of someone without a soul, of someone incapable of empathy. It put Diego on edge, and he knew The Artist could sense his anxiety like a mist of cologne in his face.

Though Diego struggled to follow along with what The Artist was saying, he understood enough to get the gist of it. He remembered what he'd seen and heard in the media about The Artist, the way he displayed his victims like art installations. Exhibits created for all to experience, each scene meticulously designed to convey The Artist's specific message, many of which were argued over by people with varying interpretations.

"They call me The Artist for obvious reasons, but

even I am regularly surprised by the way art will show itself when I least expect it. Regardless of my intentions, art has a way of revealing the truth. You just have to learn how to look for it, how to be open to it. Art bends its audience to its will, and to resist that is to deny the deepest meanings of our existence. I am The Artist, but my purpose is not to create art. My purpose is to recognize the art around me and arrange it in such a way that allows others to see it for themselves."

Diego thought back to the hospital. The way The Artist carved up the fat man. The way he expertly split James' chest open and removed the heart—the way it continued to beat in his hands as he delicately placed it into the cooler.

The wound on Diego's head started to throb, the pain taking his mind back to the elevator where he'd been pistol-whipped. To the moment that pregnant woman got pulverized by the doors. Her bulbous belly smashed again and again until her noseless baby oozed out from between her legs.

Estela, wherever you are, I'll find you, Diego thought. *I swear it. No matter what it takes. I will bring you and our baby home.*

Before taking his last job, Diego had spent days posting up flyers around the city, hoping some empathetic citizen would see Estela's photo and the detail about her being pregnant, and provide some kind of information that might point Diego in the right direction.

Though he was stuck helping The Artist, Diego remained filled with a searing urgency to find his family, the entire reason he started working for Miguel in the first place. The reason he was willing to do the kind of job James hired him for.

"Tonight… I was not motivated by artistic expression," The Artist continued. "What brought me to the hospital was far more… personal. The carnage I found inside was as much a surprise to me as it seemed to be to you. Purely coincidental, though I will admit, such a strong smell of blood in the air may have amplified my already violent intentions."

Diego wasn't sure where they were going or what was in store for him, but he wondered if he could get on The Artist's good side, if he even had one. He wondered if he might be able to convince this madman to help him. If anyone had the means of helping locate his kidnapped wife, it seemed it was The Artist. Diego had nobody else he could turn to.

But Diego wanted to try and understand him more. He wanted to see if—like James had done—he could find some sign of a heart and soul inside him.

"The man who hire me," Diego said, the still-bleeding wound on his head forgotten as he closed the distance between him and The Artist. "You knew him… no? You come to hospital to kill this man?"

"I did not intend to kill him, per se. I intended to make a statement, yes, but a statement not meant for public consumption. A statement just for him… to set in motion a series of events that would eventually cause him so much pain that he would wish for death. I knew what he was up to when he went into that hospital—he explained it to me. I assumed he only brought those other two heathens, along with you and your constituents, as a distraction so that he could accomplish his personal goal."

The Artist snickered as he thought about it, making Diego doubt that this man was capable of any kind of human emotion he could manipulate into helping him.

"Knowing James, I knew the moment I stepped foot in that hospital that his plan had gone awry. James was no saint by any means, had plenty of blood on his hands. But he was no homicidal maniac either. I can imagine how enraged he must have been when he saw the mess those animals had caused. I must admit, watching him work, putting his hands to use again, awoke a sense of nostalgia in me. So strong I nearly forgot my own agenda."

"It was the heart," Diego said, remembering the way The Artist had pierced it, squeezing the blood from it like juice from an orange. "The heart he took from doctors? I don't understand—"

"Perhaps it would be easier for me to start at the beginning," The Artist said, pausing momentarily as a horde of rats scurried past their feet.

Diego wanted to tell him there was no time for this, no time to reminisce about the past. He wanted to get whatever this job was over with so he could get back to his own mission. A mission he may already be too late to accomplish.

"I was born in filth… tossed into the trash by my mother and left for dead. The dumpster was my crib and cradle, the rats were my wet nurses." He watched the vermin disappear into a pipe, the look of longing in his eyes transforming into rage. "The man who found me, who called that alleyway home, took me and used me for his own sadistic pleasures. He kept me. For years he tortured me, from infancy to my adolescence. If he was an artist, then pain and suffering were his medium and I was his canvas. And his color palette consisted of only shades of reds and browns… with a splash of white."

Diego, for the first time, saw pain in The Artist. The human emotion gave him a slice of hope. If he was capable of being traumatized, perhaps he was capable of empathy.

"I had a darkness inside of me. I don't know if I was born with it or if a lifetime of torture and neglect injected it into me, but it became less and less possible to ignore. It spoke to me. It watched over me. It controlled me. I needed to let it out… I needed subjects. And as the man who'd lifted me from the garbage heap and crowned himself my father grew more vicious and insatiable, my rage swelled."

The Artist narrowed his eyes, a small smirk hooking the corner of his mouth.

"The darkness told me to stop letting him prey on me, and every night as he did, I grew less timid about turning the tables on him. I found a piece of metal, a shard that came off the very dumpster where I spent my first moments of life. And every night, I sharpened it, scraping it against the concrete. Thinning that edge more and more. But the night I finally found the courage to go through with it, the night I finally got that metal sharp enough… I met my mentor. The man who I would consider my *true* father…"

The Artist turned away and stared at the sewer wall as if he could see his past projected onto the slimy bricks. The way he stared made Diego feel like a ghost, an invisible spectator. The Artist was in his own world, just him and his memories.

"Your mentor… your father," Diego said, his voice seeming to startle The Artist a bit, reminding him of his presence. "This was James, no? The man who hire me… the man who—"

"The night my darkness took over, I held my first knife in hand. Squeezed so tightly it cut into my palm, but I welcomed the pain. That pain symbolized my last night as a victim, my last night allowing others to cause me harm. My time in that alley, my time in the city, I paid attention. I watched the comings and goings, witnessed the atrocities the citizens were capable of. I knew then that they needed a wakeup call, they needed a lesson. And I wanted to be their educator."

When he pulled one of his knives from its sheath and ran the edge over his fingers, Diego tensed up. Having nowhere to run, he just stood there and listened.

"I watched the monster who raised me, waiting for my moment. He rummaged through the dumpster, taking bites of rotting garbage and letting the juice run down his chin. I stalked him from behind, leaving a trail of my blood behind me as I squeezed my knife harder. And then… the ground opened up and swallowed him whole. Like a throat in the concrete. His scream echoed from below as he was dragged away… and so I followed."

The sewers… Diego thought, taking a slight step back when The Artist turned his head and glared at him, his eyes deep and showing that darkness living inside of him.

"I walked through the tunnels, following the screams. I hid in the dark as I watched my abuser's heart being cut out.

The hands that yanked it free shook uncontrollably. Like the man had an earthquake living inside him. I thought I had been holding back a gasp, but what rolled from my mouth was laughter instead. And when James turned to face me, I expected to see ferocity in his eyes. The bloodlust of a predator. But I saw tears running from those eyes. Not tears of sadness but tears of anguish and frustration. It was in that moment I knew he needed me as much as I needed him. That's when my mentorship began."

The Artist seemed to realize for the first time that they had stopped, and as he continued talking, he began walking down the tunnel. He moved slowly as he spoke, taking calm, deliberate steps as Diego followed close behind.

"James took me under his wing—he showed me how to harness my darkness, use it for a purpose. It might've been *his* purpose, but it was a purpose nonetheless." The Artist had a bit of a tremor in his voice. "I needed to let it out, and he opened my eyes. Our partnership only made sense."

The hospital, Diego thought, doing his best to follow along and put the pieces together. *The heart at the hospital…*

"You see, James was once a well-respected surgeon in this city. He worked at the very same hospital where he just spent his final moments. A neurological condition took his hands from him, caused them to shake uncontrollably. Losing his position at the hospital was a blow, but his faulty nervous system took something far more valuable."

The Artist turned and faced Diego. Locked eyes with him, freezing him in place with the intensity. "James' child, his true blood son, was born with a heart disease. A disease that would eventually require a transplant. A transplant that James could have easily performed… before his hands betrayed him. And so he did what he had to. He practiced with the faulty hands God left him with."

Diego's vision started to blur around the edges, his head injury throbbing harder than ever, begging to be addressed. He stumbled a bit but caught himself, then rubbed his fists over his eyes to clear the cobwebs. "James was a father?"

"He chose his *patients* carefully. The dregs of the city that wouldn't be missed, they would serve as practice. But, despite gathering all the required equipment over time, his hands only got worse, and so rather than wasting time practicing with his faulty fingers, he pivoted his efforts into training me instead. He taught me how to sharpen my darkness the way I sharpened my knife. Until my hands were more precise than his ever were."

Diego felt his eyes gloss over and a stinging sensation in his nose as he struggled with his emotions. "He wanted to help his child. I understand. My wife... my baby, they—"

"After a time, he became far more than a mentor to me. And he reciprocated that feeling, told me that he saw me as a second son. We were connected by blood, but not the blood in our veins... the blood we spilled together."

The Artist narrowed his eyes, the memory prodding at his core. He stopped, taking hold of the rungs.

"But as my skill grew, I saw less and less of James. And so when he began to neglect me, I grew resentful. Resentful that he was spending more time with his other son, the entire reason he taught me his trade in the first place. Resentful that he seemed to be spending all of his time planning the heist of the organ he coveted. Without that comradery we once had, I found myself turning to the only companion I ever knew. And my darkness was waiting for me with open arms. It started speaking to me, telling me I could do more with my skills. Telling me that James was only thinking selfishly. It reminded me that the city needed to see itself for what it was. It was then that The Artist was truly born."

"The heart was for his boy, and you destroy it?"

The Artist answered by looking away from Diego, staring up toward the closed manhole above the ladder.

"So now you must help—"

"No more talking," The Artist said, his voice going back to that soulless monotone pitch. "It's time to get to work."

As he started to climb the ladder, a chill ran over the back of Diego's neck. He understood that The Artist was climbing toward the promise he'd made to his mentor just a short time before he'd pulled his heart from his chest.

THE HEARTLESS

Diego stayed in the sewer, his head sticking out from the manhole as he watched The Artist approach the front porch of the house. There was one station wagon parked in the driveway and a beat-up pickup truck beside the curb with a Food Plus bumper sticker on the rear fender.

The blinds were closed on most of the windows facing the street, all but one toward the corner of the house, multicolored lights flashing from between the plastic slats.

The address was in the depths of a low-income area, the houses falling apart and weathered. Junked cars and broken appliances decorated many of the yards. Dogs barked, some glaring at The Artist and Diego from behind chain link fences.

A few people peeked out from windows or watched from their properties—many of them intimidating in their own right, the type of people Diego would cross the street to avoid in his daily life.

Yet as these people caught sight of The Artist, they seemed to sense his alpha energy. Diego doubted any of them knew who The Artist was, at least not by his appearance. He was a mysterious figure—the city's boogeyman. A faceless, formless presence who stalked the citizens. It was doubtful that he was recognizable to anyone in the city.

Yet those who laid eyes on The Artist as he stood in front of the house, studying it with a cocked head, quickly got out of sight, not wanting to draw attention to themselves. Rushing behind closed doors, leaving the Big Bad Wolf to huff and puff in any direction as long as it wasn't toward them. The people didn't fear the obvious savage, they feared the strange and unknown.

He clenched the cooler to his chest, the bloody handprints tattooed to its surface. Diego watched silently, his hands and legs starting to ache from gripping the ladder and holding himself in place. He wanted to call out to The Artist, snap him out of the trance he had fallen into. But he knew better than to interrupt the process this madman was going through. Whatever this was, Diego knew they were there because it was James' final wish.

He might be a killer, but at least he keeps his promises. At least he's a man of his word. Maybe he's the man who can help me.

For the first time since arriving in the city, Diego felt hope swelling in his chest. For the first time, he actually believed he might find his wife and finally reunite with her after so many months apart. But knowing, wherever she was, that she was on the verge of giving birth to their child, he needed more than just hope.

They came to this country for a new start, to build a future for their family, give their child the kind of chance neither of them ever had. They chose the city because it was the only place they could afford, despite all the rumors they had heard about immigrants going missing.

He only hoped she was still alive. Diego prayed that whatever hell she might be experiencing, whatever hardships she'd had to endure, that she and the baby were still healthy. Their lives were full of strife, but they always held their heads up high, always fighting to stay positive, keeping themselves focused on the future they hoped to obtain. And while Diego felt the panic rising in his belly, he tried his best to hold on to that positivity.

That hopeful, optimistic attitude.

Wherever she is, I know she's doing the same. And so I must have hope.

While he'd been telling himself this every day since she'd gone missing, this was the first time he genuinely felt hopeful. Whoever took her, whatever monsters of the city stole her away, he knew that none were as monstrous as The Artist.

He was partnered up with the apex predator. If there was anyone in the city who would be able to help him, this was the man.

The Artist finally turned away from the house and faced Diego. He beckoned him with a finger that seemed long enough to have five joints.

Before climbing out of the manhole, Diego took another look around. There was nobody in sight, not even a single dog. The neighborhood seemed to have gone silent, as if everyone but him and The Artist had disintegrated.

And whoever is inside that house.

After listening to The Artist's words, Diego had a sick feeling that James' family was inside of the home, and Diego silently prayed that he wasn't about to be an accomplice to multiple murders. He didn't imagine this man would go through the trouble of taking such good care of the heart just to kill James' wife and son, but then again, he couldn't even begin to understand the intricacies of a man such as The Artist.

After a calming breath, Diego forced himself out of his hiding spot and onto the street. His eyes darted in every direction as he crossed the road toward the house, not because he wanted to make sure the coast was clear—he was hoping there would be witnesses. Just like the hospital, he felt he was being misled into doing something his wife would find monstrous and morally malevolent.

"Don't worry, Diego," The Artist said as he joined him on the front lawn. As if he could read his thoughts and sense his trepidations. "While I understand your timidness, based on my reputation, not to mention the atrocities you've witnessed today, I can assure you that I am not here to cause harm or to send any kind of message. For once..." He trailed off a moment, a smile creeping across his face. "I am here to help. To save a life, a life I once detested and dreamed of destroying. I am here to fulfill a promise, to honor the only person who ever meant anything to me. The person who sacrificed his heart so that I could discover the existence of my own."

Diego understood most of what The Artist was saying and gave a nod, forcing a smile. He aimed to show him that he, too, was there to make good on a promise.

And if you truly have a soul, you will trade one favor for another. You will help me mend my own broken heart.

"You are a good man," The Artist said as he wrapped an arm around Diego's shoulders and ushered him toward the window with open blinds. "I could tell the moment I saw you handcuffed to that elevator. That gash on your head needs some attention. All the supplies we need should be inside. We'll take care of you first, sound good?"

"You will take care of me?" Diego asked.

"Anything you need. Consider us friends..."

Diego nodded, genuinely hoping The Artist meant it.

"Great," The Artist said with an almost childish grin. "You know, I've never had a friend before. It feels nice."

An awkward silence hung between them a moment before they peeked in through the window.

The colorful lights splashed across their faces in horizontal patterns as they peered into the bedroom. A man who looked to be in his early twenties was propped up in a hospital bed, various tubes snaking from his arms and nose to multiple beeping machines. He looked like some kind of mad scientist's test subject with his sickly skin and sunken eyes. He mashed his chapped lips together as he focused on a video game and the pixelized graphics coming from the tube television sitting across from him. Another wire was stretched taut between the controller in his hand and the bulky console sitting on the shelf just beneath the screen.

He was playing a driving game from the looks of it, some kind of first-person police game. Diego scoffed to himself, thinking about how the policeman in the video game was probably more likely to make an appearance in the city than the actual officers that remained. He watched the sick young man hit the buttons on his controller, choosing between a hospital sign and what looked like a shovel. Just as he selected the hospital sign, the man turned his attention toward the window, squinting with suspicion.

Diego quickly ducked down, but The Artist stayed put, holding his stare, his smile widening.

"It's okay, he can't see us. Just his own sad reflection." The Artist leaned in closer, his breath fogging the glass. "Don't worry, Eli. It will all be better soon."

AN UNEXPECTED VISITOR

As The Artist finished picking the lock and pushing the front door in, the hinges squealed like baby pigs, making Diego wince and brace himself for a confrontation.

But nobody came as they crept their way across the foyer. Diego could hear the noises from the video game coming from Eli's room, what sounded like a mixture of growling and screaming.

But that wasn't the only screaming he heard. The second series of screams didn't come from any game or television speakers. These screams were right there in the house with them—screams of passion.

"Do you hear that?" Diego whispered.

"Oh, Shelly," The Artist said in a tsk-tsk-tsk sort of tone. "You wouldn't dare. Not after everything James has sacrificed. Not with Eli in the other room."

As they neared the screams, there was the unmistakable grunts of a man mixed in. Heavy, labored breathing—the sounds of a man on the verge of climax.

Diego and The Artist stood just outside of the door. The Artist shook his head in disappointment as he spotted the discarded clothing scattered across the floor at their feet. A white, collared shirt had a nametag pinned just above the front pocket: GLENN GAITHER, Food Plus Store Manager.

"What do we do?" Diego asked with a quivering voice full of unease. "Leave and come back when—"

"I'm afraid it's now or never," The Artist said, throwing the bedroom door open as he leaped across the threshold.

Diego was hit with the smell first: shit and sweat.

The mildly obese man stood beside the king-sized bed, naked except for his black tube socks. Not a handsome man, with a balding head and swollen gut, dripping with sweat like a sperm whale pulled freshly from the sea. But his cock was long and thick, and when he pulled it from the gaping asshole of the woman bent over on the bed, Diego could see it had a dog-leg left curve to it.

The woman had her face buried into the mattress, but Glenn's eyes darted frantically between Diego and The Artist, his expression full of fear and surprise while his cock uncontrollably sprayed thick ropes of cum across Shelly's back and buttocks. Shelly's animalistic moans sounded like a donkey in heat as she reacted to the warm streams splashing against her flesh.

Glenn shuddered with orgasm, seemingly against his will, as he covered her ass cheeks with chaotic crisscross patterns like cream cheese frosting atop a couple of warm cinnamon rolls.

"What—what the fuck are you—?!" Glenn asked.

Shelly's shriek cut him off as she finally pulled her face out of the mattress and spotted the two strangers standing in the doorway of her master bedroom. Ignoring the post-coital detritus decorating her backside, she simultaneously covered her breasts and crawled across the bed toward a nightstand. She had the drawer open as Glenn was charging right at Diego, his cock solid and swinging like a Louisville Slugger.

"Now hold on just a minute, Shelly," The Artist said, his voice still somehow calm and collected. "As shocking as this discovery might've been to James, I'm only here to help."

When Shelly turned back toward The Artist, she held a revolver with both hands, no longer concerned with her nakedness. She fired a shot at the same moment Glenn's massive body collided with Diego and speared him into the floor.

The bullet hit the doorframe, just above The Artist's head, but he didn't duck or even flinch. Even as sheetrock dust rained down on him, he remained still and calm as he tried to reason with a panicking Shelly. His only movement was to move the cooler behind his back to protect it from getting shot.

Diego wrestled with Glenn, whose weight pinned him down like an anvil coated in moist blubber. As he rained down hammer blows, Diego doing his best to block them, his cock bounced and thudded against Diego's chest like a judge's gavel. Again and again, demanding order in the court.

Diego tried to get The Artist's attention, tried to beg him for help. But Glenn's weight pressed down on his lungs, and he couldn't get anything but whispered grunts past his lips.

"You don't know me, but I'm an associate of your husband. And he asked me to come here to save your son's—"

"Fuck you, freak!" Shelly roared before firing off the remaining shots until the gun was empty. Most went wide, blasting a framed family photo off the wall, the bullet punching a hole right through a younger James' smiling face, holding a gleeful baby Eli in his arms.

One bullet hit Glenn in the back of the head, splitting his skull. Blood and brains erupted from his cracked cranium and showered down onto Diego, blinding him and filling his mouth with a copper, meaty flavor. He could feel soft morsels between his teeth as he tried to spit and scream, Glenn's body even heavier now that it was dead weight.

"Glenn!" Shelly's shriek blasted through the air as she lowered her gun and stared in shock at what she'd just done. "Noooo!"

Glenn's body had remained upright as the contents of his head emptied themselves all over Diego, but then, as if from the force of Shelly's scream, his body finally tipped over. His slimy chest slammed down hard on Diego's face, reigniting the wound on his forehead while knocking what little wind he had left out of him.

The bulbous body started to spasm, the twitchy, violent movements assaulting Diego, pummeling him as he lay hopeless beneath the dead man.

"Mom?" The voice came from behind them, just outside the bedroom door.

The Artist turned to face Eli, a look of shame and regret on his face as he locked eyes with James' son—like two long-lost brothers meeting for the first time.

"Hello, Eli," The Artist said shyly. "I know you must be confused, but I'm… I'm here to save you."

"You what?!" Eli looked exhausted, on the verge of passing out. He tried to take a step toward The Artist, but his legs wobbled beneath him. And when The Artist rushed forward to catch him, Shelly screamed for him to take his goddamn hands off her son. Ignoring her demands, Eli's limp body collided with the Artist's tool belt. A cracking noise signified the shattering of one of the glass vials between their bodies.

Diego saw it happen, but pinned beneath Glenn, he could only watch as a strange gas erupted and quickly filled the air.

The last thing Diego saw before losing consciousness was The Artist pulling his gas mask over his head.

HELP

When Diego regained consciousness, he was met with a pounding headache that started at his wound and radiated out to the rest of his skull. He tried to groan in pain, but the effort of doing so magnified the agony, and he quickly chewed it back to a light whimper.

"Good, you're awake," The Artist said.

Diego found himself lying on the floor but not in the same room. Sitting right across from him was the same tube television he saw Eli playing his video game on. The screen was empty now, without power, and Diego could see his reflection in the black mirror. His wound looked worse, wider from the blows he'd taken from Glenn—he could tell the fleshy divot would need stitches. His face and hair were coated in Glenn's blood and brain matter.

There was no sign of Shelly or Glenn. Other than the bloody stamp left behind by his own gore-soaked body, the floor was clean.

Along with the steady, rhythmic *beep* of medical equipment across the room, there was a wet, meaty sound. Like someone kneading raw ground beef.

"Diego," The Artist said over his shoulder, his back to him. He stood at the side of the hospital bed, no longer wearing his gas mask—from Diego's view he could only see Eli's socked feet hanging a few inches off the end of the mattress. The Artist's face was spattered with fresh blood, but just a bit, as if he'd walked through a red mist. "I need you to fetch me some clean towels, please."

When he said this, he gestured with his hands, showing Diego how bloody they were. Like he was wearing crimson-colored gloves up to his mid-forearms.

Diego winced and groaned as he climbed to his feet, getting a better view of the bed. Eli lay on his back, even paler than before. His chest cavity was split wide open, the ribs cut and separated, the same way James' were when The Artist was done with him. Tubes and wires connected Eli to a machine—the source of the beeping—that resembled an oven with monitors and pumps and dials that whirred and hissed.

"What—what is that?" Diego asked through a groan, doing his best to fight through the throbbing pain in his head.

The Artist stayed focused on his work as he spoke, pulling Eli's still heart from his chest, separated from the blood vessels. He held it in his hands like a baby bird, staring at it with fascination.

"It's called a cardiopulmonary bypass pump, or a heart-lung machine. It keeps the blood pumping and oxygenated during the procedure. Something James had been building, piece by piece, for years. I can't believe he actually finished it. I can't help but admire such patience… if only he'd been a little more patient with our relationship."

Diego stood silently as he studied Eli's face, a tube hanging out of his open mouth, resting on the bottom row of his teeth. His mind again wandered to Estela and their unborn child. His chest swelled with emotion as he thought about the sacrifice James had made to save his son's life. Even though he'd never met his child, he knew he would do the same without hesitation. But would he kill to save his family if that's what it came to? It was a question he still battled with.

"Diego?" The Artist's voice had its usual calmness but with a small hint of annoyance.

"Sí?" Diego absently answered back, having to force himself to look from Eli to The Artist.

"Towels."

"Yes… no problem," Diego said as he trudged his way out of the room and into the hallway.

He aimlessly wandered down the hall, searching for a bathroom or the kitchen. Every step he took felt wobblier than the last, his knees threatening to buckle as his head wound pulsed and thrummed with ache.

As he passed rooms, he'd pause long enough to peek in through the door. There was an office, a guest bedroom, a room full of ceramic figures in glass cases. When he came to the master bedroom and Glenn's blood-drenched corpse lying face-down on the carpet, Diego paused. He spotted the door to the master bath across the room and quickly crossed the threshold, never taking his eyes off Glenn.

What did he do with Shelly? Diego thought as he traipsed through the room and shoved the bathroom door open.

It was a mess inside, discarded clothing and used towels scattered across the floor. He opened cabinets and drawers but found not a single clean towel or rag.

Shit.

Not wanting to keep The Artist waiting, Diego picked up his pace as he rushed back through the bedroom, this time keeping his eyes averted away from Glenn's obliterated head and rotund body. Diego caught a quick glance at Glenn's massive cock, which stuck out from beneath his crushed house of a body like one of the Wicked Witch of the East's legs.

He noticed, leading from the edge of the bed to the door, a trail of bloody footprints. He figured they could have belonged to The Artist, but they were too small, and he could tell from the toe imprints that this person had been barefooted.

If I was able to wake up after breathing in that gas, then that means…

Diego followed the footprints past the threshold and back into the hallway. He heard the rapid footsteps racing toward him and saw the glint of the knife before he had a chance to react.

Shelly, still fully nude, screeched as she lifted the butcher knife high over her head, racing toward him with her teeth bared into a snarl.

"Espera!" Diego shouted as he backpedaled, shielding his face with his hands. "Por favor—!"

"You son-of-a-bitch!"

Despite her thin frame, her momentum knocked Diego onto his back. She fell on top of him, thrusting her knife toward his face.

He caught both of her wrists just in time, the knife's point centimeters away from the tip of his nose.

Shelly leaned in, pushing with all of her weight, as she roared into Diego's face, spittle spraying from her mouth like foam from a rabid dog. Her nest of pubic hair scraped across Diego's torso like steel wool.

"We only try to help!"

"Stop… fucking… saying that!"

Shelly found a surge of adrenaline, shoving the knife so it poked Diego's forehead. The tip of the blade stirred and prodded at the widened gap of his already-existing wound, sending hot volts of fresh pain crackling through his skull.

With a growl of agony, Diego found his own burst of energy as he planted his foot into Shelly's midsection and tossed her up and over, making her flip and crash to the floor. She grunted and gasped as her body tumbled across the hallway, rolling onto her belly. Her back and buttocks were still encrusted with Glenn's dried semen like off-white grout caulk.

Diego, panting, struggled to stand up. The moment he was on his feet, he lost his balance and crashed down to his hands and knees. His vision started to blur as unconsciousness threatened to pull him back under. His head wound felt brain-deep as his migraine intensified to an almost supernatural level.

Shaking his head and taking deep, controlled breaths, he managed to rise again, using the wall to keep him steady. A few feet away, Shelly was also struggling to stand. With her back hunched over, she clutched her stomach with both hands.

Blood dotted the carpet between her feet as it cascaded down her torso. Her clawed hands were painted red as they wrapped around the black hilt of the knife buried deep into her belly.

"Ay, Dios mío," Diego uttered as he watched her shakily pull the knife free, her naval expelling a torrent of blood that gushed down her pubis and thighs. "I'm sorry, I didn't mean to…"

Shelly's eyes flickered with hurt. "This—this is how you h-help?"

"You try to stab me! I have no choi—"

With a raspy howl, Shelly ran at Diego again, pointing the knife at him like a spear. Her other hand clutched her bleeding stomach, but it did nothing to slow her down.

Diego ran screaming as Shelly chased him down the hallway. He knocked over picture frames and vases and lamps in hopes of slowing her down, but she trampled the glass and ceramic shards with her bare feet, jacked-up on adrenaline and showing no signs of pain. All that seemed to matter to her was catching up to Diego and burying that knife in his flesh.

The hallway led to the dining room, a large table with four chairs sitting at the center. Diego could tell this table was never used, more a decoration than anything. As he passed, he overturned one of the chairs, knocking it into Shelly's shins hard enough to break the wood.

Shelly yelped as she crashed to the floor, tangled up with the remnants of the chair, but she was regaining her footing quickly.

Diego rushed through the dining room and found himself in the kitchen. As his eyes frantically scanned it in search of a weapon, he spotted the knife block across the counter, but it was too far to reach before the pursuing Shelly caught up to him.

"Please!" he shrieked, knowing it was futile to reason with this woman.

He found the stovetop, where a cast iron skillet sat atop the oven range—a mound of fluffy scrambled eggs sat uneaten at its center. Just as he felt the bite of the knife entering his shoulder from behind, he wrapped his fingers around the skillet's handle. Swinging it with all the momentum of his spinning body, he connected.

The pan clocked her sideways in the mouth, the rough iron edge breaking teeth and shredding her cheek—egg curds splashed across her face and plopped onto the floor. She made a choking sound as she stumbled backward, tripping over her own feet as blood fountained from her kisser, loose teeth rattling across the kitchen tile.

When she fell, the side of her head collided with the edge of the counter, making a moist *thunk* sound like a honeydew melon breaking open.

As her body hit the floor, it spasmed and bucked, the knife still somehow in her hand, scraping and clicking against the tile. Blood spewed equally from her mouth and the dent in her head, a noise gurgling from her throat that made it sound like she was speaking in tongues underwater.

Diego just stood there, watching with a slack jaw, the cast iron skillet hanging at his side.

He wasn't sure how long it took for her body to finally go still, but when it did, he dropped the pan as his mind repeated to him, again and again: *It's not your fault, it's not your fault, it's not your fault.*

Suddenly, Diego had learned whether or not he could kill for his family—and much quicker than he ever could've imagined. He didn't want to admit it, but in a way, he was grateful for the horrifying experience. If he was to rescue

Estela, it would take an effort that far exceeded the one transpiring before him.

As he glared down at the pile of violence, his mind drifted to the man who'd initially hired him. Diego didn't know James, and though this woman was clearly cheating on him while he literally gave his life for his family, she didn't deserve a death sentence.

As he stared down at her dead body, he had a vision of his wife lying in her place. Estela, with her pregnant belly, lying bloody and lifeless on the floor—he shook the image away.

There's no time to feel bad. I'll deal with these feelings once I've got my family back.

His eyes landed on the spattered blood on the counter where Shelly's head impacted it. And sitting a short distance away was a heap of clean towels. He grabbed the whole stack and raced back toward Eli's bedroom.

HEARTACHE

When Diego burst into the bedroom, The Artist was already sewing Eli's chest back up. He had a satisfied grin on his face, then cocked his head when he saw Diego standing just inside the doorway.

"What happened to you?" The Artist asked before turning his focus back to his work. Pushing the needle through the bloody lips of Eli's torso skin, then pulling it taut. "You missed it. It was magnificent. It filled me with… something new. Something no exhibit could ever provide."

The heart monitor beside the bed was silent, the green line running across it straight and unmoving.

"Here are the towels." Diego, out of breath, shakily handed over the towels. He kept one for himself, pressing it against the stab wound on his shoulder.

The Artist only glanced at the towels. "Oh, those won't be necessary. We're all done here."

He snipped the suture and stepped away from the bed, standing side by side with Diego as the two of them watched Eli.

Lying motionless in his hospital bed, Eli's skin was as pale as paper. His mouth still hung open, his dry tongue resting against his lip.

Diego's eyes bounced from the heart monitor to Eli, finding himself rooting for the procedure to be a success. He had no emotional ties to anyone in this family, but after everything he'd been through, it would be nice to see that it all meant something.

"Just give it a moment," The Artist said, rubbing his hands in anticipation, staying optimistic. He bounced excitedly from his heels to his toes. And then—

Beep… beep… beep…

The green line became sharp spikes as it rose and dipped across the screen.

Eli's face twitched once, a slight grimace manifesting as he seemed to regain consciousness. His belly started to rise and fall as he took in air.

"There he is," The Artist said, wrapping an arm around Diego's shoulders, making him squeal in pain from the pressure on his new wound. "If you can hear me, James, I told you I'd keep my promise. Your sacrifice will not be—"

Eli groaned, low and whispery, just before his belly went still and his body went limp.

Beeeeeeep…

The spikes on the heart monitor went flat again as the long, maddening tone filled the air in the bedroom.

"—in vain…" The Artist sighed with disappointment and let his arm fall away from Diego.

They just stood there for a while, staring at Eli's dead body. That never-ending beep drilling into their ears.

"I'm sorry," Diego said, and truly meant it.

The Artist crossed the room and yanked the heart monitor's cord from the wall, cutting off the incessant beeping.

"Well," The Artist said with another long sigh. "I guess there's nothing left to do but head home."

Diego just nodded and followed The Artist out of the house and back into the street.

As they climbed down the ladder back toward the sewer, Diego thought he could sense sadness in The Artist. As if he truly wanted to do something good but it still ended in blood and devastation.

As The Artist lowered himself to the platform below the ladder, he extended his hand and helped Diego down. It was then that The Artist locked eyes with Diego and suddenly the defeat in his pupils morphed into a strange excitement. The Artist lit up, as if he'd suddenly remembered something. "Before the… procedure, you'd mentioned you had a wife—a wife and a child, yes?"

"Yes," Diego said, his voice cracking at the very mention of his family. "My wife, she is pregnant. They are missing and—"

"Missing?!" The volume of The Artist's voice made Diego flinch. "Not for long, my friend. I failed James… I failed Eli. But I will not fail you, Diego."

"You—you will help me?" Diego wondered if getting help from this man was wise after what had just happened.

What if he is cursed for all the evil he has done? What if everything he touches turns to shit?

Diego knew he had to take that chance. Without The Artist, he feared he might never see Estela again. Might never get the chance to meet his baby.

"Tell me everything," The Artist said as he led Diego through the sewer tunnel.

WHERE THE MAGIC HAPPENS

Diego followed as The Artist turned into a tunnel just to the left of the main corridor. A dim light emanated from somewhere within that tunnel, a faint orange that oozed out like evaporated ectoplasm. A few roaches scuttled across the bricks that surrounded the opening like gray teeth covered in plaque.

"What are we doing?" Diego asked, completely out of patience. Now that he had The Artist on his side, he was done waiting.

"There's something I have to do first," The Artist said. "Not to mention we've got to mend those wounds of yours. You lose too much blood and you won't be a help to anyone."

As he followed The Artist, the light growing brighter, Diego hoped some of this man's bravery and confidence would rub off on him. Estela and the baby needed him to be brave. If he let the potent fear in his chest take him over, it would doom every one of them.

I promised her a ring, Diego thought. *And one way or another, I will keep that promise.*

As they reached the end of the tunnel, a chemical scent tickled his nose, swirling through the air and mixing with the stench of the sewer.

"Welcome to my home," The Artist said as he stepped out of the tunnel and into the antechamber. Various pipes decorated the walls, some of them with a constant trickle of water spilling from the ends.

Diego stood just inside the mouth of the tunnel, hesitating before crossing the threshold. His eyes scanned the room—the killer's lair. It looked like a Morlock version of a small apartment, equipped with a bed, stacks of crates full of various items, even a miniature refrigerator. The place was rigged with wires and cables that extended up into the walls, like straws sucking power from the veins of the city above. Strings of lights were threaded around the room, hung along the stone walls near the ceiling. The bulbs were the size of golf balls, a few of them dead here and there, the rest buzzing and emitting light the color of egg yolk.

"Come on in," The Artist said as he draped his overcoat on a mannequin's shoulders and pulled his gas mask over its head—another gas mask hung from its hip. Once he was down to just pants, boots, and the straps full of tools and cannisters wrapped around his torso, he opened the small fridge and pulled out two cans of tomato juice.

He tossed one to Diego, who wasn't prepared for it. It smacked him in the chest and hit the ground, making a hissing sound as red liquid bubbled and foamed around the aluminum tab. The can spun in place between Diego's feet, and when he heard The Artist pop his can open and take a long, satisfying drink, Diego reached down and picked it up.

He snapped it open and sipped it despite his usual distaste for tomatoes. He hadn't realized how thirsty he was, how dry and shriveled his tongue had become during the chaotic ordeal at the hospital and house. The juice was cold and wet, and that was good enough for him as he chugged it, emptying the can in only a few gulps.

"There you go, get that down. It'll give you a little boost of energy. It's full of antioxidants that'll help with rejuvenation. Speaking of which." He moved some crates to get at a red plastic one near the center of the stack. He pulled out a small first aid kit. "We'll deal with that gash on your head first, then close up your shoulder."

When he tossed the kit, Diego was ready this time. He caught it and opened it up. He used the handheld mirror inside to inspect his throbbing wound. Dark, coagulated blood coated the jammy gouge, and just looking at it made his vision start to swim again.

As he dug through, the sudden eruption of sound—shrieks of pain and bawling babies—startled Diego and made him drop the kit, spilling bandages, antiseptics, and various other supplies.

The Artist sat cross-legged on his small bed, not much more than a cot that squeaked under his weight. Beside him sat a crate full of art supplies that he dug through, pulling out a block of gray clay and a makeshift armature. The violent sounds were being emitted from the speaker of an old cassette recorder that sat in his lap. The screams and cries sounded tinny and muffled as they oozed from the aged, dented speaker, but they were unmistakably the recorded soundtrack of the mayhem at the hospital.

The Artist reached toward his left flank, where he unclasped a length of razor wire with two weighted metal balls on either end. He used it to easily cut the block of clay in two, then mashed the top half over the armature before tossing the rest back into the crate.

As The Artist listened to the audio, he continuously hit the fast forward button, his eyes squeezed shut as he concentrated, searching for some specific moment.

"We have no time for this," Diego pleaded, ready to grab The Artist by the neck if he didn't hurry it up. "We have to hurry—"

The object sitting beside the bed on a small wooden table caught his attention and cut off his words. It appeared to be some kind of statue. Something made of leather that shone in the dim, yellow light. When Diego realized what he was looking at, he had to chew down the gasp that nearly spewed from his throat.

The severed leg looked preserved, glistening with some kind of gloss finish. The section of the limb spanned from just above the knee down to the foot. The stump was clean and smooth as if the edge had been precisely cut with a laser.

After everything I've seen today… I guess a severed leg isn't so bad, he told himself, wondering what significance this leg held for The Artist. *Because everything means something to this man. Nothing is random.*

Diego realized he was still standing inside the tunnel, and as the screams and sounds of gunfire filled the air and bounced between the stone walls, he finally stepped out of the tunnel and crossed toward the center of the room. When he faced the mouth of the tunnel he'd just entered through, his wound was momentarily forgotten as he stared up at what was decorating the wall. Above and all around the opening, stretching out across the stones on either side, were various sheets of paper.

The parchment was of all different sizes and shades of yellow, each etched with an elaborate charcoal drawing. Diego studied the dark renderings, each depicting a specific scene, so detailed they almost looked like black and white photographs. Like peeling wallpaper, the drawings covered the blocks all around him, fluttering as sewer gas blew through the room like a fume-filled breeze.

He really is a talented artist. Despite the horrific images depicted on each sheet of parchment: the carnage, the expressions of panic and horror stretched across the faces of each of his subjects.

Along the far wall was a shallow recess that was carved out from the gray bricks—a smaller room with a low ceiling that looked just tall enough to fit The Artist without him having to crouch. The lights were brightest there, strung up along the stone ceiling like glowing spiderwebs, illuminating the various tables beneath, each littered with what appeared to be the type of equipment one might find in a mad scientist's lab: glass tubes and jars full of multi-colored fluids, along with various tools and electric devices Diego didn't recognize. A chalkboard was hung along one wall within the recess, covered in scribbled equations and chemical recipes.

Across the room, The Artist hit the play button and focused in on the audio seeping from the speaker. It was silent at first, maybe some light breathing. Then Diego realized the breathing was actually whispering voices, too quiet and distant to decipher the words being spoken. But the emotion behind the words was clear. When the voices became loud enough to make out, Diego recognized them.

"You have to promise me," James' voice said, simultaneously stern and shaky, a man doing his best to hold back his tears. Diego remembered the look on his face as he stared up at The Artist standing over him. The rib cutters gripped in his hands, blood dripping down from The Artist's knuckles against James' chest. As if drawing a bullseye over his heart.

"I promise," The Artist's voice said. It had that same emptiness that coated every word his mouth uttered, but there was something extra there. Very subtle, almost undetectable, but Diego heard a slight tremble. The tiniest hint of feeling behind those two little words.

Diego remembered how he thought he saw a physical change in The Artist in that moment as he watched this interaction play out from across the maternity ward. The Artist still moved in that smooth, silky way, but his back took on a slight arch to it, as if his heart had grown two sizes and the weight of it was too much to bear.

After what transpired at the house, The Artist looked defeated, sitting slumped over as he listened to the audio. Though no tears spilled, Diego could feel his grief.

Diego stayed in his place at the center of the room, his eyes darting between the twisted art on the walls and the man who drew them. As The Artist now shaped the clay with both hands, a wrinkle of intensity took hold of him. He pinched and pressed the material, his tongue clamped between his teeth like a bubble of chewing gum that had just been popped.

The hushed voices and emotional promises emitting from the tape recorder turned to grunts and gurgles over the gory score of wet cutting. The moist sounds of the blade slicing through human flesh, squealing when it hit bone. The meaty snap of the rib cutters opening the ribcage. Though the dissection was loud in the foreground, the cries of the babies thrashing in their plastic cribs was ever present.

It made Diego think of Estela again. He instantly recalled their discussions about the birth: what to expect, what to prepare for. How dead-set she had been about having a natural birth, nervous about complications that might lead to an emergency C-section. Terrified of the idea of some random doctor slicing her open, reaching into her body, and pulling their baby out of her womb.

I'll find you, no matter what it takes.

Diego wanted to remind The Artist that time was of the essence, but one look at the man's face and he knew better.

The Artist ran his clay-coated fingertips across the dented speaker of the tape recorder. Shutting his eyes as the vibrations of James' heart being surgically removed transferred into his flesh, riding his fingers.

"You did what you could," Diego said. "You did good."

The statement made The Artist open his eyes and pull his hand away from the speaker. He glanced up at Diego for a brief moment before going back to his sculpture. As he worked, his hands moving with fast precision, the piece started to take shape.

A human heart, bisected down the center like a pregnant belly with a second, smaller heart lying inside. His eyes sparkled with a hint of longing as he tweaked the details of the valves and aorta.

The Artist finished his sculpture just as the audio of James' death reached its end. He held the heart in front of him, turning it to inspect his work. He hit the rewind button on the tape recorder before crossing the room toward a blank area on the wall, taking an empty crate with him. A gush of water erupted from one of the higher pipes, creating a waterfall that splashed into the gray pool beneath it.

Diego followed The Artist, now right beside the recessed area full of lab equipment. Some of the fluids within the glass tubes seemed to glow, giving off a toxic light along with their sharp chemical smell. On one table, Diego spotted a pile of black pills he recognized as lobo, a drug he had never heard of before arriving in the city. A drug that had a tighter grip on the citizens than meth, crack, or heroin, taking over their every thought, controlling every choice they made.

Diego had seen his boss, Miguel, use the pills to manipulate and control his workers, promising it would help them forget their fears so they could focus on getting their jobs done quicker. Diego had refused when it was offered to him. He wanted to feel his fear and experience the pain of losing his family so that he would always be motivated to find them, no matter how hard it got, no matter how impossible it seemed. His trauma kept him going, refusing to let him give up.

"I'd never wanted to do good," The Artist said as he positioned his sculpture on the crate beneath a blank section of wall. The heart was now mixed in at the end of the existing series of drawings. "Until today. This feeling inside me is… unfamiliar."

He glided toward the opposite end of the room, where the drawings were far cruder, done by the hand of an artist still finding themself, still honing their craft. The paper was more weathered and tattered, some drawn with what looked like dirt and filth rather than charcoal.

As he stared up at the drawings, focusing in on the very first one and walking down the line, taking each one in a sheet at a time, Diego thought back to what The Artist had told him about his traumatic upbringing.

The first drawing was done with dark grime on a sheet of wrinkled newspaper. A young boy, his face swollen and beaten, lay in a pool of blood that seemed to be leaking from his rear end. His pants were torn to shreds and pulled down to his knees, which he cradled against his chest as if rocking himself. The shadow of a large man spread over him like a storm cloud threatening to precipitate violence down on him.

The next drawing was done on what looked like a used dinner napkin—torn and frayed, stained with smudges from saucy mouths. Drawn and smeared with cigarette ash and colored with old food was the image of a small boy sitting cross-legged. A dead rat lay on its back in front of him, its belly splayed open as the boy prodded its innards with a bony finger. A dark figure stood behind and above the boy and appeared to be emerging out of his body. Its red eyes glowed brighter than the rat's blood, seeming to watch in delight as the boy rummaged through the rat's insides.

That was his darkness.

He wondered which would be more helpful to him: The Artist who wanted to do good or The Artist possessed by the darkness?

As they walked, Diego studied the images on the wall, watching how they evolved from page to page. Each one showing different variations of what looked like heart surgeries. Subjects of all shapes and sizes, each one with their chests spread wide as their hearts were removed.

James trained him to become a surgeon, just like he was. That's how he knew what to do for Eli, even though it was a failure.

Each drawing showed not only a more precise surgery but a more detailed drawing. Showing The Artist's growth in every area.

"This is who I was. Who I still am, really, despite this strange sensation in my chest." His tone was different, low and mopey.

The Artist stepped away, leaving Diego to take in the next series of drawings. These drawings had a completely different energy than the others. Less stilted, more fluid in the line work, giving each drawing a sense of movement. Diego could see that The Artist was coming into his own when he drew these, fueled by a sense of betrayal.

The first drawing showed a man and a woman seemingly locked in a bout of sexual intercourse. The woman looked young, maybe late teens or early twenties. The man was at least middle-aged, his beer belly and balding head giving away his age. Diego furrowed his brow as he realized it was the woman who had the man bent over, gripping his hips with her dainty hands, her pelvis rocked backward as if preparing to thrust into him.

The man's mouth was agape in an agonized scream, shrieking over his shoulder as the woman fucked him with a cock the size of her arm. Even though the drawing was done with black charcoal, Diego could see the thick veins twisted around the cock like stripes on a barber pole. He could make out the glisten of the bloody pussy juice basted over the man's shaft.

Though the girl was the one doing the fucking, she had a look on her face just as troubled as the man's, maybe even worse. As if the act of fucking him was both revolting and painfully torturous.

The sudden sound of pain-stricken grunts and deep, strained growls startled Diego from behind. His heartbeat started to accelerate, and his body tightened. As Diego spun around to face the deviant noises, he wasn't expecting what he saw.

A HAUNTING HISTORY

The Artist wasn't pulling some hidden victim out from under his bed to sacrifice as Diego expected he might. Instead, he held the tape recorder in his hand, again running his fingertips across the top of the dented speaker, letting the vibrations of the screaming rumble against his touch. He shut his eyes and seemed to relish in the wails, as if remembering these specific victims. Reliving their deaths in his mind.

"Listen to their agony… their terror. I can see the bright colors of their fear, the shading of their pain."

Diego flinched as another shriek of agony exploded from the tape recorder. Mixed in with the baritone grunts of a male were the cries and whimpers of a female. A moist, rhythmic pounding played over their voices like a whisk mixing cake batter. Thick and wet.

The Artist crossed to Diego's side, holding the player between them. Close enough for Diego to feel the violent vibrations bursting from the speaker, making him wince as he realized he was hearing the scene depicted in the drawing just above him.

"They were my first as a solo artist. I call this piece 'Fucked by His Own Petard.' And as grisly as the scene was when I stumbled upon them, I instantly saw the beauty. Not in the atrocity unfolding but in its potential to send a message to both the predators and the prey of this city."

The man's voice cursed and snarled while simultaneously begging for it to stop. The girl begged all the same, and though her voice was whispery and choked with trauma, Diego thought he could hear a bit of satisfaction in her tone. Nothing sexual… the satisfaction that can only come with vengeance. A satisfaction Diego hoped to experience when his journey to find his wife finally came to an end.

"Can you hear that? It's the sound of comeuppance… the sound of taking one's trauma and weaponizing it. So many in this city have been brainwashed to think that the way to address their trauma is to numb it, to ignore it and pretend it isn't there. But that only amplifies it, gives it more power than it ever had before. I showed her how to heal by embracing that darkness, using it to evolve from prey to predator."

She doesn't sound healed, Diego thought, wishing more than anything that The Artist would shut the audio off. Diego was growing sick to his stomach hearing the mushy sounds of the fucking, the agony in their voices.

"That poor girl. When I found them, her innocence was being stolen away from her right before my eyes. With every grunting thrust that man shoved into her, a piece of her was lost forever. The little girl her parents raised, all the hopes and dreams they had for her future. All of that dashed against the wall as this filth-covered bastard shoved his disease-ridden cock into her. Sweating a salty storm over her, grinning like the monster under her bed."

Diego leaned in closer, rising onto his tiptoes, and studied the image. He felt his stomach lurch with disgust. "What… what you do to them?"

"I thought to myself… what would it be like for them to experience each other's perspective? A shift in power. And so I cut off their parts and swapped their sexual organs."

Diego covered his mouth and backed away from the drawing, the details so professionally rendered that he could almost smell it.

"Attaching the penis to the girl was simple enough. But the man? God, how he screamed as I dug him out. One bloody scoop at a time. After all, he was a well-endowed man, and the vaginal canal needed to be deep enough to take the length of his cock all in. It was a testament to the groinal gifts God had bestowed on him, though he didn't seem to appreciate it at the time. Some of my best work, I must say."

Diego stood in silence, focusing on recovering from his own horror, as the audio mercifully ended. But The Artist pulled that tape out of the recorder and replaced it with another. And another and another as he led Diego further down the wall, playing the audio to accompany each drawing. Each one more elaborate than the last.

One showed a garbage truck, the back of it filled with what appeared to be internal organs, dripping with blood and slime. The truck was parked along the curb of a residential street, multiple trash cans standing in front of the houses. When Diego looked closer, he realized the trash cans were wearing human skin like koozies on beer bottles, the mouths stretched wide around the openings, each one filled to the brim with sloppy trash. The shrieks of the garbagemen, notoriously corrupt and known for disposing of dead bodies for the criminal organizations terrorizing the city, squealed from the tape recorder.

Another showed what appeared to be a retirement home. A trio of deboned elderlies sat in wheelchairs, what remained of their frames leaning like piles of gelatinous meat. Their skeletons stood behind the wheelchairs, gripping the handles with their bony fingers. Their strained groans oozed from the speaker along with the clacking of their bones as they were cut free from the saggy flesh of their bodies.

"Age and senility are a convincing disguise for scoundrels and goons, but I wanted to show them that, in this city, there is no such thing as a statute of limitation for their crimes and sins. That the skeletons in their closets cannot be buried and will ultimately lead them to the punishments that await them in the afterlife."

Diego felt overwhelmed as he realized just how many drawings there were, the brutality of the violence rising right along with the strength of the messages. Moving quicker, Diego tried to avoid getting a deeper dive into each death. The Artist was right behind him, watching him, desperate to tell his tales.

If I have to hear any more of his tapes, I might not make it through this. I might crumble… But I can't give up now!

He reached the end of the morbid mural and felt a wave of relief wash over him. But then his eyes landed on the final piece, and he couldn't seem to peel himself away. Because it was a scene he thought he recognized, something he saw and read in the news just recently. The latest of The Artist's infamous 'exhibits.' Diego recognized the interior of Cheaters. He'd spent some time inside the strip club when he'd been hired to dig out the floor of an office. Apparently, the owner was preparing to install a new state-of-the-art safe.

Must be nice to have so much money you have to spend some to hide all of it.

The drawing showed the main floor, seemingly on a Saturday night, judging by the number of customers and dancers filling the room. All were skinned down to the muscle, looking like raw whole chickens frozen in their final moments of life.

"I call this one 'The Skin We Live In.' Where men pay for beauty and a moment of manufactured love from women who value vanity over virtue. The men flaunt their decadent riches while the women put their glittered bodies on display. I wanted to show them that beneath all of their tools of enticement—fine clothes, jewelry, surgical enhancements—they were all the same. Just piles of meat wrapped in the perishable costumes we call skin. And so I had to peel those costumes away so they could see their true selves. Animals. Slabs of raw beef, every last one of us."

The Artist played the tape before Diego could beg him not to, though this one was different. Missing the agonized screams and wails of the victims. Instead, along with the bump of the bass from the trap music playing from the DJ booth was the moist sound of cutting. The smooth glide of the filet blade separating skin from muscle and fat, along with the metallic *shing* at the end of each stroke.

Diego's vision went staticky, the charcoal images blurring into puddles of gray color. His legs wobbled beneath his weight, and he had to lean against the wall to keep from collapsing.

"This was a bit more challenging due to the sheer number of subjects inside the building. The obvious solution was to use noxious gas to knock them out so that I could do my work without hinderance, the same gas that was activated back there at James' house. But that seemed… anticlimactic. I needed them to be conscious while I worked, to feel the pain as I skinned them all alive. I had to cook up a special recipe just for them."

He nodded toward the small lab across the room. Diego wondered what each of the chemicals were used for, what awful side effects each of them caused.

"Something that would paralyze their bodies but amplify the sensitivity of their nerves. Took a bit of trial and error…" He looked to a deformed rat in a cage beside the test area. "But I eventually found a perfectly balanced recipe. The secret ingredient, the key to making it work, was the black pills that circulate through the city."

Black and white spots danced at the edges of Diego's vision, closing in, enveloping him. He tried to turn toward The Artist, tried to find the words to respond, but all that came out was a sizzling groan as his head pounded.

And then it felt like everything below his waist disappeared. He felt the sensation of freefalling before the side of his face bounced off the sewer floor, and his consciousness snapped off like a television that had its power cord yanked from the wall.

WHAT YOU'RE WIRED TO DO

"Almost done now." The voice sounded deep and echoey, like someone speaking from the bottom of a well.

As consciousness faded back in, Diego became aware of the sharp points of pain across his forehead, like a cluster of wasp stings. He groaned and reached for the searing spot on his face, his eyes struggling to pry themselves open.

A strong hand grabbed his wrist before he could make contact and eased it back down to Diego's side.

"Easy does it," The Artist said, holding Diego down with a firm palm to his chest as Diego started to resist, baring his teeth as he tried to sit up. "You keep it up and you'll pop these stitches. I got your shoulder sewn up too. You'll be good as new."

A headache hammered Diego's skull. The pressure pulsed against his freshly stitched wound, loosening the sutures. It forced Diego to stop resisting, letting gravity and The Artist's hand push him back to the cot.

"Took a nasty fall, might be a bit concussed. But don't you worry, my friend," The Artist said as he pierced the bloody lips of Diego's head gash and pulled the stitch taut, sending a jolt of electricity across his raw nerves. "When I'm done with you, you'll be stronger and more alert than ever. We'll get you in shape to find your wife… and deal with whatever else we find on the way."

"Mi… mi e-esposa…" Diego muttered, the mention of his wife filling him with adrenaline. Despite the migraine, Diego forced his eyes open. "We have to go!"

The dim light filling the room assaulted him first, each tiny bulb now seeming to possess the power of the sun. The Artist hovered above him, reaching toward his forehead with a long, curved needle stained red with Diego's blood. The man's expression remained stone still as he stuck the needle through and tugged it tight before tying it off and snipping the suture.

"You asked me before why I destroyed the heart James confiscated from the hospital. Why I took that away from him, knowing his child would die without it." The Artist looked past Diego, focusing on something just behind him. "I took it for the same reason I took his leg."

Diego turned his head to face the severed leg mounted beside the bed. Diego recalled how James would limp, then remembered the prosthetic leg clasped to his corpse in a pool of crimson.

"He betrayed me. He abandoned me. When he found out what I was doing, when he saw my exhibits and saw how I was putting all my training to use… he rejected me. He tried to walk away from me. And so I took his leg from him. To make sure that every step he took from that day forward would remind him of how he left me behind."

The Artist picked up the leg and caressed its leathery hide. His jaw muscles bulged as he clenched his teeth.

"I thought he loved me… thought he cared. But I was

disposable. I was garbage that belonged in the dumpster. My mother knew it and so did James. And I hated him for that."

The Artist rubbed his thumb over the white bone oval at the center of the leg stump. "It was my hate that drove the knife through that heart, that wanted him and his whole family to suffer. Like his first son, I, too, needed a heart transplant. Not because I was born with a faulty one but because I was born *without* one."

The Artist approached his sculpture and lightly traced the shape of both hearts with his fingertip.

Diego rose to his feet, fighting through the tremors pummeling his skull, refusing to let anything slow him down. He grimaced as he trudged his way toward The Artist's back.

"And that void in my chest was where the darkness took root, pumping inky ire through my veins. It convinced me that I deserved to be alone, wallowing in filth and bathing in the city's waste. It told me that James' pain and suffering would soothe my heartless and unloved soul. His family's devastation would be a salve for the wounds in my back where he stabbed me. And now, more than ever, I know that was a lie."

The Artist turned to face Diego, seeming momentarily surprised to find him so close. Diego's expression tightened into a mask of determination. When The Artist smiled at him, despite the obvious warmth of that smile, Diego found himself wanting to reach out, grab his lips, and rip them off.

But The Artist was oblivious to this as he closed the distance between them and took Diego by the arms. His voice now trembled with emotion—his coldness being cooked away as he told his story out loud.

"He could never love me. His heart belonged to his other son… his *real* son. And in the end, he gave it to him, didn't he. For better or for worse. He sacrificed himself because that's what a father and a husband are wired to do. Protect and defend family, to the death. And as I cut his heart from his chest, I could feel the darkness shifting inside of me. And that's when I found you, Diego, and I knew—"

With a strong and fluid motion, Diego shoved The Artist hard in the sternum before unsheathing one of his knives from his belt and pressing the point of the blade against his throat.

The Artist only grinned, his eyes wide with a mixture of shock and respect.

"No more talking! I am a husband… I am a father! And my family needs me! If I must die to save them… then I die! But we need to go. We need to go now!"

Every word erupting from his mouth caused the point of the blade to push in deeper, a millimeter at a time. A bit of blood spilled and rode the creases in The Artist's neck.

"That's just it. You were brought to me for a reason, don't you see? I've experienced a significant evolution today, and after failing to save Eli, you're my last chance to prove myself. To show that I can take control of the darkness instead of the other way around, that I can repurpose it. But there's one thing you've got wrong—"

Diego gave the knife a small twist as he bared his teeth and lowered his face an inch above The Artist's.

"You said it yourself. Your family needs you. But this rescue mission will not end in death. It will end in reunion. But believe me when I tell you…" The Artist lifted himself into the blade, letting it dig dangerously deep. "There will be sacrifice. Enough sacrifice to paper this entire sewer system."

Diego nodded as twin tears raced down his cheeks like glass pearls. He pulled the blade away from The Artist's throat. "Whatever it takes, yes?"

"Whatever it fucking takes," The Artist said through a snarling grin. "Now tell me all about this goon you've been working for."

"He take all my money. The price always go higher, and I pay, but never enough. And now I only have…" Diego reached into his pocket and pulled out Benjamin—waving the bill like a tiny desecrated flag. "Ciento dolares…"

The Artist snickered as his grin spread wider, blood smeared across his neck like warpaint. "I've got something far more persuasive than money."

PAID IN FULL

"Not enough," Miguel said in Spanish as his worker finished piling cash into his palm. He fanned the bills out with a look of disdain. "Where's the rest? Don't lie to me, Tomas."

Tomas nervously shifted his weight from boot to boot, avoiding eye contact with Miguel by looking over his shoulder at the line of other men standing behind him.

The streetlamps spilled sallow light over the Home Hardware parking lot, gusts of fog bursting from the men's mouths as they waited their turn to undoubtedly disappoint and infuriate their bossman. Just like always.

But they'll always pay, Miguel thought, enjoying watching these men squirm. *Even if I demand every last fucking penny, they'll pay it. And they'll be back for more work in the morning.*

Each one of the workers averted their gaze from Tomas' stare, minding their own business. Making sure not to draw attention to themselves and invoke Miguel's wrath.

Because they all knew what would happen if they did. They understood exactly what Miguel was capable of and the lengths he would go to prove his point.

Tomas turned and faced Miguel again, shrinking beneath

the heat of his stare. His eyes darted to the space between his feet. "Please," Tomas whimpered back in Spanish, his head hanging in shame. "My family… they're hungry. I just need to keep enough to feed them."

"And when your debt is paid, I'm sure you'll feed them well. But I tell you what." Miguel pulled out a couple of twenties with one hand and a jet-black pill with the other. "How about I give you a choice. Fill your family's bellies… or take your medicine?"

Miguel chuckled as he relished in the man's desperation. He enjoyed watching the man's morals do battle with his chemical dependency. Miguel waved the bills and rattled the pill in his palm, waggling his eyebrows like a cartoon villain. Behind the men, across the street, he thought he saw movement. Someone watching from a distance, maybe. But he turned his attention back to the man in front of him.

He knew which Tomas would choose—it was never a question. And as Miguel continued watching the man's attempts to deny the inevitable, his amusement morphed into impatience.

"Choose now or you get nothing."

Without another moment of hesitation, Tomas snatched the pill from Miguel's closing fist and scurried away as he popped it into his mouth and chewed it dry.

The rest of the line moved quicker, the workers knowing better than to ask Miguel for mercy or sympathy. Those were two things Miguel had no interest in offering.

Miguel held out his palm and watched the bills stack higher, handing out one pill to each man like junkie trick-or-treaters. Each one of them slammed their pill past their lips as fast as they could, their teeth stained black as they chewed.

Miguel, like most people in the city, had his own demons—ghosts from the past that followed and tormented him. And so, when he heard about lobo, he thought about taking it, wondering what kind of man he might be if he could experience a little bit of peace and calm every now and then.

But what Miguel valued above all else was control. He'd

been around enough lobes to know that the drug was doing all the controlling. Miguel would rather live with demons and a head full of nightmares than relinquish authority of himself.

But for a man like Miguel, Lobotozine sure was a handy tool to keep his foot pressed firmly against the necks of his workers. Each one of them in debt, and each debt's interest rate rising from month to month. Or anytime Miguel felt it necessary.

As the final worker stepped up, Miguel realized that the men he'd sent off with the older, nerdy gringo had never returned. Including that pain in the ass Diego, one of the few who'd kept himself clean, avoiding lobo so he could stay focused on his goals. Such defiance was something Miguel had to respect but couldn't tolerate. Not from him or from any of his workers. He would make sure their debts were never paid, that they never found their loved ones.

He would make sure he remained in control.

"Miguel," came a voice from behind. "You rat bastard."

Miguel turned to face his rival. "Rolando? What the fuck do you want?"

"You know exactly what I want," Rolando snarled through a deep scowl, getting chest to chest with Miguel. "Maybe you've got shit in your ears, but this is the last time I'm gonna tell you. Find another place to do business. This is my turf."

"This money in my pocket tells a different story, my friend." Miguel puffed out his chest and faced off with the man, his eyes intense and locked in like twin shotgun barrels aimed at the center of Rolando's face. "Money talks, and right now, it says that this is Miguel's turf."

But Rolando didn't back down, poking a hard finger against Miguel's chest like a miniature battering ram trying to break through a door.

"I was here first," Rolando said, his thrusting finger driving Miguel back a step at a time until he finally collided with the side of the brick building. "And if you wanna live long enough to spend that money, then you'll—"

When Rolando tried to poke him again, Miguel snatched his finger out of the air like a frog tongue catching a fly. Kicking him in the balls with a steel toe boot, Miguel then drove Rolando's finger into the brick wall, dislocating the joint at the knuckle and snapping the bone. He turned the digit into a swollen mess, instantly darkening with bruise hues.

Rolando had time to wail in pain for a few seconds before Miguel gripped the back of his head and slammed his bearded face into the wall. The collision was hard enough to crack the grout between bricks.

Miguel hammered Rolando's head against the building again and again. Each collision shattered more teeth and made Rolando's broken nose more crooked. As the assault continued, his face was painted with more blood. It gushed from his nostrils, broken mouth, and the freshly opened gouges peppering his entire head.

The extreme disfigurement didn't stop Miguel. He kept working him over, having to grip Rolando's hair to keep him upright when the man's legs started to buckle. Pulling Rolando's head back so that his face was aimed at the night sky, his breath fogged from his mouth in strained gusts as he gargled the blood.

Miguel curled his hand into a fist and hit Rolando across the jaw with such force that he left his feet. He landed awkwardly on the back of his neck, his spine making a sound like a twig snapping, before the momentum rolled him onto his belly.

Rolando writhed like an earthworm frying on a hot sidewalk, his limbs twisting and contorting as if he was drowning in slow motion.

Kneeling beside him, Miguel gripped the scruff of his neck like a mother dog lifting one of her puppies. The loose, sweaty skin folds balled up like rubber bands in Miguel's fist. He elevated his face off the pavement and forced Rolando to look at him despite his eyes being nearly swollen shut.

"You ever seen that lollipop commercial? You know, the one with that owl? What was it? How many licks does it take to get to the center of a Tootsie Pop?" Miguel leaned in closer. "Let's find out."

He smashed Rolando's face into the concrete, gripping the back of his head with both hands and grinding it like he was juicing a giant lemon. When Rolando started to thrash and buck, Miguel pummeled the back of his skull with a trio of hammer blows that made him go still, a gurgle bubbling from his throat.

Miguel planted his feet and crouched over Rolando. Grabbed hold of the hair on his scalp with one hand and the back of his neck with the other, digging his fingers in.

When he dragged Rolando's face across the asphalt, Miguel pressed down with all his weight. Locks of hair ripped free from Rolando's scalp as Miguel pushed and pulled like he was grating a block of cheddar.

"One!" Miguel cackled as he raked Rolando's raw, gory face repeatedly over the harsh surface. Streaks of blood, tufts of beard hair, and ribbons of torn skin smeared across the rough ground, leaving a sludge of violence behind.

"Two!"

Rolando slapped and punched at Miguel's hands, but his swings grew weaker as his flesh was stripped away. The screams that had been ripping from his throat were now reduced to choking coughs.

"Aaaaaaand… a three!" Miguel guffawed as he shoved Rolando's head away, wiping the blood painting his hands and arms across the back of Rolando's shirt. "Let's see how close we are."

He used the toe of his boot to kick Rolando, rolling him onto his back. Rolando's face resembled a dish of lasagna fresh out of the oven, freckled with black pebbles from the pavement.

His lips were just about gone, only frayed ribbons left behind that hung over his red teeth like torn wrapping paper. His nose had separated from his face, the left nostril hanging over the right one, a gaping hole blowing blood bubbles in its place. White bone peeked through the deepest rips in his flesh, mostly across his forehead, the exposed skull rough from being sanded down by concrete. The swollen, purple flesh around his eyes had been torn off, along with both eyelids. His cratered eyes stared unblinkingly toward the sky, the sockets filling with blood as his pupils darted back and forth like a Felix the Cat clock.

Miguel knocked his knuckles against the white bone shining through Rolando's forehead. "Nope… not even close to the center yet. Let's keep going then."

"Miguel," came a voice from across the street. The figure was draped in shadow, but Miguel could tell it was Diego by the shape of his silhouette. Diego stepped into the light of the streetlamp above him. He shouted in Spanish, "Look at this, like two pigs rolling around in shit."

"Huh?" Miguel furrowed his brow.

"You're just fighting yourself, don't you see?"

Miguel smiled, clenching his bloody hands together, rising to his feet to face Diego.

"I was wondering when you'd show up," Miguel said. He glanced at his surroundings, expecting an ambush. Diego's tone made Miguel think he and the others had come up with some kind of plan while out on their job. A plan to rob him and get payback for all the pain he'd caused them. "Where are the boys? I take it the job went well?"

"The job went just as you expected it to. And that's why I am here."

"The others?"

"Dead…" Diego's voice became something akin to a growl, making Miguel stop in his tracks a moment.

What the fuck happened to this guy? he wondered.

His defenses had ignited into overdrive. Miguel tightened his fists, ready to defend himself. A feeling he'd never had in Diego's presence before, or any of his men for that matter.

"A job is a job," Miguel said as he regained his composure and forced himself to cross the street, refusing to fear this man. "Nothing more, nothing less…"

"And a life? Does that mean anything to you?"

"That depends." Miguel narrowed his eyes as he stepped onto the blacktop. Outside of the Home Hardware parking lot, there were no cars, no headlights approaching. Just a sea of darkness with one working streetlamp that coned over Diego like a spotlight on a stage.

"Depends on what?" Diego showed no fear as Miguel approached him. Which Miguel took as an insult.

"It's simple, really. The only life that means a fucking thing to me… is my own. All the rest?" Miguel marched across the street, closing the distance between him and Diego. Grabbing the front of Diego's shirt, Miguel twisted it into a hard fabric ball in his fist. The tip of his nose wrestled with Diego's. "Expendable," he said in English. "That goes for you, your cunt wife, and anybody else who get in the way for me getting everything I fucking deserve!"

Diego didn't move, didn't even flinch. He just smiled at Miguel as a long, slender shadow fell over him. The shadow of a figure now standing directly behind Miguel.

"I thought you might say that," said the voice, speaking English, calm and monotone, as its arms wrapped around Miguel like twin pythons constricting their next meal.

And suddenly, Miguel was falling. Plummeting through the ground, down into the damp sewer beneath.

The world became black.

KING OF THE RATS

"Open your eyes," a voice said in English.

When consciousness started to blossom, Miguel felt something tickling his cheek. Like a sweet kiss from feathered lips. He heard a small squeaking sound before he had a chance to think. Then felt the searing pain tighten across his back.

When he finally got his eyes open, he was staring into blood red orbs surrounded by a face covered with white fur and streaked with dark filth. When the rat squeaked again, it leaned forward and nibbled his cheek, peppering him with more kisses. Its whiskers tickled his skin, its claws digging into his shoulder.

"What the fuck?!" Miguel tried to thrash, but his limbs and torso were held firmly in place. He realized he was nude, despite not being able to angle his neck enough to see himself. He could feel the warm breeze against his skin, the trickle of gray water falling from above and splashing against his exposed body. "Let me go, you motherfuckers!"

As he wiggled his body, he heard the music of rattling chains. The painful pull of the hooks dug into his back, holding him up like a piece of bait.

The sewer was near pitch black, the white rat seeming to glow as its mouth searched Miguel's face for food, incisors scraping against his five-o'clock shadow as its tiny tongue lapped at his perspiration.

Miguel's eyes started to adjust as he winced in disgust, and that's when he noticed the two figures standing side by side across the tunnel. A slow-moving river of filth ran between him and the figures, saturated with the city's shit and piss. The odor was thick, like vaporized yogurt years past its expiration date.

"I see you, you cocksucker!" Miguel's head was held upright, another hook piercing the loose skin that bunched up at the back of his scalp. His face felt tight against his skull as his weight pushed against the hook. "Lo juro por Dios, motherfuckers, when I get down, I gonna—"

The rat bit his ear lobe, cutting off his words as a spark of sharp pain erupted and warm blood trickled down the side of his neck. The rat stood on its hind legs, holding the fleshy morsel with both hands. Its mouth worked on it with a rabid ferocity, chewing it up and swallowing it down.

Miguel growled and squealed as he glared across at Diego, who just stood there quietly watching this happen. After a moment, Diego turned away, disgust twisting his expression. But the other man watched intently with a sinister satisfaction that Miguel knew all too well.

It was the look of someone in control.

The figure standing beside Diego was someone Miguel did not recognize, but he could feel the energy wafting off this man. It wasn't hard to sense he was a bloodthirsty savage—Miguel was conditioned to recognize his own. The intimidating man stood calmly, biding his time, as if toying with his meal before ripping it to pieces.

Who in the fuck is that? Miguel wondered.

"You're not going anywhere," the man finally said. "Not until you give what you owe."

Miguel grimaced as the rat leaned in and bit into his ear again. This time, it didn't bother tearing off a new piece but ate directly off Miguel's head. As he fought through the pain, his panic rose even further when more rats started to arrive. They swarmed beneath his feet, lapping up the blood that ran from his pierced flesh.

"I no owe shit!" Miguel yelled.

Another shriek blasted from his throat as a couple of rats climbed his legs toward his torso, their sharp nails digging and scraping as they went. They squeaked hungrily, the taste of Miguel's blood already in their mouths.

"No?" The man leaped across the river of waste. Landing on the edge of the platform with his tiptoes, he didn't seem to struggle with his balance as he leaned into Miguel. "Diego tells me different. That you're not holding up your end of the deal."

"Deal?" Miguel looked past the man toward Diego, who still seemed squeamish. "I-I tell you when you're d-debt is paid, I—"

"You would tell him who took his wife and where." The man gripped Miguel's face and forced him to focus back on him. "His *pregnant* wife! But you were never going to tell him, were you?"

"I was gonna tell him. I swear!"

"No," the man said as he cupped the back of Miguel's head with his palm and pulled him forward. Gentle at first, almost lovingly, but more violently when the hooks and chains went taut. "His wife's life means nothing to you. His baby means nothing… They are beneath you, isn't that right? Just a family of rats…"

The pressure stretched Miguel's skin, the hooks' puncture holes widening as the man pulled harder and harder. The tented flesh started to tear and gush fresh blood that bathed the growing horde of vermin. Half a dozen rats were now perched on various spots across Miguel's body, each scratching and biting. Eating at him a tiny morsel at a time.

Miguel roared with pain and panic, his body igniting with agony as new openings were scooped out of him. The man's second hand assisted the first, pulling Miguel away from the wall, turning his back into Swiss cheese.

"Okay! I admit it! I'm sorry! J-just let me down and I tell you everything! Just get these fucking things off me! *Please!*"

The man studied Miguel's eyes but didn't seem satisfied with what he found there. He noticed a clump of feces clinging to the wall. Scooping it up with his fingertips, he smeared it across Miguel's mouth, shoving his fingers past his lips and teeth to make sure he tasted it. He then gripped Miguel's jaw and pulled it hard. The hook in the back of his head strained so stiff and nearly scalped him.

"I can't trust a word you say. Your words are shit." The man knelt out of Miguel's vision. When he stood back up, he held a large rat that thrashed and squealed, desperate to bite him but just unable to reach.

The man glanced over his shoulder toward Diego, who hugged himself with an expression of revulsion. "I know this isn't pleasant to witness. But if you want to find your wife quickly, there's only one method that men like this will respond to."

Miguel watched as Diego gave the slightest of nods.

The man turned back toward Miguel and held the furious vermin up against his face. The panicked rat immediately latched its teeth onto him. The filthy creature bit deeply into his upper lip, pulling hard enough to rip it in two, giving him a cleft that gushed blood and mixed with the flavor of shit in his mouth. The man held the rat in place, letting it mangle Miguel's shrieking mouth—mutilating his lips and gums, then latching on to the septum of his nose and ripping it away before gobbling it down.

"Enough!" Miguel again looked past the man toward Diego. "I-I fuck'n tell you e'rything I know!"

More and more rats collected at their feet, somehow ignoring the man and focusing fully on the bleeding mess that Miguel had become. Fighting one another, the squealing creatures sought their chance to get a taste.

Miguel kept his pleading eyes glued to Diego, his words altered by pain and his ruined mouth. "Please make it stopf!"

The man grabbed Miguel's face with a hard grip and squeezed his cheeks together like his hand had become a giant lobster claw. As he compressed it, more blood gushed from Miguel's tattered jaws.

"Speak!"

"I t-tell you the truth, okay? His wife… I got no fuck'n idea, I swear. I sorry I lie to you."

The man looked back at Diego as if awaiting his instructions. Diego remained silent a moment, but then something in his eyes hardened, and he glared across at Miguel.

"Then you stay here," Diego said somberly, nodding toward the rats. "With them."

"*Wait!* All I know is th-they take peopfle like your wife, anyone that won' be missed—"

"Won't be missed?!" Diego roared.

The man pulled Miguel's head so hard the hook connected to his scalp ripped free, taking nearly half the skin with it. A flap of flesh hung from the back of Miguel's skull, and his head lurched forward, now disconnected from the wall.

"You know wha'mean, goddammit! They take them somewhere underground and force'm t'make it!"

The man grinned as if realizing, like the rats, Miguel was starting to squeal. "Make what, exactly?"

"Th-the fuck'n lobo! And the more't grow, the more peopfle they need. That all I know, I swear!"

"Where?!" Diego growled.

"I don't know where, I just a middleman. They don't tell me shit!"

When he felt the man's fingers dig into his head beneath the flap of scalp, his voice became more of a howl as he begged and pleaded.

"The mayor! I know she's behind it! Her family—they invent it! You want to find lobo, she'll know where. I swear that all I fuck'n know!"

When the man finally let go, Miguel wept and gasped for breath, trying to control his panic as more rats enveloped him, as gravity widened his wounds bit by agonizing bit.

"The mayor?" Diego asked.

"It adds up," the slender man replied. "I've had an eye on them for some time. Her adopted father, Horace Doyle, created the initial blueprint for Lobotozine. He ignored all the dangers and side effects found during the clinical trials, ready to move forward. But several months prior to the initial release, Mayor McKinney outed him. She stole leverage, and the public got behind her when she took up office. McKinney told everyone the formula had been refined, but as it turns out, she was about as honest as her father."

Diego clenched his fist. "And we can get to her?"

"Of course we can. And what a magnificent exhibit she'll make. Our mayor… a piece that will send a message far beyond this city."

Diego's voice took on a tone full of energy and adrenaline. "Then we waste no time. We must go."

"Wait!" Miguel screamed, spitting blood, feces, and needles of rat hair from his mouth. "Don' leave me here! I tell you what I know! Le'me down!"

Diego glared across at Miguel, seeming to consider what to do with him. He gave another slight nod toward the man.

Miguel could smell the bloodlust in the man as he leaned closer. He whimpered as he turned away from him, as far as his restraints would allow.

"You consider yourself above those you victimize. Those who will not be missed—expendable, as you call them. Using their desperation to control them, taking their money and paying them empty promises. You see them as vermin, don't you?"

Miguel tried to speak but only managed to sputter and trip over his words, unable to look this man in the eye.

"And you ruled over the vermin… a king of rats. It seems you owe them, then, don't you? You owe them all… and it's time to pay up."

The man pulled a small vial from his waist, about the size of an almond. Shook the clear liquid inside inches from Miguel's blubbering face.

"Rat pheromones. When they get a whiff of this, they won't be able to resist. Just like you couldn't resist when you smelled the hopelessness and desperation of all those you fed upon."

"No, no, no! P-please don't—"

The man twisted open the vial and sprinkled the liquid all over Miguel's face and body, stamping him with wet dots of the rat essence.

Diego watched from a distance, clearly in a hurry to get out of there but unable to peel his eyes away as the excited creatures instantly reacted.

Their chaotic movements erupted into a hurricane of frenetic energy as the scent filled their senses and unleashed a mad hunger inside of each one of them. Like furry piranhas, they swarmed Miguel's body, racing up his legs and torso and digging their teeth in anywhere they could.

As Miguel shrieked and thrashed, dozens more appeared, emerging from the darkness, pouring from pipes and tunnels. Their screeching filled the sewer, almost as loud as Miguel's wails of pain.

They shredded him, tearing ribbons of flesh away, peeling him like a human-sized potato. His blood showered down over them, but the drenched rats never slowed. And as more and more of the hungry mouths found him, Miguel's eyes became covered by their hairy bodies. Blocking his vision, his nose and tongue were molested by their scent and flavor. When he tried to scream again, a fat rodent drove its peg teeth deep into his tongue, flaying the muscle on its way deeper down Miguel's throat.

The rats became his universe as they consumed him. The rats were all that existed. All Miguel could do was hope they made quick work of him.

SWEET SIBLINGS

"What was that?" Mason Moons asked.

"Huh?" Mayor Freya McKinney asked.

Mason looked around the curtain he'd pulled aside. *Ain't no mutha fucka gettin' the drop on me,* he thought.

The Drip Man pulled his bejeweled pistol from his holster, resting his finger on the hammer. "Maybe I'll have a look outside anyhow."

"Nonsense," Freya said. "Saul and the other men are roaming the grounds. There's nothing to fear."

"I say I was scared?"

"I didn't mean it like—"

"I fear no man, I'm just prepared. Them fuckin' rent-a-cops you got outside ain't gonna do shit."

Freya chuckled. "They're perfectly capable and have served me well for years. I think you're just not accustomed to the sounds of nature. All the smog in that city's gone to your head."

He looked behind him, quickly surveying the room and noticing that the vault door down the hallway was partially open. "The fuck is the vault open for?"

"A bit later this evening, Saul is loading the funds courtesy of Garland Pharmaceuticals. If the campaign donation and Lobotozine royalties continue like this, we might need a bigger vault."

Mason hovered by the window, returning his gaze through the glass, still unsure if he should go check things out.

"Just relax and finish pouring our drinks." Freya set the needle to the record, not about to let a random noise ruin the evening. Listening with a grin, the romantic music bled from the speakers. She had a look like her heart was fluttering—like it was about to jump through her silk robe any second. She turned sideways, gazing upon the source of her excitement.

The Drip Man had put away his piece and returned to the minibar. He was in the process of topping off the second glass full of ice with some Amaretto. His wolfskin furs and hat rested on the coatrack behind him, but his jewelry remained in place.

"Those look lovely," Freya whispered.

"Not as lovely as you, sweet thang," Mason replied.

"What do you say we just go upstairs?"

Mason grinned, the platinum in his grill sparkling. "Didn't you just drop a needle on that wax?"

"I did, but I have a surprise for you," Freya said. "And I can't pretend like I don't for another minute."

The smile melted off Mason's face, and his tone grew cold. "I don't like surprises."

"I think you'll like this one."

The Drip Man gave her a look like he'd damn-well better before handing her one of the drinks.

Freya led him from the living room to the foyer, up the stairs, and into her bedroom. When the door opened, the massive bed and lavish details of the room were revealed.

Mason's jaw dropped. But it wasn't *what* was inside the room that stunned him, it was *who.*

Mason's eyes lit ablaze with fire, the mere sight of the man before him filling his chest with wrath. While the man didn't look the way he remembered, the face was unmistakable. Deep inside his entrails, it sickened him. "The fuck happened to him?"

The elderly and shriveled white man sat motionless in his wheelchair. Former Mayor Horace Doyle showed no semblance of emotion—his vegetative state didn't seem like it would allow for it.

"Daddy's encountered some health issues," Freya said.

"That ain't my fuckin' daddy," The Drip Man said with a scowl of disgust.

Freya rolled her eyes. "You know what I mean, call him what you will."

"How'd you even find him?"

"Dumb luck, really." Freya sipped her drink. "After he had the little episode that turned him into a vegetable, he landed in the hospital."

"And?"

"Well, he never updated his emergency contacts, so they called me. Imagine that? He vanished from the face of the Earth for nearly a decade. Father Time's never lost, though, I guess."

The Drip Man couldn't help but laugh. "Stupid bastard."

"Yeah, but we knew that already," Freya said. "He wasn't smart enough to keep his scandals from going public and ruining his career. And wasn't smart enough to realize that we weren't just his props. I was destined to run the office, and you were destined to run the streets. Even as retarded as he is now, I'm sure his Jell-O brain can still see that." She squatted, glaring at his eyes. "Isn't that right, Daddy?" She tapped her finger against his forehead as she spelled out in singsong, "J-E-L-L-O."

"I been waiting for this day for a long time," Mason said, glaring at Horace. "You thought you was real smart, didn't you?" Mason swung the knuckles on the back of his hand, connecting them with the bridge of Horace's nose and busting it. As the blood dribbled down the old man's lips, he remained reactionless. "Thought you could buy yourself a couple niggas and take care of 'em like pets to get you that black vote. It worked for a while, but just cuz you seen us as monkeys didn't make it so."

Mason thought back to when he and Freya had first been placed together in Horace's care. A young boy and a young girl who were almost the same age but from two different orphanages. It was only natural they might be attracted to each other. The temptation wasn't just derived from their physical attributes but also what they'd experienced.

They both intimately understood the cold cut of rejection and, even worse, the synthetic façade of 'family.' They'd been shoehorned into everything for their entire lives. So when they encountered each other via a natural means, their bond was galvanized.

Mason wanted to hit Horace again as he quickly relived their childhoods of slavery and abuse.

"He did," Freya said, "but in a way, it was a good thing. Because his fuck-ups only served to foster my accolades. The old fool's skeletons produced the pity needed to replace him."

"We were his skeletons," Mason said.

He continued to think back to their youth—when Horace viewed both of them as meat puppets. They were dragged around in front of political pundits, cameras, and rallies, uttering the phrases they'd been trained to say. The emotionless slogans beaten into them. Chained up, they were held captive inside a luxurious house. Horace enjoyed the finest elements of life, while they were pounded with ridicule and fed gruel from golden dishes.

It was only once they were older that it became obvious they'd outgrown their use. Besides, their 'father' had become more fixated on the developmental drug he was working on: Lobotozine. If he could get the population to take their medicine, then there'd be no need to adopt minority children and parade them around. The dog and pony shows would be dead… forever. If he could create a city of zombies, then there would be no one for him to answer to. But

Horace didn't quite get far enough to implement his master plan.

"You thought we was stupid," Mason growled. He whipped out his pistol and pointed it at the old man's face. "Who's the fuckin' dummy now?"

"No!" Freya yelled.

After years of obedience, Mason recalled when they were finally given the freedom to have their own lives. But Horace hadn't counted on their resolve. On the outside, they were very much the zombies that Horace aspired to have roaming the entire city. But on the inside, the children he'd molded waited for the perfect moment.

Every time Mason and Freya had been beaten and berated, they plotted. Knowing there was opportunity afoot, patience had been their only virtue. Until the day finally came when they'd learned enough about Horace's malicious pharmaceutical ventures and gathered enough evidence to expose him.

Horace was banished. Publicly besmirched, he not only lost his position as mayor but also his partnership with Garland Pharmaceuticals.

"Why?" Mason asked, keeping his barrel square on the old bastard.

"Because he doesn't deserve it," Freya said. "After everything he did to us, he's not getting off that easy."

Mason lowered his gun, agreeing with her sentiment. Freya wasn't his blood sister, but he'd always been publicly positioned that way. Even currently, he was regulated to the city's underbelly, while Freya played politics. Just like all those years under Horace's rotten thumb, their love remained forbidden, hidden from the public eye.

In a way, she still felt like family. So much so that sometimes he felt funny fucking her for that very reason. He couldn't have been prouder of her and the way they were able to supplant themselves in each of Horace's loafers. They'd not only stolen his empire, they'd brought it to new heights.

After they'd outed the old man, Freya had swooped in, seamlessly playing the role of the city's next great hope. She couldn't possibly be the same as the rest of the crooked politicians—she was too busy exposing them. And it didn't matter how close they were, she'd blown the whistle on her own adopted father. She would stop at nothing to bring credibility and transparency into the decayed hierarchy. Or at least, that's what she told everyone.

They could've easily done the opposite of what Horace had. Reversed the downward trend and focused on real solutions to help combat the violence and poverty that infected every corner of the community. They could've made a difference. But if Horace had taught them one thing under his harsh rule, it was to look out for themselves because no one else was going to. In the end, The Devil's fruit was too juicy to turn down.

Freya convinced everyone that Lobotozine was going to be 'revamped' before its public release. They would ensure that the positive effects of the drug wouldn't be squandered while, at the same time, reappraising the dangerous side effects Horace was willing to move forward with until they were eradicated. That's what she told them at least.

But by the time the truth was discovered, The Drip Man and Mayor McKinney had ensured the majority of the population was already under their spell.

The city of fear was born.

"He never wanted us to touch," Freya said, licking her lips. She nibbled on Mason's ear, unbuttoning his shirt and sliding it off. "But there isn't a whole lot he can do to stop us now." Toying with the gold and platinum necklaces resting against his bare chest, Freya's eyes glimmered. Her hand slid over the dual gun holsters before returning to his skin. She let her silk robe fall from her body and pool at her feet.

The Drip Man felt a sense of pride. They'd come so far. They weren't the people getting shit on any longer, they were doing the shitting.

"Fuck me, baby," Freya begged. "Fuck me right here, in front of—"

Several loud bangs suddenly erupted outside of the bedroom. An incessant thrashing that sounded like it was right outside the door.

"Who the fuck was that?" Mason asked, pulling his strap.

"Saul?" Freya called out.

There was no response.

Mason wasn't the type to wait. He held his burner tight and opened the door. But when he stepped outside, he immediately slipped in a puddle of warm blood that coated the floor.

"What is it?" Freya asked.

The Drip Man backed away when he located the source of the blood, pulling the second pistol from its holster.

Mason exhaled. "We gonna have to handle some shit."

FACE OFF

Resting on the floor between the banister and the bedroom door was Saul's severed head. His handgun had been shoved up through the ragged stump of his neck so the barrel stuck out from his mouth. Two bloody, unfired bullets were lodged into his eyes.

The word BOUGHT was carved into his forehead.

"What—what the fuck is going on?!" Freya shrieked from across the room as she quickly threw her robe back on and tied it shut.

"Stay here," Mason whispered over his shoulder through his clenched platinum teeth. Fearless, he stepped over Saul's head, pointing his bedazzled pistols in every direction.

"Fuck you stay here," Freya scoffed.

Mason's jaw muscles bulged in frustration as he watched her rush to her bed and pull out a double-barrel shotgun from beneath the mattress.

"The fuck you doin'?" Mason grumbled. "It ain't safe, just lock the doors and keep your ass behind 'em."

Freya cracked the shotgun open to make sure it was loaded, then pumped it before joining Mason. "We stick together, understand? Just like always."

Mason sighed as he sized her up—studying the determined look on her face and how steadily she held her weapon. Even though he hated it, he nodded for her to follow as he crept toward the stairway leading to the foyer and the front double doors.

On their way down the stairs, Mason noticed blood splashed everywhere. When they reached the first floor, he spotted three of Freya's other security guards. Or their heads, anyway.

One head was stuck on the end of an AR-15 like a marshmallow on a stick. Another had a steel baton shoved through its ears and eyes, the bone broken so it could be threaded like a metal shoelace: in one ear, out one eye, in one eye, out one ear. The third had the top of its skull sliced off, like a jar of pickles without the lid. The brains were replaced with a cluster of hand grenades like a nest of deadly bird's eggs.

Carved across each forehead were the words PAID FOR.

"Jesus Christ!" Freya pointed her shotgun at each head as if expecting them to leap at her. The gun shook in her grip—the steadiness of her hands was replaced by quivering fear.

"You mutha fuckas think you can scare me?!" Mason circled in place, both pistols extended in front of him. He lifted one arm and fired a shot into the ceiling, making Freya flinch and nearly pull her own trigger. "You ain't shit, you hear me?! You come for The Drip Man, but it's you bitches that get dripped! *Guaranteed!*"

A hard knock from the front door made them both jump, and this time, Freya's finger slipped and fired a shot. The slug hit the head full of grenades, shattering the handle and pin of one.

The blast of the gun instinctively caused Mason to take cover. He managed to dive behind the nearest pillar, but Freya wasn't so lucky.

Kabooom!

Mason curled into a ball behind the pillar, helpless as he watched his sister get thrown off her feet by the explosion that rocked the house and echoed through the foyer. His head was filled with a sharp ringing sound as rubble rained down around him, the windows shattering and the front doors hanging crooked from their hinges.

"Freya!" Mason called out, his own voice muted in his ears. "Say somethin'!"

Her prone body lay sprawled out across the room, limbs crooked and cut-up from the flying shrapnel. Her robe was blasted halfway up her body, her blood-spattered buttocks exposed and slightly charred. The sheer force of the explosion projected the shotgun, causing it to land a few feet away from her.

Mason located both of his guns lying a short distance in front of him. He dug his fingers into his ears and shook his head, but the shrill tone continued to assault his brain as he crawled toward his gats and wrapped his fists around the handles.

He wanted to check on Freya but thought protecting her first was more urgent. He wasn't no doctor anyhow. As he crept toward the door, he used his pistols to lead the way.

"Anybody out there, you fixin' to get bodied, bitch! Best believe that!"

Mason hyped himself up with three rapid breaths, then leapt over the threshold and pointed both barrels, his fingers ready, begging to squeeze.

There was nobody there. But whoever had just knocked had left them a message. Mason growled through his grill when he saw it.

Stuck to the door by a small black pin was Benjamin. The bill looked like it'd been through some shit, crumpled and folded, stained with what looked like blood and shit. But something else stood out too. Written in black charcoal, just beside Ben Franklin's head, were the words THIS IS YOUR GOD.

A scream rang out from upstairs. Even from that distance, and with the ringing in his ears, he recognized that voice: Horace.

Ignoring his aching body and the throbbing pain growing in his ears, Mason backtracked. Taking the stairs two at a time, he was ready to confront whoever the fuck thought they could get the drop on him.

When he reached the second floor, he pressed his back against the wall right outside Freya's bedroom. He pulled the hammers back on both his pistols. After three deep breaths—

"Got you, mutha—"

Mason felt the pain ignite in his hand before he saw the blade sticking through it. The long filet knife wiggled like a diving board as his gun dropped to the floor.

On impact, the pistol fired a shot that hit Horace in the knee, the old man positioned in the same spot they'd left him. Though he couldn't move, his wide, frantic eyes expressed his pain as blood gushed from the obliterated flesh pocket where his kneecap used to be.

"Fuuuuck!" Mason had no time to pull the knife free as his eyes scanned the room for whoever had thrown it. His remaining gun swung from corner to corner. "Where you at, huh?! Come out and face me like a man, pussy!"

He saw it coming this time but still was powerless to stop it. The knife shot out from under the bed as if it were fired from a crossbow. This one hit him in the forearm, but he managed to keep his grip on the gat.

The figure slid out from the bed and behind Horace's wheelchair like a liquid shadow, so quick Mason nearly missed it.

When the wheelchair raced across the room toward Mason, he lifted his freshly-stabbed arm—the knife shoved all the way through—and pulled the trigger as fast as his finger would allow.

The bullets punched through Horace's chest, spattering his limp, tilted head with blood moments before the chair collided with Mason and sent him backpedaling.

The impact shoved him back against the banister just outside the bedroom, but he refused to let go of his pistol.

He had just enough time to lock eyes with Horace, who was still somehow clinging to life, before a pair of rough hands grabbed hold of him and spun him around to face the one-story drop to the first floor.

One of those hands took hold of the collection of chains around Mason's neck while the other yanked the knife from his arm, making him growl with agony.

"A family that chokes together," a voice whispered into his ear, "croaks together."

The other end of the chains was wrapped around Horace's neck before the chair was turned so it was back-to-back with Mason as he was shoved over the rail.

The chains went taut and squeezed Mason's trachea—the sound of Horace's neck breaking penetrated his muted ears. As he clawed at his throat and kicked his legs, he could hear the squeaking of the wheelchair, Horace's flailing making the seat rock.

A slender man in an open overcoat appeared, clutching the bottom of the banister so his body swung beside him, smiling with a conceitedness that filled Mason with rage.

"Apologies for the clumsy rhyme," the man said through his infuriating grin. "I'm an artist, not a poet."

Mason's vision started to blur as his air supply was cut off by his glimmering accessories. Still clutching one of his pistols, he lifted his weakened arm and pressed the muzzle against the chains. While it pained him to do so, he fired a shot into the jewels that he felt naked without. Instantly, he was met with two sensations: relief from the pressure around his neck and the feeling of free-falling.

His body hit the first floor feet-first, and his legs crumbled beneath him. Mason gasped for breath as his vision started to clear, immediately searching around for the gun he no longer held.

"I know you." The voice came from behind him. Mason turned to face the slender man, pulling the blade from his hand and wielding it. "But I don't believe we've had the pleasure of meeting."

"You're him, ain't you?" Mason gripped the blade tight, pointing at the man with it, refusing to show fear as he caught his breath. "The one everybody's talkin' about."

The Artist only smiled and gave a slight bow, now holding two longer knives in both hands.

"So, what, you thought you'd come here? Turn me and my sister into one of your little exhibits?"

The Artist twirled the blades in his palms and caught them with a *shing!* "I figured someone who calls himself The Drip Man and our campaigning mayor would appreciate the attention. Imagine all those admiring eyes. But for once, this isn't about me…"

The Drip Man spat a wad of blood to the floor, then locked eyes with The Artist. "Come get it, bitch."

The Artist sprang forward with supernatural speed, slicing into Mason's oblique, then again across the back of his thigh.

Mason grunted, more from anger than agony, and when The Artist darted back in, Mason bobbed and weaved and slashed with The Artist's knife he'd pulled from his hand.

The blade stuck hilt-deep into The Artist's ribs, and Mason gave it a hard twist before releasing his grip. A guttural chuckle seeped from his lips as he watched the man drop to the floor and clutch at the knife, a look of surprised panic on his face.

"You see, mutha fucka," The Drip Man said as he pursued The Artist, who was now on his back, kicking away and scooting backward across the floor. "You came up in here thinkin' you was untouchable. Like you ain't have shit to fear. But can't nobody get the drop on The Drip Man."

The Artist tried to slash out with his knives, but Mason dodged them, then kicked him under his chin, throwing his head back and causing it to crack against the floor. Both knives clattered away, out of reach.

"You like art, nigga?" Mason reached into his pocket and slid his fingers into his decked-out brass knuckles. The instrument of violence looked like it belonged in a jewelry case. He kneeled down close to The Artist, who had lifted himself to his hands and knees. "Well, let's paint that mutha fuckin' face of yours."

Whack!

Mason smashed the sparkling knuckles against The Artist's cheekbone, flinging him violently back to the floor. As The Artist tried to crawl away, Mason followed, hitting him again and again, each blow more devastating than the last.

"Oh, you thought you was the shit, huh? You thought you was top dawg." Mason's platinum grill twinkled between his grinning lips. "I run this city, bitch."

Mason reached his thumb toward his palm, where he gripped the golden brass knuckles, feeling around. He pressed a small button at the base of the brass, triggering four spikes to protract from the metal.

"The Drip Man is the *ultimate* apex predator."

Mason hit The Artist with a sharp jab to the forehead that threw an arc of blood into the air before splashing across the floor.

"Drip."

Mason waited, allowing The Artist to rise shakily to his feet before rushing him. Driving his spiked fist into the man's gut, he followed up with a hard uppercut that threw him off his feet, then crashing back to the floor.

"Drip!"

The Artist's puncture wounds bled profusely as he scrambled away. Despite the damage, when he locked gazes with Mason, there was still no fear in his eyes.

As Mason took another step toward him, he spotted one of his gats lying on the floor nearby. He laughed as The Artist reached toward his utility belt, strapped around his torso, almost wanting the son-of-a-bitch to pull more knives out.

With his pistol back in his hand, he turned and pointed it just as The Artist unclasped something from the belt.

"This my paintbrush. And that wall behind you's my canvas." Mason cocked back the hammer and started to squeezed the trigger. "And guess who's supplyin' the paint?"

Before he could fire, The Artist's hand blurred with a quick flick as he flung something toward Mason. The razor wire glimmered in the dim lighting as it wrapped itself around Mason's wrist, the heavy metal balls on either end twirling and pulling the wire tighter.

The pressure of the momentum pushed the wires through Mason's tissue with ease. His hand was severed so cleanly, he didn't feel the pain until he was staring at it lying at his feet, his beloved gun still clutched in the twitching fingers.

The Artist crossed the room and lifted his ruby wire from the floor, blood still dripping from his various wounds. He grinned with a mouthful of red-stained teeth.

"Fuckin' cocksucker!" Mason swung out with his free hand, the spiked, sparkling brass knuckles still clutched in his fist.

Shunk!

In one rapid motion, The Artist looped the razor wire over Mason's arm at the elbow and severed it.

Mason nearly slipped on his own blood when he staggered away, back toward the stairs. As he climbed, his wrist and arm stumps furiously pumped blood.

The Artist was right on his tail. "You and that lovely sister of yours turned this city into a rotting corpse."

Mason, desperate, kicked out at The Artist, but he paid for it with his foot. In a flash, he was tangled in the wire, and watching the filled shoe tumble down the stairs, throwing rooster tails of blood.

"And piece by piece, you made that decay fester, profiting off the putridity. A pair of maggots growing fat while you suckled from the city's suffering."

Mason kicked his way to the second floor, smacking his bloody stumps against the ground as he inched his way across, thrashing like an oversized larva.

"You both thought you could fly," The Artist said as he crept along, slowly following Mason across the floor. "But it was only a matter of time before someone came along and clipped your wings."

The last thing he saw before he felt the razor wire tighten around his neck was Horace Doyle's pale, lifeless face. His milky cataracts stared down at Mason, and though they were dead, he could have sworn he saw a sparkle of satisfaction behind their stare.

Mason grimaced. *I'll see you in Hell, you fuckin' bastard.*

VAULT OF SECRETS

"Drip."

As Freya started to regain consciousness, her body ablaze with agony, she was sure the voice she heard was Mason's.

"Drip."

Though the voice didn't sound like his, she figured she was just disoriented from the blast. The last thing she remembered was pulling the trigger and watching a tidal wave of fire roaring toward her.

"Drip."

Along with the voice was a wet, rhythmic cutting sound. Freya sat up, pulling her robe down and shaking her head to clear the cobwebs in her brain.

Her vision was blurry as she faced the voice, which was coming from above. She glanced up toward the second floor, and as she'd expected, she saw the back of her brother's head. But what she didn't expect was the other man standing over him. Moving his hands back and forth, he sawed into Mason's neck with what looked like metal wire.

The man's predatory eyes landed on her just as Mason's head detached from his neck and plummeted toward the first floor.

"Drop," the man said with a grin.

The head smacked the floor and rolled toward her, coming to rest between her legs. Mason's dead eyes, one eyelid pinched shut, stared up at Freya as a shriek erupted from her throat and she scrambled away.

The slender man climbed up onto the banister as easily as a cat, opening his trench coat to reveal rows of knives strapped to his torso. He pulled one free, long and curved, and pointed it down at Freya.

"Ms. Mayor," he said as he walked the banister like a tight rope, his balance impeccable. "I was wondering if you wouldn't mind answering a few questions."

He grinned impossibly wide as a deep chuckle rattled from his chest.

Freya spotted her shotgun and dove for it. She lifted it, aimed at the man, and pulled the trigger, but it clicked empty. Which only made the man laugh harder as he stalked her from above.

Freya tossed the gun and sprinted away, down the hallway toward her vault. She thought about making a dash for it through the front door, but she worried she wouldn't be able to outrun the slender man after getting a firsthand gander at his athleticism.

By the time she reached her vault, she could hear the rapid footsteps chasing her from behind. She saw a flash of movement as she wrestled with the heavy iron door. She caught a quick glimpse of the man's smiling face just before slamming and locking the vault—sealing herself inside.

She backed away from the door, trembling. As the fear rumbled inside her, she realized that this man took out her security team—a team of highly skilled soldiers she'd chosen herself.

He killed Mason, she thought. *He killed my love!*

It didn't take long to discover that she was not alone in the vault.

The headless bodies of her security guards were arranged in a circle, on their knees and bent forward like worshippers in a sacred temple. They all held hands with one another, their fingers interlocked. And sitting in a pile at the center of them was their God: stacks of coins and gold bars along with countless bundles of cash. Sitting on the very top of the stack was the silver key to the city, gleaming in the fluorescent lights.

Freya became hypnotized by the scene, frozen in place as she took it in. The man was toying with her. He seemed to have some kind of personal vendetta. It didn't surprise her, but she never imagined anyone would have the balls to do something like this.

Freya stumbled over the slumped bodies before crashing into the mound of gold and money. Scrambling her way across the vault toward the far wall, she opened a hidden keypad. Quickly, she punched in her secret code.

Her shaking fingers made it difficult to hit the right numbers. The first attempt failed, causing the light above the keypad to flash red. She took a deep, calming breath and made a second attempt.

The light turned green just as she noticed the shadow cast against the wall in front of her. The shadow of a figure rising behind her. She turned to find one of the security guards standing, the shirt pulled high to conceal his head while he was kneeling on the ground with the others.

As his head emerged, Freya didn't recognize the Guatemalan face that scowled back at her. He snarled, his bloody countenance burning with hatred.

"Who… who the fuck are you?!" she asked.

His fist exploded from his side and collided with her face, filling her nasal cavity with blood. Freya flew backward and crashed into the wall.

"Where is my wife?" the man said as he picked up a gold bar from the pile.

"I-I have no idea what you're—"

Whack!

The gold bar slammed into the side of her head, and Freya's vision went black for a moment as the impact reverberated through her bones. She suddenly felt tired, the throbbing pain in her skull shoving her toward unconsciousness.

But strong hands grabbed her by the hair and lifted her back to her feet like a marionette. When the man hit her again, her body smacked the wall hard enough to shove it inward. But it wasn't a wall, it was the hidden door to her panic room that she'd unlocked only moments before. Her limp body collapsed into it, throwing the door open.

The light spilling from the monitors illuminated the room, the brightness making Freya squint as her headache intensified. Blood dripped from her head down into her eyes, giving everything a rosy hue.

Across from the wall of monitors were shelves filled to capacity. The bottles of Lobotozine were countless—the root of her chokehold on the city.

As Freya propped herself up and cradled her bleeding head, the man in the security uniform stepped in. His eyes transfixed to the monitors, where live footage was playing, showing various angles of dozens and dozens of people working. All were stripped down to their underwear, each playing a crucial part in the Lobotozine production assembly line. Processing, pressing, packaging. Each face with a hint of fear and panic as they worked, men and women of all ages and ethnicities.

"What… what is this…?" the man asked with a heavy accent, his voice quivering with shock and rage.

"My baby," Freya said, refusing to give this son-of-a-bitch the satisfaction of seeing her scared. "The miracle drug of all miracle drugs. But you should know miracles don't just happen, they're manufactured."

The man growled and spun on his heels to face Freya. Wrapping his fingers around her throat, he squeezed, pinching her windpipe shut as he glared into her eyes.

"My wife…! Todo lo que quiero es mi esposa!"

Freya could just barely get her words past the pressure around her throat. "If your w-wife is like y-you… she was perfect for my factory."

The man loosened his grip on her throat, eager to hear more. Freya didn't know exactly what he wanted to hear, but she had to tell him something.

"The forgotten ones, I call them. Immigrants, homeless… those assumed dead from overdose. Too much lobo puts the body into hibernation. The user loses control of all bodily functions. Like being dead-alive."

She was now starting to babble, saying things just to say them, hoping to figure the man out without saying too much. Still, Freya couldn't help but be proud when she considered all she'd built.

Grinning at her own ingenuity, she recalled stumbling on the side effect during clinical trials. "They're easy to mistake for dead. Nobody misses them… Nobody important, anyway… We aren't doing anything wrong, just putting them to work is all—"

The man lifted the gold bar over his head and slammed it down on Freya's face. Even through the pain, as he hit her again and again, Freya laughed at him. She spat a mist of blood into his face as the lumps swelled up on hers.

He growled with frustration and threw the brick into the monitors, breaking the glass and killing the picture in a couple of them. Fists resting against the desk, he faced the remaining screens. Suddenly, he perked up, defeating his slouch and becoming a rigid statue of hope.

"Estela?" He ran his fingers across a woman's face projected on the screen. A woman with a bulbous belly, clearly full-term pregnant. She wept as she packed the pills into bottles, armed guards watching from every angle.

The man sobbed and pressed his forehead against the image moments before the angle switched and showed another group of workers.

"Estela?!"

He turned to face Freya again, retrieving the bar from the shattered monitor screen, his chest heaving as he glared down at her. The gold brick shook in his fist as he closed the distance between them.

"Where is she?"

"Where she belongs," Freya growled through her teeth. "Where she'll die, her and that border baby inside her!"

There was a flash of gold before the bar slammed into the side of her head. Several follow-up shots thudded into the middle of her face.

Freya held on to a shred of consciousness as she collapsed to the floor, squirming as she tried to crawl away. But the next thing she knew, she was yanked back up and slammed against the wall.

The gold bar was shoved into her mouth, scraping against her already bloody, chipped enamel. As it was crammed deeper, it stretched her cheeks, tearing the corners of her mouth to make room for its girth.

The man roared and sobbed as he wiggled the brick back and forth, shoving it deeper. Until he leaned on it so hard that her jaw *popped,* disconnecting and hanging loose from her head. Within the now gaping hole, Freya's tongue writhed, drowning in a pool of blood and teeth shards.

Retracting the gold bar, the man tossed it aside and reached toward the shelves above Freya's head. Pulling down armfuls of Lobotozine, he tore the packages open. Then, like an excited child, he began dumping the black pills down her throat, filling her wide-open mouth. He used his fist to shove them deeper, making room for more to enter.

"This is what you care about," the man whispered.

Freya couldn't help but swallow them down, her broken nose making it near impossible to breathe.

It didn't take long before she felt the effects of the drug ripping through her system, flooding her with chemicals.

For a brief moment, everything felt okay. All of her troubles and worries seemed to float away.

But then a potent fear grabbed hold of her mind and burrowed to the core. An inhuman dread manifested, something meant only for the damned souls in Hell to experience.

An infinite, eternal fear that sank its fangs and talons into Freya's spirit and dragged her into the darkness.

VÁMONOS

Diego watched the last bit of life dissolve from the mayor's eyes, her mouth resembling a candy dispenser filled to the brim with black licorice. A white and gray foam bubbled up around the pile of pills crammed into her bloody throat, collapsing as the moisture dissolved them.

He turned away from her, realizing his fists were curled so tight his nails were digging into his palms. Facing the monitors, he noticed half of them now either grayed out or fuzzy and distorted. But from what he could see, the displays showed dozens and dozens of faces. Diego scanned them, hoping to catch another glimpse of his wife. He couldn't help but wonder if maybe she had been a figment of his imagination. A quick flash of hope conjured by his mind to justify the atrocious acts he'd just committed.

No... I saw her, he thought. *I know I did. I saw how much her belly has grown. I saw my baby...*

Diego never had a chance to find out their child's sex. He didn't know how to imagine his baby's face. But he took a small measure of comfort in knowing his seed was still alive and on the verge of pushing itself into the world.

"Te encontraré," Diego said as he ran his fingertips across the screens, smearing blood across them. "Lo juro por Dios."

He heard a tapping from the vault door. "Still alive in there?" a muffled voice asked from the other side.

Diego crossed the vault and opened the door, revealing The Artist, who cringed slightly from a plethora of new injuries.

"Well, look at this." The Artist stepped into the room, an amused expression on his face as he took in the aftermath. He was finishing up using a small tube of super glue to seal his wounds shut, showing no signs of discomfort as he pinched the punctures closed. "I see she fell into our trap, hm?"

As The Artist inspected the aftermath, Diego kept his back to him while he continued studying the screens. Still, he struggled to spot Estela again, becoming more and more convinced he never saw her in the first place.

"A bit sloppy, but you got the job done," The Artist said, crouching beside the mayor and inspecting the details of her death like a judge at a murder pageant. "As an artist, you're still at that scribbling stage. We've just got to work on coloring inside the lines, yes?"

"I saw her," Diego said, his frustration reaching a breaking point. He slammed his fist against the desk below the screens, making the wood groan.

The impact of the punch caused a small drawer to slide open. Inside lay a metal box the size of a lunch pail. Diego grabbed it and tried to pry it open, but it was locked tight. Something rattled inside when he shook it.

The Artist approached Diego, staring at the monitors. Cocking his head, he watched the live footage showing countless victims forced to work alongside teams of armed guards who watched their every move.

"I've heard whisperings about this operation," The Artist said, more fascinated than concerned for Diego's family. "I pride myself in knowing this city inside and out, but even I've never run across it. Are you sure this is where they're keeping your wife?"

Diego nodded, finally turning away from the locked box to face The Artist, whose hand now gripped his shoulder. Panic blossomed in his chest when he saw the look on the blood-spattered killer's face. A look with doom written all over it.

"What is it?" Diego asked.

"I've only heard things… what they do with their workers who refuse to obey, who step out of line. Who outlive their usefulness."

"No!"

Diego shoved The Artist's hand off his shoulder, refusing to listen. Refusing to even consider what he was saying. He couldn't get this close only to run out of time right at the finish line.

Fueled with a new burst of adrenaline, he started tearing the room apart, searching for a key to the box. Diego tossed shelves full of pills to the ground and ripped the monitors off the walls but found nothing.

He pushed past The Artist and into the vault. Quickly, he checked the pockets of the dead security guards until his eyes landed on the mound of the mayor's riches. The key to the city shone from the top of the pile. It meant nothing when he'd placed it atop the pile before, but now, he grabbed it with enthusiasm.

Diego heard The Artist speaking to him, but it was just garbled noise behind him as he raced back into the panic room and picked up the metal box.

He held his breath with anticipation as he jammed the key into the hole and turned it. The box unlocked and popped open. When he found a folded-up piece of paper inside, Diego's heart raced. He quickly tore it open and spread it out on the desk.

He couldn't help but smile as he studied the details of the elaborate map. A trio of red Xs marked specific spots around the city—presumably entry points. The Artist pointed to one that appeared to be hidden deep beneath a large structure.

"That's not far from the police station," The Artist said, standing just behind Diego as he loomed over him and pointed toward the X on the map again. "Got to hand it to her"—he glanced at Mayor McKinney's bloody corpse—"not the first place you'd think to look."

Diego folded the map back up and faced The Artist. He was ready to do anything it took to finish what they'd started. He'd spent his life trying to be a good man, an honorable person. He'd tried to follow his wife's footsteps.

But this was not a job for *that* Diego. This was a job for the *new* Diego. The Diego who followed The Artist's example. Who was ready to take the paintbrush into his own hands and splash some fucking color.

While his exhibit would be hidden beneath the city, its message would change it forever.

"Vámonos."

Diego stormed out of the mayor's vault and toward the front door. But before he stepped off the porch, suddenly he froze. His eyes darted down, and he spotted Benjamin still held to the door. He unpinned the money and stuffed it into his pocket. The bill would be the last money he ever earned in this godforsaken place.

Ready for war, he marched toward the glowing lights of the city's heart.

THE FORGOTTEN THINGS

The gas filled the charred police building like a rolling fog, clouding the air with chemicals before anyone inside had a chance to react. By the time they saw or smelled it, they found themselves paralyzed on the floor.

Police officers and desk workers—the few that remained—and various citizens who were either being booked or reporting a crime, collapsed onto the floor. They all lay helpless and still aside from the rising and falling of their bellies and the frantic darting of their eyes.

Diego and The Artist stepped through the fog, both wearing gas masks. Stepping over the prone bodies, they rushed their way through what remained of the building—the heavily damaged, missing, and burned areas were blocked off by large sheets of plastic.

Diego looked around, still not seeing what he was

hoping to. The Artist stepped forward, and Diego let him, hoping he'd have better luck figuring it out.

"It's further ahead," The Artist said, and when he turned to show Diego, he found him crouched beside one of the officers, removing a pistol from the cop's holster.

"I see the men in the video," Diego said as he checked the magazine for bullets. "They had weapons… big guns."

"I told you not to worry," The Artist replied. "I know where the armory is. While I won't partake in the use of such crass weaponry, I'm not a fool either. If we're going to walk out of those tunnels alive, we'll need to arm you with something that packs a little more punch than the mayor's security team."

Diego pulled another gun from a second officer, the older man's eyes glaring at Diego and The Artist, clearly wanting to do something to stop them. But he remained helpless, trapped inside his poisoned body. Diego held the pistol out for The Artist.

"Did you not hear me?" he asked, turning his nose up at the gun as if using it was beneath him. "I have my own tools of choice. But again, while I might disparage the presence of such an uncivilized instrument, I understand your situation may warrant its use. However… if you want to survive, you'll need to do better than that."

They walked deeper into the police station, passing the rows of holding cells. The inmates behind the bars were equally paralyzed by the gas.

The Artist finally slowed his stride outside a large metal door with a brass placard above it that read ARMORY.

"Ah, here we are," The Artist said.

A police officer was propped up against the wall beside the door, seemingly guarding it before the vapors hit him.

The Artist reached toward the officer and yanked a set of keys from the belt loop of his slacks. He had to try a few keys before finally finding the right one. When he unlocked the door, he turned back to Diego.

"After you, killer."

Diego didn't hesitate a second before stepping up and shoving the door open. He pointed the guns as he rushed across the threshold, prepared for a brigade of officers to be waiting for them inside. But the only thing beyond that door was enough guns to invade a country with. Arranged in neat rows in every direction, grouped by their size and potential for destruction.

One look at the collection and Diego set his handguns down. Spinning in place, he took it all in, suddenly feeling a bit better about what he was about to do.

"Even I have to admit," The Artist said as he stepped into the armory, "the selection is pretty impressive."

Diego's breath fogged the goggles of his gas mask, making it difficult to see clearly. Beads of sweat rolled down his face and neck.

He spotted a gun belt and strapped it over his waist. After finding a magnum pistol, he shoved it into one of the holsters. He then grabbed a shotgun and an assault rifle with a shoulder strap.

"Do you know how to load or even use those?" The Artist asked with fascination as he watched.

Diego answered with silence, holding his arsenal awkwardly.

"Here." The Artist moved quickly as he loaded each gun, making sure to pack some extra ammo, as much as Diego could carry without slowing him down. He gave him some brief instruction on using the weaponry before pulling a bulletproof vest off the wall and slipping it onto Diego's torso.

"You hardly look human anymore," The Artist said with a chuckle as he cocked his head and studied battle-ready Diego. The gas mask made him look like some kind of bird of prey from a dystopian world. "Are you prepared for what we might find down there?"

"Sí." Diego slung the assault rifle over his shoulder and racked the shotgun. "Estoy listo."

"Good." The Artist reached inside his jacket and extracted the mayor's map. Holding the paper up, he traced his finger from the location of the police station to the red X some distance away. "Follow me."

Diego did his best to keep up, his new weapons weighing him down, as The Artist moved toward an exit door and threw it open. The winter air felt good against Diego's skin since he was already sweating beneath the vest.

Now outside, both men removed their gas masks. Diego was relieved to get it off, relishing in the fresh, cool air.

"There," The Artist said and pointed to a seemingly abandoned structure in the near distance. Close enough to see in the dark but far enough away to be easily overlooked. "Looks like this building was once an evidence storage facility of some kind. According to the map, it's now used for more sinister purposes. The placement of this location doesn't paint the prior police department leadership in a good light. I wonder if the current regime will ever even find out, or worse, if they already know but aren't planning on doing anything about it. With the headquarters looking the way it does, nothing would surprise me."

He showed Diego the map and pointed to the red X.

"Let's go." Diego marched straight for the building, ignoring his screaming nerves.

When The Artist found the heavy chains wrapped around the front doors, he scratched his head. "Maybe this is an old, unused entrance into the tunnel system?"

Diego shrugged.

The Artist snickered as he pulled out his lockpick and made quick work of it. He had to hold Diego back from rushing inside.

"I understand your eagerness, but don't let your haste be our downfall. We go together, calm and collected. Yes?"

Diego wanted to shove him aside and storm his way into the structure, guns blazing. But he took a deep breath and nodded, allowing The Artist to take the lead.

The interior of the building was dark and coated in thick layers of dust and cobwebs. Spiders and roaches scurried in every direction as the two men crept through.

The Artist looked the room over, sliding his hands over the walls and various surfaces. Then he toed a small divot in a steel section of the floor. He crouched as he pulled his mini crowbar from his tool belt, the same one he used to pry open manhole covers. Angling it just right and pressing down, he lifted the secret opening in the floor. A gust of warm wind blasted out of the opening like the exhalation of a giant beast luring them to step inside its mouth and travel into its belly.

The Artist glanced toward Diego and gave him a slight nod before climbing into the hole and out of sight. Diego took another deep, calming breath and then followed.

The ladder that led from the trap door into the darkness of this underground place was long and seemed to stretch on forever. Diego could hear The Artist's footsteps clinging against the metal rungs but couldn't see him. The scent of decay wafted into his face, growing stronger the deeper he went. His stomach churned with anxiety as his mind played out scenarios like movie clips:

His wife lying dead with her stomach torn open, their baby red and motionless beside her like a cherry gummy bear. The workers lined up behind his wife, taking turns savagely raping her, breaking her water with their thrusting cocks.

He even imagined his wife alive and well but furious with him for taking so long to find her, for letting this happen to her and their child. Heartache poked about in his chest as he imagined her refusing to go with him, blaming him for everything.

"Easy now," The Artist said, his voice seeping from the dark.

Diego had been so in his own head that he didn't realize he'd reached the end of the ladder. A soft light glowing beneath him illuminated the dirt tunnel that stretched into the darkness ahead.

The Artist stood just below, holding out a hand to help Diego down.

Once on the ground, Diego immediately aimed his shotgun in every direction, prepared to start shooting if he saw the slightest movement.

The air was thick and dry. Sweat poured off Diego's face and head as he wiped his brow with his shirt sleeve.

"I heard something up ahead," The Artist said, holding a long knife in each hand, his eyes narrowed and pointed down the tunnel. "Voices. At least three, maybe more."

"Then we must go," Diego said, gripping his shotgun with both hands and clenching his teeth. "Andale!"

Diego didn't wait for The Artist to respond as he jogged forward, the images of his wife being gangraped quickening his pace.

The tunnel wound like the body of a coiled snake, taking them deeper and deeper beneath the city. Every turn was blind, and Diego kept his shotgun aimed just in case he ran into whoever those voices belonged to.

When he finally found them, he didn't fire his gun. Instead, he screeched to a halt and had to use the gun to hold himself up—the mere sight of what lay ahead nearly making his knees collapse.

They hung from the dirt walls on either side of him, displayed in such a manner that Diego wondered if The Artist was responsible. Maybe the killer behind him had been leading Diego along the whole time, manipulating him, waiting for the right moment to strike.

But as he stared, he could tell this was done by a much cruder hand than The Artist's. The display lacked precision and attention to detail.

Like dissected frogs mangled by the hands of juveniles, the walls were lined with the mutilated bodies of countless men and women. Pinned to the walls by nails and chains, each body displayed a different degree of depravity.

The corpses Diego first encountered were aged to the point of mummification, eye sockets empty, lips pulled back to show their teeth, flesh gray and dried out like paper mâché. Some of them were missing limbs, others had their torsos split open and emptied.

The odor of rot became unbearable, nearly choking Diego as he kept walking, passing mangled body after mangled body. The deeper he went, the fresher the bodies became. His pulse pounded in his ears as he checked the faces of each corpse, anticipating spotting the face of his wife. For those without heads or faces, he examined their bodies, searching for any familiar attributes.

"This was done to make a statement," The Artist said as he caught up with Diego. His voice made Diego turn on his heels and aim his gun, completely on edge. The Artist didn't bat an eye as he reached up and studied one of the bodies. "A message to the others under their rule. To show them what would happen if they dared to rebel or showed any signs of insubordination."

Diego clenched his teeth tighter, his imagination running wild as he realized that the men responsible for these horrific acts had held his wife and unborn child captive for many months.

"We have to stop them…" Diego said.

Diego reached up toward the nearest corpse, its face peeled back like a banana. The torso was splayed open, the intestines stretched out and staked to the wall making it look like an octopus was bursting free from the belly. The genitals were shredded into thin ribbons that hung from the groin like a blood-soaked pompom.

When Diego's hand made the slightest contact with one of the fleshy gut ropes, the corpse took in a sudden inhalation of breath that sounded dry and painful. Its skeletal face choked and grunted as its body writhed against the dirt wall, the teeth clicking together.

The sound of its wailing woke a few of the others, who whined and squealed with agony as they thrashed against their restraints, each display grislier than the last. Barely clinging to consciousness, they'd been kept alive for the sake of cruelty alone. As their raw nerves blasted with unspeakable pain, Diego's eyes glossed over a bit.

The chorus of torture filled the air, making Diego wince and grimace as he walked past them. When they finally reached the massive metal door at the end of the tunnel, he felt a bit of reprieve. But just as he laid eyes on the door… the lever turned and it started to swing open.

The man stepped out, assault rifle in hand. He and Diego locked eyes. The man didn't have time to show his surprise before The Artist leapt on him, easing the door shut while simultaneously driving the blade of his knife through the man's head. Before the guard could raise his gun, The Artist had pushed the steel through the flesh beneath his chin and worked the tip into the base of his brain. A quick, silent death—despite the way the man's body convulsed, his boots clattering against the ground like galloping horse hooves. When he finally went still, The Artist laid him to the dirt. He hissed and winced, the wounds on his face weeping blood despite the glue that had previously been holding them shut.

"I've got another vial of my sleeping gas," he whispered as he reached toward his belt. "Enough to drop every person on the other side of this door. We can be in and out in no time. Wouldn't even have to fire a single shot—"

The Artist furrowed his brow as he patted his belt, searching to no avail. "Strange… I must've dropped it back at the station. We could always go back to the sewers first if—"

"No. My wife and baby inside. It not worth the risk."

The Artist nodded. "Then we have to kill them all ourselves. Are you ready for that?"

Diego didn't hesitate this time. "Whatever you need. I will do the job."

The Artist cocked his head, studying Diego again. A grin spread across his face as he nodded his approval.

"Splendid."

THE WOMB IN THE TOMB

Estela did her best to hide the pain as another contraction erupted across her abdomen. She clenched her jaw and ground her teeth, fighting to keep her expression blank as she counted out the pills and vacuum sealed them into bags.

A small gasp escaped her lips, and she gripped the edge of the table. She quickly glanced toward the guards nearest her and held her breath as the contraction eased up and gave her a temporary moment of relief. A moment she knew would pass quickly.

"Hey," one of the guards said. His eyes narrowed as he glared across the room at Estela.

Estela braced herself. Her eyes fluttered once as she felt her baby shift inside her belly, as if positioning itself for another push.

No… not yet. Not here, she thought.

"Speed it up!" The guard thrust his gun toward her to emphasize his words, then moved on.

Estela gently breathed a sigh of relief and went back to work, moving as fast as she could to keep any attention away from her.

The other workers around her kept their eyes averted. They didn't look at the guards or one another. Instead, they kept to themselves as they worked, either praying for rescue or death.

Just as Estela wondered, for what felt like the millionth time, if Diego would ever come for her, if he was out there looking for her—

—she felt a warmth pour across her feet and legs. Like someone had spilled a hot bowl of soup on her. But more than feeling the temperature, she heard the splash.

And so did everyone else.

Several heads in the room turned toward Estela. A guard lifted his gun, pointing the business end toward the sound. Every worker suddenly stopped what they were doing to get a look.

Estela's first instinct was to join them. It took her a moment to realize the liquid had come out of her. She felt the soaked fabric of her dress and lifted her feet from the puddle of translucent fluid pooling around her.

"Nnnggghhh!" Another contraction—the most violent one yet—took hold of her and twisted. It brought her to her knees, dropping down onto the puddle. She growled through her teeth, no longer able to hold it in.

"Get that bitch," one of the guards said, his voice flat and without empathy. "The rest of you keep working!"

As a trio of the armed guards made their way toward Estela, she saw past them. Saw what they were too distracted to notice.

The large door that was the only way in or out eased open. She thought it was a trick of the light at first but then saw a figure dart into the room. Like the shadow of an alley cat, moving fast and almost impossible to keep up. As it closed in and slid inside, it kept low to the ground, moving like black water.

"Let's go," one of the guards said as he grabbed Estela by the arm and lifted her to her feet. "Time to stick you and that fuckin' mongrel baby onto the wall."

The other two guards laughed, both aiming their guns at Estela. One at her head, the other at her belly.

They didn't notice the figure as it stood up behind them. It was tall and slim—somehow cloaked in shadow despite the light in the room. The eyes seemed impossibly darker, making the shadow around them look light gray.

A flash of metal like silver lightning. And then a wave of red gushing from the throat of the guard who had his gun aimed at Estela's unborn.

The guard didn't seem to realize he'd been slashed. He just stood there, eyes wide and mouth agape, as the blood pumped from the gash across his neck. By the time his legs went out from under him, the other two guards had already been cut. One stabbed at the base of his skull, the other through the ribs and into his heart.

Blood collectively erupted from their bodies, spraying across the tables and workers. Splashing over hundreds and hundreds of ebony pills.

The workers all panicked together, screaming and scrambling to get away from the killer who stood at the center of the dead guards. The other gunmen in the room came for him, all of them aiming their barrels—ready to shoot.

But the shadowy figure only smiled, holding up his knife and watching the blood drip from its edge. He had various wounds across his face and body, some open and oozing blood. The pain didn't seem to slow him.

"You motherfuck—" the guard closest to the door started to say.

But a second figure that had entered the room shut him up. This figure didn't bother sneaking, instead choosing to kick the door in and let off a bright flash of fire from what looked like a machine gun.

The guard's head turned into a red mist like an aerosol spray. His finger twitched and squeezed down on the trigger of his assault rifle, making the second mysterious figure drop to his stomach to duck for cover. The headless gunman's legs kept working despite having no brain to send them signals, taking shaky, sloppy steps like a newborn gazelle, circling in place as he sprayed the room with bullets.

Multiple workers took the hot lead to the chest and stomach, bloody flowers blooming across their torsos before they collapsed in heaps to the floor.

Just before the headless guard finally fell over, his finger fired off one more bullet that punched a hole right through another guard's face, from his left eye to the back of his skull. The last burst of life he had was spent flopping around on the floor as his brains leaked from his widened eye socket like gray and red soft serve.

Estela screamed, partly because of the chaos around her but mostly because her baby was coming, and it felt like it had grown porcupine quills.

Estela crawled toward another woman with a gunshot wound in the center of her chest. She pressed down on the bleeding hole with both hands as the woman choked and convulsed. But when the next violent contraction hit her, she shoved away from the dying woman and collapsed to her back, clawing at the floor as she squirmed with agony. Her hips felt ready to crack in half, her legs spread wide as her heels dragged.

She couldn't help anyone. She couldn't even move. When she glanced at the woman, who was now clearly dead and staring blankly at the ceiling, Estela couldn't help but wonder if she was the lucky one.

As her baby started to crown, widening her vagina to its limit, her frantic eyes darted around the room.

The tall man now had two knives, one in each hand. Both blades were stabbed to the hilt, resting inside a pair of guards. The first deep in the gut of one man, the other through the cheeks of the second man, whose teeth scraped against the red steel.

When a third guard came charging at him, the tall man grimaced as he yanked his knife from the guard's stomach, unzipping his flesh as he dragged the blade across his belly, and then flung it. It zipped through the air and buried itself through the incoming guard's nasal cavity, the tip bursting out the back of his head. The unzipped guard's innards poured over the floor in front of him a moment before the deadweight of his body collapsed down on top of it with a squish.

The tall man seemed to struggle a bit as he pulled his other knife from the remaining guard's cheeks in an outward motion, bestowing him with a bloody Cheshire grin. The tall man dug his fingertips up under the flesh of the dangling skin. Giving it a hard yank, he peeled the face halfway off, from his upper lip to the bridge of his nose. Another tug pulled the skin the rest of the way, the face and scalp hanging off the back of his bloody skull like a leathery hood.

The tall man glanced over at Estela as if he could feel her watching him. She was taken aback when he winked at her, clearly feeling the pain of his wounds that bled more profusely.

Rapid gunfire erupted as the guards moved in toward the man in the blood-soaked trench coat. Their bullets peppered the floor and shredded the wall behind him. But somehow, the hail of shots missed the tall man, as if the bullets themselves were too scared to touch him.

All of the workers were down on the ground now, their screams drowned out by the gunfire as they covered themselves. Fragments of black pills and powder flew everywhere, bouncing off the ground or poofing into the air as the room was annihilated.

The second figure was still ducked near the door, and when he stood up again, he was already firing his weapon. Semi-automatic bursts erupted from his gun as he sprayed a cluster of guards, dotting them with bloody holes that made them look like red domino tiles.

A few guards turned their attention toward the gunman while the rest continued their attack on the tall man.

Estela squealed as another surge swept over her. She could feel the head pushing its way out as she reached down and pressed against it, trying to delay the birth. She wanted to do her best to protect her baby from being born into such pandemonium.

But it was useless to resist it. This baby was determined to exist, and Estela was helpless to do anything but lie there and let it happen.

When the gunman rose up again and fired at the guards, Estela was sure she was seeing things. What her eyes were telling her must've been skewed by the stress of the situation. Perhaps trying to calm her by projecting her dreams from the last nine months—injecting a little hope into such a dire predicament.

"D-Diego…?" Estela whispered.

Though she kept repeating to herself that it wasn't possible for her husband to be there, there was no denying that the man locked in a gunfight was a spitting image of him. He was a sweet, loving man, but that look on his face was something she'd never seen before. Even when they journeyed from Guatemala to the States, surrounded by danger at every turn. The day he found out Estela was pregnant with their first child. When they were penniless in a city that lured the lost with promises of a brighter future only to suck the juice from their bodies, leaving dried out husks behind. Even then, Diego didn't wear the mask of rage he wore now.

That expression on Diego's face was the expression of a man with something to lose. After a lifetime of having nothing, Diego was the kind of man who would protect his own until his last breath.

He's really here…

Diego dropped out of sight, hiding behind a cement panel on the stairs by the door. The guards fired, cracking the slab, dust and cement chips flying into the air. When he rose back up, he held a shotgun with both hands, firing at the nearest goon.

The shot hit the guard in the neck, blowing off two thirds of it and creating a crimson shower of meat. His head hung from the remaining flesh and tendon, the mouth stretched into a scream that lacked the vocal cords to accomplish it.

One bullet hit Diego in the shoulder. Blood misted into the air a moment before he dropped back behind his barricade.

"Diego!" Estela shrieked from the pit of her stomach, using her pain to give it power. But her baby demanded her full attention as it started shoving its way out. She reached down and felt its head, now fully emerged. A new level of pain crackled across her body like volts of electricity as the shoulders of the fetus worked their way out a torturous centimeter at a time.

When her eyes were finally able to crack open, she caught sight of the tall man, who seemed to spin in place like a cyclone with fangs and claws. The guards were shredded and sliced to bloody ribbons, their bodies lying all around him.

Hunched sideways, the man was clearly in agony as he pressed the base of his knife against one of his bloody wounds as if trying to stop the bleeding. Shaking off the injury, the man forced himself to stand tall, knives extending from his hands like they were part of him. He flicked his wrists, throwing arcs of blood across the floor almost as if he was signing his work. A splattery signature that he admired with a cocked head.

"Help him!" Estela roared, now cradling her slimy baby with both hands down between her widely spread legs.

The tall man's face whipped in her direction. He seemed to snap out of his trance when he saw that Diego was still locked in a gunfight with a couple of guards. The last two monsters, the only thing standing in the way of freedom.

He stuck both of his knives into the strap across his torso, then reached deeper into his coat, toward his back.

His hand emerged wrapped around the hilt of a long, slender machete. If his other knives were children, this one was their mother.

The tall man gave Estela a quick nod before he took off across the room like a panther, wearing the shadows around him like warpaint.

The last two guards never saw him coming.

With one hard yet graceful swing, he took off both legs of the first guard like they were made of clay. The legs dropped out from under him, the bloody stumps of his thighs so cleanly cut that he stayed upright when they hit the floor.

The tall man spun and drove the tip of the blade into the second guard's lower back, next to the base of his spine, yanking upward in a smooth, violent motion.

The steel cut through the guard's body like a moist birthday cake, bursting out the top of his skull, sending a geyser of blood into the air like a fountain outside a casino.

The guard's two equal halves, sliced vertically, drooped to either side of him as his legs stumbled and staggered a few steps. Slimy viscera poured from his bisected body in a sloppy pile at his feet, and when he stepped on it, he finally crashed to the floor. The fingers of both hands kept curling and uncurling like they were trying to grab hold of something.

"Please!" the legless goon sobbed, still somehow propped up on his stumps. "You can't fucking do this—!"

The tall man had his machete raised, ready to silence the last guard, but he never got a chance to.

A gunshot exploded behind him, the bullet driving a hole into the guard's forehead, making his eyes cross before he collapsed backward.

But Diego wasn't satisfied.

He leapt over the cement barricade with a massive magnum in his hands, pushed past the tall man, and fired the gun into the guard. Diego blew a wide, gaping hole into the man's face as he marched toward him, but he kept firing.

When he finished, when the hand cannon finally clicked empty, he had the barrel pressed into the minced meat that used to be a face. Breathing heavily through his clenched teeth, face covered in a mask of blood, he looked lost.

"Diego!" Estela screamed. She pleaded to him with her eyes. When he finally turned and saw her, he could see their baby had pulled free, the umbilical cord still inside of her.

Her face slick with tears, snot, and sweat, she wept as she finally held her baby in her arms, fresh and warm and wet with blood and fluid.

Diego sprinted across the room, dropping his weapons and ignoring the pain of his bleeding shoulder. It was like nothing existed anymore except his family. Not the tall man, not the guards, not any of the other panicking workers.

"Estela!" he bellowed through his sobbing mouth as he dropped to his knees beside her and wrapped his arms around her and their newborn. "Lo siento, mi amor… lo siento mucho…"

He bawled into her neck as he nestled into her, kissing her frantically. And despite the pain still radiating across her body, Estela reached up and held him tight. Finally reunited—finally rescued.

As if to signal their unification, the baby's first cry wailed from her tiny throat. It was a messy moment, but Estela couldn't have wished for anything more perfect.

"Nuestro bebe," Diego said, and then hugged them tighter.

Their family was finally whole. Estela was ready to leave their bloody past behind and walk into a brighter future, hand in hand. But Diego leaned in close and pressed his mouth to her ear.

"You and the baby get out," he whispered in Spanish. "I'll be right behind you."

THE FINAL EXHIBIT

The Artist watched from across the room, letting Diego have his moment with the family he'd fought so hard to win back. He'd earned this moment. Killed for it.

As he observed them, he felt just the slightest flutter in his chest. Where his heart might be if he had one. A flutter of joy with just a hint of envy.

He knew he would never have what Diego had. What James had—or what he thought he had, anyway. He would be alone in the darkness of the sewer with only the rats and roaches to keep him company.

And his art.

His fingers tingled as he imagined how he would depict the scenes he had to add to the collection.

And I think I'll draw one in honor of Diego and his family, he thought. *Why not?*

The Artist knew this would be the last he ever saw of Diego. There was no reason to stay in touch, especially with a new baby.

I'll find others to help. Really help. Maybe I'm done killing. Maybe it's time to leave death behind and start embracing life.

The thought made him smile, watching Diego hug his wife and child with a strong sense of pride. The kind of pride he thought James must have felt when he was teaching him through the years.

Soon, he knew, he would have to see to Diego's wife. Make sure any injuries to her or the baby were addressed. He'd have to ensure that she birthed the placenta and sever the umbilical cord.

The Artist turned away from them, giving them their privacy, enjoying the fantasy in his mind of the new life that lay ahead of him.

Perhaps this is the end. My final exhibit.

The thought made him smile.

He heard the large door open, but when he glanced toward it, he only saw Diego's wife, cradling the baby in her arms. She staggered her way through the opening and out of sight.

The Artist turned to find Diego standing behind him, pulling his gas mask over his head while simultaneously plucking the missing vial of gas from his shirt pocket.

Very clever, my friend.

The Artist nodded in approval, made eye contact with Diego through the cloudy goggles of the Guatemalan's mask.

The split-second wouldn't have been enough to avoid the trap. Instead of fighting it, The Artist watched Diego smashed the vial against the floor, releasing an instant cloud of chemical gas that swept over the room like a ghostly tidal wave.

The Artist smiled even wider than before. The only emotion he felt in that moment as he closed his eyes and let the cloud envelope him was pride.

Diego was protecting his family. Because that's what husbands and fathers are wired to do.

And The Artist could do nothing but respect it.

When the cloud dissipated, The Artist found himself lying on his back, staring up at the ceiling. Though he knew he was still conscious and inside his body, it felt like he was floating. Like he was a spirit free from its physical form.

When Diego appeared above The Artist, his face still behind the gas mask, he wanted to smile and tell him he understood. But he could do nothing but stare and hope that Diego could sense it.

"You help me get back my family… and I will always remember that," Diego said as he reached toward The Artist's belt and picked up the machete. "But…"

Diego lowered himself to his knees beside The Artist and lifted the machete over his head, the tip of the blade pointed at the center of The Artist's chest.

"All that matters now is to keep them safe. And that will not be possible if someone like you is living." Diego's eyes glossed over. "I hope you will understand…"

I do… and I'm proud of you. I'm honored to be the subject of such an exhibit. It's just a shame the world will never get a chance to see it.

"I'm sorry."

Diego drove the blade through The Artist's chest, pinning him to the floor.

The last thing The Artist saw as the squirming darkness closed in on him was Diego walking through the door, leaving the hatred behind and moving forward with love.

It was the happiest The Artist had ever been as he faded away, drifting toward the dumpster in the sky.

ONE LAST STOP

"Shouldn't we go to the hospital?" Estela asked in Spanish as she cradled their baby in Diego's undershirt. He had changed out of his blood-spattered button-up shirt, now wearing a cheap T-shirt he bought from a corner store with a broken window.

"No!" Diego didn't mean to shout, but imagining taking his wife and child anywhere near that hospital, or any facility in the city, filled him with instant panic.

"Trust me," he said, relieved to speak his native tongue again with the most important person in his life, "we don't want to go there. Let's sleep tonight. Get cleaned up. And in the morning, we leave this fucking city. Find a new home."

"But where?" Estela asked.

Diego remained stoic. "*Anywhere* but here."

Estela looked ready to ask more questions, but she just didn't have the energy. She leaned against a building and collected herself. Wincing, she caught her breath, looking down at her dress soaked with blood and birth fluids.

Their baby slept, bundled up in the shirt and pressed lovingly to Estela's chest. Still covered in muck and chunks of coagulated blood, but peaceful nonetheless.

"Just… just give me a moment, okay?" Estela asked.

Diego nodded and rubbed gentle circles over her back. He peppered her head with kisses, then leaned over and planted a light peck on the baby's head. The baby swirled and blurred in his vision as tears started to well up.

They were only a few blocks away from his tiny efficiency apartment, but Diego knew he couldn't take them there. Not because the place was embarrassingly cramped and untidy but because the other people who lived in that building were some of the city's most vicious.

"How much further?" Estela asked, her voice whispery from exhaustion.

Diego peered into the distance in the direction of his apartment building but then looked away. He caught sight of a manhole cover just ahead in the street.

"Not far at all."

As she continued to recover, clearly in a lot of pain, Diego's eyes darted in every direction. He felt exposed out in the open, right in the heart of the city. Feeling the presence of monsters all around them.

But one thing he no longer felt was fear. He almost dared them to try something with his adrenaline still pumping. He'd gone from slayer mode to protective husband and father mode, both of which were equally deadly.

He realized Estela was leaning on the brick wall of a pawn shop, its neon signs burning brightly. He'd been too distracted to notice it, and when he saw the word JEWELRY lit up in bright green font, he remembered a promise he had made to Estela when they got married in Guatemala, mere days before their trip to the States.

I'm sorry I can't afford a ring, he had told her, his chest tight with shame.

I need nothing from you except your heart, Estela had said.

Her sweetness knew no bounds. All that she wanted was to spend the rest of her life with him, to start a family together.

When we get to America, I will work and make enough money to buy you the ring you deserve, Diego had said. *I promise you.*

Diego shoved his hand into his pocket and pulled out Benjamin. The bill filled him with dread, brought all the trauma from the past day to the forefront of his mind. The moment he was in the presence of Benjamin—whether in his possession or James'—his life took several turns he would've never imagined.

I got my family back. Nothing else matters.

Using Benjamin to fulfill that promise felt fitting somehow, the perfect way to end this hellacious chapter in their lives. The perfect symbol to detach from the past and soar toward their future.

"Stay right here," Diego said before kissing Estela on the forehead. "I'll be right back."

Before Estela could say a word, Diego threw the pawn shop door open and darted inside.

Through a plate glass window in the shop, he could still see Estela. He made sure to keep his eye on her even as he crossed the store toward the counter.

An Asian woman was already there, finishing her purchase with the clerk. She was thin, had a faraway look in her eye that he recognized as a side effect of the lobo. He recalled seeing it in the eyes of Miguel's other workers time and time again.

When the clerk handed her a small brown paper bag, she snatched it with a look of relief. Heavily exhaling, she clutched it to her chest and smiled to herself, oblivious of Diego's presence as he passed her on his way to the counter.

A television played from a shelf behind the clerk—the evening news. A reporter was interviewing a hysterical woman in a nurse's uniform, and though Diego didn't recognize her, a surge of anxiety filled his chest when he realized she was standing in front of Memorial Hospital. A graphic at the bottom of the screen gave the nurse's name: RENE WHITE.

"Dr. Finkelstein, he… he was a great man," the woman said through her sobs. "He didn't deserve what happened to him. Murdered by an ex-surgeon, jealous of his success. He… he tied me up, and he—"

The video cut to the anchor, who seemed almost annoyed at Rene's panicked tone. "Another tragedy befalls our once great city. One bright spot, most newborns were found unharmed…"

The anchor's voice trailed off in Diego's mind as he remembered the shrieking, noseless baby rolling from its mother's cold, dead birth canal. He couldn't help but feel guilt and wonder if he could've done more.

"Help you?" an Indian man with the nametag SINGH said, seeming frustrated to have another customer to deal with.

Diego slapped Benjamin on the counter and slid it toward the clerk, into the metal bin. "I need a ring—a wedding ring."

The clerk took one look at the bill and scoffed.

"If that's all you got, you came to the wrong shop, amigo. I suggest you find a toy store—you can get a whole bag of plastic rings." He adjusted his turban and looked up from the bill. "Now quit wasting my time."

Diego's cheeks flushed as he took Benjamin back, his pulse pounding as he glared across at the clerk, who went back to his crossword puzzle. He felt an urge to break through that bulletproof glass, grab the son-of-a-bitch by the head, and wring his neck. But even if he were Superman, he'd seen enough violence for a lifetime already.

Diego's shoulders slacked, and he turned to the window, looking out into the alley at his weathered wife. She smiled at him. He forced a smile back, but the look of worry and sadness in his eyes projected how he really felt.

"Excuse me?"

The voice was weak, the voice of a ghost. When a finger tapped Diego on the shoulder, he turned and found the woman standing behind him. Still clutching her paper bag to her chest, she had a different look on her face now, one that was full of kindness and concern.

"Is that your wife outside?" She pointed toward Estela's silhouette still leaning against the glass.

Diego nodded, on edge and prepared for anything.

"The ring you wanted… was it for her?"

"Sí… She give birth to our baby, and I promise her, one day, I would—"

"Here," the woman said, cutting off Diego as she thrust her paper bag toward him. "I want you to have this."

Diego frowned, reluctant to touch the bag in case it was some kind of trick.

"My husband gave me this ring. He was a good man… and you… you seem like a good man too. It used to mean the world to me, but… I think I've finally realized that I don't need it anymore." She forced the bag into Diego's hands.

"Hey!" Singh scowled. He pointed at them angrily. "No one does business in my store except me!"

The woman narrowed her sunken eyes at the man and flipped him the middle finger, then smiled at Diego and nodded for him to follow her.

They stepped outside, the cool air welcoming them back to its chilly embrace.

Estela frowned when she saw the woman with Diego, instantly becoming a mama bear as she wrapped her arms around the baby a bit tighter, neither of them having the capacity for trust at the moment.

Diego gave her an assuring nod and then faced the woman as he reached into the bag. When he pulled out the diamond ring, the neon light sparkled rainbow colors across the stone's surface. Diego couldn't help it when a small gasp escaped his lips.

His eyes widened as he tried to hold back his emotion. "You can't… I can't—"

"Yes, you can," the woman interrupted. "It would mean a lot to me if you'd take…" The woman's words trailed off as she spotted the baby. Her eyes instantly welled up with tears as she started to approach Estela, but then she stopped herself when she noticed Estela's nerves. "What's his name?"

"It's a girl," Estela said as she positioned herself behind Diego, her suspicious eyes locked onto this woman.

"A... a girl?" A tear rolled from the woman's eye, and she seemed lost in a memory. It took a moment before she snapped out of it and wiped the tear away. She forced another smile. "Then I must insist. The ring belongs with you." She turned to Diego. "With your wife."

Diego was at a loss for words. He had to stop himself from hugging the woman. All he could think of was to show his gratitude via the only means he had. Pulling out Benjamin, he held the cash out for her.

"Here. Please, you take it."

"Oh no. That's not necessary, I just wanted to—"

"Please!" Diego thrust the bill toward her, desperate to be free of it. "You must."

The woman hesitated but then nodded when she saw the determination on his face. She took the bill and grinned at Diego and his family.

"Thank you," Diego said. He reached out and gave the woman's shoulder a squeeze before turning and facing his wife.

"Good luck to you," the woman said as she clutched Benjamin in her fist. She watched them a moment before finally tearing herself away, forcing her eyes off their baby girl.

As Diego lifted Estela's hand, she looked confused, frowning and shaking her head as he slid the ring over her finger.

"Diego, what is—?"

He silenced her with a kiss, and after a second of resistance, she kissed him back. Long and loving. She smiled at him when he pulled away, then finally admired the ring.

"It's beautiful."

"Not as beautiful as you," Diego said as he cupped her face, beyond grateful to feel her touch again. "I love you."

"I love you too, Daddy."

Diego pulled his wife and baby into his arms. And he made a silent promise to never let them go again.

THE UNITED STATES OF AMERICA
THIS IS YOUR GOD
WASHINGTON, D.C.
ONE HUNDRED DOLLARS
100

PART 5:

MESSAGE IN A BLOODBATH

A LONELY ROAD

As Lola walked away from the pawn shop, a melancholic feeling saddled her. She could still feel the warmth and wetness of the cum between her legs. It had taken a lot to raise enough money to get the ring back. She'd never fucked so much in such a short period of time. From cocks speckled with warts to oozing sores, she'd taken it all on, possessed by the desire to regain Gabriel's gift.

Still, after all the scrambling and screwing, the epiphany struck her: it wasn't about her ring, it was about her actions.

Lola thought back to the shop and the emotion on the faces of the immigrants. Such an act of kindness hadn't been conjured in her brain in some time. It felt good to give that man the ring. Not to mention the woman and her baby. When she saw the newborn child, she couldn't help but think of her own. Lola knew that look in the man's eyes—it was the same way Gabriel looked at her when Tanya was just a seed in her belly. It was beautiful.

It's what Gabriel would've wanted.

The bond that she shared with her late husband no longer required a symbol, but that family's bond did. For

Lola, the ring was now just a trinket of nostalgia. But those feelings and memories were still alive in her bosom. *That* was the only important thing.

Besides, bringing back the wedding band wasn't going to change how Tanya looked at her. She'd be a fool to think that. What was done was done. Lola knew the truth.

The rattle of the pills echoed in her broken brain. She reached into her purse and extracted the bottle. Looking down at her demon in disgust, she knew what her daughter wanted.

She wanted her to care.

She wanted her to be aware.

She wanted her mother back.

Tanya could no longer handle this zombified version of her mother that was too much of a coward to face reality. Lola had fostered an environment that allowed her daughter to sink into the gutter. She thought about the gun Tanya had pulled back inside the house.

That's not the girl I raised.

She slipped the pills back into her pocketbook and continued walking. As much as she wanted to blame Tanya for not absorbing the lessons bestowed on her, Lola knew it was her own selfish behavior that led to her blind spot. There was no question, *she* was responsible for that gun being in Tanya's hands.

As she closed in on her house, she looked down at the bloodstains on the ground and the broken glass. The remnants of the drive-by shooting served as a painful reminder. She may not have liked her daughter's boyfriend, but Chino wasn't the worst guy. He certainly didn't deserve to go out the way he had. And Tanya didn't deserve to deal with the trauma of the aftermath.

When the foggy ordeal with Sierra and the rest of the day crew concluded, Tanya had given it to her. She'd screamed something hellish, and if anything wasn't clear before, it was certainly clear after.

When she'd reached for another lobo, that was the

trigger. The memory of the exchange replayed in her head.

You put that fucking pill in your mouth and you'll never see me again, Tanya had said.

What do you mean? Lola asked. *This is my medication. I-I need it—*

And I need my goddamn mother! But you don't give a shit about anyone but yourself.

Tanya had ripped the bottle of Lobotozine out of her hand and flung it. The barrage of capsules smashed into the wall and fell like hail onto the floor.

That's an illusion, Tanya said. *You think that gives you a pass to do anything. You think working at a strip club is setting a good example?*

Lola's eyes had widened with confusion.

I-I do that for you, Lola whispered. *I don't have a choice—*

There's always a choice! Tanya yelled. *Selling the ring my dead father gave you was a choice. Being so fucked up all the time that you don't even realize what's going on around you is a choice.*

Lola had stayed quiet.

I didn't steal that gun to protect you. I took it because I didn't wanna be here anymore. Around you, or around anyone.

Tears had welled up in Lola's eyes, and her bottom lip started to shake.

But I didn't have the guts to pull the trigger. And now, Chino's dead because of it!

The tears in her recollection now matched the ones she produced as she walked over the busted glass. There was a whole different dimension of Tanya that she was finally experiencing. One that she'd been completely disregarding. Whether Chino filled a void of love, lust, or lonesomeness for Tanya was irrelevant. Lola had ignored her daughter's agony in striving for her own obliviousness.

She glanced to the other side of the street. The pair of grungy bums in the alley getting warm near the flaming trash can stirred her memories. She thought back to her childhood in the Philippines. The campfires in her village, where she'd grown close with her family.

Her own name was a symbol of how close her mother and grandmother had been. In Filipino, Lola literally stood for grandma. When Lola was in utero, her grandmother had passed away. She was given the name because she'd never get to meet her and because her mother never wanted her to be forgotten. Lola wished she could've had such a connection with her own daughter. The distance between them sickened her.

I failed my family.

The bums glared at Lola. She turned her head, looking away from the fire.

But I don't have to keep failing them.

How could she face the present when she hadn't come to grips with her past? That would be the first dragon she'd slay. That's what Tanya needed, not the ring.

Lola removed the pills from her purse again, but this time, she found the strength to open them. She looked down at the sewer gridding expelling smog beneath her feet. She could already feel herself starting to sweat. The shakes weren't far off. The glistening meat from inside Cheaters, the sharp blade, and the waves of blood awaited. Or Gabriel's hospital bed, malnourished frame, and sunken eyes. A mountainous reel of motherly failures was always ready to be replayed. The memories of sadness and depravity were always just right around the corner.

She knew without the lobo, her brain would soon be raped. Dominated by foul thoughts and restless nights. But if that was the path to mending the fence between her and Tanya, she was ready. If the terrible weekend had taught her anything, it was that.

Listening to the sound of each of the pills she'd picked up off her bedroom floor slide out of the bottle both terrified and excited her. As they fell through the grid and into the sewer water, Lola listened to the sound of her freedom flourish. But home was where most of her stash remained. Once she got back, flushing the rest in front of Tanya would be the best way to send a bold message about her newfound commitment.

It was a new night.

"That's the best thing I've seen in a while," a voice said.

Lola looked up from the smoking sewer, toward the entrance of her house. Looming in the darkness, near the front door, stood Sierra. Her fingers were wrapped around the gold crucifix that hung from her neck. Holding the piece tightly, she looked to be searching for strength.

"I'm sorry about before," Sierra whispered. "I was only thinking about the money. I was wrong."

Lola approached her. "Well, did you find what you were looking for?"

Sierra put her head down and shook it. "Found a lot more than just that, unfortunately." Sierra stepped up and took hold of Lola's hand.

Lola felt something sharp and cold. When she looked down, a blood-speckled diamond the size of a small pear glimmered in the moonlight.

"I want you to have this," Sierra said.

"My god," Lola said. "Is this real?"

Sierra's eyes glossed over. "It sure better be."

Turning, Sierra headed for the street.

As Lola watched her walk away, she couldn't help but feel her heart race. The idea that, after everything she'd been through, something so valuable could just be dropped in her hand was unfathomable. And for the first time, she wasn't thinking about how much lobo she'd score after she fenced it. She was thinking about turning the heat back on in her house and filling the refrigerator. Maybe taking a trip with Tanya if she could get straight—no, *when* she got straight. Somewhere far away. Where they could feel the grass under their feet and dance under the stars.

The crimson jewel represented more than money. It represented an opportunity to mend their fractured relationship. But amid all the excitement remained a mystery.

"Wait," Lola said.

Sierra stopped but didn't turn back.

"Why are you giving me this?"

"Because no jewel or any amount of money can save me. Only God can save me."

Lola had more questions, but as Sierra disappeared into the darkness, she realized it was too late to ask.

MAKING THINGS RIGHT

The vomit was still leaking out of Tanya's mouth when Lola entered. Her daughter's eyes were wide and lost, her body still and motionless. The fight and everything else inside her had stopped. Just when things were finally about to change and everything seemed clear, the darkness that haunted Lola had resurfaced.

"Tanya, baby!" Lola cried, falling to her knees.

She cradled her daughter's sweat-soaked head and gazed into her blank eyes. The empty lobo bottles lay on the floor—one floating in the chunky pool of puke. Lola's sadness was amplified by the vile smell coming from her daughter's nether regions.

Tanya's jogging pants were saturated with fecal matter and urine. The explosion of brown painted the floorboards near her daughter's bed. Lola's face snarled in disgust as the rancid odor molested her nasal cavity, but the smell was the least of her worries.

"W-what did you do?! What the fuck did you do?!"

Her words were hollow. They fell upon the ears of a lost soul. A frozen husk that had no way of reciprocating. Lola leaned up against the foot of the bed, caressing the moist clumps of hair as the vomit oozed onto her lap. She would've given anything to feel Tanya's pulse.

"No," Lola shook her head. "It's not what you did, it's what I did." She stroked the side of Tanya's face but was unable to look at it. Instead, Lola stared vacantly as she spoke. "This is all my fault. Y-you didn't do anything wrong, you were…" Her lip quivered. "You *are* an angel. My angel."

The flashes of her little girl, once happy and energetic, illuminated her mind. Long before things had gotten so warped. Before the world as a whole seemed to lose its mind. Before their American dream had become a nightmare.

"I just wish I got to show you how perfect you are. How I finally saw that and… and how I was finally ready to change. I know you probably don't believe me—how could you after everything I put you through?"

Tears rained from her eyes as she sniffled. With the lobo withdrawal looming, her agony was that much more amplified.

Lola emptied her pocketbook. Benjamin fell into the vomit near the pill bottle as she lifted the massive stone.

"You see?"

Lola held the valuable gem in front of Tanya's dead gaze.

"I dumped all my pills into the sewer. I was going to use this to—to get us out of this place. So we could start over. So we could start right. I thought that God himself had dropped this in my lap to give me what I needed to make things right with you. But now, you're gone…"

Lola's eyes widened as she looked at the sharp, pear-shaped end of the stone. Repositioning her grip, she clasped the larger part of the gem.

"But why should I let that stop me?"

She pressed the pointed end of the stone at the top of her wrist.

"When your papa died in that bed, I wanted to do what you did… to go away forever. I didn't, though. I couldn't leave you behind. That wouldn't have been fair."

Lola shook her head. "Still, in so many ways, I left you behind anyway. I should've been stronger. But I can be strong now. Maybe… maybe I can still make things right."

As Lola pushed the sharp gem into her flesh and parted it, she thought about Tanya. The wonderful times they'd had were far and few as of late, but the memories of the magic moments made her feel drunk with joy.

It was a feeling she wasn't accustomed to.

As she moved onto the other wrist, she felt the warmth of her blood pooling over her dress.

"We'll be together," she whispered as a sniffle of sadness escaped her. "One way or another, we'll be together."

AMERICAN NIGHTMARE

Listening to her mother apologize and acknowledge all the gripes that infuriated her while not being able to respond was a cruel and unusual form of torture. It was almost as agonizing as knowing a reservoir of blood was exiting her mother's body and there wasn't a thing that she could do about it.

It wasn't long until Tanya heard the beating heart that gave life to her mother slowly die out. Her mother's shivering frame lost its vibrations. The labored breaths laced with stress and worry had finally ceased.

Now, she lay helpless in her dead mother's arms.

Even despite the nightmarish scenario, Tanya remained grateful. In so many ways, she'd believed her mother to already be dead. Dead to her, dead to the world. She'd been a walking zombie for so long, just going through the motions, no inkling of metamorphosis looming. As a depressed parasite, she had nothing to offer in life that she couldn't in death.

Tanya's mind battled with her heart.

Why don't I care? she wondered.

Then suddenly, it struck her.

This is why she did it.

The drugs kept Tanya's mind in a quiet state of euphoria. It didn't matter that she was trapped in a horrible scenario that should have left her both screaming and crying in her own head. The lobo kept her detached and subconsciously subdued.

Suddenly, it made sense. If Tanya could swallow being a fly on the wall during her own mother's suicide, she could comprehend the allure of lobo. It's what would've helped her mother to avoid agonizing every waking moment when she looked at her wedding band. It's what would've helped her forget the gristly memories of hiding beneath the stage to avoid the gaze of The Artist as he peeled the skin from her friends' bodies. It's what helped calm her incessant paranoia.

Even as Tanya considered the points in her own mind, she felt a certain measure of guilt. If she just would've tried to talk with her mother, just waited one more night, there was a possibility that they'd have been on their way to a better life. Instead, they were bleeding and puking in a pile of shit as they died together.

Or so she thought.

AMERICAN NIGHTMARE CONTINUED

Tanya couldn't be sure if it was the massive surge of lobo quelling her emotions, but during the hours of purgatorial paralysis, she'd found a way to come to grips with it. The cold shower helped awaken her. And as she washed the blood, vomit, and shit off her shivering body, she finally understood her mother's perspective—she understood it more intimately than she'd ever hoped to.

As she stared down at the blood-drenched diamond, dressed in a fresh set of clothes, Tanya's eyes shifted to her mother's pale body. There was no way of knowing if the things she'd said while bleeding out were more hollow promises or solid words to build upon. Tanya felt fortunate that she was numb enough not to care.

The moment her mother believed her to be dead and promptly made the decision to follow suit, Tanya suddenly comprehended just how much her mother cared.

Might not have been the best at showing it, but she cared, Tanya thought. Bending down, Tanya slid her fingers over her mother's eyelids and kissed her on the cheek.

She was a braver woman than me.

"I-I'm sorry, Mom," Tanya whispered. "But I can't return the favor."

When Tanya lifted the diamond off the floor, within the massive pool of blood lumped with her vomit, she saw Benjamin. The words written in black that read THIS IS YOUR GOD popped out from the mess. Benjamin disgusted her—the bill was saturated with nearly every bodily fluid imaginable.

Gonna need a little cash to get wherever I'm going. But it needs to be cleaned…

She took Benjamin along with the stone into the bathroom. After running them both under water, she used a towel to dry them off. The stone looked like it came out of a jewelry shop. Benjamin, however, remained stained with various human juices.

"What the hell?" Tanya said.

Tanya tried running Benjamin under the water again, and while she was able to get more of the filth off, a sizable amount remained.

It's like it doesn't wanna let go.

Tanya understood the feeling. She dried it off again and stuffed the bill inside the front pouch of a small backpack. She took some toiletry supplies before returning to her bedroom for some clothing. After adding a few outfits, Tanya stopped dead in her tracks.

Slowly, she turned back to her mother's lifeless body and looked at the few remaining pills that she hadn't consumed during her suicide attempt. They were slathered in the repugnant mixture of her mother's blood and Tanya's own vomit and shit.

Using an open pill bottle, she fished the tainted tabs of lobo out of the puddle, then capped it.

Tanya slipped the bottle into the front pouch of the backpack and looked at her mother one last time.

"I guess we've got more in common than I thought."

THE STREETS ARE WATCHING

As Tanya made her way out of the house, the anxiety crippled her. When she hit the street, her heart felt like an engine without oil. She reached for her chest as the images of Chino's gory expression flickered inside her brain. Soon after, the murderous image was overlayed with one showing her mother's pale skin and dead eyes.

How far detached from a dose was she? It was hard to tell the amount of lobo she'd registered. She'd swallowed an absurd number of pills but didn't know how many were regurgitated via her vomit spell.

Is this how Mom felt when she needed a fix? she wondered.

Without even thinking about it, her shaky hand was already inside the front pouch of the backpack, uncorking the bottle of pills she'd scooped out of the nasty scene inside the house.

Looking at the gunky medication, Tanya shook her head, kicking herself for not thinking to wash them off. As her body trembled, tears started to run down her face. The thoughts inside her brain only intensified. Chino's face was quaking. Various bugs transversed his decaying flesh as he screamed at her.

"You took my gun, bitch!" Chino wailed. "I'm fuckin' dead because of you!"

Her mother interjected next, foggy eyes peeling open. "You spoiled cunt! I killed myself because of you! The least you can do is join me!"

"No, no, no!" Tanya screamed, shoveling a pair of pills into her mouth.

"Everything okay?" a voice asked.

Tanya turned and was faced with a pair of homeless men peering around the corner of an alley just a few yards away. The grubby bums did nothing to quell her anxiety—they only intensified it.

"What's wrong?" the man continued.

She didn't answer them. Shoving the bottle back into the open pouch, she zipped up the bag. Tanya then turned in the opposite direction of the alley and took off into the night.

A FAREWELL TO FAÇADES

Crane watched Hector scratch the final ticket and discard it on the ground.

"Fuck, another loser," Hector mumbled. "Nine tickets and not a single goddamn dollar back."

"Shocking," Crane replied, rolling his eyes. As he reset his gaze, he saw a girl venturing out into the street just a short distance from the alley. His eyes widened.

She removed the pill bottle from her bag, too excited by the allure of the drugs in her grasp to notice Benjamin slip out and fall onto the ground.

"No, no, no!" she screamed.

Hector peered around the corner just as she tossed the pills into her mouth.

"Everything okay?" Hector asked.

The men watched on as she turned toward them. The

girl didn't answer his question. The look of panic in her swelling pupils was as close as she came.

"What's wrong?" Hector persisted.

The girl suddenly broke out of her frozen stance, and Crane watched her take off into the night. It was as if she was being chased by every demon in the city. In many ways, he was sure she was.

"Fuckin' weird," Hector said, looking back at Crane. "What the hell are we still waiting around here for, anyway?"

Refocusing on Benjamin, Crane kept a careful eye on the bill while he fished a few coins out of his pocket and approached a payphone.

Hector shoved his hands inside the pockets of the warm jacket Crane had blessed him with. "Well? I'm fuckin' cold, man."

"We're not," Crane replied, dialing a number.

Furrowing his brow, Hector still couldn't figure him out.

"Five minutes," Crane said into the phone. "No, it's just down the street from where you dropped me off." He hung up the phone and returned his attention to Hector.

"What?" Hector asked.

"You asked me what we're waiting around for." Crane walked over to the sidewalk and lifted Benjamin off the cold concrete. The bill was in a foul state, but that did nothing to deter him from making contact. "I said, we're not. You've fulfilled your end of the bargain. You're free to go."

Hector's eyes popped. "Holy shit, did you really just find a hundred?"

"I did, and I certainly haven't forgotten the kindness you showed me when you found *this* very bill."

Hector squinted in disbelief. Amid the mishmash of bodily stains and scribbles, he saw the lipstick impressed upon it. "What? How's that possible?"

"Anything's possible," Crane replied.

Hector crimped his lips in disgust and shook his head. He looked at the charcoal scribbled onto Benjamin. "It looks kinda different than when I had it."

Crane grinned, his white teeth glowing in the moonlight. "That's the nature of money. Doesn't make it worth any less, does it?"

"I guess not."

Holding up Benjamin, Crane examined the filth. "In a way, it's symbolic of society. The devolution of man is quite similar. Eventually, everything rots."

Crane looked down toward the worthless scratch tickets that Hector had tossed in the alley and nodded. "That's why I didn't understand when you bought those."

Looking back at the tickets, Hector sucked his teeth. "Yeah, you were right. They were duds."

"No, that's not what I mean. You should be glad you lost. You don't understand how good you've got it. Sometimes, winning only complicates things."

"Yeah, but it'd be nice to eat a hot meal once in a while."

"I've been around you long enough now to know you don't miss dinner. You don't *need* this." He held up Benjamin. "Because you *always* find a way. Whether you've begged your way to a breakfast or stolen supper, you fill your belly. And that's worth more than any bank can hold."

A pair of headlights came into focus at the end of the street, gradually drawing closer.

Crane pointed to the bill. "This is weight. Heavy as chains. The burden of burdens."

Hector looked at the headlights and then back at Crane. "The fuck are you talkin' about, man?"

"I'm telling you to use your fucking eyes! You showed me this godforsaken city! Not the other way around!"

"What the fuck does that have to do with anything?"

The headlights stopped beside Crane. He watched as Hector's eyes bulged at the sight of the vehicle. The driver's side door of the black stretch limousine opened, and a well-dressed chauffeur stepped out.

"May I take your coat, Mr. Starks?" the driver asked.

"Just open the door, please," Crane replied.

Hector glared. It was hard to tell if he was upset or excited by what he was seeing. "The fuck is this? That's... that's yours?"

Crane moved in, getting face to face with him, and nodded. "It is." He held up Benjamin. "And *this* is yours."

Benjamin fell and Crane observed Hector's jaw drop as the bill connected with his palm. He turned away from the stunned transient and approached the chauffeur holding open the back door of the limo. But just as he was about to get inside, Crane stopped and looked back.

"But just remember, it's only yours if you want it," Crane said. "Because..." He looked at the heavens as if praying to be gifted the right articulation. "That face you're making right now when you look at me, it's the same one I make when I look at you."

PARTING WAYS

Hector remained speechless as he watched Crane enter the limo. He had many questions, but also one answer that seemed to invalidate everything he wanted to ask. He looked up from Benjamin to the driver as he tipped his cap at him and shut the doors.

The hunger in Hector's belly resurfaced, but as he watched the limo disappear at the end of the street, he couldn't help but think about what Crane had said.

Hector shook his head side to side.

Suddenly, Benjamin's weight felt much heavier than before. The texture of the bill wasn't just rough, it was almost acidic. An unnatural sensation took hold of him.

Hector looked away from the bill to the worthless scratch tickets in the alley. He looked down the road at the glowing sign of Fast Cash.

Tomorrow's a whole new day, Hector thought. *I got more time than I need. I'll figure it out then.*

But there was one thing he knew that he didn't have to figure out any longer—one thing he was now certain of. Hector looked back at the scratch tickets and started to hack up some phlegm. Once he'd collected enough in his mouth, he spat a clam on the ground.

It's time to go home.

Hector crumbled up Benjamin and tossed the bill onto the pavement.

THE UNITED STATES OF AMERICA
100
100
100
100

THE END?

FATEFUL EVENTS

BY SHANE McKENZIE

So you've made it to the end. We hope you enjoyed your experience with Benjamin. We know *we* did! But not only was this project a huge undertaking to create, it was a long and strange road to even happen at all.

I started writing and getting published in 2010, which eventually led me to Hollywood, where I switched my focus from writing books and comics to writing solely screenplays. I had a good run with lots of exciting opportunities thrown my way. I got to write a web series for Warner Bros, got to pitch to people like Eli Roth, Salma Hayek, and Jennifer Lopez (their companies, anyway), plus studios like Universal, Sony, SpectreVision, and more. I wrote two movies for Blumhouse, one of which was killed by COVID, the other of which was produced and is now streaming as an Amazon Original.

I only mention all of that because when you're working as a screenwriter, what you're doing more than anything by far is writing pitches. One-pagers and look books and pitch decks and whatever else you want to call it. You are always trying to come up with new, fresh ideas that you can pitch to companies because once you've had a project made, you have to capitalize on the leverage of that as soon as possible, because it's very much a what-have-you-done-for-me-lately kinda business.

So, you have to come up with ideas that are original and exciting but also feasible. You can't write up the next Lord of the Rings and expect anyone to take that seriously if you're still a new writer earning your place. And so you take things into consideration like budget and subject matter, so that if you get the chance to pitch to a big Hollywood company, they have a reason to even consider your pitch.

I'm thinking rated R or TVMA type stories, which means I can get away with certain things but not others. And then, when it comes to budget, I always tried to come up with ideas that would require minimal locations, minimal cast, and minimal special effects.

One of those ideas I knew ticked all those boxes was something I was calling BENJAMIN. The idea was very similar to what you just read, but I wasn't necessarily trying to connect the stories as much as they are connected now. I just loved the idea of following a $100 bill around as it was passed from person to person, leading the money back to the original person who lost it in the first place. I remember I had a bank robbery, a drug bust, an alternate version of the stripper story, and I think I even had something that involved a kid's birthday magician.

I pitched this story around and got interest right away because I had learned how to pitch projects that would get attention. What I hadn't learned yet, and am still learning, is how to go from interest to production. There's really no surefire way to make this happen, as far as I can tell, anyway.

Benjamin was nearly a movie, then it was nearly a comic book, then nearly a movie again. It never got past the interest phase though, and so I put it on the backburner. But it's just always been one of those projects that refuses to go away. It was always in the back of my mind, poking at me, telling me that it really wanted to exist.

Then the year 2023 happens. There is a huge writers' strike in Hollywood, and I was forbidden by the Writer's

Guild of America to do any screenwriting work. Even for projects I was already contracted to do. So I was using this time to write scripts on my own, getting things ready for when the strike eventually ended. During this time, KillerCon in Austin happened, which is an extreme horror convention that my buddy Wrath James White puts on and is one of the major highlights of my year, every year.

This particular year, Aron Beauregard was a guest of honor, and while I had heard his name, I wasn't all that familiar with him. We knew a lot of the same people and were part of the same community, but by this time, I hadn't written any new fiction in eight years and was still very much a screenwriter.

Well, we met and hung out quite a bit, talking about the business and getting to know each other, along with Kristopher Triana, who's been a buddy of mine since the very beginning. Aron had mentioned that if I ever wanted to get into more detail about the way he does business, I could travel to his house in Rhode Island any time, and we could get into it.

Now, I've had a handful of similar interactions over the years, where you hit it off with someone and start making plans, but then they just never happen. I'm not really the kind of guy who just travels to visit people, so I assumed it would be years if this happened at all.

So Saturday night. We are all at the after party following the infamous Gross Out Contest. We're having a good time. My wife is there and she's dressed to impress because she and I had gone to a concert earlier that evening. At one point in the night, one of our fellow writers, who I had just met that weekend and who was drunk off his fucking ass, started making lewd comments about my wife. I did my best to be cool, but before long I was in this guy's face basically ready to cave his skull in if he said even one more comment.

To our left was Aron, who was watching all this unfold and took it upon himself to remove this person to make sure it didn't go any further.

Now, if you know, you know, but I'm not gonna name this person. We have since buried the hatchet and are on good terms… and here's why.

Aron offered to reach out to me and send this person's apology. And this is why I bring this up at all. Because if this incident hadn't happened, it's very possible that this book would have never happened.

When Aron emailed me, it turned into an email chain, which turned into a phone call. I was telling Aron that he should consider writing screenplays, and then he explained to me how the publishing business has changed since I'd left it eight years ago. This led to me actually booking a flight to stay with him in Rhode Island so he could show me the details of how he was doing business because I was intrigued and had been missing writing books for some time. And since I wasn't allowed to write screenplays, the timing just sort of worked out.

While in Rhode Island, we were hanging out one night, watching *Wishmaster 4* and intoxicating ourselves. And we just started talking about book ideas we've had that we hadn't gotten around to writing yet. And so I brought up Benjamin.

Aron sat up and gave me a crazy look. "No fucking way. I had the exact same idea."

Not only had he come up with the idea to follow a $100 bill around from person to person, but he, too, was calling it BENJAMIN.

We agreed right then and there that we would have to collaborate on this thing. It truly felt like fate. Like this book wanted to exist and was using us to make that happen.

This book just feels meant to be. I'll just give one more strange example. January of 2024, I put together a writers' retreat at my grandmother's lake house. Aron, Kristopher Triana, Judith Sonnet, Wrath James White, Lucas Mangum, and I stayed at this house over the weekend and wrote our asses off. Truly one of the best weeks of my life.

This is where we started writing *Benjamin*. We spent hours and hours and hours drinking and smoking on the front porch, going over every detail again and again.

When we returned to Austin from our trip, Aron and Kris found out their flight had been canceled. So they ended up staying at my house for an extra day.

We decided to go check out a horror merchandise store called Pallbearer Press. I made arrangements for my mom to watch my kids and we headed over, all excited to spend some money… and it was closed.

Then I thought, I could take them to The Gas Station, which is the actual gas station used in *The Texas Chainsaw Massacre* that has been converted into a horror merchandise shop… and it was closed.

"Are there any other horror related places we could go?" Kris asked.

The only other place I could think of was The Museum of the Weird in downtown Austin. I had been there before and knew it was a pretty rad place, but most importantly… it was open!

So, we headed over there. We were having a great time walking through the exhibits and reading about all kinds of crazy shit. There was even an actual frozen bigfoot type creature there called The Minnesota Ice Man, and they had the *Unsolved Mysteries* episode about it playing on a loop.

While checking out some of the exhibits, Aron and I both noticed something strange and random just sitting on top of one of the glass cases. It wasn't part of the exhibit, it was just sorta… there. Staring at us.

If that ain't fate, I don't know what is!

ABOUT THE AUTHOR

Aron Beauregard is the guy who usually pees in the alley next to Columbia Liquors off Broad Street. He survives on a diet that mostly consists of river water and the contents of used diapers he finds around the city. Manhole was not only his nickname in high school but is now also where he 'lives.' Constantly in the grips of lobo withdrawal, when he's not offering to suck cock for pills, he's haunted by nightmarish visions of a time in the distant past when he was a reasonably successful writer.

ABOUT THE AUTHOR

Shane McKenzie smells like a shit-caked dick, but that has nothing to do with the shit caked around his penis. The smell comes from the dumpster sludge he uses as a blanket every night that also serves as his breakfast the next morning. The shit on his dick... to be honest, he doesn't really know how that shit got there. His only friends are his own demons that never stop chasing him, and he'd fuck a stray dog in the ass just for one hit of lobo to get even a moment's reprieve. Oh wait, that's where that shit came from!

FILM & TV RIGHTS

'Benjamin' was written with both the big and small screen in mind. For inquiries on obtaining film or television rights, please email: FollowBenjaminRights@gmail.com

SERIOUS INQUIRIES ONLY.

Printed in Great Britain
by Amazon

57666236R00260